Paradise Acres:
The Stry-Ker Family Saga

Canada

*The Publishers gratefully acknowledge the financial assistance of the
Government of Canada through the Book Publishing Industry Development
Program (BPIDP) for our publishing activities.*

National Library of Canada Cataloguing in Publication Data

Warring, Molly-Ann, 1937-
   Paradise acres / Molly-Ann Warring.

ISBN 0-88887-312-3 (bound). — ISBN 0-88887-308-5 (pbk.)

   1. Austrians—Canada—History—Fiction. 2. Frontier and
pioneer life—Prairie Provinces—Fiction. I. Title

PS8645.A77P37 2005   C813'.6   C2005-900728-1

*Painting by Gracie Generoux
Cover design by Bull's Eye Design, Ottawa
Printed and bound in Canada on acid free paper.*

Paradise Acres:
The Stry-Ker Family Saga

Molly Anne Warring

Molly A. Warring
Enjoy the read!

Borealis Press,
Ottawa, Canada
2006

I humbly dedicate this book to my late grandmother, Palahia, and my father, Mike Zarusky . . . the two best story tellers that I have ever met

ACKNOWLEDGEMENTS

This novel has taken me over ten years to complete. I did not work on writing it for the entire time . . . only when I could get away to Kona, Hawaii, where I am inspired to write. So my greatest thanks go to my God and the ancient Hawaiians who used to worship at the bay where I write. Their spirits live on . . . welcoming people such as I to share in the outstanding beauty and tranquility of these islands.

I sincerely thank my publisher Borealis Press, Dr. Frank Tierney and Dr. Glenn Clever, for supporting my story and publishing it. My thanks also go to my fabulous editor, Janet Shorten, with whom it was a delight to work; my husband Lou, who has supported me morally throughout this time and beyond; my son Barry Basaraba for his legal research; and Susan Basaraba, my grand-daughter, who read the first cut of the story and told me she enjoyed reading it so much that when her dad told her to turn out the lights and go to sleep, she continued to read the manuscript under the covers with a flashlight . . . when she finished she phoned me and said, "Baba, that's a great story!" My thanks also to Elizabeth Basaraba, my 16-year-old granddaughter who helped with proofreading; and to Paul and Elena Napora, who have been my dearest friends for over forty years and have supported me throughout this time. Paul is a famous psychic and an author of many books; his latest, now in production, is entitled *You Through Your Dreams: A Psychic Dream Book*; Elena helped me with the initial editing and proofreading. Thanks to Liz Sliwa for her support; to Pat White of the Billfisher at Kona for always welcoming me with open arms; and to Tom Chambers for geology advice.

I am grateful to Gracie Jane Generoux, who designed and painted the cover design. Gracie is a well-known artist in Alberta and has reached international acclaim by painting *The Tear of Hope* depicting the statue of liberty with a teardrop on her cheek. This painting honoured the firefighters who died in New York during 9/11.

My gratitude also to my benefactors: Sine Chadi; John Chomiak; my cousins Sally and Ron Starchuk; and Duncan Stewart.

To Barb Hatfield who word-processed the original writing before I learned to use the computer; to Cherry Robinson who helped with the publishers' list and distribution; to Winnie Bogosoff who helped with input and changes to the manuscript; and to Mabs Murji and Paul Linton of Speedy Copy, who did all my duplications and the original copy for the cover design. To Myrna Howell, my dear friend, for final proofreading and Lyan Redekopp.

My research sources were Stella Devanthey, RCMP; Father Bill, Mundare Monastery; Reimer Express Lines; *The Canadian Encyclopedia*; Alberta Report Book Series; *Edmonton Journal*; *Edmonton Sun*; *Heavy Horses* by Grant MacEwan; and the Edmonton Public Library.

CONTENTS

CHAPTER ONE

It was already dawn as Evan Stracher stumbled down the long dirt path that led to his home. The path branched off the main road in the village of Sosnitcha. Even though everyone called it a road, the only road in the entire village, it was still just a wide path by most standards.

Sosnitcha was a squalid, dirty, depressing little Galician village in Austria. According to the last census, taken by command of Emperor Franz Josef, the Austrian ruler of the time, there were 256 Austrian citizens of Ukrainian descent living there. There were 31 weather-beaten, straw-roofed huts in the village with a barn attached to almost every home. Some of the houses even had a privy, but most people used the barn as their toilet facility. In the middle of the village was an onion-domed Byzantine church, with a separate belfry. This was the place of worship, attended by every villager, from old to young.

At one end of the village was a fieldstone flour mill. Two strong oxen drove the grinder stones each day. A hempseed oil extraction mill was located at the opposite end of the village. Along the main street was a general store, which carried all the basic items for the villagers' use—items such as salt, candles, and spikes for building, along with hammers, shovels, hoes, and cross saws. Beside the church was a stick-built community hall in a sad state of repair. This hall was used for gatherings of major importance, usually when the Pun made announcements that would affect the villagers' lives. Not far from the hall stood the blacksmith shop, where horses were shod and basic farm implements were made and tool blades sharpened. Next to the hall was a shoemaker, who made all the boots for people who could afford them and repaired others until there was no boot left to repair—for people who were poor. This included everyone except the Pun and the local priest.

Most times there was a pungent odour of animal manure in Sosnitcha because cattle, pigs, and chickens roamed freely in the village. The only people who were poorer than the villagers were the roaming gypsies from Hungary whose caravans travelled from one village to the other in search of food, clothing, and anything else that they could find or steal. If something wasn't nailed or screwed down, the gypsies soon became its possessors. Even a dead chicken discarded by a villager and thrown in the ditch to rot would be picked up by these people. They were such awful scavengers that they picked maggots off the dead bird and threw them into their large boiling kettles before quickly devouring every last piece of the bird's flesh.

The house in which Evan Stracher lived was like any other in the village. It was certainly not comfortable accommodation, but it was bearable. This was the way of life in Sosnitcha in the early 1900s. It was a hard life for the villagers, but what other choice did they have?

Evan Stracher worked hard at his weaving shop during the day. He would always start work around mid-day because he stayed up most of the night drinking and visiting at the *korshma*, the village pub. After work, he would go home and prepare a meagre meal, usually consisting of black bread, boiled potatoes, and fried eggs. Sometimes he would complement this with sauerkraut mixed with hempseed oil and raw onion. Once in a while, Evan would treat himself to *slunena*, pickled pork back fat. But this was only on those occasions when someone in the village butchered a pig and was kind enough to give him some of the fat.

On this day, as was his routine, Evan left work as soon as darkness approached. But instead of first turning toward home, he headed straight for the korshma, where he intended to remain until dawn. Today he had endured a very depressing experience and felt the need to drown his sorrows and be consoled by his friends.

The korshma, well over fifty years old and in much need of repair, stood on rotting timbers that seemed to be held together by the thatched straw roof. When it rained, the water would stream down the straw bundles, dripping onto the tables and onto the faded and scuffed timber floor. The patrons didn't mind, though, because it was a happy place and the little bit of rain on their heads was "good luck," they would always say.

Evan now entered the korshma, his broad shoulders and barrel chest momentarily filling the doorway. He shuffled across the small, crowded room to one of the crude, handcrafted, rectangular wooden tables and settled himself heavily on one of the stools. His back was to the large stone fireplace along one wall where, as always, a pig carcass was cooking to perfection on the spit.

Without looking around or speaking to any of the other half-dozen men drinking and eating at nearby tables, he ordered himself a glass of beer. You could drink beer or wine at the korshma and eat the pork meat and black bread. Any man with a few pennies (women never visited the korshma in Sosnitcha) could have a meal, but today Evan was not one of them. He was not in the mood to eat; he was here to drink. When his beer arrived, he began to drink, first one . . . then another . . . and then another.

As he drained his third glass, Saska, who had been serving him, approached him. Saska was the pretty daughter of Kozal, the burly, gray-haired owner. She had a sympathetic ear and could make any customer laugh and forget his troubles. And, as the men in this village had many troubles, the place was always busy.

Normally Evan would let Saska sit on his knee, ruffling the unruly blonde curls on his head or tugging jokingly at his blond, walrus mustache, and together they would sing and laugh happily. Though Evan was not a particularly handsome man, there was something about him—perhaps his crude charm, perhaps his sex appeal—that attracted women's attention. Not more than five-feet six-inches tall when he straightened his husky frame, Evan's presence nonetheless drew attention. And he normally enjoyed giving the lovely Saska attention, but not today.

Saska was not amused by Evan's bad disposition. "Why are you in such a bad mood today? You certainly are not as pleasant as you usually are!"

"If it was any of your business, Saska, I would tell you. But it is not!" He said roughly, in his deep baritone voice. "So leave me alone. Go to some other man, you flirt."

Saska continued to stand there, shocked at his rudeness. "Go on! Go! Did you not hear me?" he shouted, waving her away, his high cheekbones red with emotion, and the nostrils of his aquiline nose flaring like those of a wild Viking.

Kozal, standing behind the tall table which served as bar, looked up in surprise when he heard Evan's shouts. Saska came up to him, anger and bewilderment in her lovely brown eyes. "What the hell is bothering him today?" she asked her father, one hand on her hip, the other pointing in a sweeping motion toward Evan, who was now drinking with a few other men at his table.

Kozal shrugged philosophically. "Who knows what bothers most of these burdened men?" He grabbed a clean rag and began polishing the table. "Maybe it's

Sosnitcha, Saska. Maybe we should move to Canada and start another business there, don't you think?" He straightened, looking at her closely as he mopped his thick brow with the rag.

Saska shook her head and waved her hand, showing she did not take him seriously. "Father, you always say that, but it never happens." She looked around her at the customers as they smoked their home-grown tobacco. "Only some of the villagers have the courage to emigrate to Canada. I don't think we will ever go . . . and neither will Evan. He is just like one of them!" Her smooth, tanned arms swept the room contemptuously. "He is just a coward!"

"Shh!" Kozal whispered fiercely, wringing the rag in his hands and looking around at the tables worriedly. "Be quiet or someone will hear you!"

Saska threw back her long golden braids unconcernedly and left to refill the wine of a customer who was calling out to her in good-natured impatience.

Evan looked gruffly in her direction, then got up, said a few words to his companions and, with the measured strides of a panther, left the korshma. As he headed for home, he knew he could not live long in this hopeless condition. He began to cough raggedly, stopping to lean down for a moment on a nearby tree stump to catch his breath again. His cough was getting worse, which added to his worries; his roving eye and womanizing ways had not abated, which added to his guilt. Evan had always blamed the Austrian army for his indiscretions, but how long could one keep blaming something else for what was essentially your own failure?

The past twenty-four hours had been filled with despair, anguish, anger, and ultimately excitement. Evan's day had started much like most days. He slept until midday, long after his wife had left to work at daybreak in the sugar beet fields. He slept until the middle of the day because he usually got home from the korshma at dawn after a night of boozing. Only this day was different. He had visited Pun Doctor Illia, who had been very blunt with him and told him that he was dying. What else was there to do after this devastating news, except to go to the korshma and talk to his friends, who he hoped would console him? Except that didn't happen . . . instead they told him to follow Pun Doctor Illia's advice and move to Canada . . . and they praised Canada as never before. This advice from his friends made him very angry, because that wasn't what he wanted to hear at this time, so he took his anger out on Saska. But now, several hours later, he was starting to become excited, because somewhere during the night he had made up his mind to begin plans to emigrate to Canada.

Evan stumbled along the narrow path winding around the majestic oak tree standing watch over his tiny home—a hut with a straw-thatched roof. He heard the beautiful red-, black- and gold-feathered rooster already at his post, crowing away, waking everyone to begin their day. Ko-Koo-ree—Koo! Ko-Koo-ree-Koo! he crowed proudly. Evan had always admired the spirit and persistence of this creature. Usually when he didn't come home until morning, he wished the rooster would just be quiet so that Tainka would not see him enter, but today his heart lifted and sang with the beautiful creature.

Sparing barely a glance at the tall, welcoming sunflowers that hugged the sides of the hut, Evan grabbed the rickety wooden latch and let himself into his small, dank, crowded home. Tainka, with baby Maria at her side, was still asleep, one of the child's hands held lovingly in her own. Fortunately the old rooster hadn't awakened either of them. Evan stood still for a moment as he watched mother and child, his "two doves" as he called them, sleeping peacefully under the colourful patterned blanket which Tainka's mother had given her daughter as a wedding present.

His thoughts went back to 1902, when he and Tainka were first married in their little village church. He had been so proud of his beautiful wife. Slightly taller than he, Tainka was tall for women in these parts. Ten years younger than he, she had sky-blue eyes and raven hair, which she refused to shroud with a babushka (kerchief), as did most of the other women. Also, whereas the leathery, weather-beaten faces of the other women were the evidence of the hard work they had to endure, Tainka's complexion was smooth and extraordinarily light, even though she worked as hard as they did. Not only was she beautiful, though, she was also educated, having completed eight levels of schooling. She read fluently and wrote well, not in Austrian, but in Ukrainian, the language which was used in these parts. Yes, Evan was very proud of his wife.

He lowered himself quietly to the edge of the rickety bed, momentarily blocking the early rays of the sun warming the blanket. Soon Tainka would have to be wakened to go to work in the fields, and Maria would have to be taken to her grandmother's house for the day. Evan's big hand reached out to rest briefly on their hands. He knew he wanted a better life for both of them. His heart filled with emotion.

With a soulful sigh, he started to rise. Tainka stirred. Her lovely blue eyes, shaded by thick black lashes, slowly focused on his face.

"Evan, are you sick again? Have you had trouble sleeping again?" She sat up gently so as not to disturb her sleeping child. "Evan?" she repeated softly, angling her head to look at him closely. She knew how bad his cough was getting and what bad news this could bring. For the past two years Evan had had the cough, its intensity increasing as the days went by. He was also wheezing so badly that at times he sounded as though he was going to die at any moment, unable to catch his breath. They both knew what this meant, as people all around them were dying of consumption—of tuberculosis. Evan had been spitting up blood with every cough recently. And his condition was worsening as the days went by, to the point where he was no longer able to endure the condition and had finally decided to go see a doctor in the village.

Evan held her hands in his own soothingly and looked into her eyes. "No, Tainka, I haven't slept. I'm a little drunk, but mostly I'm so excited!" He positioned his body more comfortably on the small, creaky bed. "Let me tell you what happened, and I hope you will be excited with me!" Tainka nodded earnestly and listened.

"You know Pun Doctor Illia, don't you?"

Yes, Tainka knew him. There were qualified physicians living in Lviv, 40 kilometers away. Pun Doctor Illia was not a qualified physician, but he was brilliant and self-taught. Midwives delivered most babies in Sosnitcha in their crowded, squalid little huts. Some were competent, but most were not, causing two out of every ten mothers to die, leaving fathers to scrape a living and care for the surviving motherless children. Many of the fathers remarried, usually to unattractive old maids who were left in the village because no man wanted them in the first go-around. But many of these women made excellent mothers to the children, cooking well for them and serving the family with even more care than the first wives.

Tainka knew that when Pun Doctor Illia delivered a baby, though, both mother and child would survive. But the problem with many of the village women was that they were too embarrassed to have a strange man see their genital area and so would insist on midwives attending to their delivery. To many, their embarrassment would be a fatal mistake.

Tainka's thoughts and attention came back to Evan as he began to relate what had happened at Pun Doctor Illia's home.

Upon his arrival, Staffka, the doctor's wife, dressed in a crisp blue frock and wearing a white, clean apron, had courteously ushered him in. Evan had been painfully conscious of his own sloppy white linen shirt with the black drawstring at the neck and of faded black trousers torn at the knees. He had woven both garments himself but knew that they badly needed to be replaced. Also, his Austrian army boots had holes, which he had tried to seal by lining them with pieces of leather from the shoemaker's scrap pile. Evan had felt that his health was in the same sad condition as his clothes.

A fit of coughing overtook him as he followed Staffka into the parlour where the doctor would be examining him.

"How long have you had this cough, Evan?" she asked him, concern and sympathy in her kind eyes as she noted that he was coughing up blood.

Evan drew in shaky breaths, thumping his chest slowly as though that would make things right inside. "For about two years," he answered, willing his body to relax.

"For two years?" They both turned around at the sound of the deep, resonating voice that was in such direct contrast to the short, wiry man that accompanied the tone. The doctor nodded to his wife; she gave his patient a reassuring smile and left them.

It took less than three minutes of questions and examination for Pun Doctor Illia to deliver the expected, but nonetheless shocking, blow. "Evan Stracher, you will be dead before you reach 35 years of your life!" His piercing brown eyes bore into Evan's and saw his body momentarily recoil from the bluntly delivered warning. "You will die of consumption!"

I have just two more years to live, Evan's brain repeated in a dull haze. He had been married for less than one year. His spirit sank even lower in depression, an odd sort of emptiness enveloping him. He was dying both physically and psychologically. What was there for him? Illiterate, unable to do any work other than weaving, what could he do? He could not farm for he hated the dust and the sweat and toil. It was Tainka who loved the land; it was she who loved nurturing things and watching them grow. How I wish I had been born into a rich family, Evan thought in weary despair. His tired, lifeless brown eyes rested on Pun Doctor Illia for a moment as if awaiting some small reprieve from his death sentence.

The doctor put his hand on Evan's shoulder and squeezed gently in encouragement, willing Evan not to sink into hopelessness. "Come, let's sit for a moment." He patted his patient's big shoulders and urged him toward one of the two chairs in the room. Sitting down in the other, he rested the palms of his hands on his thin legs and leaned earnestly toward the other man. "I may have a solution to your problems, Evan," he said. "I hear there are golden opportunities in the new country . . . in Canada. I also hear their government is giving away land to new settlers from other countries who are willing to clear the bush and make the land arable so that the rich soil will be productive. I hear that the soil in Canada is so rich that only the best crops grow there. And you will likely be much healthier there!" He nodded in emphasis as he saw Evan's eyes focus on him, a ray of hope in their brown depths. "I hear that there is so much land in Canada that not even in your wildest imagination can you picture so much land!"

Evan quashed the ray of hope for a moment. "But, Pun Doctor, you know what a poor farmer I would make. I don't like anything about farming—I'm a weaver!" His tone suddenly filled with self-disgust. "Why, even Tainka, my wife, who is a woman, knows more about farming than me. All I'm good for is weaving fabric and being a good soldier, as I was in Franz Josef's army." Evan had completed the obligatory four years in the Emperor's army. His chief duty had been to play the reveille in the morning. He shook his head in self-deprecation. He had always thought that he served the same purpose as the old rooster did with his crowing. He was an outstanding bugler, but that did not put food on the table for a poor man's family.

The doctor dismissed his concerns with a simple wave of the hand. "Evan, if only your partying and merry-making could provide a living, you would never have a worry in the world. But here in this miserable village in Austria's outback, it counts for nothing!" He leaned closer to the other man. "Evan, don't you see there is opportunity and adventure waiting for you in Canada?" Then he slyly played the ace card, knowing he had to reach Evan's ego to move him to save his own life. "There is opportunity there in Canada, Evan, but only if you are brave . . . only then."

Evan looked at the doctor piercingly, the small ray of hope in his eyes igniting once again. He knew that to travel half-way around the world with a young wife and baby would be hard. He knew that not being able to read or write or even speak the language would be harder. But he also knew he was a brave man! No one could ever accuse him of not being a brave man!

"I have heard of your many courageous exploits in the army," Pun Doctor Illia echoed his thoughts. "Others have also said you are as stubborn as a mule. That stubbornness should help you in this situation." Standing up abruptly, he signalled to Evan that the visit was over, knowing that this was the point where the younger man would have to seriously consider the option he had been given.

And consider it seriously Evan did. Rather than heading home, he headed straight for the korshma, the doctor's words of advice echoing in his mind. At the korshma, the other patrons agreed whole-heartedly with the good doctor and urged Evan to follow his advice. "Do you remember the Pushinskys?" his neighbour, Petro, asked him. "They emigrated to Canada and they have written that it is a fabulous place, that it's well worth going to. They wrote that the fields were as wide as your eye could see and that the open prairie provided good, black, fertile soil."

"That's right," confirmed Kozal, coming to stand beside their table, the ever-present rag hanging from his burly hands. "They said that the soil could produce enough wheat to feed ten families, not just one!" He held up both hands, fingers spread wide. "All an immigrant needs is ten dollars to register his homestead. One hundred and sixty acres, Evan." He leaned down, eye to eye with the young man. "Think about it . . . one hundred and sixty acres!"

And so it was, with visions of rich black soil, blue skies, and golden opportunities, that Evan had headed back home to his straw-thatched hut and to Tainka.

CHAPTER TWO

Evan and Tainka talked for several hours on that morning when he came home excited—which was a rare occasion. He told Tainka about his dreams for himself and her . . . but mostly for Maria and other children he knew they would have. He told her about what Pushinsky's cousin had said about Canada. How there was so much rich, black soil . . . the soil was under the bushes that had to be cleared. Bush meant there was lots of wood to build from and wood to burn for fuel.

When Tainka heard about the rich, black soil she became very interested. She knew that the more good soil you had, the more grain you could grow. She knew that grain, especially wheat, could be sold to people who lived in towns and cities to provide them with bread. How much money they could make! She also had read about Canada in the Lviv newspaper, whenever someone from Sosnitcha brought a paper back on their return from the market.

Her experience in farming with Evan's brother, Yatsko, had prepared her. She was not afraid of farming . . . farming anywhere in the world. Canada was just as good as anywhere else, as far as she was concerned.

Tainka loved Evan more than words could describe, but when she thought about the prospect of emigrating to Canada and leaving her mother and sister behind, perhaps never to see either one of them again, the thought overwhelmed her. But she also knew that Pun Doctor Illia was a brilliant man and that what he had revealed to Evan about his constant coughing was a brutal reality. She had seen in the village young people and old dying of consumption. Evan had to be her first consideration. If Evan were to die then she had no future here anyway. However, her love for her widowed mother, Maria Greshko, was also very strong. To abandon her mother, whose husband had drowned while crossing the Dniepre River in the spring of 1899 when the waters were the most turbulent, would be unconscionable.

Since that morning when Evan had come home drunker than usual, about four weeks had passed and there had been much soul-searching by Evan and Tainka. Finally the decision was made . . . they would indeed emigrate to Canada. Tainka knew in her heart that if she emigrated, she would never come back to this country again. She looked around the squalor of their little house, with their old, handmade furniture, and determined to go. Her decision became clearer as the days passed. She knew that if there was any better opportunity for Evan to survive and for Maria to have a better life than she had, it would not be here . . . not in Sosnitcha. She had also considered Evan's womanizing and how badly it had hurt her when she caught him making love to a young woman from another village. This incident had taken place in his weaving shop. Tainka had been eight months pregnant. Perhaps, if they moved to Canada, he would start a new life; perhaps he would no longer be interested in other women. This thought had been the deciding factor. Yes, she would agree to emigrate to Canada.

Canada, even with all its mystery and uncertainty, was beckoning. Her mother was another matter. How was she to explain to her mother that she would never be seeing her again? It was almost like foretelling a slow death. She was sure that if she ever got to Canada, there was no coming back. Now three months had gone by since that morning when Evan had come home drunk and Canada had been discussed by the two of them. Now the emigration plans were taking shape in earnest.

Tainka had broken the news to her mother about emigrating to Canada. As expected, Maria Greshko was crushed. She fell into a deep depression and could only sigh deeply wherever she went.

The Strachers packed the big, wooden trunk anyway. The trunk, known as a *scranya,* would serve as Tainka's security anchor, where her valuable and irreplaceable possessions would always remain. Clothing, pieces of household items, an oak hand-hewn bathtub to bathe Maria, her precious multi-coloured woolen sash which Evan had woven for her as a wedding present. Seeds for her garden in Canada, a few meagre possessions for Maria, including a small sheepskin coat with the sheep's wool turned inside to keep her warm during Canada's cold winters. They had heard that Canadian winters could get very cold, unlike the Austrian winters in Sosnitcha, where temperatures dipped only to -15°C.

Even though Tainka's mother hoped and prayed that the Strachers would change their mind about emigrating to Canada, it was not to be.

The morning of departure arrived. It was February 1903. Tainka's brother-in-law, Mike Yaworsky, volunteered to drive Evan, Tainka, and little Maria to Lviv. There the Strachers would board the train to Hamburg. At the Hamburg harbour they would climb aboard the ship that would transport them across the Atlantic to Halifax, Canada.

Tainka's sister, Helenka, was ready to deliver her first child any day now, so the 40 kilometre journey was too difficult for her to travel at this time. Mike Yaworsky and Tainka's mother drove up to the Stracher house where Evan, Tainka, and little Maria were waiting. Tainka showed her reluctance, and little Maria could sense this.

The usually quiet, even-tempered child cried and fussed. No matter who held her, she cried deep, teary sobs. Maria Greshko was a large, handsome woman with an ample bosom. As delicate and pretty as was Tainka, Maria Greshko was the opposite. Everyone thought Maria Greshko was a tough old woman because of her size and the fact that she had survived as a widow for the past few years without much difficulty. People, however, did not realize that Maria's children were the reason for her whole existence. "This is a very bad omen," she warned her daughter. "The child is sensing something bad will happen . . . it's not a good thing. Why are you going to this . . . this wild, unknown place—this Canada? Wild animals will surely eat you alive . . . or the Indians that live there will kill you!" She began to cry and howl and this, in turn, made Tainka cry even louder. Now all three generations of females were sobbing incontrollably.

Mike Yaworsky could see the difficult position Evan was in. He felt that if this continued Tainka might change her mind and not emigrate to Canada, even though the small hut the Strachers lived in was already sold, as were their one and a half morgs of land. Evan's brother, Yatsko, had bought both and had paid premium dollar for their properties. The proceeds of the sale were paying for the train fare from Lviv to Hamburg, for the Trans-Atlantic fare, and for the train fare from Halifax to Western Canada. It also left $50 for other needs, including $10 to register a homestead in Canada.

Mike Yaworsky quickly took matters into his own hands. "Now, now, is this the way to treat your daughter as she leaves?" he admonished Maria Greshko. "She and her children will have a wonderful opportunity in Canada, can't you see that? The kind of opportunity that we here in Austria will never have. I'm sorry, Mother, but you are being very unfair," he told her gently but firmly.

"Now let's finish packing this wooden *scranya* and place it on my wagon, and we'll set out for Lviv. If we don't do it now, they will miss their train!"

"You are a cruel man, Mike Yaworsky," Maria told him. "How can you talk to me like that? You are showing me no respect . . . no respect!" She was now hurt and angry but she stopped crying and, with that, so did Tainka and little Maria.

Evan, who didn't know what to do, was relieved as soon as he saw his wife packing the last items into the waiting wagon. Maria Greshko refused to travel to Lviv with Mike Yaworsky, saying she would rather stay with her other daughter, Helenka, Mike's wife. "It's right for one of us to stay with Helenka. Just suppose she has the baby when you're gone." Maria Greshko was still angry and frustrated because she had not managed to change her daughter Tainka's mind. Mostly, however, she was simply depressed.

Mike Yaworsky and Evan Stracher were relieved that the women stopped their tears and shenanigans. Mike dropped Maria Greshko at his home to be with his pregnant wife, Helenka. Everyone came into the house. As Tainka hugged her expectant sister, more tears were shed. Then she hugged her mother and asked God to bless them both. As she looked at her mother's sad face, she knew in her heart that she was seeing her for the last time.

Mike Yaworsky summoned the Strachers to climb aboard his new wagon or they would not reach Lviv before sunset. As the wagon rattled along the main road leading from Sosnitcha to Lviv, the two huge horses easily pulled their heavy load. Mike Yaworsky owned two gelded Shire horses. This team was the envy of all the men in the village. Mike had acquired them because of his bravery in the Austrian army, when he saved the life of one of the senior commanding officers and a crew of men working on a project. The army had been contracted to repair some deteriorating portions of the Franz Josef rail line, which linked the Austrian capital, Vienna, to Belgrade in the Balkans.

The incident occurred as work was progressing on the Franz Josef rail line through a mountain pass. A flatbed car loaded with timbers for use on the rail bed was parked on the finished rail tracks. Nearby, soldiers were using dynamite to blast their way through large boulders that blocked the path of the planned railway. Suddenly the braces holding the timbers in place on the rail flatbed broke, pinning the commanding officer under so that he could not move. Simultaneously, a soldier lit a stick of dynamite near the blast site, too close to the car where the officer was pinned under the timbers.

Mike Yaworsky watched in horror as this series of events occurred. Quick as lightning, he dove towards the soldier, grabbed the stick of dynamite with the burning fuse, and threw it at superhuman speed a hundred meters away. He saved the life of the officer, as well as the lives of the rest of the crew. The dynamite would have blown the officer and the others to bits. When Mike was asked what could be done for him in gratitude, he said a good horse would be appreciated upon his discharge from the army. One year after this incident, Mike Yaworsky had been honourably discharged and, as he walked out the gates of the barracks, a team of the most beautiful Shire geldings was waiting for him.

As they drove toward Lviv, Evan could not help envying Mike Yaworsky's magnificent team of horses. He made a mental note that some day in Canada he would surely own a similar team of these incredibly beautiful and powerful horses. When Evan made mental notes, he did so in great detail. He could picture Canada, the territories to where he and Tainka were headed, as a beautiful, vast land with luscious green forests in many hues of green. He could see evergreens and leafy deciduous trees in many shapes and sizes near a blue, pure-water lake. And there, in the middle of this forest and lake, he imagined a palace with many windows and a circular driveway in the front of the building. His dream palace looked like the many beautiful, stately homes he had seen in Vienna when he was serving in the Imperial Army of Franz Josef. At the front door of the palace, inside this circular driveway, was a beautiful team of huge tan-coloured horses. Evan's dream was that this was his very own team of horses in Canada. His dreaming was interrupted by Mike Yaworsky's voice, telling him how he and Helenka had also talked about emigrating to Canada in the near future. Tainka heard this and gave Evan a frightened look. Evan knew why Tainka was so concerned . . . she was worried about what would happen to her mother, Maria Greshko, if both her daughters abandoned her.

"As soon as I can save enough money to go and it is safe for my new baby and Helenka to travel, we will join you in Canada. I swear that I'll also leave this dreadful, hopeless place!" Mike vowed.

Soon they reached Lviv and the train station. The Strachers had six hours to wait until the train to Hamburg departed. Mike Yaworsky wished them God's blessings, good health, and good fortune. He needed to get back to Sosnitcha and to his pregnant wife.

The Strachers had bought their passage in advance, but when they arrived at the train station to board the train, their names could not be found, no matter how Evan, who spoke Austrian very poorly, tried to communicate. He could only speak Ukrainian fluently. Tainka tried to help and eventually they achieved a low level of communication.

The ticket agent finally found a hyphenated name on the passenger list. "It says Stry-Ker here. Could that be you?" He asked, perplexed. "Stry-Ker?"

"Yes, yes, Stracher," Evan nodded impatiently. By this time he was very frustrated. Tainka tried to intervene, to calm him down, but with no luck. "Stry-Ker is what I said!" the agent insisted angrily. "Oh Evan, let it be Stry-Ker—Stry-Ker. I'm not going to argue with him . . . let it be Stry-Ker. We know who we are!" Tainka pleaded with him.

They boarded the train and were seated in the lowest economy class. Austrian trains had the reputation at the turn of the century—in fact, since the mid-1800s—of being the most advanced rail lines and coaches in all of Europe. So even the lowest economy class provided a comfortable ride. As soon as they were seated the train started gently pulling out of the Lviv station and heading toward Hamburg. Little Maria fell fast asleep with the rocking motion of the train. This was her first train ride, as it was also for Tainka. Evan had ridden the train many times during his service in Franz Josef's army, when his regiment was transferred from one location to another. He felt he was a seasoned traveller. He wondered what adventures awaited him. Clickety-click, clickety-click, the train rocked toward Hamburg. Soon Evan was also fast asleep. Tainka, however, could not sleep. It was a wonderful adventure seeing the countryside . . . a view she had never seen before. As the train left the Austrian border, the terrain did not change much except that the countryside in Germany seemed to be more prosperous. The farmhouses were bigger and more livestock seemed to be pasturing in the fields. As they passed village after village, she saw that the places looked a lot cleaner than Sosnitcha had, and a lot more prosperous, too.

Tainka found the train to be extremely comfortable and relaxing. She was pretty well read, but she was not aware of the proud history which was associated with the Austrian rail lines.

The first steam railway in Austria was the Kaiser Ferdin and Nordbahn, opened in 1837. The rail line ran northward from Vienna into what was later known as Czechoslovakia. The state took a lead in the next decade or so and various railways, including the famous Semmering main line (1851) over the mountains, linking Vienna into what is now Trieste and Italy, were constructed under its auspices. In later years private enterprise took over and developed some important lines, such as the Kaiserin Elizabeth Railways from Vienna to Salzburg in 1852 and the Franz Josef line, linking the capital to Belgrade, in 1860. Finally, in 1880 the KK St B state system was formed. This organization gradually took over all the private lines, including the Semmering, one of the earliest state lines which however strayed away from the stateowned system and became the Sudbahn. In 1889 the opening of the 6.3-mile Arlberg tunnel completed rail communication from the Swiss Frontier at Buchs right across the country.

That was 12 years ago, when Tainka was only 11 years old. She was now 23, a beautiful woman in the prime of life, contemplating her future with much excitement, but even more reluctance. In Hamburg the Strachers hired a livery service to take them to the Kaiser Wilhelm der Grosse berth at the Port of Hamburg, one of the busiest port cities in all of Europe. Most central European immigrants departed from the Port of Hamburg. As the train pulled into the station Tainka was in complete awe of the hustle and bustle around her.

How could anyone live among all this noise and confusion? Horses, buggies, and dray wagons were everywhere. People were yelling and shaking their fists at one another because someone had gotten in front of them and cut them off in transit.

The buildings were much taller than she could imagine; some were up to ten stories high. There was the smell of the ocean, a salty acrid smell—a smell she had never experienced before. Along with the smell of the ocean, there were cooking odours and plain old manure smells from all the horses in the streets. Evan found all this exciting, as he liked city life. Maria was angelic and slept through it all. There the Strachers spent their first unpleasant night in a foreign country, with the officious German security personnel herding the peasant emigrants with less respect than cattle would have received. Evan tried to tell the officials at the registration window of the Kaiser Wilhelm der Grosse Station that he had a baby girl and asked where he could buy some food for her, Tainka, and himself. Once again, all the official was interested in was his name. Evan stated he was Evan Stracher and attempted to spell it in the Cyrillic alphabet, but the official did not understand and again the problem with their name ensued. The official had a pre-paid ticket for the Strachers.

"Yes, Herr Stry-Ker, you, your wife Tainka, and your baby daughter Maria are listed here," the official told them rudely. "Our ship sails tomorrow at 9:00 a.m. We are not responsible for food or lodging until tomorrow." Then he rudely muttered under his breath. "Dumbkopf Austrik, dumbkopf!"

Evan understood the insult perfectly. *Dumbkopf* meant the same thing in both the German and Austrian languages. He had heard *dumbkopf* enough times when he had served in the Austrian army. And at this point he was feeling very dumb. In fact, his normally positive constitution was reaching a new low . . . and it was too late to change his mind. He felt as if he was slowly drowning. Feeling totally dejected with his lack of success in procuring food or a place to sleep and again being referred to as Stry-Ker, Evan returned to Tainka's side. Being called a dumbkopf, on top of having your last name mispronounced over and over again, added insult to injury, he thought dejectedly. But on seeing Tainka's tears streaming down her face as she watched Maria, asleep on her lap, Evan did not burden his wife with his own feelings of depression and fear—fear of the unknown, fear of failure yet again. This was becoming an adventure which he liked less and less. "Oh, if I could only speak German," he thought hopelessly.

"My dreams and hopes were so real . . . I could imagine so vividly. I knew I was doing the right thing by wanting to go with my family to Canada. But now, looking at Tainka crying so bitterly . . . I am not able to talk to anyone . . . to help her . . . I don't know . . . I don't know if I made the right decision . . . Why did I decide to leave the security of Sosnitcha?" his thoughts tormented him. "Why, even if I carried on as a weaver and died of consumption, Tainka's mother would have looked after her daughter and her little granddaughter. Perhaps that would have been better than taking Tainka and my child on this wild adventure. What is Canada anyway? Maybe we all three will die in that land of uncertainty." Evan's normally optimistic disposition was being assailed unmercifully by doubts and regret. "Maybe we'll even die before we get there!" He thought darkly.

Suddenly he heard his name being called. "Stracher, Stracher, is that really you?" It was Petro Eliuk, who had served in the Austrian army with him. He came from the village of Parameshly, near the Russian border, but still in the Province of Galicia, Austria.

"*Shluck trafit* . . . may a curse blast . . . it's really you, Petro! To see you at this time is like seeing Jesus Christ himself! What are you doing here?" Evan slapped him on the back excitedly.

"We . . . my wife Mary and I . . . are emigrating to Canada. We are sailing tomorrow morning at nine on the Kaiser Wilhelm der Grosse to Halifax, in Canada!" explained Petro Eliuk, grinning widely. "And you?"

"What a blessing. We are also sailing tomorrow on the Kaiser Wilhelm der Grosse. We too are going to Canada!" Evan could hardly contain himself. Seeing Petro Eliuk at this time, when he was so deeply depressed, was truly a godsend. Surely, he felt, this was a good omen.

"Where were you going, Evan?" Petro asked, pleased to see a familiar face. He had always liked Evan.

"To buy some food for Tainka and Maria," Evan replied. "You will soon meet them both."

"I'll go with you. I already know where to go," Petro assured him. He was considerably more fluent in the Austrian language, having served as a message carrier for the Austrian commanding officer of his regiment. He and Evan walked about three blocks from the shipyard to a small front-side delicatessen, where a jolly German butcher sold pork back fat, seasoned with much paprika, at only a quarter of a mark per pound. They also bought a loaf of black rye bread. They hurried back to the reception area of the Kaiser Wilhelm der Grosse station. Petro brought his wife, Mary, to meet Tainka and little Maria. The women liked each other immediately. Mary, who was childless, fell in love with little Maria. She lovingly reached for the child and hugged and kissed her as if she were her own. Tainka was so pleased to meet the Eliuks.

Mary Eliuk took little Maria to a large bathhouse that was there for the use of the passengers and gave her a warm, soothing bath. She changed her into the clean clothes which Tainka had given her. After she had dried and clothed Maria, she washed the baby's soiled clothing in the bathwater and came back to Tainka, Evan, and her husband Petro. Tainka was so relieved to have someone else caring for the baby. Now relaxed, she nursed and fed some moistened rye bread to little Maria, who immediately fell fast asleep. The four adults sat and visited half the night, quietly sharing their hopes and their dreams. Then they wished each other a good rest and went to sleep on the public benches for the remainder of the night.

The next morning everyone got ready to board the huge ship. The gangplanks were lowered and, as names were called, people began boarding. First to go on board were the 558 first-class passengers, then 338 second-class passengers, and lastly all the 1,074 steerage passengers— the Eliuks and Strachers among them. A crew of 488 members was on board to serve the passengers and operate this magnificent vessel.

Vulcan built the Kaiser Wilhelm der Grosse at the Stettin yard in 1897. Its maiden voyage took place on September 19, 1897, from Bremerhaven to New York. It was the world's largest ship at the time. It was the first German ship to succeed in capturing the 'Blue Riband' with 22.35 km between Sandy Hook and the Needles. It displayed four huge stakes and two magnificent cranes for loading and off-loading cargo.

Tainka and Evan, along with Mary and Petro, were awestruck at the site of this huge, magnificent ship, their transportation to the new land—their new land, Canada.

Each class of passengers was called in alphabetical order; when the steerage were called, the Eliuks boarded well before Tainka and Evan Strachers' name was called.

When Strachers' name was called it was once again pronounced "Stry-Ker," "Stry-Ker." Evan first exploded with indignation, but soon sighed resignedly. "Let it be already . . . we'll change our name back to Stracher when we get to Canada. That will definitely change in Canada!" Tainka agreed and the three climbed onto the gangplank and into the spacious *Kaiser Wilhelm der Grosse*. It was at this point that the Strachers became Stry-Ker even though their intention was to maintain the name Stracher in Canada. That, unfortunately, was never to be.

Petro and Mary Eliuk were waiting for Evan, Tainka, and little Maria on board the ship. Soon the gangplanks were lifted and the anchors pulled. Shortly after, the large horns blasted as the *Kaiser Wilhelm der Grosse* pulled away from its berth. Soon the little tugboats pulled the magnificent sea vessel into the deep water of the cold Atlantic Ocean. In half a day the ship was out to sea and in four directions all one could see on the horizon was ocean—a rough, dark, navy blue, angry ocean. Evan took deep breaths of the ocean air, its salty sea smell invigorating him as he felt his lungs expanding to draw it in.

Tainka, however, became seasick almost immediately. She could neither eat nor drink. If she tried to force herself she would heave and vomit. Exhausted, dehydrated, and weak, all she wanted to do was lie in bed all day. Within two days she had lost all her milk. Mary Eliuk coaxed Petro to speak to the German crew, to convince them to find a nipple and bottle so that baby Maria could receive some much-needed nourishment.

An elderly German lady who was also immigrating to Canada with her daughter and granddaughter overheard their conversation and solved their problem. Her daughter had not one but two bottles and nipples fashioned of little pottery clay tips—perfect little nipples for babies to suck on and obtain nourishment. The German *Oma,* grandmother, soon came forward with some milk laced with honey. Little Maria suckled hungrily, seeming to enjoy this concoction even more than her own mother's milk.

Because Tainka was so sick that she could not provide for little Maria's needs, Mary Eliuk and Evan took over her care. Petro Eliuk also helped, for he loved children as much as his wife did and he was looking forward to having his own in Canada. It would be a fresh start . . . a great opportunity for their children. So much better than what he and Mary had experienced in their own childhood in Parameshly, Austria, in the province of Galicia.

As Evan Stry-Ker and Petro Eliuk mingled in the steerage class they discovered over fifty emigrants headed for the Canadian Territories amongst the passengers. Most spoke Ukrainian, although many spoke different dialects because they came from the Province of Bukovyna. The Bukovynans were a happier, merrier group of people than were the Galicians. They partied from morning until night on board ship and well into the wee hours of the morning. They brought with them home brew (moonshine whiskey), which they had brewed in their various villages. This supply was to tide them over while on this transatlantic journey. It helped prevent seasickness and helped dull the pain of leaving their homeland. It also helped them to more readily accept the uncertain future which they would all face in their new home, Canada.

Petro and Evan joined the partying on many nights while Mary Eliuk cared for little Maria. At a few of the parties they met Olana Hapko, a young Bokovynan widow from the village of Chernivchee. Olana was the happiest woman that Evan and Petro had met so far on this ship. Evan secretly yearned for a woman like this. She danced, even joined the men in dancing the *Hopak*, a Ukrainian dance where a person balances himself on the floor by using only his hands and, at the same time, kicks his legs up without falling or touching the floor with his feet. She would hike her skirt up to her waist so it would not hinder her kicking motions, and then she would get down on the floor with the men to dance. She didn't mind showing off her black bloomers. She didn't care who saw them.

"If they have never seen women's bloomers before this, let them look!" She would declare unabashedly. "If they have, then that's nothing new to them!" Then she'd sing along while dancing. "Hobze, Hobze, Chee, Chee, Chee!" She would sing joyously in her lovely voice. Her cheery disposition brightened everyone's spirits and made them feel more optimistic about their future. And when they heard the stories of her life's tragedies, they all felt humbled and even more fortunate to be who they were.

A marauding group of gypsies had ruthlessly murdered Olana's husband and their baby daughter, whom he was carrying in his arms, simply for the clothes on their backs. The gypsies were never apprehended. Olana had suffered a nervous breakdown. When she was finally able to accept life again, she decided she could no longer live in Chernivchee where memories caused grief beyond endurance. She also began to look at life differently, to live every hour to its fullest. And that was exactly what she was doing on this journey.

All the emigrants spoke mostly Ukrainian, very little Austrian. English, however, was completely foreign to them. Yet the country they were coming to was an English colony. Queen Victoria, a benevolent Queen who had opened the borders to these central Europeans, had died just a year ago leaving her son, Edward VII, as the ruling monarch. Edward VII continued his mother's practice of allowing entry to as many able-bodied central European immigrants as wanted to come. This agreement was of mutual advantage. Canada was developing its land in Rupert's Land in the Canadian Territories—today known as the provinces of Manitoba, Saskatchewan, and farthest to the west, Alberta. The central Europeans' most valuable possession was land, land which would produce grain crops the envy of many other regions in the world. As Petro Eliuk and Evan Stry-Ker talked to their fellow Galicians and Bukovynans, especially Olana Hapko, their hearts were lifted. For every one of these emigrants was in the same circumstances. Yes, the emigrants were all fearful of what awaited them but, because there were so many of them, they felt more secure and more determined to survive.

Olana Hapko would remain with the group until they reached Winnipeg, in the newly formed province of Manitoba, the place to which her sister and her husband had emigrated in 1900.

CHAPTER THREE

For the next twelve days, the ship made its way across the Atlantic Ocean en route to Halifax. The night before they would step on the soil of their new homeland the immigrants partied particularly hard. Even Olana Hapko became very tired and hung over from the excessive drinking. In fact, she had been able to outdrink the men.

So the morning that the magnificent *Kaiser Wilhelm der Grosse* was to dock at Halifax harbour, she was somewhat less cheerful than she had been throughout the Atlantic crossing. Such was the case also with Evan and Petro. Just a short hour ago, they were sicker than Tainka had been during the entire journey. Their condition, however, could be attributed to drunkenness, not seasickness.

When the *Kaiser Wilhelm der Grosse* finally docked at Port Halifax, Evan Stry-Ker and Petro Eliuk, blurry-eyed and heavy-headed, were forced to gather all their belongings and guide Tainka off the gangplank because Mary was carrying little Maria. Their hungover condition made this simple task almost insurmountable. The moment Tainka got her land legs, she instantly came to life again, particularly when she saw the condition in which Evan and Petro had been reduced by their overindulgence the previous night. She blessed Mary Eliuk for all her help during the ocean crossing, vowed to God that she would never again set foot on a sea vessel, got down on her knees, and kissed the ground passionately. This was the ground of her new country, Canada.

Now the processing of immigrants began. At the immigration-processing centre, not much to their surprise, the only language to be spoken was English. Passengers headed for the Territories were herded into one area. One of the Ukrainians, who had been exposed to a little English through his work as postmaster in the village of Valsilka, Austria, stepped forward to help translate for the immigrants. Some English words he had retained; some he only understood. But this was enough to help his fellow travellers with communication.

In the processing centre, all of them were asked to strip and were examined from their heads to their toes. Their teeth were examined carefully. Most had very few left, as dental hygiene was never a priority in Galicia or Bukovyna. The stench about them was unbearably strong. Many had been seasick during the long voyage and vomit had dried onto the one set of clothing which most of them wore during the voyage. They had no choice but to follow the officials' orders.

Evan and Petro were furious at the shabby treatment they received. "Why are we being herded like the army used to herd the horses into corrals?" demanded Evan. But he did not show his boiling anger to the authorities. He simply made a further mental note. He would fight for justice in this country . . . justice for people who were underprivileged, justice for people who were being treated shabbily, as they were now.

There was an attitude of impatience and condescension among the officials. The old country postmaster whom they had met on the ship overheard two officials talking and translated what they were saying. "These stalwart peasants are good for Canada. Even though they wear their ugly, dirty sheepskin coats, they don't need much. They will work like horses on clearing the bush off the lands in the west. Yeah, I heard most of them work like horses. Goddamn, they all stink like horses too! After all, most of their forefathers have been farmers for ten generations. If nothing else . . . they do know how to farm." When Evan heard about the comments, he knew he was not in that category. He knew nothing about farming . . . but he would learn. Even if it killed him, he would learn.

Names were called, again in alphabetical order. The Eliuks went first, while the Stry-Kers waited their turn. Tainka, who had now regained a lot of her strength, was having no problem caring for little Maria. Her body, however, was dehydrated. Evan continued to feel fragile. They both needed to eat and replenish their strength. Water was available in the processing centre in huge stone crocks with a spout in the bottom, where a sprocket dispensed it.

Once again their name was called and once again the caller clearly announced Stry-Ker, Evan, Tainka, and infant Maria. Evan and Tainka looked at each other in despair. "What's the use, we're in our new country and if they too wish us to be Stry-Ker, then so be it," Evan told Tainka.

"God bless us and thank Him for a safe journey . . . that is what's important. And if we are called Stry-Ker, then let it be." Tainka agreed. And so the Stry-Kers of Canada were born.

In the midst of all this commotion, the old country postmaster found an English newspaper in the Immigration Centre which stated that in March 1903 the number of immigrants coming to Canada totalled 121,500. Great Britain contributed over 47,000, while almost 40,000 came from the U.S.A. The rest—34,500— came from central Europe. He related this information to his fellow travellers and explained that there were almost as many immigrants from their part of the world as there were Americans coming to Canada. It was truly a patchwork of different languages and nationalities.

Even though the Canadian government officials treated these immigrants with disdain, they were nevertheless impressed with the healthy influx of them. They realized that within a few years the northwest, where the Stry-Kers were headed, would become a productive agricultural area and a market for eastern Canadian manufactured goods. Hence, the officials realized at this point that the Homestead Act was working in their favour and Canada would indeed become a nation from sea to sea. Most of the immigrants were attracted by the virtually free land which was being offered by the Canadian government.

The train voyage was much more pleasant for Tainka and she became more hopeful for a better life in Canada. She took over Maria's care entirely. The Canadian trains bore no comparison to the modern Austrian trains. Canadian trains in 1903 were called "Iron Horses." The huge steam-powered engines looked fierce as they gobbled up the coal which converted water into the steam power that propelled them. Large steel cattle guards were located in the front of each steam engine. These guards came to a "V" point and cleared most debris on the rail tracks. Unlike Austrian trains, the Canadian Pacific rail trains pulled passenger cars and freight cars at the same time. They stopped at most large centres.

The Stry-Kers marvelled at the vastness of their new country. "So much land, so much water and bush . . . I could never imagine such a wondrous sight!" exclaimed Evan. "We are so fortunate!" As they travelled through Quebec, they noticed a number of churches. Each church held a large cross at the peak of the steeple. The steeples were not the onion domes which were customary in Central European villages. It pleased the Stry-Kers because they were both very religious in the Ukrainian Greek Catholic faith, although they were not Roman

Catholic. However, the Pope in Rome was the head of their church as well and they respected him as such. They passed the majestic Ontario hills and the Great Lakes which, as the conductor announced to everyone, formed the largest body of fresh water anywhere in the world. Evan marvelled at this sight as the train passed Lake Superior. "This water could provide enough moisture to grow crops and gardens for all of Austria!" he exclaimed. "I wonder if where we're going also has fresh water . . . for us and for watering your garden, Tainka."

"I'm sure there must be, Evan. After all, this is Canada, and it's probably the same all over," Tainka assured him.

The train entered the Province of Manitoba. As it puffed along the rails, Evan and Tainka were surprised at little Maria's excellent behaviour. Their baby looked out the train window as though she understood that this beautiful, vast territory was also her new home. The train continued into the Territories and headed toward their destination. Now it only stopped to take on water, in order to drive the steam engine, and coal to fire the engine. They crossed a large plains area, which would later be known as Saskatchewan. Here they saw fewer and fewer settlers. Evan hoped there would be more settlers where they were going. Upon finally arriving at Strathcona Station in Edmonton, the Stry-Kers felt an immense relief. It had been a long, arduous journey. Here they bade their friends, Petro and Mary Eliuk, a tearful goodbye and vowed to continue to be lifelong friends. It was March 1903, and it was so cold . . . -10° Fahrenheit. Canada was like Britain, in that measurements and weights were calculated in the Imperial System; temperature was measured on the Fahrenheit scale.

The Kuriak family was there to greet them. This family had emigrated in 1899 from the same village of

Sosnitcha, in the old country, and had settled around Star, Alberta. They were distant relatives, second cousins on Tainka's side. This is where the Stry-Kers spent the next six months of their lives. During those months, Evan and Tainka watched the Kuriaks seed their grain and watched it grow. The Kuriaks had already cleared 80 acres of their 160-acre homestead. Tainka admired the rich black soil. The Kuriak land was almost entirely rich black soil. She hoped that Evan and she could have the same type of soil on their homestead, as she knew enough about farming to know that rich black loam was the best for growing crops and gardens.

In September of 1903, against the advice of the Kuriaks and their warning about the bitter Canadian winters, Evan set out impatiently for his own homestead. His cousins, the Pushinskys, who were the four brothers who had written all those encouraging letters to Sosnitcha—letters which were primarily responsible for the Stry-Kers' emigration—had settled around Shady Hollow, some 70 miles northeast of Edmonton.

Evan purchased a wagon and one horse which he named Yapa after one of his drinking buddies at the korshma in Sosnitcha. They packed their few belongings, which were in the *scranya*, and began their journey to Shady Hollow. The roads were little more than cutlines in the bush, truly a disaster, and Maria cried the entire trip to Shady Hollow. En route, as they camped under the wagon, coyotes howled all night. Tainka thought they would surely not survive. She thought back to her mother's warnings that the wild animals would eat them alive. After a very unpleasant three-day journey, which started each day at sunrise and ended at sunset, they reached Peter Pushinsky's homestead. Evan went to register his land claim the next day and was given the claim to his own homestead. The condition of his Homestead

Agreement was that one acre of land per year must be cleared for the next ten years before they would be given clear title to the land. He also paid the officials the ten dollars which was part of the Homestead Agreement.

If he had taken Tainka along with him, they might have selected a better parcel of land, but Evan's only requirements were that the land have much firewood and water. Firewood was plentiful. It would be used for warmth and for building a shelter for themselves and their livestock. He also wanted a steady supply of water. The sad part of these two requirements was that he got one of the most unproductive pieces of land around Shady Hollow. The hills, although breathtaking in scenery, were steep and contained many gullies. As beautiful as this area was, it was simply unproductive land. The soil was a black loam in only about one-third of the claim. The rest was clay, sand, and muskeg. There was, however, an artesian well, which trickled summer and winter. The water bubbled and sprang to the surface in an ongoing stream. It was the best and freshest-tasting water that anyone could ever have wanted. And the quarter section was covered in aspen, spruce, and willows. A creek ran through the property in the northeastern section of the homestead.

For their first home in Canada, the Stry-Kers dug a cave into the side of one of the many steep hills on the property and built a lean-to onto this cave. This was to be their home for the upcoming winter. They had no idea how accurate the Kuriaks' warnings about winter survival actually were. Little did they know how severe Alberta winters could be in reality.

Tainka was accustomed to washing clothes at the riverbank in the old country. She continued washing clothes outside at the artesian well. The well was fine until November but then the temperature dipped to

-40°F. Still she continued to go there every week to wash. This week, as she neared the cave which they called home, she collapsed. She had gotten so cold that she suffered a severe case of hypothermia.

Evan was looking after Maria, keeping himself and the baby as warm as humanly possible in this dark, dank, horrible little cave. Evan had bought a small, round tin heater and fashioned tin pipes, which were elbowed to the outside of the cave in order to allow the smoke to escape. The tin heater had to be kept fuelled with wood day and night, otherwise the Stry-Kers would certainly have frozen. The heater was also used to cook their food, mostly rabbits, which Evan shot during the cold, dreary days. The cave was no more than five feet deep and seven feet wide. The ceiling was low, no more than five feet high. Evan and Tainka were forced to crouch all of the time. Most nights the bedding froze onto the dirt walls. A feather quilt, which the Kiriuks had given to the Stry-Kers upon their departure, possibly saved their lives the first winter of their Canadian existence. Their bed was located in one corner of the cave. It was made of green poplar branches and a straw mattress Evan had fashioned, using straw which they got from their neighbours, the Borischuks. The opening into the cave was covered in spruce branches woven together tightly using spruce boughs and willow branches. This was one place where Evan's weaving skills came in handy.

Evan revived Tainka by putting her to bed and warming her under the feather quilt, where he placed flat, hot rocks which had been heated atop the tin heater. The hot rocks were a life-saver that first winter in Canada. The Stry-Ker land certainly had a lot of rocks. Actually, there were more stones than there was arable soil! Tainka was stricken with a death of a cold. It could even have been pneumonia. She would have died had Evan not taken her and Maria to the Borischuks, who lived on the next quarter, half a mile east and a quarter of a mile north, down a steep hill on a pretty, scenic homestead. The Borischuks had lived there for over two years and were quite well established, even though their house was a sparse little shack with a thatched straw roof. Theodore Borischuk drove his tiny one-horse sleigh to the Stry-Ker homestead and to the cave where they lived. He and Evan tightly wrapped Tainka in the feather quilt. Theodore had also heated some rocks before he left home as his wife Pashka had instructed him to do. They were still hot when they placed Tainka, wrapped in the quilt, to sit on these rocks a half-hour later.

Pashka and Theodore Borischuk were in their late forties. Pashka Borischuk was a medium-sized woman. She was shorter than Tainka by two inches. She measured five feet five inches. She weighed about one hundred and forty pounds. Pashka's face was her crowning glory. She wore a constant, sunny smile with dimples in both cheeks. Even on rare occasions when she frowned, her dimples were still prevalent on her kindly, rather than beautiful, face. However, this saintly woman had an inner beauty that shone like a beacon. Theodore Borischuk was short—five feet two inches tall—and weighed about the same as Pashka. He had prematurely grey hair and a grey full mustache. His eyes were happy, even when he squinted. A soulmate to Pashka, he enjoyed with her a good and loving marriage. Never blessed with children of her own, Pashka Borischuk acted as the midwife for most of the homesteader women in the region. She also knew much about using local herbs and roots for medicinal purposes. Miraculously, her skills, determination, and perseverance brought Tainka back to life. Pashka did not sleep for forty-eight hours until Tainka's fever broke and she knew she would survive. She insisted on keeping Tainka until she fully recovered. She also insisted on keeping little Maria for the rest of the winter until the Stry-Kers could build a more decent house in which to live. This occurred in the spring of 1904.

CHAPTER FOUR

Spring in Alberta does not usually occur until late April and the frost can come as late as June. Evan and Tainka busied themselves during the milder weather by cutting down the abundant spruce trees on their homestead, scaling the bark with the drawing knife, and hewing the logs in readiness for stacking them into a comfortable home. The Borischuks were excellent advisors and helpers. Having lived in this region since 1901, they considered themselves to be quite an authority. By spring of 1904, the Stry-Ker cabin was complete. It was a crude little one-room shack, but to Evan and Tainka it was a palace. The logs were chinked with clay, dry grass and manure, and the roof was thatched with straw. It had one window, which was purchased in Lamont, Alberta. Lamont was some thirty miles away, across the North Saskatchewan River from where the Stry-Kers lived. The shack also had the luxury of a wooden floor. Other settlers in the area had dirt floors. Evan had acquired a knack for carpentry. He was, in fact, enjoying this work and found that Theodore was a good instructor. Nonetheless, Evan still did not enjoy field work one little bit.

Pashka gave Tainka a clucking hen and twelve fertile chicken eggs. She showed Tainka how to set the clucking hen on the eggs. She instructed her that the hen was to be kept in a dark room and taken off the eggs twice a day so that she could eat and drink water. The cave in which the Stry-Kers spent their winter was perfect for this purpose. Three weeks after setting, eleven chicks hatched; only one egg failed to hatch because it was infertile. The chicks were like cuddly balls of fluff and little Maria, who was now two years old, was very excited about these beautiful little creatures that chirped and scrambled around the yard. Evan bought a milking cow (and named her Kalena or Cranberry) from his cousin, Peter Pushinsky. The cow was a deep wine colour—hence the name Cranberry. He also bought a pregnant sow from the Borischuks. The kindly Theodore Borischuk told him he could pay him back whenever he had the money. Thus life on the homestead began for Tainka, Evan, and Maria Stry-Ker.

The clearing of ten acres of land in the designated ten years as required by the Homestead Agreement had begun in earnest that spring. A small patch of land was cleared and ploughed with the new walking plough Evan bought in Edmonton for $15. Tainka planted a garden, carefully unwrapping the precious seeds which her mother, Maria Greshko, had carefully packed for her when she left the old country. Her mother's words now rang clearly in her mind. "Oh, daughter of mine . . . you are lost to me forever!" her mother had cried as the priest blessed the seeds. Tainka felt so terribly sad at this point, after having spent a miserable winter in the horrible little cave. Nothing in Sosnitcha was as bad as their life so far in Canada. Nothing! Why had she come?! Oh, why indeed!

As she unwrapped the canvas bundle of seeds, tears streamed down her face. She did try to be hopeful in her new country, but this experience of examining the seeds which her mother had lovingly given her in the old country made Tainka realize that she would never again see her mother alive, and depression overcame her. "Oh, mother, mother of mine," she sobbed brokenly. "I shall never see you again. Oh God, if only you knew how I miss you, mother, my dear mother. Had I known what

life was like here in Canada, I never would have come!"
After a long crying session she wiped her eyes, straightened her *babushka*, which was tied behind her head, and
began to examine the seeds, smelling every tiny package
for some hint of her mother's fragrance. There were car-
rot, beet, pea, poppy, bean, and cabbage seeds. She made
a makeshift *russadnik* (greenhouse) with the rotten
manure she had gotten from Pashka Borischuk. Pashka
also gave her a bucket of red potatoes for seeding. She
told Tainka these were early potatoes; they would be
ready to eat in mid-July. Tainka remembered Pashka in
her prayers every night, asking God to give this wonderful woman good health and happiness . . . oh yes, these
blessings in Canada were most essential. Pashka was like
a mother to Tainka, as she was fifteen years her senior.

With Tainka's help, Evan and Yapa the horse became
a formidable work team. They cleared one acre of land
quite handily and completed seeding the garden by the
end of the summer of 1904. They then began to seed
wheat on the small strip of land left from their clearing
efforts. Evan and Tainka both hoped there would be
enough wheat to mill into flour for bread during the
coming winter. Evan built a *peech*, an outdoor oven, for
Tainka. It was built in the shape of a half-moon by weaving willows into half-circles and binding these half-circles
in a perpendicular direction with willow branches. These
binding branches were then attached to the half-circular
shapes. The *peech* measured ten feet by six feet and was
five feet high on the outer measurements. The inside
capacity, when complete, could bake about twenty loaves
of bread at one time. A platform was built inside this
structure about two feet off the ground. This would create the oven inside the structure. A large opening was left
on the front of the structure. Then the outside and inside
of the *peech* were plastered with the clay that was so

abundant on the Stry-Ker homestead. A *peech* was one of the essential things needed by a Ukrainian pioneer, for it cooked and baked practically all their food. The inside of this huge clay oven could reach temperatures of up to 400°F. In preparation for baking, dry wood would first be placed in the oven to heat it. After the wood was burnt to embers and the heat made intense, the embers would be removed and the unbaked risen dough, formed into individual loaves of bread, would be set inside the oven. In summer the loaves were placed on cabbage leaves; in winter, women placed them on flat pieces of tin. Then the outside of the oven was sealed with a large wood and tin oven cover. The little spaces between the oven cover and the *peech* itself were sealed together with wet clay. It would take a little over one hour to bake a batch of bread in this airtight oven—the most delicious bread anyone would ever wish to eat.

When the clucking hens were finished hatching the eggs into fuzzy little chicks, the cave would be used as a barn for the sow who had borne ten piglets. The family was now living in their one-room cabin. Another spruce bough and willow shed, which Evan had again woven for the walls and ceiling, was built for Kalena the cow and Yapa the horse. A smaller shed was built for the chickens. Ten chicks survived; one had been captured by a roaming coyote.

Three months went by and Tainka was not menstruating. She discovered she was pregnant again and expected that the baby would be born six months later, sometime in December of 1904. Evan was pleased and hoped the child would be a boy, as he wanted a son to carry on the family name and help with the farming operations.

The Stry-Kers badly needed more cash. The cash that Evan had brought from the old country was now depleted. They had brought fifty dollars with them, after having paid for their train and ship passages. Evan had bought Yapa the horse; a walking plough; some crude tools, such as an axe and pick; a buck saw; shovel; hammer; drawing knife to debark lumber; grub hoe; and a wagon, which Yapa pulled. He still owed the Pushinskys ten dollars for Kalena, the cow. Evan was very concerned because without money in Canada one would certainly starve. There were no government relief programs, as the expectation was that the immigrants would fend for themselves. And most of them did just that. They survived . . . but barely. Evan had heard there were many jobs in Southern Alberta with wages of $5 a month for labourers. He was forced to make a painful decision. Should he leave Tainka in her present state or should they continue to live in bitter poverty for another year? He decided to discuss the matter with Tainka, as ultimately she would be the one most affected.

Tainka was pondering what to do, when Pashka Borischuk walked through the cabin door. "Tainka, my poor child, what worries you so on such a pleasant and blessed day?" Pashka asked her friend.

"Evan can get work in the brickyards of Medicine Hat. We need money desperately because not only do we owe Peter Pushinsky for buying Kalena the cow from him, we also owe you money for the sow. But we will also need more grain seed for next spring to plant the other acre we will have cleared. I'm pregnant . . . the baby is due sometime in December. I am afraid to be here by myself with little Maria because I've seen a few Indians walking by our house. What will they do to us when Evan is not around?" Tainka wailed at her plight. The Borischuks were their closest neighbours, living less than one mile away. South of the Stry-Kers, only half a mile away, a new family of homesteaders had just settled. Their name was Lupski.

The wise Pashka pointed out a few facts. "What, indeed," she began. "First, your fears seem to be about the Indians. Let me assure you, they were here before I or you got here. We are all living in their country. I have never heard of any attack by Indians on people in this area. And these Indians are Wood Crees. They are a very peaceful and passive people. Your homestead sits on their trail. This was the trail which they have walked on for ages to get to the trading post at Pakan. They trade their furs for supplies which they need. There are also rumours that their burial grounds are on the steep hill just above your artesian well. There are large rises in the earth over there that I noticed, and I also have seen the Indians stop there for quite a long time when they pass by. Don't be rude to them and they will respond accordingly," she advised Tainka gently. "As far as your pregnancy is concerned, I think it is a serious matter but you are a healthy woman and there should not be any complications. My experience tells me that you will have an easy childbirth. Furthermore, I have delivered more babies around here than I can count, so I should know. We live so close to you, and Theodore or I will check on you and Maria often. And you are right . . . you do need money in this country. That's the way of life here. We all arrived here and have supported ourselves—Evan and you will do the same."

And so it was decided. Evan would go to work in Medicine Hat. He had to walk to Lamont, as Yapa the horse was left for Tainka's use. He would then catch a CPR train to Edmonton and continue on to Medicine Hat. It took him almost two days to walk to Lamont. He had no nourishment with him and lived off the land. He picked berries or he killed a rabbit and cooked it on a campfire. He always took a slingshot with him. When he couldn't find rabbits, he picked wild duck eggs out of their nests and cooked those eggs by boiling them in the metal can which he always had with him. He managed to survive in this manner. His shoes were always worn out. He could not afford to buy new ones for the first few months when he started working.

Medicine Hat was indeed newsworthy in Canada, as drillers who were drilling for oil had discovered a tremendous flow of natural gas. It was expected then that some day there would be an oil boom on these lands.

It would take Evan ten days to get to his destination. The Canadian National Railway (CNR) would not arrive at Shady Hollow until 1918. It would serve the towns of Gibbons, Radway Centre, Waskateneau, Ralston, Shady Hollow, Smoky Lake, and Edwund, ending in St. Paul.

* * *

It was December 1, 1904. Evan had now been working for over five months. He was home only once in all that time. He managed to save $15, which he kept in the sole of his shoe in a special pouch, as he did not trust any banking institution nor did he trust his roommate at the brickyards.

Evan had remained faithful in the marriage from the time they set foot in Canada until he left for Medicine Hat. He might have had a sexual relationship during the voyage across the Atlantic Ocean. He had propositioned Olana Hapko, the cheerful Bukuvynan widow from Chernivchee, but she would have nothing to do with a married man. But in Medicine Hat, because of his insatiable sexual appetite, he did find a woman who sold sexual favours. He knew her as Madame Sooka. She was a widow who had lost her husband as a result of an accident at the brickyards. A large pallet of bricks had fallen on him and crushed him to death. Madame Sooka was left with four small children. In order for the five of them to survive, Madam Sooka sold herself to many of the men who worked at the brickyards. Her rate was fifty cents per favour. Evan had become her regular weekly customer. When he considered that his savings amounted to only fifteen dollars in five months he felt awful that he was paying two dollars per month strictly for his own sexual gratification. However, he justified his actions because, in his mind, he was helping Madame Sooka and her children to be fed and sheltered.

One morning Pashka came faithfully to check on Tainka as she or Theodore had done daily for the past five months. Tainka had started her labour. Pashka immediately ran home to tell Theodore to come and mind Maria while she attended to Tainka's needs. It took seven hours before the baby—a healthy fair-haired boy— was born. He had many of Evan's features: fair skin and hair, dark blue eyes which would turn to brown in later years, a cleft chin, and strong lungs. Evan's lungs too had become healthy again since coming to Canada. Tainka was amazed at the ease with which this baby arrived and thought surely that Pashka was the best midwife in the world! What a difference from the hard labour she had endured when Maria was born in the old country.

Evan came home for a week during the English Christmas, December 25 on the Gregorian calendar. He was ecstatic to have a son and was particularly pleased that the baby's facial features were like his. They named him Mikhail. Evan was also very pleased that, since he arrived in Canada, there had been no further signs of tuberculosis.

While he was at home, Evan hitched Yapa to the wagon and drove to Pakan (named after the great Indian

Chief) to pick up the mail. It would take Evan all day to reach Pakan and get home again because the roads which led to the trading post were rough and bumpy forest roads. Although the cutlines were wide enough to accommodate an ox cart or a wagon, travel on these roads was not easy, as the stumps, mud holes, and corduroy over low spots created extreme problems for travellers. As well, there were numerous creeks to cross en route, creeks which did not have bridges and had to be forded. Most supplies and mail to the Fort at Pakan were delivered by barge or boat on the North Saskatchewan River from Edmonton, some sixty miles down the river.

Evan brought home a letter from Tainka's mother in the old country. The news was very bad. The letter began, "My dearest daughter, Tainka, and granddaughter, Maria." Maria Greshko never mentioned Evan in her letters because she blamed him entirely for the loss of her eldest daughter to Canada. She also felt that Tainka married far below her station and never changed her mind about that. Maria Greshko regarded Evan as nothing more than a drunken, uneducated bum. She was convinced that her lovely daughter could have married a rich Pun or at least a physician. So as far as she was concerned, Evan did not exist.

Maria Gresko went on, "Today I write to you with a very heavy heart. The news here in Sosnitcha is very bad. Your sister, Helenka, died while giving birth to her son. He was a very big baby and the good midwife from our village was away. Mike tried to get another midwife from the next village, and he did, but the woman knew practically nothing about delivering babies. She could only pull the big baby out of Helenka. Thank God, at least he is alive, but Helenka bled to death. The funeral was very sad. I fainted many times and so did Mike. We buried Helenka next to your father's grave. There is yet room for me at the cemetery and I pray to God every day that he takes me soon. With both my daughters gone, what is there to live for? Right now I am caring for little Mikhail. That's what Mike named him. Now I have two grandsons named Mikhail, yours and Yaworskys'. I know that Mike will find a woman to marry soon and she will look after the baby so why is there any reason for me to live? I am sorry to be sending you this bad news but someone has to tell you. I hope Maria is fine and growing healthy and I also pray for you. God bless you both. *Mamunia*."

This tragic news affected Tainka so adversely that she could not continue nursing her own baby, Mikhail, past the second month. She lost all her milk as she had done when crossing the Atlantic with little Maria. Pashka again came to the rescue. She ordered Theodore to travel to Edmonton and buy nursing nipples and bottles because the Pakan Trading Post had none, nor were there any at Lamont. While he was gone, Pashka and Tainka wet a soft cloth in milk and let the baby suck on the wet cloth. A week later Theodore returned from Edmonton with two porcelain nipples, and Pashka prepared a formula of cow's milk and some honey, which was given to baby Mikhail upon demand. Theodore brought back not only the nipple and a special glass container to hold the cow's milk but also some colourful fabric for Pashka and Tainka so they could sew new Sunday dresses. The cow's milk was to be fresh at all times and so Kalena the cow was milked frequently. The baby survived; in fact, he thrived. He became a chubby and cuddly baby with a healthy appetite and a wild little temper! He was a scrapper and full of determination, yet he was very lovable.

A year had gone by since Evan started work in the brickyards. Tainka managed the homestead well by herself. She did, however, receive much help from the Borischuks. In the spring Tainka and Theodore seeded the land by hand. Theodore owned a simple machine to broadcast the seeds. He put the seeds into a small receptacle and strapped the machine around his neck. As he turned the crank of the machine with his right arm he walked at a steady pace; as a result, the seed was evenly broadcast in the field. The two cultivated acres were seeded easily in one day. The wheat was bought from the Pushinskys, who most times had the best crops around Shady Hollow. The two-acre parcel had been cleared according to the terms required in the Settlement Agreement. The Pushinskys were reasonable about payments, since Evan could not yet pay them for last year's seed grain. Kalena had delivered a calf, a heifer, which was the Stry-Kers' first-born animal that they could call their very own. They named her *krasaw*, meaning "spotted" in Ukrainian, because she had huge brown spots on her white body.

It was July and the wheat was heading out beautifully. This would be a great crop. Perhaps Evan could stop working and devote his energies to farming and caring for the livestock. Tainka was outside tending to her garden patch with Maria and Baby Mikhail. The baby was now crawling in the dirt in a little dress which Tainka had sewn for him. He looked like a true, dirty ragamuffin but he was having great fun, giggling and crawling as little Maria tickled his chubby legs.

Tainka, amused by their antics, took a few moments to relax. Looking up, she saw one female and four male Indians approaching from the north. The men were dressed in their rawhide trousers and shirts, their long black braids on either sides of their heads adorned with beaded headbands. All four were tall and slender and their dark-skinned faces were very handsome. The woman was dressed in a fringed rawhide dress. All wore new, beautifully beaded moccasins.

Not being able to speak Cree or even a word of English, Tainka could not communicate with them. Furthermore, she was very frightened. Grabbing both children, who by now were howling because they could sense their mother's fear, she fled into the house. The Indian passers-by followed them. When they came to the closed door, they knocked. Tainka thought they would surely scalp her and the children, judging from stories that she had heard from various people in the old country. Most of all she remembered her mother's warning, given just when they were leaving Austria to come to Canada . . . "If the wild animals don't eat you, then the Indians will kill you!" Tainka summoned enough courage to open the door slowly, her hand shaking visibly. She motioned them to enter.

The Indian woman was the first to try communicating with her. She tried to introduce herself. "Me Mary . . . Me Mary," she repeated slowly several times, pointing at herself. Then she pointed to the men. "This Paul, this Louis, this Cochees, and this Gabriel." The only name Tainka could remember was the woman's name, because it sounded like her favourite saint, the Virgin Mary. Mary held out a tiny bag and motioned for Tainka to open it. Tainka opened the bag and looked inside. She had never seen anything like this . . . black, dried-up leaves which had a surprisingly nice fragrance. Tainka had never seen tea leaves before, although she had read about *chi* (tea) in the old country. She had no idea how this beverage was to be made or what was the proper way to prepare it. Sensing that the Indian visitors meant no harm, she relaxed. From their sign language she realized that they wished to rest. The woman, Mary, motioned for Tainka to stoke up the fire and soon the kettle (which Tainka called a samovar) was boiling. Tainka then scooped up a big handful of tea leaves, placed these in the bottom of a pot, and then poured the boiling water from the kettle over them. This created a pot full of tea leaves with very little liquid left to drink. What liquid was left tasted as strong as tar.

Mary gently nudged Tainka aside and motioned that she would do the job. Some more water was boiled. She then took three small pinches of tea leaves and indicated with a hand-to-eyes motion that she wished Tainka to pay attention so she could learn just how few tea leaves are needed to brew tea. She then poured the boiling water on the dried leaves. The Indians let the tea brew for a few minutes, then helped themselves to the second-hand cups which Evan had purchased at an auction sale somewhere on his travels in the south. Drinking their tea and smoking their pipes as they sat in a circle on the Stry-Kers' shack floor, they tried to talk to Tainka, but she could not understand them nor could they understand her.

After a while they rose. In gratitude they left the rest of the black tea leaves for Tainka and some berries which they had picked for the children. The fragrance of their rawhide clothing and pipe smoke lingered for quite some time after they were gone. The scent pleased Tainka. After this day the Indians made the Stry-Kers' home a regular stopover on their way to the Pakan trading post. Tainka learned to make the best tea, and she enjoyed their company immensely. She now remembered their names and associated each one with their proper name. They were indeed gentle, friendly, and compassionate people. After a while she even learned to speak some Cree. Throughout her life, Tainka never discriminated against any colour, race, or creed, and she tried to instill this quality in all her children. She also learned how to use roots and herbs for healing purposes, both from the Indians and from Pashka Borischuk.

CHAPTER FIVE

In 1905, Alberta was inaugurated as a province (and no longer was known as the Territories), with proper status in the Confederation. Great ceremonies took place in Edmonton. Wilfrid Laurier was the Prime Minister. Upon inauguration, the first Alberta Premier to be appointed was Rutherford. Laurier was accommodated at the regal Alberta Hotel on 97 Street and Jasper Avenue during the time he was in Edmonton to attend the ceremonies. Evan was on his way to Medicine Hat, going back to the brickyards. Before catching the train to Medicine Hat he stopped at the Turkish baths located near 97 Street. He had started to indulge in his womanizing ways in Edmonton as well as with Madame Sooka in Medicine Hat. Hence, he did not visit the steam bath alone, but with a woman whose reputation was neither savoury nor honourable. There was such a hullabaloo outside the baths that Evan rushed outside along with other patrons and got a glimpse of Prime Minister Laurier as he was being driven to his hotel after the inaugural ceremonies. Sir Wilfrid—as he was eventually knighted by the king—was a tall regal-looking man, handsome with his distinct French features. Later, in the steam baths, the clients who had attended the inaugural ceremonies explained what the Prime Minister had told the crowd.

Most of the men were very impressed with Prime Minister Laurier's speech. It stated in part, "We do not want nor wish that any individual should forget the land of his origin. Let them look to the past, but let them still more look to the future . . . let them become Canadians,

British subjects, and give their heart and soul, their energy, and all their power to Canada, to its institution and to its King!"

These words were particularly meaningful to Evan, as he was a proud immigrant. However, he did wish to forget his country of origin because it held so many bitter memories for him. He just wanted to forget his past and look ahead to his family's future.

Tainka continued to manage the farm. A weasel killed two-thirds of her chickens in the spring of 1905, when it got into the chicken coop and sucked the life out of twenty of her best laying hens and prime roasting roosters. It broke her heart to look at the lifeless birds as she buried them. She could have thrown them into the gully near the farmstead, but this would just have encouraged the masses of roaming coyotes to come back for more and kill the chickens that had survived. She would wait for some of the remaining ten chickens to start laying eggs and then place a few clucking hens on the fertile eggs to hatch more chicks. Once again, Pashka Borischuk provided three dozen fertile eggs and three clucking hens which were set on the eggs to begin their labour of hatching. In three weeks' time the chicks would come to life. The old cave up on the hill, the Stry-Kers' first home, was the best place to set clucking hens because it was dark and warm at this time of year. This time, all thirty chicks hatched—twenty female and ten male chicks. All but one of the male chicks would be used for eating; one would be left to help the hens produce fertilized eggs. There were no commercial hatcheries at Shady Hollow or even in Edmonton in those days.

This time the chickens were penned in a screened area. Theodore Borischuk had bought some fine chicken wire in Edmonton a few years previously when a weasel had devastated his flock. Whatever wire was left was used for the Stry-Kers' chicken pen. When Evan came home on one of his infrequent visits, the pen was already built. Tainka was becoming virtually self-sufficient. She did have Theodore and Pashka to help her; however, there were many days when she did not even think about Evan. Deep down in her heart she suspected that Evan was being unfaithful to her for she knew what his sexual demands were when they were together. Now he had been away for almost two years. She knew that he could not have been celibate all that time, considering the few visits he made home.

Tainka continued becoming a stronger person in her own right. She was losing the passive, submissive nature which she had exhibited in the old country. Much of this change could be attributed to necessity. If she didn't become self-sufficient then she would not survive. And she had no intention of giving up at this point—she had too much to lose. Her children were depending on her. There was no one else, as Evan was away. Every night in her prayers she asked God to be merciful and, above all, to give her strength to carry on. Obviously God was listening to her prayers.

CHAPTER SIX

Tainka received a letter from her brother-in-law, Mike Yaworsky, in the old country. The news was black indeed. Her mother, Maria Greshko, had died of a broken heart, he said. On her deathbed she had lamented that she had lost both her daughters—one to death and the other to Canada—so she had no reason to continue living. Mike had found her dead on one of his visits. She had died peacefully in her sleep at the age of 46.

Though burning tears ran uncontrollably down her cheeks, Tainka was not entirely surprised at the tragic news. Her mother's last letter had indicated that she had no more will to live and that she would welcome death. Mike Yaworsky had also written that he was remarrying, as he had found a dear lady who was willing to take on the duties of a stepmother and care for his baby, Mikhail, Tainka's little nephew. He further revealed that, now that Mother had died, they were planning to emigrate to Canada.

In 1906, Tainka gave birth to another child. She named her Helenka after her own sister, Helenka Yaworsky, who had died giving birth to Mikhail. Baby Helenka was a colicky baby and was very difficult to rear. She was not at all like Tainka's firstborn, Maria, who was a gentle, quiet soul. After watching this fretting, constantly howling child, Pashka Borischuk concocted a healing brew for Helenka to drink. Then Helenka slept for three days. All Tainka knew was that the drink contained some amount of poppy seed juice. After this long sleep, Helenka's colic disappeared and her constant crying ceased. She only cried on occasion, as did other babies.

Evan by this time had stopped working away from home and was dedicating his time to clearing more land. Yapa, the horse, and he were away from the house most days, leaving Tainka with the baby and minding the other two children as well as tending her garden and doing the farm chores with the animals. There were no more children at the Stry-Kers' until November 1, 1910, when Katayna was born.

Evan was frequenting the Turkish baths in Edmonton more often now than he had before Helenka's birth. The visits were always about a week long. He would explain to Tainka that his blood was bad and he needed a treatment. The treatment, he told her, consisted of using leeches to draw out his bad blood. Tainka eyed her husband with suspicion. She knew all about Evan's roving eye for attractive women and now realized that he would never change. He had not been faithful to her since she first met him in his days in the Austrian army. *Why did I ever marry him?* She now wondered, finally understanding why her mother had never liked him. Consequently, she did not accept his explanations about leeches sucking out his bad blood as a reason to go to Edmonton.

Tainka's mother had known that Evan had roguish tendencies. Coupled with that, he had an extremely charming personality . . . . especially with attractive women. But perhaps that was why Tainka had married him, much against her mother's wishes. Evan had learned early in life that a charming personality was the secret to survival—it had helped him survive being orphaned at twelve years of age. Evan used to pick up any paying job he could find in the village. During his childhood, he had worked for widows and old maids; for a few years, he had also tended the priest's sheep. When he turned sixteen he had joined the Austrian army.

Pashka Borischuk continued to be Tainka's midwife, close friend, and confidante. On October 15, 1913, another boy was born to Tainka. He was named Paul. The baby was dark-haired and blue-eyed, just like his mother. A passive, introverted little boy, he would hide in the corner whenever a stranger came to the house. This was also the year Mike Yaworsky and his new wife emigrated to Canada. Tainka vowed that this was the end of her childbearing.

CHAPTER SEVEN

The Ukrainian Catholic community was a very close-knit group, possibly because many of them were related in one way or another in the old country. Most of them came from the same village; if not, they all came from the Province of Galicia in Austria.

All were fiercely religious. Evan would not permit any work to be done on Sundays, particularly if it could be done on any other weekday. Work such as sewing, knitting, canning fruit and vegetables, or even using scissors to cut fabric or paper was strictly prohibited in the house. The only exception was tending to the daily farm chores and working with the farm animals . . . feeding and milking the cows, slopping the pigs, and feeding the chickens.

Every Sunday Evan would push a chair over to the shelf located near the ceiling of the porch which had been added to the house. He would reach for his Holy Liturgy Mass book. He would then sing the entire Mass. Even though he had trouble reading, he could read every word of the Mass book. His Mass book was one of the most important books in his life, even more than the Bible. Because he couldn't read, the Bible was just too much to memorize. Of course, he had memorized the passages of the Mass book as he still could not read Ukrainian with any fluency, but he was learning English. He would sing and chant the part normally taken by the priest while Tainka and the children responded to the parts normally taken by the congregation. His patience grew thin when the response sounded insincere. He would stop the Mass and bark at his wife and children to be more serious and earnest about how they replied.

The men who were Ukrainian Greek Catholic in the community—which was most of them—called several meetings at the Stry-Kers' home. The parishioners decided that a church must be built. And so in 1910, the year Katayna was born, a church was built. Mr. Joseph Chomiak, a neighbour of the Stry-Kers, donated three acres of land to the project. His land was very similar to the Stry-Kers', with deep gullies and rolling hills. The site for the church was the most peaceful, enchanting place in the whole area. It was situated on top of the highest hill in the region with beautiful aspen, willow, and spruce trees surrounding it. Looking down the rolling hills toward the base of the valley was the slow-running White Sands Creek, a tranquil ribbon of blue from the church's vantage point.

Tiger lilies and violets bloomed in profusion in the months of July and August. The men cleared half an acre of land for the actual church site; the remainder was to be used for the cemetery.

A priest of German ancestry, who spoke broken Ukrainian, was the priest designated for the Parish of St. Olga by the bishop who lived in Winnipeg. The designated priest for the parish resided in Mundare, Alberta, at St. Basil's Basilian Monastery. He served the whole area encompassing about sixty square miles. His name was Father Ruhr. Until now, he had conducted masses about once a month in the homes of the parishioners.

Father Ruhr was a gifted person in many ways, even though his Ukrainian left a lot to be desired. One ability with which he was blessed was his architectural skills. He drew plans for the first little church. It was to contain seven hundred square feet in total, with one large onion dome in the centre of the structure.

The project took several years to complete. Each item was donated—lumber, glass windows, and nails. The inside was finished in tongue-and-groove boards; the outside was covered with cedar siding. This siding, imported from British Columbia, was the most durable. The tongue-and-groove boards were painted first by the church members. This did not require any great skills. The main colours were yellow and blue, the colours of the Ukrainian Nationalists. The final work inside the church was left to a fine iconist from Edmonton. He painted the insides of most of the churches in the area, whether they were Russian Orthodox, or Ukrainian Catholic, or Ukrainian Orthodox, or Romanian. All the icons were similarly beautiful with their crisp, bright colours. Many had gold paint around the subjects' heads to indicate halos. Usually the iconist painted baby cherubs into each of his icons.

This church was to be the greatest gathering place for the parishioners. Even the Stry-Kers' neighbours, who were Polish and by tradition therefore Roman Catholic, chose to come to St. Olga's to celebrate Christmas on the 7th of January in the new church. They did on all other occasions throughout the rest of the year follow the Gregorian calendar. The bell tower was erected about two hundred yards from the church. The huge bronze bell, made at a foundry in Winnipeg, Manitoba, was shipped to Edmonton by the CPR train. A wagon and four horses were needed to haul it from the Strathcona Station in Edmonton to Shady Hollow. Theodore and Pashka Borischuk made a generous donation of $100 toward the purchase of the bell. They explained that they had no children and wished to contribute to the enhancement of the lives of their friends and their children at Shady Hollow. On October 11, 1911, the Bishop responsible for the diocese arrived from Winnipeg to bless the church and conduct official commemorating ceremonies. People from everywhere came in their horse-drawn wagons, or the more sophisticated democrats. Even Mrs. Makovitsky's son, Billy, drove her to these special ceremonies. She owned a General Store in Shady Hollow and was much more prosperous than most people in this area. The family even owned a Model T Ford. While driving through the badly maintained roads, Billy hit a mud puddle. He shifted into first gear. "Why do you keep pushing on that stick all the time?" his mother demanded.

"Mother, I am shifting gears!" he explained.

"My dear son, may God forgive you!" she admonished him. "Could you not have shifted those gears on Saturday? Why would you choose to do this task on the holy Sabbath day?" Mrs. Makovitsky was very much like Evan Stry-Ker. She did not believe any work should be done on Sundays.

The church bell was loud and could be heard for miles around. It was used to notify people that someone in the neighbourhood had died, and it was used during all other church services, funerals, weddings, and christenings. If the bell rang on days other than Sunday or holy days everyone knew there was a death in the area or an emergency summoning people to gather at the church.

CHAPTER EIGHT

In 1913 a school was built. It was the next large undertaking in the community. However, this time the community involvement was much greater, as it included everyone regardless of his or her religious affiliation.

The Shady Hollow Municipality was established in 1915. There were schools south, southwest, and southeast in the municipality, but no schools in the northeast or northwest where there certainly were children of school age. For instance, Maria was now eleven years old, yet she had never attended school.

Again land was donated, this time by Mr. Lupski, the Polish neighbour. He gave two acres of his quarter section, in the extreme northeast corner of his homestead.

It was convenient for the Stry-Ker children, as the distance was only a quarter of a mile from their home. They could, and did, come home for lunch.

School was taught in those years only during non-seasonal work months, primarily October to April. The homesteaders relied on their children to help with farm work. Evan and Tainka had different points of view on schooling. She wanted her children to know how to read and write in English even though she took no initiative to properly learn English herself. Evan, on the other hand, felt that developing the homestead was much more important. And girls had no reason to go to school anyway. After all, they would only marry, have babies, and be their husband's helpmate.

The one-room school was completed one and a half years after construction began. All children in the area attended, regardless of their religion or background.

They spoke different Ukrainian dialects: Bukuvynian, Hadiski, Broschakee, and Lambkee.

The Stry-Ker children—Maria, Mikhail, and Helenka—all went to school. They were all placed in grade one, even though there were six years separating the eldest from the youngest. The teacher's name was Mr. David Newhouse.

He was intellectually articulate and came from Drumheller, Alberta. Before a teacherage could be built, he received his room and board from the Borischuks, as they had no children of their own and had the additional room.

The children spoke no English; Mr. Newhouse spoke little Ukrainian. He did speak French, English, Hebrew, and Latin fluently, having been educated in Montreal where his family lived before moving to Alberta. In order to teach the children to speak English, he quickly made a rule that no Ukrainian was to be spoken in the schoolyard during school hours.

Mr. Newhouse was a tall, slim, delicate-looking man with a high hairline and reddish- brown curly hair. His nose was thin and aquiline with a slight hook at the end. His nostrils flared and his freckled skin turned a beet red when he got angry, which was not often. He wore round, wire-rimmed glasses which fell to the end of his nose as the day went on, and he had a habit of constantly pushing them back up to the bridge of his nose.

Every day he was dressed immaculately. His high, starched collar was always crisp and white; he wore a vest, dress suit, and polished shoes that were covered by grey spats.

He avoided visiting most of the homesteaders, as certainly he would have soiled his clean shoes and spats had he even come close to the farmyards, because the cows, pigs, and chickens roamed around quite freely in most farmers' yards. This was no different than in Sosnitcha, even though people now lived in Canada. Everywhere you stepped there were some form of animal droppings! The Stry-Kers and the Borischuks were the exceptions because their pigs and chickens were penned separately.

His class numbered thirty-five and the ages ranged from six years to fourteen. Rosie Soova was fourteen going on fifteen. Her family lived across the road from the Lupskis (on whose farm the school stood) and kitty-corner from the Stry-Kers.

Mr. Newhouse taught English, reading, writing, arithmetic, history, and geography. Physical education or sports were not his forte as he was a bookworm more than an athlete.

His patience was tried on many occasions, as he needed to place these thirty-five children at different levels. One common problem was that none of them spoke any English. However, some were very good in arithmetic. Some began to read English more quickly than others.

He finally placed them into four groups, with some levels having up to twelve children. Each group was taught English at the same time.

Rosie Soova was attractive for her age. She had a full, round face, blue eyes, a tiny nose, straight white teeth, and sweetheart lips. She had a well-developed figure for a fourteen-year-old, with a particularly large bosom. She was only about five feet two inches tall. Good-natured and constantly smiling, Rosie was particularly bright and learned quickly. She took instruction well and idolized Mr. Newhouse. When he spoke to Rosie, his tone of voice changed. It was obvious he adored Rosie as well.

After six months, Rosie was reading at a grade three level. For homework, she voluntarily studied the Oxford dictionary, which Mr. Newhouse loaned to her. On many days she was forced to miss school, as she was the eldest of the Soova children and her parents needed her help, either to mind the younger children or help with the farm work. Mrs. Soova was pregnant frequently and was at this time carrying their ninth child.

CHAPTER NINE

The second school year began in October 1915. Mr. Newhouse was contracted to teach another year. Evan was the school councillor, a position which he had held since the school was started. It was the councillors who established the teacher's wages. As financial resources were limited, it was found the teacher's wages could not be raised that year. David Newhouse agreed to teach for the same amount for one more term.

The men in the community built a one-room teacherage over the summer months and David Newhouse now had his own residence. His contract for the entire year amounted to $150. He was docked $25 for the rent of the new teacherage.

David Newhouse was now twenty-five years old. His mother, Rachel Newhouse, came with him from Drumheller to set up house in the new teacherage. She stayed for only one week, but during that time made an effort to meet Evan and Tainka, the Borischuks, the Lupskis, and the Soovas. To everyone's surprise and delight she spoke some Ukrainian.

The Newhouse family, before moving to Drumheller, had operated a General Store in Mundare, Alberta, a predominantly Ukrainian community. Everyone was most impressed with Rachel Newhouse's charming personality. She was about forty-five years old, with dark hair and eyes and an infectious smile. However, her steel determination was evident. She showed much interest in everyone she spoke with but had very little patience for anyone making a genuinely ignorant statement—as Mr. Soova had a habit of doing.

Rachel Newhouse drove a Model T Ford. She made it well known that the family was of Jewish faith. Judaism was their religion and it was the most important thing in their lives. She left a Torah and a Menorah in the teacherage for her son to use during prayer times and holy days. He also wore a Yarmulka during prayer times, but—he made it very clear to his mother—he would not be wearing it when he taught school.

While visiting the Soovas' home, Rachel Newhouse met Rosie as well as Rosie's father and mother, Metro and Olga Soova. Olga Soova was a meek, quiet woman totally dominated by her oversexed and ignorant husband. She appeared to be sixty but in reality was only thirty-two, the same age as Tainka.

Mrs. Newhouse greeted them. "My son David tells me your Rosie is a very smart girl. Perhaps you should consider sending her to higher school and she could come back here as a teacher," she offered.

"To hiyear schoola? Whad for, to hiyear schoola!! She vill be rady to mary and to having babies just lik her mudder. See whad so bad about her mudder!" Metro Soova said, and leered at his wife. Olga never contradicted him, but the sorrowful and hopeless look on her face told the whole depressing story.

Olga Soova was in her ninth month of pregnancy. She was clad in a washed-out, torn, calico-printed smock over which she wore a large soiled apron. Her head was wrapped in a black *babushka*. Her weather-beaten, wrinkled face with sunken eyes was a testimonial to her misery as she sat quietly on a homemade bench rubbing together her swollen hands. The skin on her hands was chapped and cracked on every finger. They looked as if they had never stopped working. She was barefoot. A lone tear dropped on her cheek as she turned her face away.

Mrs. Newhouse looked at Metro Soova with contempt and disgust. She could see that this lecherous man lived to fornicate and if it wasn't with his wife it was with any other female who was willing or convenient. She looked around the one-room shack with a dirt floor and marvelled at how ten people could survive under these conditions.

When Rosie offered to make some tea, Mrs. Newhouse declined politely and made the excuse of having to pack for her journey back to Drumheller the following day.

CHAPTER TEN

On October 15, 1915, Metro Soova came running to the Borischuks to summon Pashka to deliver the baby. "Quick, Pashka," he gibbered excitedly. "The wife is ready to have the baby!"

Pashka grabbed her sash, clean linen, a small bottle of moonshine whiskey, and some dried puffball powder, which was used to congeal blood. She piled these items in her carpetbag and climbed into his rickety wagon. He beat his roan horse and the animal reared, almost causing whiplash to Pashka's neck as they drove off to his homestead.

When Pashka arrived, she found Olga Soova swollen beyond recognition. Her face had ballooned and her hands and feet looked dangerously bloated. Pashka became very concerned. She knew there would be serious complications and expressed her concerns to Metro Soova.

"Metro, as you can see, Olga is having more serious problems than I am capable of dealing with. Please go get the doctor from Lamont. If you hurry it may not be too late!" she pleaded.

"What, are you crazy or what . . . I not be going to Lamont for a wife who's only having a baby. She already had eight. What's one more . . . it will be like pulling a stone out of a plum! No don't be worried . . . and do your work, woman!" He yelled.

"Metro, you don't understand. Olga is more serious this time . . . she's much weaker. I'm telling you, please get a doctor!" Her cries fell on deaf ears.

Olga Soova had a serious toxemia problem. She also had lost all will to live and had no energy to push when it was time to deliver the baby. The baby was situated in a breech position and started coming with its feet first. Midway through the delivery she stopped pushing altogether. When Pashka urged Olga Soova to continue to push hard she could see that there was no breath left. Pashka forcibly pulled the baby out of Olga's dead body. But the baby was dead also. Pashka tried blowing her own breath into the baby's lifeless body but the tiny infant boy was already gone to join his mother in death. He would have been a healthy boy had his mother not expired.

When Metro Soova learned that his wife and son had both died he raged like a mad bull. "You killed my wife and my baby boy. You are a witch and a demon! How could you have taken my wife from me and left me with all these children!" He raved on and on.

Pashka Borischuk was totally distraught. She who would have given her own life to save someone else was being accused falsely and unfairly. She tried to defend herself. "Metro, please listen, please . . . I pleaded for you to get a doctor; don't you understand?" She collected her things in her carpetbag and walked to her home. Rather than considering the source of these horrid accusations, she took it personally. Her grief cut so deeply that she went into a chronic depression. Theodore came to the Stry-Kers' and asked Tainka to come to Pashka's aid as she needed reassurance badly.

The huge church bell rang solemnly. All through the area the homesteaders knew there had been a death because the bell tolled in a slow fashion. In an emergency the bell was rung in a quick stream of rings. Most of the people ran to the churchyard and learned from Evan, who was ringing the bell, about Olga Soova's death. Arrangements for the funeral had begun.

Soova commanded the women in the area to prepare his wife's and baby's bodies for burial. The men built a coffin—a very plain, large, rectangular, pine wood box. Olga and her baby were buried together.

The sorrow was overwhelming. As the Soova children huddled around the coffin, their tear-stained faces showed the terrible grief they were enduring.

The priest was dressed in black; all the women were in their black dresses and black *babushkas*. Olga Soova and her baby had their grave hand dug by the churchmen using spades, pikes, and shovels. First the bodies lay in the house for three days, where a vigil was kept day and night. During the vigil, people from everywhere in the community came to pay their last respects. The Bukuvynian women chanted sad chants. "Ooyee, Ooyee . . . Olga, Olga, why did you take your baby and leave us? Ooyee, why did you leave these little orphans behind? Open your eyes and come back to us!" The chants made a sad situation even sadder and everyone howled louder in sorrow. The little Soova children's hearts were simply broken. Their father was no consolation, as he did not know how to show affection. Not only was he incapable of consoling anyone—he was still angry that his wife had died and dared to leave him with all these children.

The funeral procession wound its way to the new St. Olga's church on the top of the hill for the burial mass. The choir sang the mass in special intonements for funerals. Everyone sang in slow, deep, sorrowful voices.

Mrs. Olga Soova and her baby were the first parishioners to be buried at St Olga's cemetery. In most cases the baby would have been buried on the outside of the churchyard because he was not baptized and could not be accepted inside the yard, but this rule was suspended in this case, because people loved Olga Soova and did not wish to separate her baby from her in death. It was an old church rule*, which the settlers brought from the old country.

CHAPTER ELEVEN

Rosie Soova was taken out of school by her father to help him on the farm and mind her younger brothers and sisters. There were five boys and three girls, ranging in age from one to fifteen. The seven- and ten-year-old boys continued to attend school whenever their father felt like sending them.

Rosie was heartbroken by her mother's death. When she realized she could not attend school any longer, her spirit was completely broken.

Maria Stry-Ker, now 13 years old, became a close friend of Rosie. She told Mr. Newhouse about Rosie's dilemma.

After giving the matter much consideration and realizing he very much missed Rosie's presence at school, David Newhouse worked out a compromise. If Mr. Soova was willing to allow Rosie to come to the teacherage after her work was finished for the day, he would be willing to give her private tutoring.

Soova would not even consider this proposal. He said the work was never done and Rosie would soon be marrying and needed no education for what would be expected of her. No matter how Rosie pleaded with him, she could find no agreement to Mr. Newhouse's proposal.

One evening she met Maria Stry-Ker on the road. Maria had just chased the cows back to the pasture after their evening milking and was coming home for supper.

---

* This insensitive ruling took a long time to change, but in 1960 the innocent babies who were stillborn or died before being baptized were allowed to be buried in their usual family plots.

"It breaks my heart to see you so sad," Maria said with the deepest sincerity. Slowly, between many sobs, Rosie told Maria the whole story, about how much she missed her mother and how her father refused to allow her to take private lessons with David Newhouse.

"There must be some way he will consent to let you study with Mr. Newhouse, maybe twice or three times a week. What is his greatest objection?" Maria inquired.

"He says there is always work to be done and I'm wasting my time with education," Rosie sobbed.

"So it's the work that you wouldn't be doing that he objects to most strenuously!" stressed Maria. "Let me discuss this with my mother. She always seems to find solutions to problems. Meet me here tomorrow and we'll discuss this further."

She went home and related Rosie's dilemma to Tainka. They pondered for a long while how to convince Soova to let his daughter continue her learning. Maria was the first to suggest a possible solution.

"Why don't I go to Soova's two or three times a week for one or two hours after I chase the cows to the pasture at night and take Rosie's place? I'll do her work and mind her younger sisters and brothers," Maria suggested.

"My dear child," Tainka said, "you work so hard at home and attend school also, that would be too hard on you." Tainka was always more concerned about Maria. It was very evident that Maria was her favourite child, perhaps because she was her first-born and was named after Tainka's mother. Maria was also a very agreeable and obliging person with a heart of gold.

"Child, if you want to do this for your friend, I'll discuss it with your father. You know he has to make the final decision," her mother reminded her.

That night, when the children were asleep in the new addition of the Stry-Ker house, Tainka broached the subject with Evan. Evan had built the addition to the one-room shack, the shack in which they had lived for the past ten years. At first he wouldn't hear of it, saying that Maria had her own responsibilities at home. It was simply an impossible idea. Evan had another concern which he did not wish to raise. He had grave concerns that the lecherous Soova might attempt to rape Maria.

Tainka pushed the subject, now playing on his spiritual Christian beliefs. "What kind of a Christian are you? You know the hardships that poor Rosie has suffered by losing her mother and by having to take over her mother's duties. Don't you have any pity for that child? I know you don't have a rock for a heart, Evan, do you?"

Evan knew that Tainka was not going to let this subject die, so he mentioned Maria's safety around Soova. He had very little tolerance for this crude, insensitive man.

Tainka shed some further light on this. "Evan, you don't have to worry about his sexual needs . . . Soova has been seeing the Widow Litikiw who lives across the creek. He started searching for Olga's replacement one week after she was buried. Soova and the widow are planning to marry soon, according to what I hear from the ladies."

"I still think he may try something with Maria. He is so oversexed I wouldn't trust him with our sow!" Spat Evan. However, after much more discussion, he finally agreed to go over to Soova and offer Maria's help to him.

The next morning, Tainka told Maria that her father had agreed to her offer but cautioned Maria about Evan's concerns. She assured Maria that her father would handle the situation and discuss the offer personally with Soova.

Soova had taken to excessive drinking after losing his wife, and in order to have a steady supply had started distilling his own moonshine whiskey. This morning he was in a visibly inebriated state, the after-effect of moonshine whiskey still very evident.

Evan explained the idea Tainka and Maria had to enable Rosie to continue her education. He mentioned Rosie's incredible ability to learn and praised him for having such a brilliant child. He used his position as a councillor of the school and said he endorsed the idea if Mr. Newhouse was willing to give up his free time to teach Rosie.

The one thing Soova respected was Evan's size, intelligence, and position in the community. What did he have to lose? Yes, it was a good idea. A young girl was coming to take Rosie's place for one to two hours twice a week . . . and there might be possibilities. Before he could fantasize any further, Evan interrupted his thoughts.

"Soova, you should know I have some serious concerns about letting Maria come here because it is well known what your mind is on constantly. But, let me tell you here and now, that if you even lay one hand on my daughter, I will personally kill you with these bare hands. Maria is an innocent child and a virgin and that's how she will remain!" Oh . . . what prophetic words these were to be.

When Rosie heard of the arrangements which her father had agreed to she was ecstatic. She hugged and kissed Maria and told her she would be forever grateful to her. It was agreed amongst all concerned that Tuesdays and Thursdays would be the two days each week that Maria would go to Soovas while Rosie went to school to take instruction from Mr. Newhouse.

After the first Tuesday's instruction Rosie came back punctually after two hours. She had a glow on her face, which Maria was pleased to see, as Rosie had been chronically depressed since her mother died. Metro Soova was not at home. He was spending more and more time at the widow Litikiw's. Plans for a second wedding for these two were imminent. Maria enjoyed the seven Soova children, especially little Yurkiw, who was now one and a half years old and a totally loving little boy.

At eight o'clock, Rosie would return from her lessons and Maria would say she should be going home. Every time Rosie returned she was simply radiant and on this, the third Tuesday of instruction, Rosie was just bursting to tell Maria how things were progressing. Maria noted the excitement. "What did you learn today?" she asked.

"Oh, Maria, in all my sorrow over mother I thought God had abandoned me . . . but he hasn't. I think I love Mr. Newhouse!" Rosie burst. "He is the kindest person I have ever met and he treats me like I was really important!" She continued.

If you are comparing the man to your father then you did not need much for an improvement, thought Maria.

"Maria, remember this is our secret. When I first went to school three weeks ago Mr. Newhouse was very pleased to see me. He hugged me and said he was sorry about my mother and brother's death. When he hugged me, something inside me stirred like nothing I have ever experienced on earth. We started the lesson and he told me I had progressed beyond grade seven in reading and my arithmetic was also at that level. He gave me some books to read on geography and history. All through the lesson we couldn't take our eyes off each other. When the lesson ended I was going to put on my coat. He took it from me and helped me put it on. I have never seen a man do that before. As he put on my coat he kissed my cheek. I couldn't resist him, nor did I want to. I grabbed him and hugged him tight. We hugged and kissed so passionately. When he broke the kisses, he said he should never have done that and we should stop now. I reluctantly agreed and went home. The next Thursday when I came, he was very reserved and the lesson continued. I could see that he blushed every time he looked at me. At the end of the lesson he once more helped me with my coat but he was just shaking. I grabbed him and hugged him again. Again I told him how much I cared for him. He told me he thought I was also a special person and he cared for me very deeply. He said he liked me from the first day of school last year. He said next time I came for a lesson we would discuss our feelings some more. Last Tuesday, when I went to him all we did was discuss our situation. He told me he was Jewish and about the inflexibility of his religion, Judaism. He realized I was Catholic. He said his mother was an Orthodox Jew and it would break her heart if he got involved with a Gentile. We went to the teacherage where he lives and he showed me the Torah, his holy book—like our Bible—and his Yarmulke and Menorah. He lights the Menorah during Hanukkah, their holy holiday which comes every year just around our Christmas. When he prays he wears his Yarmulke. He tried to explain the difference between Judaism and Christianity. It's so complex that I have difficulty understanding. I said to him, 'In my view we all believe in one God. Why should there be such a difference? We also honour the same Ten Commandments, don't we?' We kissed ever so softly, and he walked me to the school gate. I know how difficult the situation is for him. Religion is so restrictive. You know how your dad and mine feel about the Russian Orthodox Church. They would curse until there were no more '*sluk trafits*' (may a curse fall upon you), if they ever knew I was involved with a Jew!" Rosie wisely concluded.

Maria went home and contemplated life as she

walked along the short distance to the Stry-Ker home. What does life hold for me, she wondered? She wasn't an unhappy person. She was always thankful to God for whatever blessings were bestowed upon her. She was always healthy, although naïve. Tainka never told her about menstruation or sex. This subject was never discussed and there were no books at the school which covered the human physical anatomy or reproduction of humans. Although she had seen many of the farm animals mating and watched their young being born, her mother always said a stork brought the babies whenever she asked about where babies came from.

At thirteen she still had not started menstruating and was dreading the day she would. Rosie Soova was older and much more knowledgeable. She explained the menstruation process to Maria, that it occurs once a month and lasts about four to five days. During this period blood comes out of your bottom somewhere. Maria thought about Rosie and David Newhouse and was pleased that her trusted friend had taken her into her confidence.

CHAPTER TWELVE

Christmas 1915

The Christmas concert was a highlight at White Sands Creek School. Even though he did not celebrate Christmas, Mr. Newhouse taught the children some English Christmas carols and let them sing carols in Ukrainian. One of the highlights of the concert was the Nativity of Jesus. The children performed the Nativity dressed in whatever costumes they could muster. Mr. Newhouse had brought back some inexpensive fabric from his parents' store in Drumheller and some of the ladies in the school community had managed to conjure some very impressive costumes.

Rosie was also to appear in the concert. Her part was to lead the Christmas carols. She had a good soprano singing voice, and the other children and the audience followed her with ease.

Mr. Newhouse brought back some silky fabric just for Rosie so that she could make herself a Christmas dress. The sapphire blue dress with white lace enhanced Rosie's blue eyes and brightened her skin. She was very pleased with her appearance and could see that Mr. Newhouse looked at her even more often than he normally did.

All the families in the area attended the concert. Metro Soova and the Widow Litikiw were there, along with the widow's six children and the Soovas' eight. Soova and Widow Litikiw were planning to be married right after Ukrainian Christmas, January 7 on the Julian calendar, when the priest came to perform the Christmas mass.

After the concert David Newhouse distributed little bags of peanuts in the shell and hard rock candy, something the children had never seen or tasted. The concert was held on December 20. A two-week Christmas vacation was to take place after the concert. Mr. Newhouse planned to go to Drumheller to spend his two-week vacation with his family.

Everyone helped to disassemble the stage. It had been put together with strong fir planks placed on top of sawhorses. The tables and benches were put back in place in readiness for the school session in January. The Soovas left in a hurry, as the Widow Litikiw was staying with them overnight. Rosie told them she would walk home, as she wanted to help Mr. Newhouse put all the costumes away neatly. As she and David Newhouse walked into the teacherage they found that the fire in the small rectangular cast iron heater had almost died and the temperature in the teacherage was almost as cold as it was outside . . . -40F. David Newhouse stoked up the fire. He put some paper and dry wood on the embers, then liberally sprinkled some coal oil as he ignited a match and threw it at the open cast iron heater door. A big *whoom!* was heard and the fire licked his face and hands, singeing them, as he fell backwards onto the floor. This scared Rosie enormously. When she saw David Newhouse's singed hair and pink complexion, caused by a slight burn to his skin, she ran to him and cupped his face in her hands.

"David," she wailed, "are you badly burned?"

He looked at her concerned lovely face and could no longer resist her. They began kissing and caressing each other feverishly. Soon his hands were groping at her full breasts and down to her skirt and the plain flour sack petticoat. There was no resistance from Rosie. In fact, she encouraged him by removing her long bloomers, brown stockings, and leather boots. They were now on the floor, rolling around and kissing constantly.

"Do you want me to make love to you?" he whispered in a raspy voice.

"Yes, yes," she whispered hoarsely. She could now feel his manhood.

David Newhouse discovered Rosie was not a virgin.

* * *

The Ukrainian Christmas came and once again it was the happiest day of the year. This year it was the Stry-Kers' turn to host Christmas Eve and Christmas Day festivities. The Yaworskys, Tainka's brother-in-law and his second wife Pearl, and their family arrived. They now had grown to five, including Tainka's dead sister's son, Mikhail. They had settled in the Radway Centre area some twenty-five miles away. The Borischuks and the Kuriaks from Star, Alberta, also came. The Kuriaks had been good friends of the Stry-Kers since 1903 when the Stry-Kers first arrived in Canada and lived with them. The Stry-Kers had more room for overnight guests this year because of the new addition to their house. The overflow would stay with the Borischuks, who had three extra beds.

When the first star in the east appeared it was time to start the Christmas Eve celebrations. The table was set with hay under the tablecloth cover. Hay symbolized the manger in which Jesus was born. Evan went outside and came back bringing the *koluchi* (round braided bread), a candle, and a sheaf of grain.

"*Xristous Ruzdieitshaw*" (Christ is born), Evan said, and then he chanted more incantations. Tainka responded by saying "*Slavitee Iho*" (praise him—Jesus) and we praise his birth. A group prayer followed. What a wonderful celebration it was! The meal started with the traditional piece of apple for everyone present. The apple symbolized the complete circle and the hope that the same circle of relatives and friends would endure for the following year.

This was followed by wheat, poppy seed, and honey (*kutia*). There were twelve lenten dishes in all to symbolize the twelve apostles of Jesus: dried mushrooms in a rich brown gravy that had been gathered in the area during the previous spring and summer, boiled and then jellied fish, and fish fried in *olle* (hemp seed oil). Mr. Borischuk caught the fish in White Sands Creek, which was well stocked and flowed through the Stry-Kers' and his farms. He had built a fish trap using fine chicken wire. The variety of fish included Suckers, which were excellent for making the jellied fish. There was also Northern Pike and Pickerel; these were best fried. The meal consisted of *kwos* (sauerkraut juice with rice and mushrooms), potato *pyrogies* (round dough usually with fillings of potatoes and cottage cheese), *holuptsi* (cabbage rolls), sauerkraut and chickpeas (*kapusta*), white beans with garlic, and *cebulnick*, a flat bread covered in fried onions, almost like an onion pizza. Everyone's favourite was blueberries, lowbush cranberries, and dried apple made into fruit compote. No animal fat or eggs were allowed during this special meal. Tainka had picked many berries during the summer and fall. The raspberries made excellent wine and this raspberry wine was saved for the Christmas season. All the children were allowed to have a small glass.

Evan bought a gallon of moonshine from Metro Soova, who by this time was distilling a good-quality moonshine whiskey. Tainka's Indian friends always left some tobacco for Evan. It had a pungent smell but the men savoured this treat, as they were all heavy smokers.

After the meal was finished an empty plate was left at the table for the spirits of the relatives who had died in past years. No one hurried on Christmas Eve; they relaxed, smoked, and drank moonshine. The men exchanged stories about their days in the Austrian army and at the various posts they had served. Mike Yaworsky had served at a post near Turkey and talked about the strange customs the people there observed. He said everyone celebrated when someone died, as they believed that the soul had gone on to much greater things than anything imaginable on earth. They discussed the First World War in detail. Evan would imitate a trumpet with his lips and Theodore Borischuk used his fingers to thump on the table imitating a drum. The women chattered about babies, news from the old country, and what the war was doing to families in Europe. Their gardens were also a major topic. Then eventually the men would talk about their favourite subject—ghosts and how this was an unexplained phenomenon. Evan mentioned that there was a very bright light that had started appearing half a mile west of their homestead. The light started appearing after a road was completed to serve the ever-expanding area to the northwest of the Stry-Kers. The light looked like one headlight of Makovitsky's Model T Ford. When someone came close to it, it disappeared and then reappeared a few hundred yards away. No one could venture a guess what this may be, except that it must be a lost spirit.

Another favourite story they constantly repeated was about the miller's daughter who had died in the old country. She was buried in her wedding dress because she was of a marrying age. Every day at sunset her spirit walked to the flour mill which her father operated. One day one of the men in the village made a bet. If one of the brave young men would catch the apparition he would be paid fifty dollars, which the men collectively threw into a pot. So one evening as the sun set, the ghost of the miller's daughter floated down the road, as it often had since the funeral. One young man of the village had plied himself with copious quantities of liquor, to give him more courage. He ran after the ghost. As he neared it he tried to grab hold of her, and then his arms clasped but there was nothing but vapour. He fainted. When the others came running to him they saw that the fear in his face was overwhelming. He lost all of his hair in a matter of one month. No one ever chased the ghost of the miller's daughter again, and she continued to make her daily visits to the mill. No one ever claimed the fifty dollars and, after a year, it was given to a number of very poor families.

The children sat listening to the men's stories simply spellbound! Many of them could not bring themselves to go to the outdoor privy after hearing these stories. Then one of the children looked out the window and saw a ghost. The boys got the attention of the men, who by this time were quite drunk themselves. They had consumed almost all of Soova's moonshine whiskey.

"You say there's a ghost . . . a spirit out there? Well, let's go see!" Evan drunkenly coaxed the frightened children.

Sure enough, as all four men looked out the window there it was, white legs and arms waving, coming toward the house. It had no face. Evan grabbed his rabbit shotgun and fired a shot. It didn't disappear, so he fired again.

By this time Tainka was alerted. As she looked outside she saw the commotion. "You fools!" she yelled. "That's your underwear, Evan, hanging on the clothesline!"

Christmas Day came and Evan conducted the mass. It was more special than normal masses, as this was Christmas. It took him at least a half-hour longer. There were many more people in attendance to reply and Evan was pleased that everyone was responding in earnest. A large dinner followed the mass. Tainka roasted three of her large roosters and served them with all the trimmings. The mass at the church was scheduled for the third day after Christmas, which was the feast day of St. Stephan. It was also the day Metro Soova was to marry Widow Litikiw.

CHAPTER THIRTEEN

The Soova Wedding

The world was in turmoil as Britain declared war on Germany on August 14, 1914. Canada was committed to follow Britain into a conflict that would see 48,885 of Alberta's most able men enlisted. Most of them would serve in front-line trenches or man primitive fighter planes. Some worked in field hospitals; others manned artillery batteries. These men fought in Ypres, the Somme, Vimy Ridge, and the muddy slaughterhouse of Passchendaele, France. In 1916 there were 24 Alberta battalions, each numbering about 1,000 men. Before the war ended, 6,140 of Alberta's best died on the battlefields.

It was in 1916, too, that prohibition would be the law of the land as a result of a vote by Albertans the previous year. Prohibition would become law on July 1, and it would last for the next five years. Rum runners and bootleggers would become more popular than ever before, and Metro Soova, with his superior moonshine, would become a rich man.

On January 9, 1916, Metro Soova stood in his Sunday best at the altar of St. Olga's church. He was only five feet six inches tall but his frame was husky and his shoulders were broad. He had big hands and feet. His neck was thick, his nose was big and bulbous, and his forehead was narrow. He had combed and sleeked his blonde hair back. It appeared that he had washed himself too, at least where it was visible.

The widow Litikiw was also dressed as well as possible. She was a large woman with very ample breasts and buttocks. She had a broad face with a large nose turned up at the end, her cheeks were always highly coloured, and she had a very full mouth. The widow Litikiw smiled constantly. It was quite obvious that she was already pregnant.

During the ceremony the new priest, Father Kohot, led them around the altar three times. The couple wore golden crowns on their heads. This was part of the wedding ceremony. The large bronze bell in the belfry, which the Borischuks had donated to the church, tolled outside. Father Kohot could see there would soon be a christening, which he would be attending at the Soovas'.

He pronounced Metro and Domka Soova man and wife. All the combined children of Domka and Metro were there, fifteen in all. The Stry-Kers, the Pushinskys, and even the Polish Lupskis attended. The Chomiaks attended too, as Joseph Chomiak was the *starcey braut* (the elder who serves the priest). Teckla, his wife, always volunteered to wash the church table linens and usually organized the cleaning of the church with the ladies of the church community.

The Borischuks did not attend, as Pashka could not forgive Metro Soova's insults when his first wife, Olga, died. A person everyone was surprised to see was Mr. Newhouse, as they all knew he was Jewish and they thought he wouldn't attend a Catholic Church. Little did they know his interests did not lie with the church at all, but with the lovely Rosie Soova.

Everyone went back to Soovas' to celebrate. Domka was part Romanian and part Ukrainian, of Bukuvynian origin. She was an excellent cook and had prepared a delicious wedding feast. The meal started with the traditional *borsch* (beet soup) made with white beans and a meat stock. There was roasted pork and chicken, carrots, turnips, *kolasha* (a special cornmeal dish), *holubtsi*, pyrogies, and fresh white bread. For dessert she had made deep fried buns with high-bush cranberries called *pompuski* (sweet bread buns). The food was cooked in the outside *peech*. Metro Soova's moonshine flowed in abundance. The hooch was gaining notoriety as being the best quality in these parts. After all, it was now fetching twenty-five cents for a 16-ounce, pop-sized bottle.

There was no room to sit because of the large number of people in attendance. Some went into a granary which Soova had built during the summer and in which he had installed a round metal heater. In any case, most people had to stand. Even though one guest had brought along a fiddle, there was no room to dance.

David Newhouse came to the rescue and suggested that the school would be a fine place for dancing. Metro Soova looked at him with great contempt—he did not like David Newhouse—and quickly declined the offer. He said that the dancing could wait until summer when the new house he was building would be finished.

After several hours of merriment Maria Stry-Ker saw David Newhouse leave Soovas' and about half an hour later she saw Rosie leave the house. She suspected where she was going but said nothing to anyone.

CHAPTER FOURTEEN

After Metro Soova married Domka, Maria was no longer required to go to take Rosie's place while she took her lessons. Metro Soova was still in a mellow mood because of his new-found happiness with his new wife. Metro finally met his match—Domka was oversexed just as he was. As a result Metro was starting to look like a worn-out rag, grey in colour and walking a little humpbacked. He did not object to Rosie's lessons twice a week.

Rosie continued to visit Mr. Newhouse on Tuesdays and Thursdays. She was now reading and doing arithmetic lessons at a grade eight level. Her knowledge of geography and history increased immensely. Her interest in learning was intense, but not half as intense as her interest in David Newhouse. Their intimate liaisons continued each time she visited him and their trysts lasted up to an hour. Consequently, Rosie was coming home about half an hour late after each lesson.

In March, Metro Soova suspected something might be happening and asked his thirteen-year-old and eleven-year-old sons to go see where Rosie was. The boys scurried to the school, where a coal oil lamp shone. They knocked on the door several times. There was no answer. They opened the door but could not see Rosie or Mr. Newhouse. They ran to the teacherage, there was only a glimmer of light coming from the one window in the small shack. The shade was drawn but there was a space between the shade and window frame, so the window was not completely covered. They peered in and saw Rosie and Mr. Newhouse making love on the Winnipeg couch. The springs on the couch were squeaking very loudly. George and Peter Soova then knocked on the door and heard scurrying inside the teacherage, but no one answered. They ran home and excitedly announced to the entire household what they had witnessed. George, being the eldest, blurted, "Rosie is foocking that Jewish teacher!"

"Yes, yes she is," seconded his brother, Peter Soova.

"Whad is youse telling!!" Soova was enraged. "He's foocking Rosie?" He started to curse . . . "*Sluck, Yahoo trafit* (may a curse hit him). Some-a-bish!" He was now learning how to swear in English. He grabbed his hatchet and ran off in the direction of the school while Domka, his wife, yelled after him to control his temper.

In the meantime, Rosie knew that her real problems were about to begin—also her lover's, if her father found out about their relationship. She had heard her brothers banging on the door. She and David Newhouse dressed and escaped out of the teacherage just as Metro Soova was making his entrance into the schoolyard. He went to the school and whacked the door with his hatchet as the door flew open. When he found no one there he raged over to the teacherage and began chopping down the door on the shack. Rosie and David Newhouse were hiding behind the woodpile.

They could see that when Soova found no one in the teacherage he would start looking around the yard, so they crawled on their bellies to the nearest stand of bush, which was about one hundred yards away. When they reached the safety of the bush they decided on a course of action. The Borischuks would protect David Newhouse because they had become close friends since he had lived with them last season. And Soova wouldn't dare enter the Borischuks' land because of his dispute with Pashka. Rosie would run to her friend Maria Stry-Ker's place where she knew she would also be safe.

As she banged on the Stry-Kers' door, Rosie was summoned to come in. Everyone could see the girl was panic-stricken.

"My father wants to kill me and Mr. Newhouse!" she blurted out. "He's mad about my lessons . . . he's coming after me with an axe. Please hide me, please!" she ended desperately

"Daughter, daughter!" Evan regarded Rosie as close as any daughter could be. "What reason does he have to kill you? Didn't he agree to your school lessons?" he questioned.

"Mr. Newhouse and I have a closer relationship than teacher and student," she tearfully admitted. She didn't have to say more. Tainka and Evan knew what she meant and Maria knew it for a fact, because Rosie had confessed to her a long time ago. The younger Stry-Ker children gawked; perhaps they understood, but they said nothing.

Within half an hour Metro Soova was at the Stry-Kers' door, pounding on the solid wooden door like a madman. Evan knew he would have to do some fancy talking to calm down this unreasonable man, who was like a raging bull. He told the children and Rosie to hide under the beds in the second room.

"Soova, you old bull, what in the hell are you scaring my family for?" Evan demanded as he opened the door. "Must I always put up with your crazy behaviour?"

"That *kurva* (whore) of a daughter of mine has been fornicating with that rotten Jewish teacher and I'll kill her before I let my name be dragged down with the likes of him!" Metro Soova roared.

"You idiot!" Evan looked at Metro with contempt. "And who the hell do you think you are, Soova? Your name is no better or worse than Newhouse or Stry-Ker. Whatever you think your daughter was doing is now done. Not you or me or anyone else can change that. If you ever want to see your daughter again, you start acting like a man, not like a beast!" Evan was trying to control himself, but was quickly losing his temper.

Still fuming, Metro Soova cursed Rosie and screamed that he did not want the whore to blacken his doorstep again as long as he was alive. His temples were pulsating with all the stress he'd brought upon himself and others. His face was still a flaming red.

"Stry-Ker, I do not appreciate your meddling in my family's affairs, and since you have, you bastard, I tell you now you can keep the whore!" screamed Metro Soova. "I renounce her as my daughter."

Evan could not tolerate anyone calling him a "bastard." He told Tainka later it reflected on his mother and not on the person being called the name. To him his mother was saintly even though he couldn't remember her. He grabbed Soova around his thick neck and was ready to choke him. Tainka intervened and yelled at both of them to come to their senses. With that Evan pushed Metro Soova out the door and yelled at him to never come back.

"May all the curses of hell be on you and your family!" Soova declared as he swiftly stalked away.

Meanwhile, David Newhouse explained briefly to the Borischuks that he and Rosie were in love. He was planning to marry her. Mrs. Borischuk realized what incredible obstacles these two young people were facing. The matter of religion just could not be overlooked. She wondered if David Newhouse determinedly facing his mother and trying to convince her was a good plan. But she said only "May God bless both of you, as you have a difficult path ahead."

Theodore Borischuk needed to talk to Evan, as he was still the councillor of the school. A plan had to be worked out because now that Metro Soova with his uncontrollable temper was after Mr. Newhouse, neither he nor the children were safe at the school.

He did not want to leave Pashka and Mr. Newhouse by themselves in case Soova did actually get the courage to enter the Borischuk yard. It was no more than an hour until Evan came to the Borischuks' and a meeting took place. Mr. Newhouse realized the serious scandal his behaviour with Rosie would create and was first to suggest that his contract be terminated by the school board. Evan and Theodore Borischuk agreed. Evan would call together the other fathers in the area and work out a plan to keep the school open until May.

The problem of Rosie and Mr. Newhouse's immediate safety had to be addressed. They all walked back to the Stry-Kers'. It was nearing three in the morning but Maria and Rosie were sitting up waiting. Both were crying, and Tainka was trying to calm them down. Rosie sobbed that she never wanted to go home again after hearing the dreadful comments her father had made.

The plan they concocted was that when the Christmas holidays were over, Evan would go to the school and tell the children that Mr. Newhouse was called away suddenly for personal reasons and would not be returning. They would be notified when another teacher would take over. At the same time Pashka and Theodore Borischuk hitched their horses to a hay wagon. They hid Rosie and David Newhouse in the hay and drove them to Shady Hollow. David Newhouse hired Billy Makovitsky to drive them both to Edmonton in his mother's Model T Ford. The scandal hit Shady Hollow like a prairie brush fire, fuelled mostly by Metro Soova.

Very little conversation took place during the journey to Edmonton. Billy Makovitsky knew something was wrong because Rosie cried all the way, while David

Newhouse attempted to console her, although it was obvious that he too was distressed. He saw also that neither one had any luggage. He was instructed by Mr. Newhouse to drive them to the newly built MacDonald Hotel. After paying Billy, they went inside the hotel, where David registered them in two different rooms under their proper names. He told Rosie he would see her after they had a chance to clean up.

This was Rosie's first trip into Edmonton. She had never seen electric lights or indoor plumbing. She went to her room and fumbled with the key, finally managing to open the door. Once inside she was in a foreign environment. It was getting dark and she could see no coal oil lamp to light. She needed to urinate but could see no privy. "Oh God!" she thought. "Whatever am I going to do!" She saw a sink and the toilet. She looked at the toilet and saw the water in the bowl. This was certainly a well and the sink must be a new kind of privy so, with relief, she urinated in the sink.

Mr. Newhouse knocked on the door about two hours later. He had gone shopping and bought Rosie a beautiful navy blue suit and hat, an ivory satin blouse with lace, a fancy petticoat, bloomers, silk stockings, shoes, and gloves. She was overwhelmed with his attention and was extremely grateful. No one in her entire life had ever treated her this well.

"David, how can I ever thank you enough? I shall love you as long as I live!" she declared.

"Rosie," he said as he cupped her face in his delicate hands. "I love you more than life itself and I would be the happiest man in the world if you consented to marry me." He spoke with such utter tenderness and sincerity that Rosie knew he meant what he was saying.

"I'll marry you. I could live in any corner of the world with you!" Rosie said, filled with ecstasy.

After realizing Rosie had never been exposed to modern facilities, David apologized for being so insensitive and drew a bath for her. He also showed her how the toilet and sink worked. She was too embarrassed to tell him she had urinated in the sink. After taking a leisurely bath and using the perfumed soap to wash her hair and body, Rosie knew she preferred this lifestyle to anything she had ever dreamed about in Shady Hollow, at the poverty-stricken Soova homestead.

She dressed in her new clothes, looking every bit a sophisticated lady. David took her to the Wedgwood Dining Room for dinner. Rosie felt very insecure in this elegant room with high ceilings painted green and white. The sculptured white Wedgwood design around the vaulted ceiling was so beautiful; it was beyond anything Rosie had ever imagined.

She watched everything David did and the way he handled his cutlery and followed his actions exactly, as his manners were impeccable. She was starved by this time, as she hadn't eaten anything for almost forty-eight hours. But she ate slowly like David and chewed her food well. She would not have embarrassed him for anything in the world. But after all, she had never been exposed to any culture or sophistication in her short life at Shady Hollow.

When they finished dinner, David walked her back to her room. "Boy, oh boy, am I in lots of trouble, David," said Rosie. "Will you see that no harm comes to me?"

"Rosie, as long as we shall both live I will be there for you," David vowed. After holding each other tenderly for a long while they went to bed and made passionate love. Then they lay in bed and talked about their future. They both realized neither one could go back to Shady Hollow under the present circumstances, as long as Rosie's father was alive.

In the morning they would board the CPR train for Calgary. Rosie would wait in Calgary while David travelled to Drumheller to tell his mother about their engagement and plans to marry. They boarded the train at Strathcona in south Edmonton. The ride was exciting, as Rosie had never ridden on a train before. She watched the landscape as the powerful steam engine puffed its way through the countryside. It stopped at Wetaskiwin, Lacombe, Red Deer, Olds, and Crossfield before reaching Calgary eight hours later. Once there, David took her to a rooming house owned by some of his friends and boarded the next train to Drumheller.

Two days later David appeared at the rooming house with his mother. He looked bedraggled and his face was tear-stained. He was frustrated and appeared to be browbeaten. The spokesperson was Rachel Newhouse, his mother.

"I will come right to the point, Rosie. You know how it is. We are of two different worlds. It is not fair to David or you to marry one another. As you are aware, we are Jewish and practice Judaism. We have our strict traditions, and you are Ukrainian Catholic and must observe your beliefs. Should you have children, what would they be? They wouldn't know if they were fish or fowl!" Her preaching continued and it made some sense, but Rosie was flabbergasted. David said nothing as he sat on a chair looking down at the floor, but his anger was becoming more and more evident. His nostrils started flaring and his complexion was turning a beet red. How he controlled his temper was beyond Rosie's understanding, but control it he did. One didn't have to be a genius to realize he was submitting to his mother's demands. "However, I do have a proposal for both of you to consider," Rachel Newhouse continued. "My son Abraham, David's older brother, needs help with his business in

Montreal. His wife has been stricken with tuberculosis and is away at a sanitarium. He wants David to come and help him. This is a fine opportunity for David. Why not let him go for one year and if after that time you both feel the same about each other then you could marry. What do you think, Rosie? Is this proposal something to consider?"

What was there to consider? She had already made up her mind and his. The shock of this revelation left Rosie almost speechless. The only question she could ask was of David.

"Is this what you want, David?" Rosie asked quietly with all of the strength she could find within herself. By this time his anger had subsided.

"One year isn't that long, Rosie. I promise you I will be back," he replied firmly. He left Rosie one hundred dollars for train fare back to Edmonton and for living expenses until she could get a job. Mrs. Newhouse departed along with her son, who was looking back pleadingly at Rosie. It took only two days until David was on the train headed for Montreal. It was one month later that Rosie realized that she was pregnant.

World news in Shady Hollow travelled slowly. But any local scandal was well discussed and the moccasin express, by which one neighbour ran to the other, was very effective. The Rosie Soova and David Newhouse scandal would soon be everywhere. During this time the world was in turmoil, particularly in Europe. The Germans were at war, and so was the Austro-Hungarian Empire. Britain and all its colonies, including Canada, were their enemies, so many of the Ukrainian settlers, being of Austrian origin, were interned in concentration camps across Canada.

It was morning and Theodore Borischuk came running into the Stry-Kers' yard. He had just read that

Ukrainians were being sent to prison camps. Most of the internees, "enemy aliens" as they were called, were Ukrainians guilty of nothing more than being in the wrong place at the wrong time and having immigration papers that read "Austrian citizen." There were 24 such camps all across Canada. Over 8,579 men were interned. Accompanying them voluntarily were 81 women and 156 children.

The government of Sir Wilfrid Laurier had urged Slavic peasants to settle the prairies. But after the war broke out in August of 1914, a surge of patriotism led many Canadians to look on immigrants from Eastern Europe with deep suspicion. And in the wake of an economic slump, many of the men who had answered Laurier's call were unemployed.

The 24 internment camps set up across the country served many purposes. They enabled the federal government to remove "suspicious" foreigners from public view; they reduced unemployment in the cities; and in the Rockies, northern Ontario, and northern Quebec they provided a cheap way to open up the wilderness.

Up to 800 prisoners held in a camp near Castle Mountain at Banff, Alberta, helped build the Banff Springs Hotel, a golf course, and the Cave and Basin Mineral Hot Springs swimming pool. Another 200 kept in a camp near Jasper worked on road building, clearing projects, and building the Miette Mineral Hot Springs swimming pool.

After the scandal of David Newhouse, life at Shady Hollow went on in a pretty normal fashion. In 1918 a heavy hailstorm brought destruction to the Stry-Kers' crops. It was July 15 and Evan was admiring his sixty acres of land, which he had carefully cleared and then planted forty acres of prime golden wheat and twenty acres of malting barley. Both crops were ready to harvest.

A few minutes later, after admiring his bumper crop, Evan came back to the house, just before a thunderous hailstorm erupted and ravaged almost every head of grain on the Stry-Ker homestead. The next morning, there was a sickening smell of rotting vegetation. It made Evan and Tainka cry as they realized it was the end of a dream of prosperity for that crop year. Wheat was selling for $2.21 per bushel and the heavy crop would have yielded about twenty-six bushels to an acre. They were devastated, but the grace of God sustained them. They had gone through much harder times—a hailstorm was not going to destroy them or their family.

In 1919 Mikhail, Helenka, and Paul continued to attend school. The School Board had hired a spinster teacher from Edmonton by the name of Miss Brownlee after Mr. Newhouse's sudden departure. She continued to teach at White Sands School for several years.

In 1919 Katayna entered her first year of school. She became the teacher's pet almost instantly. Maria had completed her eighth grade in 1918 and was now helping Evan and Tainka on the homestead. Anywhere she was needed she would go. If Evan asked her to help with the brushing, ploughing, seeding, cutting grain, or farm chores she would help. When Tainka asked her to help with the housework she would never refuse or object. Maria had turned into a beauty. Her hair was now a golden blonde and her eyes were turquoise. She had fine features; her face was full at the cheekbones; her nose was like her mother's. But Maria's greatest beauty was inside. She didn't have a malicious bone in her body. She was goodness personified.

She also had a new interest. Now seventeen, Maria had a beau. It was Chomiak's eldest son, Stephen. He was Maria's age. They had attended school and church together. They had been good friends all through school and enjoyed each other's company. Their courting took a few years, as theirs was a platonic relationship. Their close friendship continued. Even though there had never been any feelings of intimacy between the two in the past year, they had started loving each other, and marriage was now in their discussions. Tainka and Evan approved of Stephen; Joseph and Teckla Chomiak loved Maria.

Joseph Chomiak bought a homestead for his son. It was located three miles north and one mile west of the family farmstead. The land was inferior to the home place but it would be excellent for hay meadows and raising cattle. This was the area where the blueberries and low-bush cranberries grew in abundance. This was also the area where the native Indians harvested seneca root for medicinal purposes. The drive by horse and buggy to Chomiak's new homestead was a beautiful experience, particularly in the fall when the leaves turned colour. The crude one-horse trail wound up and down hills and very deep gullies, making the journey dangerous in spots. It passed the Romanian settlement and beyond where white and black aspen and willows flowed into jackpines, spruce trees, and birch tree stands. There were also Saskatoon, choke cherry, high-bush cranberry, and raspberry bushes everywhere. There were various kinds of grasses: alfalfa and clover smelled like fragrant perfume. The leaves after the first frost in fall turned to many shades of gold, crimson reds, and oranges. It was a heavenly sight.

This day, as Stephen drove to his new homestead with his grey two-horse team and hayrack attached, he marvelled at the beauty of nature. His constitution was very much like Maria's. He appreciated life and felt he was blessed for every day that God granted him. He was particularly happy these days as he knew he had met his soul mate in Maria and they would indeed have a very good life together.

His land was abundant in strong, tall jackpine that whispered when the wind blew and almost sang to him. There were also tamarack tree stands. The jackpine would make excellent fence posts and the tamarack could be used for fence rails. Stephen had decided where he would build their new home. There was a high hill on the northeast portion of the quarter section, which overlooked the entire valley. He named his homestead "Maria's Valley of Paradise." He wanted to show Maria this incredibly beautiful spot. He wanted to share his admiration and enthusiasm for this place with her.

* * *

In 1919 the Spanish flu epidemic struck the world, with devastating consequences. Death was everywhere. Shady Hollow was no exception. Evan was frightened for the safety of his wife and children. He had learned in the army that in order to ward off disease, people would have turpentine simmering on the stove at all times. Also, eating copious amounts of garlic would help. The smell of the simmering turpentine was so atrocious that the demon himself would not have approached the home. That, and the powerful odour of garlic, prevented the flu from attacking the Stry-Kers' home.

All around them in Shady Hollow, people were dying. There were several Romanian families who had settled around White Sands Creek. Their homesteads were two and three miles away from the Stry-Kers'. The creek was the same creek which crossed theirs. The Ordeljes family had eight children. One day, as the Ordeljes family was driving back on the wagon drawn by two horses—the same wagon that had carried two small caskets only three hours earlier—they heard terrifying screams coming from their house. The woman who had stayed behind to watch the third flu-stricken child came running out, screaming that the third Ordeljes child had just died. The family's grief was unbearable. Evan had helped them dig the graves. He had also attended and sung at each burial service, even though the service was in the Russian Orthodox Church. The church which most of the Romanian families attended was the same as the Catholics' except in the parts of the service where the church hierarchy was mentioned. The Catholics mentioned the Pope, but the Orthodox mentioned their head of the church. Otherwise the service was the same so Evan could participate in the entire offering to God.

The tragic sadness at these funerals was something Evan would never forget. He wondered when the pain for all these new Canadians would end. He didn't realize that the Spanish Influenza was a worldwide epidemic.

CHAPTER FIFTEEN

The next three years at the Stry-Kers' continued normally. Every day Evan and Tainka toiled at their daily chores. By now they had cleared one hundred acres of their homestead. They chose to brush the area which they felt was the most arable. The remaining sixty acres were muskeg and could only be used for pastureland. In 1922, Evan bought an additional quarter section of land kitty-corner from his homestead, land which had been abandoned by one of the Romanian families. This family simply could not survive on a site that was mostly non-productive muskeg. The land was being sold for taxes and it cost Evan twenty-five dollars. Tamarack and spruce trees grew on the land. There were about sixty acres cleared, and some rangeland grass seed had been planted. Cattle enjoyed pasturing the young, succulent foxtail grass even though it grew wild. However, it was a nuisance when it reached maturity. Coarse, barley-like, bushy heads were carried by the wind to every corner of the land and then reproduced in abundance the following year.

This would be the year Maria and Stephen were to be married. Stephen had built a small two-room house in the location which he first chose. Maria loved their Valley of Paradise as much as Stephen did. The year before, in preparation for the wedding, Evan had started building a new five-room house himself. The home would be fancy. It would be built on top of the hill where the well stood. No one would have to bail water with a pulley and rope any longer. There would be a pump in the kitchen. The house would have two stories, with dormers on the upstairs windows. On the main floor there would be a large kitchen, which would accommodate the round table seating eight people. There would be cupboards for all the pots and pans, dishes, and even a tin-lined flour bin. A new cast iron cook stove with a large water reservoir would stand in the corner by itself. The second room was the parlour and a large, separate room would be Evan and Tainka's bedroom. The ceilings would be covered with tongue and groove boards and the floors would be finely sanded birchwood. There would also be a veranda, creating additional room. It would extend along the entire front of the house on the main floor. For now, it would not be winterized.

On the second floor would be two large bedrooms, each with a dormer. There would be one bedroom for Maria, Helenka, and Katayna, but Maria would soon be married and leaving to live in her own place. Mikhail and Paul would sleep in the other room. A wall would separate the rooms and there would be storage cupboards along the dividing wall. A stairwell was planned to come up along the north wall.

The house would also have a large root cellar for storing potatoes, carrots, and turnips for the family's use and sugar beets for the cows to eat during the winter months.

Construction started after harvest in 1921 and got as far as the cellar being dug. A horse was used initially, pulling a huge scoop shovel. This was how basements usually were started. Then the men refined the job using picks and shovels. A sub floor was built, then vertical logs were erected around the perimeter of the house. The room dividers on the main floor were constructed of the same type of vertical logs.

After the spring work of 1922, the men in the community held several *klutkas* (building work bees). The rafters were built and raised. Then the roof was covered

with one-inch by four-inch boards. Now they were ready
for the biggest *klutka* of all. This was to chink the logs.
Most of the church parishioners and parents who had children in school came. The women brought many varieties
of food, ranging from *borsch* to main course items such as
roasted chickens, leg of pork, cabbage rolls, and *pyrogies*.
Some even brought sweet breads (*babka*). The children
particularly enjoyed this *klutka* because they could stomp
around in the clay mud used for the chinking. Their little
feet were used as the mixers. A six-foot by six-foot pit was
dug in the ground. This was used as the large container
where gumbo clay, straw, and warm water were mixed to a
supple consistency that provided the high-grade chinking
used between the logs. The men were given buckets to
carry the clay from the pit to the house under construction. They used their hands to chink the cracks in the
vertical logs. In a smaller pit only clay was mixed with
water. This was used as a wall plaster on the inside walls.
After the chinking was done, the women did their work.
They would prepare very fine clay mud from the smaller
pit and make this substance much thinner than the chinking. Then they smoothed this fine mud over the chinked
surfaces. They were more fussy and expert in finishing the
walls so as to level each surface as straight as possible.

There were forty-five adults and fifty children. The
Soovas did not attend. Evan and Metro Soova had not
spoken since the night Rosie Soova and David Newhouse
left Shady Hollow. The *klutka* was a day of great achievement but it was also a day of celebration. A day similar
to a wedding . . . a prelude to Maria and Stephen's wedding, which was now scheduled for July 15, 1922.

The chinking and plastering was completed within a
day, after which time the party began. The men drank
moonshine and sang Ukrainian songs. The women
talked about Maria's pending wedding. Where was Maria

getting her wedding dress? Who were the bridesmaids? Did Tainka need help with the wedding feast? They all clucked about this being the first Stry-Ker wedding—it should be a very special occasion. Their conversation covered many areas. They discussed the spinster schoolteacher, Miss Jane Brownlee, who came from Edmonton, and how anti-social she had been. After all, she'd been teaching here for over three years and had never visited even one home. Tainka told them she had come to the Stry-Kers' place only to sign her contract for each year and receive her cheque for the previous year. A few ladies said they saw Billy Makovitsky's mother's car parked at the teacherage several times.

Eventually, the conversation got to Rosie Soova and David Newhouse. The women were not sympathetic to Rosie's plight and agreed with Soova's evaluation of his daughter. She was nothing but a cheap little tramp. After all, it was she who must have encouraged David Newhouse with her big breasts and with her wiggling her ass with every step she took. They didn't know that Rosie was writing letters to Maria. Evan and Tainka knew but said nothing. When Maria could not listen to any more of this gossip she sprang to Rosie's defence.

"How can you talk about someone when that person is not here to defend herself?" she demanded. "You should all know that Rosie is a friend of mine and we write letters regularly and she will always be my friend! So let's not make her sound worse than she is. Rosie has had some difficult times to face and it isn't fair to condemn her until you know the entire story. Why do you gossip so much?" With that Maria walked out of the old house, followed by Helenka and Katayna. All the women looked at each other. This was so out of character for Maria. Nevertheless, when they were gone the women continued to pursue the subject with Tainka.

"What has Rosie been writing to Maria? Where is she? Did she ever marry that Jew?" Tainka also wished to discontinue this subject as gracefully as possible. "Maria does not tell me what Rosie writes and, as you know, I do not read English, so even if I wanted to I could not read Rosie's letters!" She replied in such a way as to discourage further discussion and yet without sounding rude.

They then went on to discuss the upcoming church picnic at St. Olga's, which would take place on *Zelenee Shvata* (Green Holidays) in June. This was the annual feast day of the church. It was also the day of the church picnic. Much time had passed—the children were tired and slept in wagons and on all the available beds at the Stry-Kers'. Other children slept under the benches and even in the hayloft. It was dawn when the last wagon pulled out of the yard, homeward bound.

CHAPTER SIXTEEN

The church picnic was especially enjoyable in 1922 for Maria and Stephen, as their wedding would be the next special occasion at St. Olga's. The church gates were adorned in young, white aspen trees to make a *brama* (a specially decorated entrance gate usually for weddings). Green Holidays symbolized the dawning of new life, of yet another spring. The Stry-Kers did not decorate their gate for Green Holidays this year, as in a few weeks they would be making a *brama* for Maria's wedding. A wedding *brama* was different from the one for Green Holidays. Maria's *brama* would be made of spruce boughs on which brightly coloured strips of crepe paper were hung; waxed crepe paper roses were attached to the boughs.

During the previous winter many of the church ladies used to gather at the Stry-Kers' to make flowers for the church decorations, for the wagons, for the *brama*, and for the many special guests who would be attending. These were called *bouketa* (corsages). One group of women would cut the crepe paper in three-inch strips; others would notch the strips of paper, which were stacked in layers of five. The more experienced women would twist the roses into shape, starting with the fine petals inside the rose and extending it to the full larger petals on the outside edges. Beeswax was kept warm on the side of the stove and any flowers that were finished were dipped into the warm wax. This created a rich, brilliantly coloured rose which would last a few years, and could even be used for other weddings in the family.

One day a parcel arrived for Maria from Edmonton. In it were six yards of beautiful, ivory-coloured silk.

There were also three yards of white damask netting for the veil. A small note inside read:

"To my dearest friend, Maria. Here is my wedding present to you. Sincerely, Rosie."

Maria was overwhelmed. She certainly had never expected to be wearing silk for her wedding and the fine damask must be very expensive. This was indeed an extravagant gift, and extremely appreciated. An excellent seamstress lived at Radway, a Finnish woman, Sara Houskinen. Pearl Yaworsky told Maria and Tainka about her and said she could do justice even to cotton sacking. If she worked with silk the dress was sure to be divine.

Tainka and her eldest and favourite daughter Maria set out to drive to Radway. It took the full day for the return trip. They were pleased with Mrs. Houskinen's work. She showed them someone else's wedding gown, which she was sewing at the time. She would use tiny mother-of-pearl buttons on Maria's silk dress. Mrs. Houskinen was impressed with the quality of silk Rosie had sent.

Maria and Evan had driven around the community one month before the wedding and invited all the guests they wished to have attend Maria's special day. Maria begged Evan to invite the Soovas, but he would not.

It was now two weeks before the wedding. Mrs. Borischuk had a myrtle plant and would braid the *venok* (wedding headdress). Everyone was getting excited, especially Maria. They all worked at a feverish pace to finish building the new house and prepare for the wedding. Maria was whitewashing the inside of the new house using a lime whitewash with some laundry bluing added to make it look a brilliant white. She was perspiring heavily and continually drinking the ice-cold water out of the new kitchen pump. That night she woke up with a heaviness in her chest and an extremely sore throat.

"It must be the fumes from the lime that are making my chest hurt," she said to her mother. "I have no time to be sick now. There is so much more to do." Tainka also had not looked well the last three or four months. She looked as if she was gaining weight. In any case, she comforted Maria and said she and Helenka would finish the whitewashing and that Maria should rest in bed and get well. The following day Maria could not even talk and she had started coughing. Her eyes looked sunken and she had started running a very high fever. When Stephen came over he was shocked at her condition. He insisted on taking her to Dr. Liston, who had just opened a practice in Shady Hollow. He claimed he was a qualified medical doctor. He had healed a few horses already. Maria kept insisting there was nothing wrong, that it would get better in a day or two. Tainka, however, could see that Maria was sicker than she had ever seen her.

Stephen and Tainka drove Maria to Shady Hollow. Dr. Liston diagnosed her, and confirmed she was indeed running a very high temperature, and said that eating some ice would help bring down the fever. When they brought Maria home, Tainka sent Evan to the *lidowna* (ice house) to chip some ice for Maria. He came back with half a bucket.

Maria couldn't bear the high fever. She started eating the ice as quickly as she could swallow it. The next morning Tainka's favourite daughter Maria was so ill she could not lift her head off the pillow. Evan hitched the horses to the wagon, carefully placed Maria on a woolen quilt, and along with Tainka he galloped the team to Shady Hollow, where he hired Billy Makovitsky to drive them to Lamont. A new hospital had opened there recently. As they were crossing the North Saskatchewan River on the ferry at Pakan, Maria took her last breath. She lay peacefully cradled in her mother's arms, her face looking like an angel. Tainka started shaking her hysterically, shouting and yelling. "No, no, no, you can't die, Maria! Maria, how will I live without you, my wonderful child? No, no, don't leave us! Maria . . . . Maria . . . .Maria . . . Maria . . . .!!" Evan sat in the front seat with Billy. He too could not control his tears. Neither Tainka nor anyone else had ever seen him cry because it wasn't manly to cry, but Evan could not control his emotions . . . his firstborn was dead. How could this have happened? Had God abandoned them? voices inside him yelled. "No, not Maria . . . not Maria!!"

Pashka Borischuk was sitting at her kitchen table looking at the huge myrtle plant, figuring out which would be the best stems to pick for Maria's venok. Suddenly a small sparrow crouched on the window frame and pecked on her kitchen window several times. She instantly knew this was a bad omen. It always meant death. She hadn't visited the Stry-Kers during the past week and did not even know that Maria had been ill.

She was puzzling who this death sign was meant for when Theodore came into the house. He could see Pashka was deeply troubled. "What is worrying you?" he asked her.

"I cannot understand, but something dreadful is about to happen. My heart has been heavy for almost a week. My ambition to make Maria's venok has not been there and just now a bird pecked on our window! That troubles me deeply. I know it means someone will die." she explained. Theodore knew better than to question his wise wife. Her psychic abilities had been too accurate during the forty years they had been married to be dismissed as nonsense.

After an hour or two the big bronze bell at St. Olga's church began to toll mournfully. They knew that someone from the parish had died.

Theodore ran over to the Stry-Kers to see if they had heard anything. He knew something was dreadfully wrong when he heard the wailing as he entered the yard. They had brought Maria's body back home and laid her gently on the bed in the second room of the old house. Everyone was hysterical by now. Tainka was screaming with grief, totally out of control. Helenka, Katayna, Mikhail, and Paul were huddled around the body crying uncontrollably. Stephen, Maria's betrothed, was there, standing motionless, his face drained of any colour. He appeared to be in deep shock. Evan, whom Theodore had never seen cry, continued to cry uncontrollably.

Theodore ran home to tell Pashka the dreadful news. She began to scream. "Oh, not Maria, my little Maria. All these years she has been like my own flesh and blood. What are you saying, Theodore? Are you sure . . . are you positive?" Pashka continued to make ridiculous comments. Theodore knew they both had to gain control of themselves and be strong at this time. The Stry-Kers needed them now more than ever before.

He started shaking her. "Pashka, my dear wife, you are always so wise . . . you are the pillar of strength. You must come to your senses. Tainka needs you more than ever, so does Evan. Don't you think this untimely death has destroyed them? You must stop your hysterics!" Pashka stopped making irrational comments, sat down, and cried loudly for two hours. Then there were no more tears left; she could not cry any more. "Now we must both go to Stry-Kers!" she told her husband. She felt more sorrowful than she had ever felt before. She wasn't sure if she was strong enough to handle this awful tragedy.

Nevertheless, they both took over matters at the Stry-Kers'. Pashka hugged Tainka, who didn't even recognize her best friend. She hugged all the children and Evan, who was also oblivious to her. Pashka didn't have to say how her heart ached about Maria's death because her face showed it all. With that, she disappeared into the kitchen.

Soon the pots were rattling as she started preparing food. She knew this funeral would attract more people in the community than any funeral before in these parts and there would have to be food. Theodore went outside to look after the farm chores.

The news of Maria's death spread like a wild prairie fire. Soon people from everywhere were streaming into the yard. There simply was no room for all of them in the tiny second room of the old house. Theodore quietly went to everyone and asked them to certainly express their sympathy, but when they had done that, could they possibly come the next day and give the family their private time this evening with their beloved Maria.

Pashka forced the children to eat some chicken soup with homemade noodles. Evan and Tainka refused to eat. They just sat near Maria's body, and would not leave the room. Soon Mike and Pearl Yaworsky arrived from Radway. Billy Makovitsky had driven over to their place to let them know after he'd heard the news in Shady Hollow. Even Domka Soova came to offer her help. It didn't matter to her about the feud that Evan and her husband Metro were carrying on. She had a good heart and she thought if these two old fools wanted to continue their childish behaviour she would not be a part of it. She was pregnant for the sixth time with Soova's baby. This would be her twelfth child, and she knew it was time to stop. But she would deal with that matter at another time. As she came into the house, Tainka was being led by Pashka into the kitchen. Domka Soova grabbed her and gave her a tender, loving hug. She kissed both of Tainka's cheeks and expressed her great sorrow.

"We all loved Maria," she sobbed. "I'm here to do whatever I can to help you get through this great loss we are all feeling."

The Borischuks, Yaworskys, and Domka Soova had a discussion on how to handle matters for the funeral. There was no sense asking Evan or Tainka's advice, as they were both in severe shock and overcome with grief. Their minds were not on this earthly plane at this time.

Pashka would look after preparing the body for burial and Pearl Yaworsky would assist. They would also handle Tainka and the Stry-Ker children. Mike Yaworsky and Theodore Borischuk would look after the farm chores and burial arrangements at the church. They would also organize the new house where people could come in and pay their last respects and move out again, as they expected the whole community to attend. Domka Soova volunteered to be in charge of the cooking. Some of the neighbours were delegated to start digging the grave.

Tainka spoke a few words to Pashka and Pearl Yaworsky, after much coaxing. She wanted Maria to be buried in her new wedding dress and veil and she wanted her to have a nice coffin. A new coffin was bought in Edmonton and brought to Shady Hollow. It had white pleated satin inside with navy velvet covering the outside.

As Maria's body was prepared and laid out in the coffin the tears did not stop. Occasionally, Pearl and Pashka cried out loud, although they realized it would upset the family even more. Maria looked angelic in her ivory silk gown, with a white veil framing her face. All around the perimeter of the inside of the coffin the brilliantly coloured waxed roses were placed against the white satin lining—the flowers that were made for Maria's wedding.

It was time to place the coffin in the parlour of the new house. A high frame was built by the men and covered with white cotton cloth. The navy coffin was placed on this wooden rack. A large flat container of wheat was placed at the head of the coffin on a small table. Lit candles were inserted in the wheat, where they would continue to burn until the third day, when the burial would take place. For the next two days, as one day had already passed, a stream of friends, neighbours, and parishioners from St Olga's church streamed by the coffin paying their last respects. The Bukuvynian ladies came and chanted, as they did at all funerals.

"Ooyee, Maria, Maria, why are you lying here . . . why did you leave us . . . you should be a happy bride now . . . instead you have died and left us. See Stephen, your husband-to-be . . . see how he cries. God, please see your mother and your father . . . see how they miss you . . . Ooyee, ooyee, oyee Maria, Maria Oyee, yeew, yeew." As usual, the chanting made no common sense. It only served to upset the family and Stephen even more. But that was their custom and so it continued.

The night and day vigil continued and many people sat and mournfully talked through the night. On the third day after Maria expired, her body started changing colour. This was July and no embalming process had even been heard of in these parts. Father Kohot, dressed in his black vestments, arrived to conduct the last prayer at the house, after which the coffin was placed on a black, shrouded wagon. Young girls carried the special funeral church banners and a young man held a brass cross—they all followed the coffin. The family sat in the wagon with the coffin. The choir sang a funeral mass, a high requiem mass. As designated for funerals, the tone was mournful. The church was shrouded in black and was packed with people from near and far. Half of the churchyard was also full of people.

A mysterious lady veiled and clad totally in black, as most of the ladies in attendance were, appeared at the funeral. She arrived in a Model MacLaughlin Buick. Everyone suspected it was Rosie Soova, but they did not know for sure, as she did not lift her veil and her black dress hung very loosely on her body. Even Metro Soova attended the funeral. He had always liked and respected Maria, since she helped his family after his first wife Olga died. Also attending were Tainka's Indian friends—Mary and Paul Tatonga, Cochees Sinclair, Louis Demers, and Gabriel Laboucane. They had heard the sad news when they picked up their mail at the post office at Shady Hollow.

Tainka had refused to sleep since Maria died. Evan slept for short periods only, on the chair where he sat during the vigil. The rest of the Stry-Ker children also looked like the walking dead. Father Kohot didn't help matters much. "What sorrow this is. What dreadful grief this funeral brings, this lovely young woman at the threshold of her life," he intoned in his sermon. "God took her away from her betrothed, whom she was going to marry in one week. Away from her loving family, away from all of us to her eternal peace. We cannot question God's wisdom . . ." on and on for almost an hour. The funeral mass and sermon lasted well over three hours.

When *Vechnia Pomenit* (Forever Remembered), the customary last farewell in Ukrainian funeral services, was sung, everyone wailed. The church was filled with the smoke of the burning thurible. Father Kohot ceased using the thurible for a short while until he reached the grave. At the grave, as the coffin was being lowered onto a large pine box positioned at the bottom of the freshly dug grave, Tainka tried to jump in after the coffin.

"Maria, Maria, I can't live without you!" she yelled hysterically. "My child, why did you have to die before me?" Pearl Yaworsky and Pashka Borishuk held onto Tainka. Her sons, Mikhail and Paul, assisted them.

After the burial everyone was invited to the funeral dinner prepared by Domka Soova. The tables were set outside and most people attended the dinner. However, the lady in black did not attend, nor did Metro Soova.

Tainka's Indian friends did attend the dinner and Mary Tatonga gave Tainka a big hug. "I can't imagine your heartache, but my daughter, who is Maria's age, was taken from me by the government as a young girl and placed in a residential school," she solemnly stated as she hugged Tainka. "I don't know where she is now, because she never came back to the reservation. My heart aches for her . . . but at least I may see her someday . . . God bless you Tainka," Mary's eyes welled with tears and she turned and left with the others to travel back in a wagon drawn by one horse . . . back to the reservation, White Sands Creek Reserve.

CHAPTER SEVENTEEN

Pashka and Pearl stayed for an extra day after the funeral. They cleaned out the new house in readiness for the Stry-Kers to move in. The parlour smelled of death. There was also the lingering odour of incense from the burning thurible which the priest had used at the prayer service. There was also the scent of burned wax from the candles which had burned for three consecutive days. Evan, Mikhail, and little Paul, who was now almost ten years old, mustered up enough energy to do the chores. Helenka and Katayna also tried with all the energy in them to help Pearl and Pashka.

Tainka sobbed all morning while she knelt praying at her bed in the old house. After she finished her prayers she dressed entirely in black, including her stockings and *babushka* tied under her chin. Without a word to anyone, she walked out of the yard. Evan saw her leave and ran after her, inquiring where she was going. All she would reply was, "*na chvintar*" (to the cemetery). This was a forerunner of what her regular daily schedule would be for the next six months. She would spend an hour or two every day praying and weeping at Maria's graveside. When she came back home she did very little in the house or garden or on the farm.

That night the family was just sitting down to eat their supper, which Pashka Borischuk had prepared, when Mikhail, who was completing the chores in the barn, came running into the house. He was as white as snow. He could hardly talk but managed to stutter, "I, I j-just s-saw MaMaMa-Maria's sp-sp-spirit!"

119

This brought Tainka right to attention. "What are you talking about . . . where did you see her?" She demanded urgently. She went to fetch him a cup of cold water. She could see her eldest son, now eighteen, was in much trouble. After he had taken a drink of water, Pashka Borischuk and Tainka started rubbing his hands and applied a cold rag to his forehead.

"My son," Tainka continued, "are you sure you weren't just hallucinating?"

Mikhail spoke very quickly. "No, I was not. I was chasing Debba, the white-faced cow, out of the barn after milking and I could sense someone or something was watching me. As I looked up at the open door to the hayloft . . . there she was. She was dressed all in white, just like how we buried her . . . her face was blurred so I don't know whether it was Maria or someone else, but her dress was a glowing white. As soon as I saw her, after maybe a few seconds, she or whatever it was—maybe a ghost—disappeared!"

Tainka, Evan, Pearl, and Pashka all ran to the barn to see if they also could see anything. All they witnessed was a dark, opened door to the hayloft. No one will ever know whether Mikhail hallucinated because of the deep grief he was bearing or whether it was actually Maria's spirit coming to bid her final farewell. Throughout his life, Mikhail would maintain that he saw her. Try as Tainka would though, she could never see her beloved Maria.

Evan ordered a fancy tombstone for Maria's grave. It was a tall Gothic cross, constructed of refined cement. There was a thick facing on it that read:

Here lies Marie Stry-Ker
(Stracher)
Born 1903

Died 1922
She was a beloved daughter
of Evan and Tainka
May she rest in peace
cradled in God's love

At the top of the Ukrainian script was a black and white picture of their Maria, enclosed between two pieces of glass. They used her old country name because she was born a Stracher, as well as her Canadian name, Stry-Ker.

Evan's attitude changed drastically after the funeral. A tough taskmaster, he had always been the disciplinarian in the family, not Tainka. Evan now became a tyrant. His demands were unrealistic. Nothing the children ever did was right. His drinking and smoking habits became excessive. He would sit half the night at the kitchen table drinking moonshine and chain smoking.

A week after the funeral the Stry-Kers moved into their new home. Helenka and Katayna put all of Maria's clothes in the *scranya* (storage trunk). Her letters from Rosie Soova and Stephen, her betrothed, which she had kept in a canvas pouch, were placed there as well.

There was to be further sorrow in the community. In September, Teckla Chomiak saw her son Stephen's team and the two dapple-grey mares drive into the yard, pulling behind them a hayrack with a load of hay. Stephen was hunched over on top of the hay on the hayrack. He had been grieving deeply since Maria's death. For a month he had done nothing. However, in the last few days he had just resumed his responsibilities. It was a regular duty of his to bring home hay for the livestock from his homestead . . . his and Maria's Valley of Paradise which he no longer treasured. On these trips he took along his favourite .22 calibre rifle, as there was an abundance of partridge and prairie chickens on the road to the homestead. He normally shot two or three, which Teckla prepared with sauerkraut in a delicious dish.

The horses now pulled the wagon up to the barn and stopped. Teckla ran up to the wagon, thinking Stephen was asleep. She climbed to the top of the hay load and tried to shake him. As she did, his body tilted backwards and she saw blood had streamed down the front of his body. It was now dry—he had been dead for some time. The horses, knowing their way home, had continued to pull the wagon even though Stephen was dead. No one will ever know if his death was an accident or a deliberate suicide.

Stephen's body was laid to rest beside Maria. Mrs. Chomiak was experiencing the same degree of sorrow as Tainka. Stephen was her eldest son. Now both women visited the cemetery daily. Both dressed entirely in black and both cried till there were no tears left.

On Stephen's tombstone, which was exactly like Maria's, was written in Ukrainian script:

Here lies Stephen Chomiak
Beloved son of Teckla and Joseph
He also rests beside his beloved Maria
Born 1902
Died 1922
Rest in peace and cradled
in God's love and eternally with Maria

A picture of Stephen was encased in the cross between two pieces of glass.

CHAPTER EIGHTEEN

Tainka was three months pregnant when Maria died. She was very upset about the condition in which she found herself. She was now 39 years old and her last child had been born ten years earlier; she had been certain her childbearing days were over. This pregnancy was her worst. She lost fifteen pounds after Maria's death because she took very little nourishment. Her back ached; her feet and hands were swollen most of the time. She said nothing about her pregnancy to the children. But they could hear her scolding Evan for being an old, oversexed *boohigh* (bull) and getting her into this condition. From these one-way scoldings they knew that a new baby was soon to arrive on the scene.

The children were excited about this baby. They felt the baby might bring Tainka out of her state of grief and depression. But the grieving lessened very little and her daily trek to the cemetery continued even though November brought with it severe weather . . . -30F to -40F almost every day. Pashka Borischuk was Tainka's only consolation. Pashka kept reassuring her friend Tainka that it would be an easy birth. She kept urging Tainka to take more nourishment, but to no avail.

On December 19, Pashka came to see Tainka to check on her condition. The day of the baby's birth was fast approaching. She felt Tainka's protruding belly, checked her hands and feet, and showed some concern. She announced that it didn't appear the baby would arrive for about another week and that she was being called away to deliver a baby across the river at Andrew. She would be back in plenty of time to deliver Tainka's baby. The very next day Tainka's labour pains began. Evan was totally beside himself. Mrs. Borischuk was gone—who was going to deliver this child? He hitched up the horses and galloped them to Shady Hollow to fetch Dr. Liston, again to no avail, as the good doctor had left for a one-week trip to Edmonton to pick up supplies. As he was driving back home he met Josephina Lupski, their Polish neighbour. He told her what was happening and that Mrs. Borischuk and Dr. Liston were not available. Mrs. Lupski volunteered to come. After all, she had given birth to six children and she had delivered many farm animals, so what possible difficulty could there be?

She brought along her *kryanka* (a densely woven multi-coloured sash) and dressed herself in a clean white apron. When they got to the Stry-Kers', Tainka was in complete agony, perspiring profusely, her face badly flushed. A whole day of labour passed with no baby in sight. Another day had begun and the labour contractions were getting worse. On the morning of December 22, Mrs. Lupski was beginning to feel as helpless and desperate as everyone else in attendance. She finally asked Tainka to rise from her lying position and, using the tightly woven sash she had brought with her, tied Tainka to the heavy iron bedstead. Then she asked Evan for another sash. He gave her Tainka's *kryanka* and Josephina began tying it tightly around Tainka's pregnant belly, trying to force the baby downward. As she kept tying the *kryanka* tighter and tighter, Tainka's pain became more and more intense. Her abdomen was badly bruised and she was begging for mercy.

"Oh God, let me die!" Tainka moaned weakly.

It was at this point that Evan made God a promise. If Tainka survived (the baby's survival was not part of the promise), he would never again burden her with his sexual demands. Tainka made a promise of her own to God. "If the baby and I survive, I will make sure the child will be a servant of God." She had always hoped little Paul might lean that way, but seeing how shy he was, it wasn't likely. In her mesmerized state, she was faintly muttering to Mrs. Lupski about what promise she had just made. Josephina looked gravely at her, thinking neither Tainka nor the baby would survive. Just then an angel of mercy walked in . . . Pashka Borischuk!

She was absolutely furious when she saw what a terrible state her precious Tainka was in. She spit out orders with such rapidity that even Tainka came back to reality.

"Oyee, oyee, Pashka, is that really you?" she groaned, a slight smile on her face.

"Yes, my child, it's me. And I am amazed at what these idiots have been doing to you!" Pashka seethed. She chased everyone except Katayna out of the house; Katayna begged to stay and help in any way she could. When Pashka saw the condition Tainka was in she was deathly afraid that Tainka would suffer the same fate as Olga Soova. After all, Tainka at this point was very weak. She also was toxemic. Pashka hoped that her friend could push when it was time for the baby to be born. She then gently laid her hands on Tainka and massaged her swollen, bruised belly ever so gently with warm hempseed oil. Tainka relaxed completely and within one hour a long, thin baby boy was born.

"I shall name him Francis Nykola because it so close to Christmas." Tanika said in a feeble voice, immediately after being told the gender of the child. "He is my Christmas present. Therefore, Nykola will honour St. Nicholas. He will also reach incredible heights and be powerful just like Franz Josef, our Austrian Emperor." With that she fell asleep for two whole days, with Pashka Borischuk sitting beside her bed. She only rose briefly when Katayna brought the tiny infant to nurse. He weighed no more than six pounds and looked emaciated. That is how life began for Francis Nykola Stry-Ker.

From the beginning it was obvious Tainka would have very little to do with this child except provide him with nourishment. Francis Nykola's maternal bonding was made with Katayna, his thirteen-year-old sister, who loved him absolutely. Helenka, who was now sixteen and should have been the natural person to take over the care, showed no interest in little Francis Nykola. She no longer attended school and grudgingly looked after him during the day. Katayna cared for Francis Nykola when she got home from school and woke up at night when he cried to take him to his mother for nursing. Tainka continued her daily practice of visiting Maria's grave one week after Francis Nykola was born.

Christmas 1922 was one of the saddest the Stry-Kers had ever experienced, despite having a new little Christmas present in the form of Francis Nykola. It was not the same without Maria. All went to the Borischuks' this year to celebrate Christmas Eve. On Christmas Day the dinner was held at the Stry-Kers'. Father Kohot was coming to Shady Hollow to conduct Christmas Mass. There would not be another mass held until February. This was much too long to wait to baptize Francis Nykola. They believed that if he died, he'd never be allowed in heaven and he'd have to be buried outside the church fence. So the occasion was to be Francis Nykola's christening as well as the Christmas celebration. Tainka chose, as expected, Pashka Borischuk to be Francis Nykola's *Xristna Mawte* (godmother), and Evan chose Joseph Chomiak, the late Stephen's father and deacon at the church to be the *Xrisnee Tato* (godfather). He had the reputation of being a reliable, honest, and compassionate person. People chose godparents to be the standbys in the event the parents died. Godparents were also examples of what qualities parents would like to see in their children.

Miss Brownlee, the spinster schoolteacher, brought over a huge turkey that she had purchased from a Finnish farmer in Radway. She now owned a car, a Chevy coupe, and travelled to Edmonton once a month. Her visit to the Stry-Kers was a goodwill gesture because of all the hardships the family had suffered during the past year. Evan had resigned as Councillor of the School Board after Maria's death. But since Evan had hired her to begin with, it was important to her to show gratitude at how well he had treated her while he was the Councillor. Ever since she arrived to teach at White Sands School, Evan had always been an ally.

Miss Brownlee was invited to attend Christmas dinner and acccpted the invitation. The Stry-Ker children spoke English well and Evan's conversational English had improved a lot, so there was no problem with conversation around the table. The Chomiaks, Borischuks, and Yaworskys also attended. Everyone was seated around the large table in the parlour where Maria's body had lain. Most people in attendance had a feeling that her presence was still there.

Right after the prayer was said, Tainka burst into tears and left the table. Everyone knew why and excused her. That was the first year Rosie Soova sent the entire Stry-Ker family a written Christmas message. She wrote her address and told them she owned a rooming house in Edmonton and if any of them ever needed a place to stay when they came to Edmonton they would be very welcome. This special Christmas greeting, the first formal Christmas card they had ever received, was placed in the wooden trunk along with Maria's possessions.

In two months, Tainka had no more milk to feed baby Francis Nykola. The Borischuks had recently purchased a Jersey milking cow. The little Jersey produced milk that was incredibly rich in butterfat. Theodore brought the cow over for the Stry-Kers to use, primarily to provide the nourishment that the baby so desperately needed.

The baby gained weight much more quickly than when Tainka was providing breast milk. He received as much love as he needed from his sister Katayna. Mikhail and Paul also adored him, whereas Evan, Tainka, and Helenka paid very little attention to this little baby boy. The child must have sensed this and gave them very little trouble. He ate and slept. When he was awake he amused himself by playing with his toes as he lay in his cradle. He cried very little. He gurgled and giggled sweet little noises and sucked his thumb for security.

CHAPTER NINETEEN

One year had passed since Maria had died. Tainka shed her black clothing and went to the cemetery only once a week, on Sundays. She had given up eating her favourite fruit, strawberries, as a memorial tribute to Maria. The wild strawberries grew in abundance on the Stry-Ker farm in the sector where there was sandy soil. Not eating strawberries was one way Tainka showed sacrifice for her dead daughter, her favourite child. Life without Maria would never be the same for her.

Tainka appeared to be taking a little more interest in her home, garden, and farm in general. Certainly she was not paying any attention to her baby boy, Francis Nykola; Katayna continued to be his surrogate mother. He didn't seem to mind one bit, as it was no different than at any time since his birth. He was now six months old and starting to roll around on the floor. Francis Nykola was not a beautiful child. He was long for his age and very thin. He had a full head of brown curly hair and very dark eyes. His face was long and thin. His skin was white and pale. Katayna took him everywhere she went. When she weeded the garden, she'd place him in a large basket. Once in a while she'd place him on the grass beside her. He loved to be outside. She would even take him along when she sneaked down to the artesian well for a smoke.

All the Stry-Ker children thought smoking was a real treat. Tainka did not allow them to smoke and neither did Evan, even though he was now a chain smoker. Mikhail was the only one who was allowed to smoke Evan's tobacco and he was permitted to sit at the kitchen table and smoke at meal times. Girls, however, could not. So Helenka and Katayna smoked cigarettes which they made using old newspaper and dried leaves—usually those of the poplar trees. Once in a while they snuck Evan's tobacco from his Ogden Tobacco can and a few of his Chanteclaire papers for a huge treat. In order not to be caught stealing the tobacco, they would fluff up the remainder using Tainka's knitting needles.

As Katayna was savouring a long drag of this crude-looking cigarette, Paul came running to her. "Katayna," he accused breathlessly, "*Te Korish*! (You're smoking!) You just wait till *Mamunia* and *Tato* find out. Boy oh boy, are you ever going to get it!"

She was afraid he would go home and tattle, and Evan, with his current tyrannical behaviour, would give her a cruel beating. So she coaxed Paul to take a puff of the cigarette. "Here, you little brat, you try it—that's if you are man enough. Then you'll see why I like smoking so much! Aww, but I don't think you will. You are such a sissy!"

With that kind of a dare, Paul did take a puff and became very dizzy. "It tastes awful . . . like horseshit. I'm never going to smoke!" he groaned.

"But you already did, so if you tell *Mamunia* or *Tato* I was smoking, then I'll tell them you were too!" warned Katayna.

"Katayna, you made me do it . . . that's unfair of you!" Paul accused her.

"Always remember, little Paul, no one makes you do anything if you don't want to!" she replied smugly.

With that he ran off yelling, "I don't like you . . . I don't like you! My favourite person in the whole world is Mikhail!" But he did not report the incident to Evan or to Tainka.

CHAPTER TWENTY

1925 The Starosta

As the years passed, the older children were expected to get married, especially the girls. Helenka was now twenty years old and had a number of suitors coming to see her, but none that she wished to marry. Helenka had turned out to be a beautiful woman also. She resembled her mother. She was as tall as Tainka, but heavier set, although she had a good figure. Helenka was an excellent cook and was gifted in the crafts. She would knit wonderful sweaters with various designs and colours. Many people in the neighbourhood paid her to knit for them. She could also crochet lovely doilies, tablecloths, and dresses for young girls.

One day Petro Kuriak, Evan and Tainka's old friend from Star, Alberta, brought an affluent young man to see Helenka. In those days, the accepted custom was the use of a *starosta* (matchmaker), particularly for women who were having problems finding a mate. These women were known as *stara-divka* (old maid), and the parents usually arranged for a *starosta*. In this case, everyone suspected it was Evan's doing. Petro Kuriak brought the young man, whose name was Samenion. It was up to the starosta to do the selling job. Helenka objected to this ordeal, but Evan was such a tyrant since Maria's death that she felt it would keep peace in the house if she went through with it.

Helenka sat on a chair across the room in the parlour while Evan, Kuriak, and Samenion sat at the large dining room table used for only special occasions. Kuriak was excitedly bragging about Samenion and singing his virtues. The greatest selling feature was that he was a *boohatch* (rich man). It didn't matter that his body weighed over 200 pounds and that he measured five feet five inches. He had a round face with large spaces between his dirty, stained front teeth and his ears protruded from the sides of his head like ears on a porcelain pitcher. He was extremely shy, and while Kuriak kept waxing eloquent about his laurels, Samenion looked up at the ceiling. Once in a long while he'd sneak a glance at Helenka, who was sitting across the room and looking at the floor.

After Kuriak thought he had succeeded in selling the wonderful virtues and qualities of Samenion, he said, "Samenion, I'm sure you want to say something now, don't you, son?"

Samenion continued to stare at the ceiling for at least five more minutes, then he responded. "Well, yes, as I look around your place, Mr. Stry-Ker, your place is like ours. I see the flies shit all over your ceiling, just as they did at our place!" Then abruptly he stopped talking.

Kuriak and Evan looked at each other in utter amazement. Helenka ran out of the room bursting her sides with laughter. Samenion turned as red as a beet and clammed up. His ears turned red, blood red . . . and he never spoke another word at the Stry-Kers'. Kuriak had a few drinks of moonshine and smoked Ogden tobacco cigarettes with Evan while Samenion sat and continued looking at the ceiling. As Kuriak and Samenion left to go home, Evan told them he would let them know what Helenka's intentions were, knowing damn well what her answer would be.

He went back into the house and called Helenka into the parlour. "Why were you so rude to that young man, Helenka?" Evan asked, trying to suppress his laughter.

She had a strong will but very seldom contradicted Evan. This day she was being very assertive. "You don't seriously think I would marry that idiot . . . rich or not?" she spluttered.

Evan burst out laughing. When he finally was able to control himself, he wiped his eyes and looked at her. "No, daughter, I don't expect you to marry the likes of Samenion. But these constant offers you are getting have got to end up in some kind of a marriage. You are now twenty and I'm sick and tired of seeing a string of these men coming to our house." He gave her an ultimatum. "Either you will marry within the next year or I will have Kuriak bring someone else and this one you will marry. Ugly, stupid, or poor, you will marry! I don't want people calling you Stry-Ker's *stara-divka*. Pretty soon no one will want you. You're almost too old now . . . twenty-one. Most girls, except the real ugly ones, are married by then, and I don't see you as being ugly at all!"

Within six months Helenka married Peter and Olana Pushinsky's eldest son, Joseph. Joseph was a gentle man. He was also attractive, with brown hair and black eyes— eyes that were happy all the time. He didn't smoke but loved to drink alcohol. Why not? He was a musician and so would attend many parties and festive occasions where liquor was served all the time. They were very distant cousins, but Father Kohot did not feel this constituted an incestuous relationship, so he blessed the marriage. Joseph was five years older than Helenka. The celebrations that had been planned for Maria's wedding were renewed: Helenka would be married on July 25, 1925.

CHAPTER TWENTY-ONE

July 25, 1925 Helenka's Wedding

Helenka's wedding was a beautiful occasion. Evan took much interest in this first wedding of a child of his. Tainka didn't help matters by groaning everywhere she went, "Oyee, Oyee, if only Maria was here to share this blessed event with us!"

Helenka felt this wasn't fair, as this was her special day. "Once in a lifetime a person marries . . . and I shall love my Joseph always! We will have a good marriage. Why can't you see that, *Mamunia?* Please be happy for me . . . just this once!" she pleaded.

Evan and Tainka, as everyone suspected, were no longer intimate. This had been the case since Francis Nykola's birth. In fact, Evan respected Tainka as the mother of his children and tolerated her morbid behaviour. He also noted that she had very little to do with Francis' rearing even though she constantly talked about how honoured the family would be when Francis became a priest.

Evan tolerated these comments from her, even though he never would have done so had they come from anyone else. But he could no longer tolerate her ridiculous behaviour just before Helenka's wedding. One month before the wedding there was a dreadful argument between them. They thought the children were asleep. However, Katayna was walking around holding little Francis, who was fussing. He slept in the girls' room upstairs from the time that he was born. Katayna heard their exchange. It sounded as though Evan was shaking Tainka, for her voice was shaky as she responded to him.

"It's four years since Maria died. Don't you think I feel as badly as you do about her death? Why have you kept everyone in this house living in a grave with Maria? For goodness sake, woman, all these children are ours. Why aren't you treating them equally?"

Evan had never yelled at Tainka or made such cruel remarks before. At first she was hurt. Then anger came over her as she bombarded him with her caustic remarks.

"You never mourned enough for Maria! Don't you think I know what you've been doing? The ladies at church stop talking when I come near them. I know they are saying things about you and the widow Hunkowski. You are nothing but a whoremaster. God punished us by taking Maria because of your oversexed behaviour," she accused him. With that final statement he could not suppress his rage. He was just as hurt as she was about Maria's death. He smacked her across the head with both fists clasped together. She flew across the room and crashed against the wall.

He yelled at her as he stomped out of the room, totally ignoring her comments about the whoremaster. "You will act like you are interested in Helenka's happiness and make this wedding a happy occasion for her sake or else I'll beat you to death!" He slept in the hayloft that night, the same loft where Mikhail claimed to have seen Maria's spirit. He hoped against hope that Maria's spirit would once again appear and make him feel better, as Maria could do when she was alive. She could make everyone feel good . . . God, what an angel she was, he thought as he drifted off to sleep. The next day when he came into the house for breakfast he noticed Tainka's badly bruised cheek, but neither of them made any further comments.

The *brama* was ready one week before the wedding. The crepe paper streamers and waxed paper roses would be hung on the spruce boughs on the day of the wedding. One month before the wedding Helenka and Joseph Pushinsky, her husband-to-be, had personally invited all the guests.

Tainka did appear to be taking more interest in the wedding plans since her encounter with Evan. She went over to the Soovas' and hired Domka to be the official cook, as it was well known that Domka was the best cook for miles around and had cooked at a number of recent weddings. Evan and Metro Soova had not spoken since the incident with his daughter Rosie and David Newhouse, but Metro held no animosity toward Tainka. In fact, within his rotten self he felt a little sorry that he had cursed the Stry-Ker family that night because he felt the curse was what killed Maria, and Maria had been so good to his family. Yes, he was sorry Maria had died . . . died because of his bad temper.

Together Domka and Tainka planned the menu. Domka told Tainka how much food would be needed and what she should have on hand to start preparations.

Joseph Pushinsky and his three younger brothers, Peter, Metro, and John, played in their own band. Along with a cousin, Alec Pushinsky, the four Pushinkys would play for the wedding. The band comprised a fiddle, a banjo, a guitar, and a *symballe* (dulcimer). Joseph played the fiddle; a cousin who could play the fiddle almost as well would replace him. Most of the Pushinsky brothers could play almost any instrument. They were very versatile. The wedding dance would take place on top of the huge new hayloft. The Stry-Kers had built a new barn two years earlier.

One day, about one week before the wedding, Tainka asked Mikhail to drive her to White Sands Creek Indian Reserve. Mikhail obliged. They travelled east and north of Stry-Kers', to where the reservation was located.

Tainka asked Mikhail to find out where Mary and Paul Tatonga lived. The Indian agent asked Mikhail why he wanted to know, whereupon Mikhail told him it was to invite them to his sister's wedding. The agent told Mikhail that Paul Tatonga was now the Chief of their reservation, and he showed him where their house was located. Tainka and Mikhail knocked on the door and were invited in. Mary and Paul Tatonga were pleased to see Tainka and Mikhail and invited them to stay for tea. She served them fresh bannock and accepted the wedding invitation with pleasure. Tainka asked that the invitation be extended also to Cochees Sinclair, Louis Demers, and Gabriel Laboucane. Paul told Tainka that Louis and Gabriel had moved off the reserve, and no one knew where they were.

The wedding dinner would be served in the parlour in three different sittings, as one sitting accommodated only fifty people and one hundred and fifty had been invited. There were long tables set all around the perimeter of the room and one short table in the middle of the room. The children would eat on the veranda, where long tables were set out. A steer, a large sow, and fifteen chickens were butchered. This looked after the meat requirements. Domka Soova roasted most of the meat in the large *peech*. At the same time, she cooked the *holuptsi* and *kolasha*. *Pyrogies* were boiled the night before the wedding. The traditional *borsch* (beet soup with white beans and pork stock) was made the day before the wedding as well, and warmed up during the day. Domka Soova learned a new way of serving potatoes. She combined cubed boiled eggs and peeled, chopped potatoes boiled in their skins and added very finely chopped onions. She placed these chopped eggs and potatoes into a small tub, salted and peppered everything well and then added a boiled salad dressing which she had made earlier.

It appeared to be a light yellowy cream colour. She would not tell anyone what was in it; this was the cook's secret. "Oh I put a little of this and a little of that," she said to anyone who asked. "I never measure anything. It just turns out this way!" But what the little of this and that was, she would never reveal. No one around Shady Hollow had ever heard of or tasted this wonderful dish before. Domka called it potato salad. This was one of the most popular dishes at the wedding besides her apple and lemon pies. Domka Soova had established a reputation everywhere in the community as being an excellent cook. She was now in demand as the chief cook for weddings as far away as Andrew, across the North Saskatchewan River. She concocted dishes that were delicious and unique. She certainly had enough testers at home. Her family had grown to six of her and Metro's children, six from her previous marriage, and eight children from Metro Soova's first marriage. Granted, six of them, like Rosie, had now left to start lives of their own. But there was still a horde that would have eaten a wolf if one was salted and cooked.

Sara Houskinen of Radway sewed Helenka's wedding dress. It was a lovely dress with mother-of-pearl buttons down the front and on the long sleeves. The only difference from Maria's dress was that Helenka's fabric was ordered from the T. Eaton's catalogue in Winnipeg, Manitoba. It was not the fine silk which Rosie Soova had sent for Maria's wedding.

The excitement was mounting as the wedding day approached. The Stry-Kers even bought a new car, a 1925 dark green Chevrolet. The car was by all intents Mikhail's, as he had taken over much of the farming operation. Evan never did learn to drive a car. He preferred horses. The car would be decorated with brightly coloured streamers and white crepe paper flowers. This would be the official bridal car. There was also a groom's car. The Pushinskys had bought a car three years before the Stry-Kers and this car would carry Joseph on his wedding day.

The custom in those days was for both families to host receptions in their respective homes. The couple would go to church in the morning. Mass would be celebrated, followed by the wedding ceremony. This took about two and a half hours. Following the church ceremonies, the bride and her attendants would go to her home to begin celebrations and the groom and his groomsmen would go to his parents' home to celebrate with their friends.

The orchestra greeted every guest who arrived. The orchestra went along with the bride to her home. Wherever she went, so did they. The groom was not to see them until after he had claimed the bride later in the day. In this case though, the orchestra consisted only of his brothers and cousin. Each guest threw money at the members of the orchestra to show their gratitude for being welcomed in such a special way. At about 4:00 p.m. the groom came to the bride's home and was met at the *brama* by the bride's parents. The bride stood in the background until she was summoned to come forward by her father. The groom had with him a gallon of wine, special bread called *koluch*, and a cup of salt. These were all symbols of health, happiness, and prosperity. He handed them to the parents and asked them to part officially with their daughter and give her into his care.

The whole day was happy and beautiful. Everything went according to plan. When Joseph came for Helenka later in the day, Evan and Tainka bestowed their blessings and ceremonially handed her to Joseph. Soon the presentation lines—*darovenia*—commenced. This gave all the guests an opportunity to present a gift to the newlyweds.

The men always gave money and their spouses or partners presented a gift . . . something the couple could use in setting up their home.

Helenka and Joseph would live on the same yard as his parents but they had built a separate small house near the big house in order to have their privacy.

During the *darovenia* the orchestra played an individual rendition for each couple that came to present their gifts, after the special singers sang an individualized Ukrainian song for each. Domka Soova again was the centre of attention as she knew many songs and had a good, and loud, Ukrainian voice. It carried for long distances. The lyrics often did not make sense but they rhymed. One favourite song was . . . "dance, dance, dance, and jump and a little more dance, the potatoes are not cooked and the corn meal has gone sour . . . dance, dance, dance, and jump and a little more dance and jump!"

Paul and Mary Tatonga attended, and so did Cochees Sinclair from the White Sands Creek Indian Reservation. They presented the couple with the most beautiful hand-beaded and embroidered moccasins made of treated rawhide. Cochees donated a hand-carved bear made out of birch wood, which he had personally carved.

As each couple came to the table to face the bride and groom, the groomsmen poured two small glasses of wine. They would drink a toast to the newlyweds and then wish them the best of luck in their marriage, wish them many healthy and happy years together, and many children. After everyone had presented their gifts, a large meal was served. This was the second large meal served that day, as one was served when the bride came back from the church in the early afternoon. After the newlyweds ate the meal, they entered the hayloft where the wedding dance was being held and danced the official first wedding dance together. After this they danced with all the "very important persons." Then it was time to leave to continue celebrations at Joseph's place.

The official traditional bows were exchanged with Tainka and Evan and the couple left with their entourage. Katayna and Mikhail were in the wedding party, along with two other girls and boys from the area. Best Man and Matron of Honour were Mike and Pearl Yaworsky from Radway. The orchestra left with them. The same celebrations would now occur at the home of Joseph Pushinsky.

There was a total of one hundred and twenty-five dollars donated at the two homes during the *darovenia*. There were also many varied and beautiful gifts, gifts of whatever anyone could afford. Many had made items, such as cross-stitched cushions, pillowslips, and table-cloths—all on pure white linen fabric. These were treasures and genuine works of art.

The celebrations at the Stry-Kers' continued until 4:00 a.m. Francis Nykola, now three years old, lasted until midnight and then fell asleep under the bench in the hayloft. Tainka noticed her little baby asleep as peaceful as an angel, so she picked him up and put him gently on his bed. He awoke slightly and asked for Katayna. Katayna was Helenka's bridesmaid and could not put him to bed as she normally did. Many children and women fell asleep but the men continued to drink moonshine, sing, and dance by themselves.

Evan, Theodore Borischuk, and another neighbour named Mike Mikalik were having a great time. These three friends were the founding members of St. Olga's church. Their friendship went back a long way, to the time they all served in the Austrian army. There were also a number of other guests who were still having fun, among them Milka and Todour Popilsky, friends and neighbours of the Stry-Kers. They continued to dance and joke. Even Tainka had let her guard down, and enjoyed herself tremendously.

CHAPTER TWENTY-TWO

The last people to leave the Stry-Kers' at 4:00 a.m. were Todour and Milka Popilsky. They lived three miles southeast of the Stry-Kers and were walking home because their fifteen-year-old son, Andrew, had driven the five younger children home several hours earlier.

Todour had been drinking moonshine all night but he was not obnoxiously intoxicated. He was having a good time singing wedding songs. Perhaps the *solonena* (pork backfat marinated with salt) cushioned his stomach against the alcohol. Todour had a good voice and sang in St. Olga church's choir. He had also been one of the *spevaki* (singers) during the presentation earlier in the evening, along with Domka Soova.

His wife, Milka, was in her third month of pregnancy. As they walked home he stumbled here and there but continued to sing at the top of his lungs. As they walked past Soovas' farm they encountered Metro Soova. He had not been invited to the wedding event, even though his wife and children had, and all had attended. He was as sore as a boil waiting to be lanced. All day and all night he watched and heard the guests as they came and went to the wedding. He could hear the music and singing because he lived only a half-mile away. He had been drinking heavily all that day. This, however, was a normal thing for Metro Soova.

He came rushing out of his yard and lunged at the Popilskys, waving an iron crowbar. "Shad-up you Som-a-na-bich." He thought he was most proficient in the English language. "You not knowing what time is it?" Soova yelled.

Popilsky had no use for Soova and yelled back at him in Ukrainian. "*Ta staray didko* (you old devil)!" he slurred. "This is a public road and we can walk on it whenever we want to! Now go back into your yard and don't bother people!"

"You Som-a-na-bich, I show you I meen buzzenezz!" Soova threatened. He swung the crowbar and Milka, trying to stop him from hitting her husband, received the blow across her left shoulder blade and dropped to the ground in sheer agony. With that, Todour Popilsky lunged at Soova with no regard for his own safety. He was not in any shape to fight a lamb, never mind this raging animal, who was as strong as a bull and had a crowbar in his grasp.

Whack, whack, whack, across the head and Todour slumped to the ground in a kneeling position as he held his hands to his head. Soova gave him yet another blow to his back and then another to the head.

"You killed him!" screamed Milka, "You creature from the bottom of hell!" This brought Soova to as many senses as was possible and he went back into his yard in a dazed state, leaving the crowbar beside Todour Popilsky. Todour's body appeared lifeless. Milka could not walk for help and futhermore would not leave Todour, so she wept and cradled him in her arms. Blood was streaming from Todour's head as a result of Soova's vicious attack. Milka was also hurt, and could no longer hold Todour as her shoulder was swelling badly.

About half an hour later, as the sun was rising, Mikhail and Katayna Stry-Ker returned in their car from Pushinskys after the wedding party there had ended. Katayna was the first to see Milka Popilsky kneeling beside Todour. She was shocked that someone would be kneeling at the side of the road. "Mikhail!" she blurted out, but he had already noticed the Popilskys. As the car rolled to a stop they both saw the seriousness of the situation. Milka was now covered in Todour's blood. She could not lift her own body. Her shoulder and her face were badly bruised and her shoulder was getting worse. One eye was now swollen and shut tight. Todour appeared to be dead.

"Holy God! Holy God . . ." Mikhail croaked out the sounds. He couldn't believe what he was seeing. "What happened here?"

Katayna turned as white as a sheet and went running to Milka, who was shaking and in deep shock. Katayna ran back to the car and grabbed a blanket from the back seat, the blanket they always kept there in case Francis Nykola ever fell asleep in the car.

Crying hysterically, Milka explained how Soova's attack happened and pleaded that they help them. Mikhail picked up Todour's lifeless body and laid it on the back seat. Milka insisted on riding in the back seat with him. Todour's body was covered in blood and the smell of blood and urine was strong. With the severe beating which Todour received, he had lost control of his vital organs. They turned the car around in Soova's gateway and drove as fast as they could to Shady Hollow, where a hospital had just opened that year. It had been relocated from Pakan to Shady Hollow, where a lively community was being quickly established. A young doctor from Edmonton, Dr. Frank Allison, had set up practice. He was a brilliant doctor, with the latest knowledge of medical technologies.

Mikhail carried Todour into the hospital. A nurse immediately began to tend to Todour and then Mikhail carried Milka in as well. By this time Milka had collapsed from her injuries and exhaustion. Katayna was dispatched to get Dr. Allison, who lived a block away. The doctor came rushing over within minutes and immediately started a blood transfusion on Todour.

Mikhail and Katayna then proceeded to notify the Royal Canadian Mounted Police. The detachment had been established in Shady Hollow in 1910. Corporal Jack Seymour was in charge, and the young constable who assisted him had just arrived one month earlier. His name was Robert McLennan—most of his friends called him Rusty. Both men were over six feet tall with wide shoulders and evidently not an ounce of fat. Together or separately they were a formidable sight. Neither appeared to have any fear nor did either show even a remote sense of humour.

When Mikhail and Katayna arrived at the police station they hammered on the door. The police lived in the same structure in which the office and jail cells were located. The first to answer the door was Constable Rusty McLennan. He was fully dressed in regulation uniform. He didn't appear to be drowsy; rather, he appeared perfectly alert.

"Good morning. I'm Constable McLennan. How can I help you?" he boomed. His height and physical build would have intimidated most people. His voice was a deep baritone and he sounded like a booming drum. Even when he tried to talk quietly it didn't come out that way.

"We have come to report a vicious beating, maybe even a murder," replied Mikhail. Katayna, in the meantime, was speechless; she thought this was certainly the most handsome man she'd ever seen in her entire life.

Constable Rusty McLennan lived up to his Scottish heritage. His hair was a mass of flaming, copper-red curls that matched the colour of his moustache. His face was angular with a strong square chin. His eyes were a dark chocolate brown but they always had a serious, no-nonsense look—piercing might be the best way to describe them. His nose was aquiline, with just an ever so slight bend to the left, a souvenir of his boxing classes at the RCMP academy in Regina, Saskatchewan. His eyelashes and brows were dark brown, complementing his copper-coloured hair and moustache.

As Mikhail was describing the incident, Corporal Seymour entered the room. Seymour had dark hair and moustache, with a handsome masculine face and a bullish neck. He looked stern and mean. The Corporal appeared first and foremost not to have a great deal of patience. He bellowed at the young policeman, "Constable McLennan! I suggest you escort these people to the office and take a written statement from them." He looked at Mikhail and Katayna in the most contemptuous manner possible.

Seymour had much resentment. He was a white Anglo-Saxon Protestant. His heritage could be traced to the Empire Loyalists in Upper Canada. He had absolutely no use for any of these "intruders," these "ignorant immigrants." On top of this built-in resentment he had been transferred to Shady Hollow from Fort McMurray, where for five years he had been in charge of all police operations for the remote northern region.

Fort McMurray had been established in 1899, four hundred miles north on the Athabasca River. The RCMP and their predecessors until 1904, the North West Mounted Police, had been there until 1917. The detachment was closed down in that year until 1920, when it was staffed with the chief officer Corporal Seymour. It was alleged that he was involved in some form of embezzlement along with the Hudson's Bay agent. The allegation was that the pair was short-changing the Indian people on their fur pelts. When they reported various incidents to Corporal Seymour he always took the side of the agent, claiming their accusations were inaccurate. The RCMP hierarchy conducted an intense internal inquiry but could not prove any wrongdoing by Seymour. If they had found definite proof of wrongdoing, he would have been dismissed from the force with dishonour. They obviously had not. He was, however, transferred to another posting . . . the new posting at Shady Hollow. This he did not appreciate. Although definite proof of wrongdoing was missing, the RCMP nevertheless took disciplinary action—Seymour did not receive his upgrading to the rank of Sergeant, after ten years of service and many extraordinary achievements.

Constable McLennan was given the posting at Shady Hollow because of his keen interest in and knowledge of moonshine stills. He was born at Buctovche, in the heart of the Acadian country. His mother was of Scottish origin. Her descendants had settled at Campbellton, New Brunswick*. Constable McLennan's father was also an RCMP officer. His claim to fame was the destruction and cleanup of the moonshine stills in the Buctovche area. Young Rusty had watched his father and was totally enamoured of the techniques his father used to find illegal stills.

RCMP officers were not, as a rule, posted in the province of their birth. At the Police Academy in Regina, Saskatchewan, Rusty's father's achievements and fine reputation were well known, and Rusty had mentioned on a number of occasions that he would appreciate a posting where the illicit moonshine industry was thriving. He was posted to Athabasca for two and a half years and then to Shady Hollow at his own request, as not many young Mounties would have chosen this place. Shady

---

* Campbellton, New Brunswick, was the site of the 16th- and 17th-century French missions which were settled by dispossessed Acadians in 1757. The settlement was named Pointe-des-Savages at that time, and renamed Campbellton in 1825 after an influx of Scots arrived.

Hollow was unofficially recognized as the moonshine capital of Alberta. There were estimated to be about fifty stills in the region. Most people, as well as the RCMP, knew about Metro Soova's moonshine operation but could never locate his still, no matter how they tried.

"This beating incident will close him down for good, should the courts see it that way," thought Corporal Seymour.

Constable McLennan took statements from Mikhail and Katayna with Corporal Seymour sitting in a chair nearby, peering at them both. It was now close to 7:00 a.m.

Before they drove home they checked back at the hospital to inquire about the Popilskys' conditions. They breathed a sigh of relief when they were told Todour Popilsky was still alive, although barely. He was in a coma. Milka, his wife, miscarried her baby and sustained a badly broken collarbone as well as a broken forearm. She was resting peacefully after the doctor had given her large quantities of morphine. It was Dr. Allison's unyielding determination that saved Todour's life. The doctor had given him a badly needed transfusion. He was the same blood type as one of the housekeepers at the hospital, who very willingly gave her blood. The doctor remained at the hospital, constantly checking on their respective conditions.

As they drove home and past the Soovas, Mikhail and Katayna found that the two RCMP officers were already there looking for Metro Soova. When they got home everyone was still asleep. They woke the family and held a meeting where they explained what had happened. Evan was in a daze, as he had drunk copious amounts of wine and moonshine. He quickly came to his senses when he heard about the tragedy. Even baby Francis Nykola woke up, and Katayna ran to pick him up. As Evan and Tainka did the Stry-Ker chores, Mikhail drove to the Popilskys' place to inform the children about the tragedy. Paul, who was by now like an extension of Mikhail, jumped into the car and drove off with him. They would help with the Popilsky chores. The whole affair was a disaster! All the younger children started crying hysterically when they heard about their parents' tragedy. The eldest, fifteen-year-old Andrew, would not show emotion as he thought it would show him to be weak. He was now totally in charge of the family, in the absence of his mother and father.

Mikhail, with Paul dragging behind him, finished the chores. They drove back home and told the family of the sad tidings at the Popilskys'. Tainka suggested that Katayna go back and stay with the children until Mrs. Popilsky's mother or other relatives could come. Next Mikhail and Paul drove to Lamont to notify the Popilskys' relatives of the sad tidings. Milka Popilsky's mother, the children's grandmother, came back with them and took over the care of the family, after first stopping at the hospital to see Todour and Milka.

The grandmother cried all the way back to Popilskys' farm. Mikhail had not slept for well over twenty-four hours. When he got home he crawled upstairs and fell on the bed. He did not wake up for the *popravene* (after-the-wedding party) but slept through to the next day. He was in a deep shock as well as being exhausted.

About seventy people came back to the Stry-Kers' the next day for popravene. Most of the conversation centred on the Popilsky tragedy.

"Did you hear about what that old, crazy Soova did to the Popilskys?" one would ask the other. If the person hadn't heard they would be told, with a little more detail added each time the story was explained, until finally when Katayna heard the story repeated to her there was little similarity to what had actually happened. According to one of the other guests, "Both Popilskys were beaten to within one inch of their lives. He had his head split open and you could see his brains, his eyes had popped out of his head, and he had lost all his teeth . . . surely he must be dead. Mrs. Popilsky had her face smashed right in and her nose was crushed beyond recognition. Most of the bones in her body are broken. She was found lying beside her husband and Soova was standing over them like a crazy, wild animal wielding an axe!"

Katayna looked in amazement at the guest and tried to explain. "No, that is not what happened!" She attempted to correct the embellished story.

"Well, that's not what I heard!" said the guest, not wishing to hear the facts. Katayna in frustration, blustered, "I don't care what you heard. That is not the way it happened. After all, I should know . . . Mikhail and I were the first to find them!"

"Oh, were you?" was the response. "Well, tell me what did happen. What is the story?" Katayna was too tired and frustrated to continue this foolish conversation so she politely excused herself.

The chief cook did not fulfill her contract. This day Domka Soova had too many other problems to be concerned about serving food for the popravene, although there was certainly enough food left over from the wedding feast.

CHAPTER TWENTY-THREE

The Arrest

When the RCMP arrived at Soova's farm, Domka had just gotten home from the Stry-Kers' after working all day cooking at the wedding. They banged on the door with such force as to arouse all the children. Domka asked them to come in. They asked to see Metro, her husband. She hadn't even noticed that he was not in the bed until she went to look for him. In all honesty, she had no idea where he could be.

"Why do you want to see him?" she inquired.

Both Corporal Seymour and Constable McLennan showed irritation and impatience at Domka. "There has been a vicious beating which occurred earlier this morning by your gate, and it is alleged your husband did it!" Seymour explained brusquely. "We are looking to question Mr. Soova!"

Domka was shocked. "Who was beaten?" she asked.

"We are not at liberty to say!" barked Seymour. With that they looked around the crowded house. Most of the twelve children were frightened and shocked as they sat up in their beds. When they finished their check of the house, Corporal Seymour and Constable McLellan continued to sweep the rest of the yard. Each was armed with a revolver to protect himself. They looked in the barn, chicken coop, cellar, and icehouse. They even shone the flashlight down the wooden cribbing of the thirty-foot well. The pail was lowered to the bottom and sat on top of the water below. But Metro Soova was nowhere to be found.

They came back and asked Domka where else she might think her husband could be. She replied that they owned a homestead in the blueberry country or that he might be at her old place where she'd lived with her first husband, the late Sam Litikiw. He might be there because she had noticed that his wagon and horses were gone.

Soon the police car roared out of the yard in a cloud of dust, headed for the northern blueberry country. When they arrived at the Litikiw homestead, they parked their car on the main road and walked into the yard, on constant alert. Both noticed a small shack which sat on a clearing about a quarter of a mile into the property. They noticed fresh wagon and horse tracks in the soft sandy road. These tracks led into a stand of thick spruce trees and birch trees. There they saw the wagon without the horses. Then they checked in the shack. Soova was not there. They came outside again and started looking at the horse hoof tracks in the sand. Following these to yet another dense part of the bush, they found Soova's two roan horses, still in their harnesses. They appeared to have been ridden hard, as their mouths were still foaming and the sweat on their bodies looked like soap lather. But there was no evidence of Soova.

As they carefully continued to walk further into the thick jackpine, birch, and spruce forest they heard many morning birds singing and chirping. The blue jays were screaming at them for invading their territory, for this was truly their domain. Every few steps they stopped and listened. Suddenly they could hear some pounding noises in the distance. As they walked toward this noise it grew more and more intense. They slipped down a sharp decline into some soft, wet muskeg, with thick willow trees raised beyond that on a small plateau. They spotted Soova holding the blunt end of his axe.

He was feverishly banging at the copper pipes and kettle of his moonshine still. The kettle had been smashed to smithereens and pieces of copper pipe were strewn everywhere. Swinging his axe, he looked like a madman.

This time the Mounties were armed with their shotguns and revolvers. Seymour and McLennan came at Soova from different directions with their guns drawn and pointed at him.

Seymour, as always, was in command. "Drop that axe immediately; you are under arrest!" he shouted at Soova.

When Soova saw who was coming at him from in front and from behind, he was at first shocked and then mystified at how anyone would find him in this, his private hide-a-way. No one ever dared come near his moonshine still. Had it been anyone else he would have given chase with his trusty axe. But Soova was basically a coward. He would attack women, children, and anyone weaker than himself. He was, however, afraid of authority. When he saw these two huge Mounties pointing their loaded guns at him, he was totally intimidated.

He immediately dropped his axe and stuck his arms in the air. "You be finding mine moonshine *fabrica* (factory) . . . you be taking me to the jail for dat ting?" he asked in a cowardly whimper.

Seymour was now clamping the handcuffs on this pathetic creature. "Mr. Soova, I'm afraid it is more serious than that. We are taking you in for questioning related to the vicious beatings of Mr. and Mrs. Popilsky earlier this morning and also for illegal production of moonshine whiskey. You should rot in jail for quite a while." They didn't even bother to ask Soova whether he'd been involved in this dastardly deed, because Soova volunteered a statement.

"Nobody making fool of Soova. I tell the Som-a-na-bich to shud-up when he walking past mine place, but he calling me names and telling me he can singing all he wanting to. He make it me so mad I could kilt him . . . and that stupid voman, she be trying to stopid me!"

"So you hit her as well, did you?" Seymour questioned, leaning closer to hear more evidence.

"You betta-your-life, no stupid voman telling Soova whad to do!"

Metro Soova was formally charged with attempted murder, aggravated assault causing bodily harm, and illegal operation of a moonshine whiskey still.

At the trial, he pleaded guilty to all charges and was sentenced to fifteen years of hard labour in the jail at Fort Saskatchewan, Alberta. Fort Saskatchewan jail was built in 1914 to incarcerate lawbreakers in Alberta, including any sentenced to capital punishment, who would be hanged by the neck until dead. In his sentence the judge also awarded fifty lashes, which were to be administered during his fifteen-year sentence.

After the trial Domka Soova, even though she told no one, felt a great sense of relief deep in her heart, as Metro's incarceration would certainly be a liberation from her annual event of unwanted pregnancies.

After the vicious beatings, it took three weeks in the hospital before Milka Popilsky was released with a heavy cast on her left arm and a sling to keep her collarbone in place. Tudour Popilsky regained consciousness one week after the beating. His physical injuries healed well after two months, but he sustained permanent brain damage and had to be placed in the Oliver Mental Institution near Edmonton, Alberta, for the rest of his natural life. Milka and her six children continued to farm the quarter section until the children were grown and then the family moved back to Lamont, where Milka would be closer to her brothers and sisters. Her mother died one year after the beatings. Many said that her heart suffered from the shock she received. She died of a massive heart attack.

CHAPTER TWENTY-FOUR

Evan's Venture into Horse Breeding

After Helenka's wedding, which occurred in 1925 during harvest, Evan and Mikhail had a serious argument. It started after Mikhail and his friends—Fred Radjec, the Romanian bachelor from across the creek, and Paul Lupski, the Polish neighbour's son—discussed the inadequacies of getting their respective crops threshed.

Peter Pushinsky, Helenka's father-in-law, owned the only steam engine and threshing machine operation for miles around. Everyone relied on him to get their stooks threshed. Of course, he would always complete his farm first and then that of his brothers, after which everyone else could get theirs done. Barley would be threshed first, followed by wheat, rye, and then oats, the main grain crops grown in these parts of the country.

Peter Pushinsky had his favourites. Stry-Ker, Lupski, and Radjec were far down on his priority list, as they never paid him more than the agreed amount. Their crops would not be threshed some years until late October, and if the snow came early, the stooks would have to wait until spring to be threshed. When this happened, as it did in the fall of 1924, there would be tremendous hardship for the families. They relied on the harvested grain to sell in part as a cash crop while the feed grains were used for feeding their livestock.

The three friends—Mikhail, Paul Lupski, and Fred Radjec—were the same age and they had attended school at the same time. They felt if one of the families were to buy a tractor, such as a McCormick Deering with lugs on the wheels, and another family would buy the threshing machine, they could do their own threshing first and then compete with Pushinsky on contract threshing. They were sure it would be a lucrative business and they figured the machinery would pay for itself within the first four years.

Mikhail knew Evan had $5,000 in his savings account in the Shady Hollow bank which had just opened. One day he had seen Evan hiding it in the pocket of his buffalo fur coat in the *scranya* (wooden chest) and sneaked in later to count it. It was some time later that Evan overcame his mistrust of banks and took the $5,000 for deposit. That was after he heard that money could bring interest and the bank would pay him two per cent just for keeping it there. Paul Lupski was sure his father, Anton, had stashed away a similar amount. The John Deere threshing machine sold for $275 in Edmonton and the McCormick Deering tractor could also be bought in Edmonton, for not more than $350.

Mikhail had all the facts when he approached Evan with his suggestion. Evan roared at him and would not even listen to reason. He said the topic was not even open for discussion and he would never, never see one of those noisemakers on his yard. He said he grudgingly agreed to purchase a car but he now had second thoughts about that purchase because a car was quite useless. A tractor or a threshing machine was out of the question.

Mikhail, with little Paul watching approvingly, decided this day to be assertive. "Why must we always be the tail on the calf? Can't we ever be the leaders?" He continued to push. "The machines would make us the leading citizens in the community."

"First of all, I told you I do not like machines. If you had suggested buying better horses than I might consider

it," Evan retorted. "Second of all, I will never be a partner of a Polack (referring to Lupski, the Polish
neighbour). They can't be trusted. Don't you know anything of history? The Ukrainians and Polish have always
been at war in the old country."

Mikhail spouted, "This is not the old country. You
are stubborn and old-fashioned; it's no wonder the
English people call us ignorant Bohunks . . . !"

He didn't finish the sentence when Evan turned
white with rage. "You piece of shit from a spotted cow! I
never want to hear you speak to me like that again . . . or
. . . or . . . or . . . *Shluck taba trafit!*" he yelled and shook
his fist at Mikhail. This was the worst curse anyone could
use. It meant serious business.

Paul ran out of the kitchen, disappearing quickly into
the *vondoll* (big valley or gulley). Mikhail could see if he
said another word, his father would certainly strike him,
so he did not say anything more. Tainka came running
into the house from the garden, where she had been digging new potatoes, to see what the commotion was about.
She could see Evan was furious; Mikhail was sitting by,
sheepishly looking at the wall. She also said nothing but
gave Evan a hostile look, turned on her heel, and walked
out again. Their argument had also scared Francis
Nykola, who was playing outside with the little wagon
that Mikhail built him. He came into the house crying.
Katayna, who was upstairs writing a letter, came running
down, grabbed him, and went outside after her mother.

Within a week, Evan had driven to Bruderheim with
his democrat and horses. He purchased two purebred
twin Clydesdale mares and a Clydesdale stallion from a
German horse breeder. It cost him $4,500 for the three
animals, which even in those days was a great bargain.
He'd first seen similar beautiful horses like these when
Mike Yaworsky had a pair of Shires in the old country.

That's when he made a mental note that someday he would own a similar pair, all of his own. He had seen Clydesdales when he worked at the brickyards in Medicine Hat. He always yearned to own a stable of them some day. That day had now arrived. He was now going to begin raising his stable of purebred Clydesdales. He named his mares *Zoria* and *Zolota* (Star and Gold). He named the stallion *Shascha* (Lucky). Next on his future purchase list were the ornamental harnesses for the mares. He would also embark on providing a studding service to the farmers in the area, even though a Clydesdale stallion was a much bigger animal than any other horse in the Shady Hollow region.

The Clydesdale horses originated in Scotland and dated back to 1352. William, Earl of Douglas, was reported to have obtained a permit from King Edward III of England to bring ten big stallions to the Valley of Clyde. It is believed that the Clydesdale originated from the big Flemish horses on the European mainland. These huge horses were bred with local mares and from this cross, big horses, mainly bays and blacks with markings, were born. Some, which were throwbacks to shires, were beige with white manes and fetlocks.

The first Clydesdale stallion from Scotland was brought to Canada in 1887 by Alex Colquhoun from Brandon, Manitoba. He paid one dollar per pound—the animal weighed 2,163 pounds.

Ed Quinn in 1888 brought Clydesdales to Alberta, to the Bow River Horse Ranch in the district of Cochrane.

The Clydesdales that Evan bought from a German farmer at Bruderheim, Alberta, were descendants of those early Clydesdales of 1888. They were all beige, blonde with white manes and fetlocks. The German farmer sold all three horses for only $4,500 because he was dying of tuberculosis. When he heard about Evan's brush with death of the same ailment and how much Evan loved these animals, he sold them to him at a bargain price. He made Evan sign a contract that when he finished raising Clydesdales he would sell, to another worthy person, two mares and a purebred stallion for the same price . . . $4,500.

The remaining $500 from his savings Evan reluctantly gave to Mikhail. "And remember this is only a loan . . . you can buy your stupid machines . . . but I want it paid back in two years with five per cent interest on the money!" he shouted, as he threw the five hundred-dollar bills at Mikhail.

CHAPTER TWENTY-FIVE

Evan Gets Involved in Politics

Mike Mikalik, Evan's Austrian army and church friend and also his neighbour, came running to the Stry-Kers' one day. Unlike Evan, he was a well-read man with the same education level that Tainka had achieved in the old country—meaning he could read the *Ukrainske Vesta* (Ukrainian news) from cover to cover.

It was well known that Mikalik was a radical Liberal and was the only politically active person in the community. The others were too busy looking after their rudimentary needs for their families to be concerned about politics. Evan had been a small-c conservative since he had come to Canada. His philosophy was to work hard and make opportunity happen. He did, however, have a social conscience, primarily expressed through his church.

Mikalik's campaign this day was geared to a provincial issue. The western Canadian provinces were demanding a constitutional amendment. The amendment focused on demands to Ottawa for the surrender of mineral, forest, and hydro resources and to give full authority to the western provincial government in power. At this time, the 1924-25 government in Ottawa under the leadership of McKenzie King was Liberal. The representative for this region was Michael Luchkovich, the first Ukrainian Member of Parliament under the United Farmer's Party. In Alberta, the government in power was the United Farmer's Party led by Premier Brownlee. There was to be a delegation going to Ottawa headed by

Premier Brownlee himself. Mike Mikalik was invited as one of the delegates.

"What this means, Stry-Ker, is that right now this young Province of Alberta owns nothing more than the top soil. The government in Ottawa owns what's underneath. The future in this province is what's underneath the ground . . . coal, oil, and gas which they have already found in Turner Valley in 1914, things like that. There's much greater wealth underneath than on top of the ground!" Mike Mikalik was a clever man who had a progressive vision of the future.

Mike enjoyed being away from home because it was well known that his tiny wife, Annie, was a tyrant. As stubborn as a mule, she ran the house and all other matters on the farm. Even though she would not admit it, she made all the decisions on the Mikaliks' yard.

Evan listened intently. Then, after some consideration, he asked how he could help . . . how he could get involved. After all, he knew many people and felt he could have some influence in the community.

The involvement of Mikalik and Evan was effective in one of the most important constitutional amendments for Western Canada. It was the triumph of twenty-four prairie farmers, Mike Mikalik being one of these delegates, who found themselves in the role of parliamentary power brokers. Prime Minister Mackenzie King courted them and tried to keep the status quo in Ottawa, but the prairie delegation drove a tough deal. They demanded and eventually received the federal government's surrender of full authority over mineral, forest, and hydro resources to the western provinces.

There was much jubilation and partying when Mikalik returned from Ottawa and told Evan how the Prime Minister himself had courted them. They drank and sang, and eventually discussed once again the fun they had in the Austrian army. Their celebration ended, as it always did, with their imitation of a drummer and bugler. The beat was far from being in unison and it sounded like noise made by two drunken men . . . which, of course, it was.

CHAPTER TWENTY-SIX

A year had gone by and Mikhail and his friends still did not have their threshing outfit purchased.

Today Mike Mikalik was to come to the Stry-Kers', where Evan would harness his beautiful Clydesdale mares, *Zolota* and *Zoria*, in their new decorative harnesses. He had just purchased these harnesses. He would hitch them to the large democrat and together they would drive to the Chomiaks'. This was an annual affair, when these three friends made beeswax candles for the church.

When Mikalik came into the house it was obvious he was upset about something. His tall body slumped and he looked sheepish. They exchanged pleasantries.

"*Slava Ichosoo Xristoo*" (Praise Jesus Christ), he greeted Evan. Evan responded, "*Slava na vikee*" (Praise him forever).

"Are you ready now or would you like a drink of coffee? Did you remember to bring your share of beeswax?" Evan asked.

"Stry-Ker, I would like a drink of something stronger than coffee. And no, I did not bring my beeswax!" Mike Mikalik angrily retorted. "I left my place in a big hurry today."

"Did Annie chase you out or did you shit the bed?" Evan asked him jokingly.

"It's not a joke, Stry-Ker. I have been annoyed for a long time at how that woman of mine has taken to making all the decisions at our house. It's humiliating, particularly after my achievements in Ottawa. And everyone knows I am nothing more than a mouse in my own home. I've tried to talk to her about how bossy she is, but she wouldn't even listen. Well, this morning, as usual, she was yapping. I couldn't stand to listen to her. Yapping, of all things, about how we should make the candles today. After all, we've only made them for twenty years, right? I couldn't listen to her much longer, so I slowly slid my shoes far under the bed and then I asked her to climb under there and get them; she knows I am too large to fit under the bed. When she climbed under there I took the heavy willow barn broom and gave her about ten strong whacks, while she screamed like a pig being slaughtered. Before she could come out from under there I ran out of the house. I think it would be wise for me to stay at your place for a few days. Would you mind?" he pleaded.

"That's what I call a real man!" Evan laughed mockingly. "Yes, yes, you stay as long as you want, but you can be sure she'll come looking for you. But we'll cross that bridge when we get to it . . . so relax." They drank two small glasses of moonshine whiskey, collected Evan's beeswax, and drove off to Chomiaks'. All day they made candles. Most of the candles they made were the thick long type to set at the altar and for the deacon to hold during the reading of the Holy Gospel.

They discussed church matters, politics, farming, and Evan's Clydesdales. Evan was bragging about the healthy colts both mares had had two months earlier. He thought that if both mares continued to have fillies, his herd would grow quickly. He also told the men about his thriving studding business. He always tempered his bragging by the preamble, "If God grants such . . . ." Many farmers were asking for Shascha, his stallion, to breed their mares. He was on the road most of the spring and summer. Because of the large Clydesdale stallion, the horses in these parts were much larger and therefore stronger for pulling equipment on the farm.

Not once was the sensitive subject of Mikalik's experience with his wife Annie even mentioned. After three days had passed, Annie came looking for her husband. One of her eyes was swollen and had turned a vicious-looking colour of black with a tinge of green and yellow. She also had bruises on both arms.

Tainka, not aware of what had happened, asked, "Annie, whatever happened to you? You're so badly bruised!"

"I ran into a bad situation, and if you don't know about it . . . it would be best left alone," Annie responded sharply. "Is Mike at your place?"

"Why yes, he was, but he is not here now." Tainka replied. "He said he wanted to stay and travel with Evan as he takes the stallion to breed some mares somewhere southeast of here. They are not coming back for another week, I do believe."

"He's a *golgone* (rascal). The least he could have done is tell me," Annie sniffed.

When Mikalik came back, he stayed another four days. After two weeks had passed, Annie came back again. This time she looked worried and apologetic. She asked her husband to talk to her privately, and after about two hours of talking she convinced Mike Mikalik to go back home. Matters at the Mikaliks' improved for the next few months. After that, however, Annie's attitude regressed to its previous form. Mike became tolerant once again of her verbal abuse.

It was Monday morning and Evan was preparing to leave for a few weeks with Shascha, his stallion, and Kudlee (Runty), the runt stallion, and his fourteen-year-old dapple-grey gelding. The gelding was Yapa's first colt.

Evan had waited ten years before he had bred his first precious mare, Yapa. He had bought her on his arrival in this country from Petro Kuriak at Star, Alberta. It was for a very sentimental reason that she was not bred. He would have felt terrible if she had died during foaling. She was bred to a small stallion so there would be as few problems as possible at birthing. Consequently, Rudy was born. He was never a prize-winning animal but he suited the work he was currently doing. Yapa enjoyed having colts and in her twenty-three years of life produced ten of them. Most of her colts turned out to be good workhorses. Evan did not want to see anything happen to his faithful horse, Yapa, the first he had ever owned in his entire life. So Yapa received care that was better than any other animal on his farm, even better than his precious Clydesdales.

Every day since he had bought *Zolota*, *Zoria*, and *Shascha*, he had performed a spiritual ritual in the barn. He would sprinkle salt around each horse every morning when he was at home and recite incantations to ward off the evil eye. In his terms, no one would *vreeche* (place a curse) on his precious animals and this practice, in his view, was working, as he now had five pure Clydesdale mares. *Zoria*, on her last foaling, had given birth to a colt. The colt was now a yearling and a farmer at Westlock, Alberta, had offered Evan $2,000 for him. He would be using the animal for studding purposes. Currently Evan was considering this offer.

Evan had bought himself a two-wheel cart with a seat on top. He would harness Rudy and hitch him to the cart. He placed a choker halter and blinders on *Shascha* and Kudlee and tied them to the back of his cart. He then made his rounds to have *Shascha* service the mares on the circuit.

On this particular Monday he had his regular run to the area north of Waskatneau. His was truly a horse and pony show. The large Clydesdale stallion with the runt cantering beside him and Evan atop the two-wheel cart pulled by Rudy, the dapple-grey gelding, was a sight to behold.

He reached his destination in the early afternoon. He had encountered a few problems along the way, when a wagon drawn by two mares came toward his entourage. One of the mares was in heat, and *Shascha* and Kudlee went wild for a while until Evan yelled at the driver to speed up his mares and get out of the area quickly or they would both be trampled to death. The mare in heat caused the two stallions more excitement than Evan could handle on a public roadway. After all, that was the whole purpose of a stallion's existence.

The first farmer had three mares to breed. Evan's fee for *Shascha's* studding services was $12 for each mare. He would not collect until he was sure each mare serviced was in foal. Shascha's success rate was 95 per cent of the mares that were bred. The five per cent that were not successful showed in most cases that they were not able to be bred. He had a firm method which he followed faithfully. He would ask each farmer to have a snorting poll ready before his arrival. When he got there he would tie *Shascha* in the barn. He would let Kudlee exercise the foreplay with the mare, which was in heat. Kudlee could never reach the mare's genitalia so he could not breed her, but he would get her very excited waiting to be bred. *Shascha* was then brought from the barn to complete the task. The mare at this point was very ready to be bred.

Shascha was much larger than any mare in the area. When Evan had him settled down to where he could control him it took only a few seconds to breed each mare. On every circuit he did no more than twenty mares. Then he would let *Shascha* rest for a month before going on another tour. Once in a while Evan would allow Kudlee to breed a runt mare for no charge in order to keep his frustrations at manageable levels.

While on the road, Evan paid farmers $1.50 per night to sleep and board him and his three horses. He never stayed away from home for more than two weeks at a time.

Upon returning from this sojourn Evan noticed the yard was deserted. Francis was not playing with his wagon near the house. He led *Shascha* and *Kudlee* into their respective pens and released Rudy into the pasture, where he joined his mother and all the other workhorses. He went into the special pen where his prize mares were kept. He saw *Zolota* and *Zoria, Patasheka* (Birdie), and the yearlings *Pischoha* (Pet) and *Velikee* (big and tall). But where was *Rebka* (Little Fish), the two-year-old mare? He could not see her anywhere. When he came into the house he could find only Tainka in the kitchen. Her voice was trembling when she told him about the misfortune *Rebka* had had.

When Paul was chasing the cows to the pasture he put a halter on *Rebka* and took her with him, hoping to break her and ride her. He apparently tried to get on her back but she bucked him off and ran away in a wild fury. She kept galloping until she ran into one of the barbed-wire fences which had half-fallen. She got tangled in the wire. The more she kicked the more tangled she became. Paul came running back when he could not release her. Mikhail and Paul went running back to the pasture to try to help her but she had lost a lot of blood. They could not get her to come home, so they came rushing home and drove to Shady Hollow to get Dr. Liston, who helped animals as well as humans. When they got back with Dr. Liston, *Rebka* was almost dead. He tried to help her but to no avail. She died that night.

Tainka said, "We left her in the pasture in case you wanted to see her before the coyotes eat her carcass," Tainka told him. Evan surprisingly was hurt much more than angry when he got to the pasture. The coyotes had already started eating the soft part of *Rebka's* carcass. When he came home, he ate no supper and said nothing to anyone. He was deeply hurt. To him, one of his prize horses was almost as precious as his own children.

The next morning he packed a few belongings and asked Mikhail to drive him to the train station at Shady Hollow. He told Tainka he needed a leech treatment for his bad blood and he would spend some time in the Turkish baths in Edmonton. Tainka thanked God for sparing everyone from a very unpleasant scene. Paul also thanked God with such sincerity that it made Mikhail's tears flow as he heard him, kneeling at his bedside in a half-whispered prayer.

"God, oh my dear God, thank you from my heart for sparing me from a sound beating by *Tato*. I honestly am so sorry for *Rebka's* death. If only I had known that she would run into that wire I would have never tried to break her . . . please, if horses go to heaven . . . please, dear God, look after her and keep her until I see her again," Paul pleaded.

Evan stayed in Edmonton for a week and came back home in a mellow mood. The family members were pleasantly surprised. They had expected Evan to be furious about the death of his prized Clydesdale mare, but he was not. He brought everyone a small present. Paul got a brand new horse halter. Francis Nykola got small candy suckers, which Evan placed at the top of each calendar nailed near the ceiling. He would only give him one per day until a week's supply was exhausted. He then pulled out two $1,000 bills. These were the proceeds he had received for selling Velikee to the Westlock farmer. He gave his consent to Mikhail to buy a threshing machine and tractor.

"With the $500 I gave you one and a half years ago, and the $2,000 which I am giving you now, you can go and buy your threshing operation. I know that will be enough and you don't have to pay me interest, but it is still a loan," Evan stated emphatically. He had looked at some machinery while in Edmonton and, in fact, had made a tentative deal in case Mikhail wanted this arrangement. However, he would not consent to go into partnership with their neighbours, Lupski and Radjec. The machinery was for Mikhail and Paul in joint partnership.

Evan then took a hammer and other tools and hitched his wagon to two workhorses. He asked Mikhail and Paul to help him fix the barbed wire fences so that no other animal suffered the fate *Rebka* had suffered.

CHAPTER TWENTY-SEVEN

1927 – Francis Goes to School

On many occasions, when Evan hitched his prize Clydesdale mares to the big democrat to go to Shady Hollow, he would take Francis Nykola with him. He had never extended this courtesy to the older children. He used to take Francis into the confectionery section at Makovitsky's store and order sausage, buns, and Orange Crush pop. The mustard was always on the table. After eating their lunch, they bought the necessary staples, collected the mail at the post office, stopped and visited with friends, and then returned to the livery stable to drive *Zolota* and *Zoria* back home. On days when Evan took the scrub team, Jessie and Frank, Francis did not get to go to town with him. On those days, Tainka was never polite to Evan when he got home. Francis could never understand the reason for this even though he did ask.

Ever since Francis' birth, Evan had had a soft spot for the boy, possibly because Tainka did not appear to, although now that the child was five going on six in December, she was starting to pay much more attention to him. Her attention, however, was not focused on the boy's immediate needs but on what she was hoping and dreaming he would become in the future. In her evening prayers, since the child had been born, she had always first thanked God for sparing the boy and herself at his birth. Her second consistent request was that God would grant him the inspiration to become a priest.

Francis Nykola was a very intelligent child. He spoke Ukrainian and English fluently. Tainka and Evan taught him to speak their mother tongue, while Katayna, Mikhail, and Paul taught him to speak English, much to Tainka's dismay. "Don't make that child into an *Angleck!*" (Englishman), she would often complain.

Everyone spoke Ukrainian only at the table during meals. Even when Francis attempted to speak English, no one responded to his questions or his chatter. They did not even acknowledge it. He knew that if he was to be included in the conversation he would have to speak Ukrainian.

As brilliant as he was, Francis was also an overly inquisitive and curious child. He had to be everywhere and asked multitudes of questions, to the point of being a nuisance. Everyone in the family commented on the problems he would create for the teachers when he got to school. They could have waited a year to send him to school as his birthday did not arrive until almost the end of the year, but Francis begged them to let him go and the new teacher, Mr. Horn, agreed to take him.

Miss Jane Brownlee had taught in White Sands School from 1919, right after Mr. Newhouse made his quick exit. She would be missed a great deal, as she had become a pillar of strength in the community. She learned to speak Ukrainian and received more invitations than she could handle to weddings, Christmas and Easter parties, and christenings. She had nineteen godchildren in the area and everyone was extremely sorry to see her leave. Not only did she handle fifty children in eight grades at school, she also taught evening classes for those adults who wished to learn to speak English. This practice had started when she first arrived in Shady Hollow and Billy Makovitsky had asked for her help. She taught him English at her teacherage. There had been many rumours that Billy and she were intimate but she paid no attention to the rumour mill as she was not even remotely interested in men.

Miss Brownlee left to begin touring the world. She explained that she had so much to see in whatever little time she had left. She was then over fifty and her first adventure was to be aboard a steamer ship to Hawaii, followed by the long journey to Australia. Not many in these parts had even heard of these far-off exotic places, never mind going there.

Mr. James Horn, the new teacher, was a stern person with a military background. He had served in the First World War from 1914 until 1919. He had negotiated with the Shady Hollow School Board that he would not teach fifty children by himself and that the school should be expanded to two rooms, a junior room for grades one to five and a senior room for grades six to ten.

Construction had begun on the addition of the second room but was not expected to be finished until this term was over next June. Paul Stry-Ker was now almost fifteen years old and did not wish to continue school as he had heard Mr. Horn was a demon to deal with. Paul was still a very shy and reserved young lad. He also felt he was going to farm with Mikhail and he had all the education he needed. Evan and Tainka agreed.

On Francis' first day of school he received the strap. He met Harry and Onyfry Kaditz, twin boys of a new family who had just moved into the area. There were also two little girls who would be in grade one with him. The girls' names were Sophie Goseniuk and Mary Soova. Sophie was an only child of Mike and Jenny Goseniuk. She was a spoiled little girl. The parents could not have any more children and Sophie had been treated like a queen bee since her birth. Mary was the daughter of Domka and Metro Soova.

Sophie was teasing Mary mercilessly about her father being in jail and saying that he was a horrid person.

"Your father is a jailbird. Your father stinks," she teased as she skipped around Mary. She teased her so much that Mary began to cry, first softly and when Sophie did not relent, out loud. In her nervousness, she wet her pants.

Francis heard and saw the whole interchange. He told Sophie to stop her teasing. When she would not, he grabbed one of her lovely, thick blonde braids and pulled it hard. Sophie screamed and tattled about the incident to Mr. Horn. Mr. Horn was angry, basically because of this large horde of children he had to teach for the next year, so when Sophie related the incident he did not even ask Francis to explain his action. He barked an order in his most militarist manner.

"Franki! . . . Come up here now! Franki Stry-Ker, I said come up here now!' And that's how his name got changed from Francis Nykola to Franki. The frightened child came sheepishly up to Mr. Horn's desk. Without much notice the teacher asked Franki to hold out his hand and whacked it as hard as he could. He left a welt on the palm of the tiny little hand. Franki came home very distressed and told Katayna what had happened. Katayna didn't even discuss the matter with her *Mamunia* or *Tato*. She ran to the school and found Mr. Horn still sitting at his desk working on assignments.

She was white with rage. "Was that any way to treat a child on his first day of school?" Katayna shouted at Mr. Horn.

"Of whom do you speak, young lady?" Horn responded in the most intimidating manner he could muster.

"How many children did you strap today?" she demanded.

"I have no regrets about strapping your little boy. There will be discipline in my classroom. I will tolerate no foolishness and, furthermore, I do not appreciate meddling parents!" he snapped.

"Francis is not my little boy. He is my brother and I will meddle all I want. You are not a very decent person. I wouldn't treat an animal the way you treat people. I'm glad you're not my teacher!" she snarled.

"I am also pleased you are not in my class, young lady, or I would be forced to teach you some manners. Now, if you'll excuse me, I have work to do! This conversation is over!" Then he pointed in the direction of the door, indicating for her to leave.

CHAPTER TWENTY-EIGHT

Franki's Adventures at School

It was a Saturday. Franki had been in school for over a month. He had become bosom buddies with Harry and Onyfry Kaditz. Onyfry was renamed by Mr. Horn, as was Franki. Onyfry he called Oni.

Mary Soova played with a little girl in grade two. She refused to play with Sophie Goseniuk. Sophie continued her trouble-making ways and was fast becoming Mr. Horn's little pet. She was an extremely attractive child. Her face was a beautiful heart shape, her blonde hair the colour of straw, an attractive widow's peak at the top of her high forehead. Her eyes were as blue as the sky. She had a pug nose and a pretty, rosebud mouth. She looked angelic, although her attitude and treatment of others was demonic.

Mostly Franki, and to some degree the Kaditz twins, received the brunt of Mr. Horn's violent temper. Much of his anger was possibly as a result of the insults Katayna had hurled at him on the first day of school. Despite Mr. Horn's attitude, Franki was an avid learner and was soon at the top of his class. Much of this was due to Katayna's constant tutoring at home. As far as Sophie was concerned, no one could be ahead of her and, when Franki got higher marks than she did in his examinations, she created many scenes through her temper tantrums.

Mr. Horn reprimanded her occasionally for her bad behaviour. But his reprimands were inconsistent and this confused the other children—until they accepted the fact that there was one set of rules for Sophie and another for all the other children.

The Kaditz twins found that learning presented great difficulty. They were the eldest in their family and spoke no English. They spoke some Hungarian, as their father was of Hungarian descent, but primarily Ukrainian, as their mother was of that origin. Annie Kaditz's father had settled on a homestead in the blueberry country. When the original family who homesteaded this piece of land encountered difficulty surviving on these scrub lands, they moved into Gibbons, Alberta, a town twenty miles north of Edmonton, where the father got a job working on the Canadian National Railroad as a labourer repairing the rail tracks.

Annie Kaditz, the twins' mother, always missed the homestead, particularly the pines that whistled when the wind blew at night. She had married Louie Kaditz, and had convinced him to move to Shady Hollow and claim back her dad's homestead, which was being sold by the municipality for tax arrears. Louie Kaditz was a cattleman and felt he could raise cattle successfully on this scrubland. The White Sands Creek flowed through the land and grass crops thrived there. Certainly there was enough pasture for cattle.

Louie Kaditz had more money than people knew about and within three years he bought three more quarter-sections adjacent to the homestead, including the quarter of the deceased Stephen Chomiak's Valley of Paradise. Joseph and Teckla Chomiak had lost total interest in this property in the last seven years, after their son Stephen's death. The Kaditzes built a large log home on the quarter, in the Valley of Paradise. Their beautiful log home was built on the same location Maria and Stephen had chosen for their first home. They demolished the one-room shack that stood on this location, which had been built by Stephen Chomiak.

Every morning, Annie Kaditz had to coax her twins to go to school. Every morning they fought with her endlessly, and each fight ended in a long crying session for the children. She asked them why they disliked school so intensely and they explained how Mr. Horn gave them a strap every day and how he never stopped yelling at them and constantly humiliated them. They told their mother that he only liked Sophie Goseniuk. Annie didn't know whether this was the truth, but she knew there was something wrong and she was going to get to the bottom of this problem.

She discussed the matter with her husband, Louie Kaditz. "I wish I knew whether they're telling the truth. Those boys of ours like to lie a little. If this is true maybe we should talk to Mr. Horn."

"You know that I have no use for teachers, especially if they are English. This Mr. Horn is someone I'd like to punch in the nose fast. If he's hitting the boys then look out!" Louie threatened.

"I'll drive the team to the Stry-Kers' today and ask them if their Franki is having problems in school," Annie decided, greatly concerned. After they ate lunch, she helped Louie hitch the wagon and she drove the three miles south to the Stry-Kers'. Tainka and Katayna were completing their task of pouring melted wax in the cracks of wooden barrels and preparing them for storing their delicious dilled cucumber pickles and sauerkraut cabbage.

Annie Kaditz drove into the yard. She slid off the wagon seat, jumped off the wagon, and tied the horses to the rail fence. "*Slava Ichosoo Xristoo* (praise Jesus Christ)," she greeted them.

Tainka and Katayna replied, "*Slava na vikee* (praise him forever)." They invited her into the house. After the normal chit-chat about how the children and Louie are, and how gardens were doing this year, they began discussing school.

"I have to fight every day with my boys—Oni, as Mr. Horn calls him, and Harry. They do not want to go to school. Is Franki having any problems?" Katayna quickly related her experience with Mr. Horn on the first day of school and all three women agreed that something must be done. This teacher was simply out of control and it was unacceptable.

Soon Evan came into the house and Tainka related their concerns to him. "How often is he strapping your boys, Annie?" Evan asked.

"They say every day, and once in a while I have seen welts on their little hands," she told him.

"Has Franki said anything more about this lately?" Evan directed the question to Tainka and Katayna.

"He hasn't said anything since I went to see Mr. Horn, but I can see he's not as happy as he was before he went to school," stated Katayna.

"This evening at suppertime we'll discuss this matter when Franki is at the table. If I find that there is reason to talk to Mr. Horn I will do that. In the meantime, I suggest you ask your boys for what reason he is strapping them, " Evan advised Annie Kaditz.

At suppertime everyone sat at the round table, Evan with Tainka next to him, Franki, Katayna, Mikhail, and Paul. They said grace and everyone crossed themselves. "*Voima chaw, e sena e shavatoo ho dooha, amin*" (in the name of the Father, the Son, and the Holy Spirit, amen). After the hot chicken soup with homemade noodles was eaten, they began to eat the main course. Then Evan started to speak; as often as he could, he would try his English skills.

"What's new in the school, Franki? Is that there Mr. Horn learning you much?" he asked, watching each facial expression of the little boy.

Franki hesitated and then stammered, "He . . . he . . . tells us to read and when we don't know the words he hits us with a yardstick over the knuckles and says we're stupid Bohunks."

"You are sure he is saying Bohunks?" That's all Evan needed to hear.

"Yes, *Tato*, he always calls us Bohunks . . . always Bohunks!" admitted Franki. The word Bohunk always made Evan see red. It was obvious his temper was rising.

"And the Kaditz boys, is it he is treating them the same as you?"

"Yes, he hits them even harder with a yardstick and with the strap," Franki responded. "He also hits Mary Soova in our grade. The only one he doesn't hit is Sophie Goseniuk."

Paul, who spoke very rarely, particularly if Mikhail didn't make the first remark, piped up, "They say that Mr. Horn is a *didko* (demon). He hits people for moving in their desks . . . that's what they say!" He never identified who "they" were but that didn't matter; he had taken part in the conversation and provided useful information.

The next morning, as soon as Evan finished helping Mikhail and Paul with the chores he changed his work shirt to a clean one and pulled on a pair of clean trousers. He wore clean shoes and walked the quarter mile in record speed. Evan had taken one year off as Councillor after Maria's death but then had been coaxed to go back to the job as he did excellent work as a community representative. Over the years elections took place and Evan was always acclaimed into the position. He now was the Municipal Councillor for the entire region of Shady Hollow.

It was morning recess. He asked Mr. Horn to tell all the children to go outside and play. Mr. Horn recognized him right away and was aware that Evan was a powerful School Trustee and Municipal Councillor and an influential person in the community. He was much more intimidated by Evan than he was by his daughter Katayna.

"What can I do for you, Mr. Stry-Ker?" he said in as pleasant a voice as he could muster.

"Answer me some questions honestly is what you can do for me," Evan replied. "Do you know it that my son, Franki, and some odder children do not like to or want to go to this school?"

"Why is that, Mr. Stry-Ker?" Mr. Horn asked.

"Because your *disiplena* (discipline) is like for criminal, in Fort Saskatchewan jail. Is it nascesayary to always hurt children who are not even seven years old?"

"We all have different degrees of discipline. Perhaps mine is harsher than your previous teachers, but that's my way!" He was sounding more assertive now.

"Is it nascesayary to call them names about our Ukrainian background?" asked Evan.

"What names am I being accused of using?" Horn replied.

"Bohunk . . . . Bohunk is what names I am meaning about!" Evan was having great difficulty containing himself and trying to speak English at the same time. If only he could speak more fluently, he thought.

"Oh, that's just a figure of speech. It means absolutely nothing, Mr. Stry-Ker!" Horn was visibly shaken.

"If it is meaning nodding, then don't be using it. It is Bohunks that hired you and us Bohunks can also fire you! If I am hearing one more time about you are being cruel like on our children, I swear it, you will be fired. Do you hear it what I am telling for you?" Evan gestured, pointing his finger in the air, his voice rising considerably.

Mr. Horn was white with rage, but he controlled his hot temper. "I apologize for using what is in your view such a hurtful word, as you put it. I will be more careful in the future," he responded coolly.

Evan served notice at the next school trustees' meeting about Mr. Horn's overly severe discipline. The trustees in the community representing White Sands School issued a stiff warning to Horn. Matters at the school improved for a few months—until after the New Year, when he once again resumed his militaristic ways. Katayna felt the only way she could change matters was to herself become a schoolteacher and teach these children whom she understood so well. She harnessed the team and drove to Shady Hollow where she met with the high school principal. He agreed to assist and guide her through a high school home correspondence course. Within one and a half years she finished her grade eleven level and was eligible to enroll at the Camrose Normal School for Teachers. Camrose, Alberta, was located forty miles southeast of Edmonton. Mostly Scandinavians from Sweden and Norway had settled there.

She enrolled the following fall in 1929. Evan supported her actions, as he felt she would have to make a very good teacher because she was totally useless as a farm hand.

In the fall of 1929, the new addition to White Sands School was finally completed, two years behind schedule. Mr. Horn was reluctantly contracted to teach for yet another year because teachers were hard to find. He was promoted to teach the older children, grades six to ten, in the senior room. Anyone wishing to complete grades eleven and twelve had to attend school in the hamlet of Shady Hollow. The new teacher hired to teach the younger children in the junior room, grades one to five, was John Starchuk. He was a local boy who had graduated in the spring from the Camrose Normal School for Teachers. He was of Ukrainian descent and was sensitive to the children's traditions and their youthful needs. He was a tall, handsome young man, with a thick head of blond, curly hair and navy blue eyes with thick, long lashes framing those eyes. The change from Mr. Horn was a phenomenal relief to all the children who had experienced his tyrannical and cruel teaching methods.

Franki, Sophie Goseniuk, and Mary Soova were starting grade three. Oni and Harry Kaditz had failed their grade in the first year so were only in grade two. However, Franki and the Kaditz twins remained the best of friends.

On the first day of school the children cheered delightedly with the knowledge they would no longer have to put up with Mr. Horn. They acted like wild urchins. When Mr. Starchuk had trouble settling down this excited lot, all he had to say was that he would call Mr. Horn to establish order. Within seconds you could have heard a pin drop.

During the lunch hour, Franki, Oni, and Harry wanted to explore the attic of the school, as it was raining outside and much too wet to play ball on the field. They leaned an old ladder to the gable end of the school where the outside door to the attic was located. All three scurried up the ladder and opened the door that led to the attic. Once up there they had difficulty adjusting their eyes to the darkness. But once they did, they found all sorts of treasures. There was, among other things, an old Ogden's tobacco tin, left behind no doubt by the workmen who built the new addition to the school.

Franki, being the leader of the pack, said, "Let's all piss in the can and then we can pour it out the door like a waterfall. Everyone will think it's raining very hard!"

"Yes, that's a good plan," agreed Oni.

"A very, very good idea," repeated Harry, who always agreed with Oni and spoke only after Oni, the firstborn twin.

As they finished the deed, they heard Mr. Starchuk's voice. He climbed up the ladder, "Boys!" he called in as stern a voice as he could manage. "Get down here right now. I don't want you falling down and breaking your necks!"

He couldn't adjust his eyes to the darkness and the boys came scrambling to the door. As they did, one of them kicked the tobacco tin over and spilled its contents. When they came into the classroom and got seated they saw the funniest sight. Sophie Goseniuk was looking up at the ceiling with an open Quink inkbottle. She thought she was catching the raindrops falling from above. The three boys began to snicker and couldn't stop, as they knew well what these raindrops were.

Mr. Starchuk was becoming a little impatient. "Boys, what's so funny? Tell the whole class so we can all laugh," he urged them sternly.

The boys were now laughing uncontrollably with each additional drop, as some drops missed the edge of the bottle and splashed on Sophie's fingers. Mr. Starchuk called them to his desk and warned them that if they didn't stop laughing he would have no alternative but to strap them. As they turned away from his desk to walk to their own, another drop came down. Sophie caught it on the edge of her inkbottle. As it splashed, she got some droplets on her face. In unison, the boys burst out laughing. Mr. Starchuk felt had no choice but to give each of them one hard strap on each hand.

This strapping psychologically hurt Mr. Starchuk more than it hurt the boys physically because he had promised himself that he would not administer corporal punishment in his teaching regime. Here it was, the first day of school, and he had strapped already. He vowed never to threaten children with the strap again.

For Franki, this was the second year that he got strapped on his first day of school. This time, however, Franki was relieved because Mr. Starchuk's strapping wasn't even painful compared to Mr. Horn's. Also, Franki felt he deserved the strap this time. Neither Franki nor the Kaditz twins reported this incident at home.

CHAPTER TWENTY-NINE

Katayna was accepted in Camrose Normal School for Teachers. She attended for one year, graduating with honours in the spring of 1930. Signs of the Great Depression were everywhere, precipitated by the stock market crash of 1929.

The Depression was caused by many factors. In the 1920s, Canada was experiencing good times. Industries such as mining, fishing, and lumbering were showing remarkable profits. Manufacturing was growing astronomically, and this sector provided opportunity for much employment. Therefore, employment was steady.

In 1928, Canada was having problems with its primary export, wheat. The farmers had overproduced and so the 1928 crops still were not sold in 1929.

In the meantime, the European countries were facing economic problems. In fact, these countries had faced economic instability since the First World War.

In the United States, factories were overproducing though there was no market for the goods produced. Therefore, the industries were stockpiling. The biggest problem was that the values of stocks on the New York Stock Exchange were hugely overvalued. Government and business were totally oblivious to these bad economic signals around them and did nothing to curtail the disaster which was soon to affect everyone.

Canada was in a vulnerable situation. Even though the country is a very large land mass, the thinly spread population numbered less than ten million. Canada's revenues to operate the government came from export sales, and these sales were in sensitive commodities such as grain, lumber products, and various mining products such as coal, nickel, and copper.

The United States bought forty per cent of Canada's exported goods. Canada counted on its American neighbours for the vital money needed for expansion. In October 1929, all the bad events that could happen economically did indeed happen. Stock markets tumbled to rock bottom. The New York Stock Exchange took a disastrous bloodbath, a sign that the American economic system had been smashed. Many prominent American and Canadian families' fortunes were wiped out overnight.

Canada's markets began to collapse. The U.S. protected itself by erecting high tariffs, thereby effectively shutting out Canadian goods. The prairie grain prices fell: wheat sold at $1.60 a bushel in 1929 and 38 cents a bushel during the Depression. This was the case at Shady Hollow, as it was throughout the rest of Canada's prairie region.

Saskatchewan, the province just east of Alberta, suffered the greatest blow. Not only did the drop in wheat prices thwart the province's economy, but God punished the people by sending down the worst drought that Canada had ever had. The fields turned to dust bowls and the dust clouds never stopped. It seemed as though the end of the world had arrived. Southern Alberta suffered the same fate . . . severe drought. Shady Hollow did not. The grain grew in abundance, but no one wanted to buy it. As Western Canada's grain economy went down, so did the rest of Canada. Farmers stopped buying. Eastern factories closed or laid off their employees in the hundreds. The building industry came to a screeching halt. Banks made no further loans; instead, they called in loans and virtually destroyed the people who could not pay the money back. Less and less money was in circulation and fewer and fewer goods were being produced because no one was buying. Why? Because they had no money to purchase goods. The rolls of the poor grew longer and longer. There was despair throughout the land.

The Depression was like a downward vortex, and no one could stop it.

Governments were forced to establish relief programs, but the assistance people got was only enough to keep them from starving. Furthermore, people refused to apply for relief because they were proud pioneers and most of them had never relied on government handouts.

Shady Hollow was no exception. A few families received relief but it was a dishonour to do so. Wheat prices were high during the First World War and this led to expansion based on wheat, but during the 1930s Depression that was now starting, most farmers began to diversify and began mixed farming operations in order to save the family farm. Many did not succeed. The Stry-Kers, however, succeeded very nicely.

The School Board was forced to cut the teachers' wages by fifty per cent. Mr. Horn refused to return. He emphatically stated that his teaching skills were worth much more than $500 a year and that the offer was, indeed, an insult. This arrangement suited Katayna very well and she agreed to teach for $250 annually. Mr. Starchuk was also willing to stay on because he lived at home and didn't have to pay room and board. He was promoted to the senior room and made principal of the school. He was paid $25 more for this promotion. This still saved the school board $225 for the year, enough to cover its yearly maintenance costs. Katayna was very pleased to sign a contract to teach the junior room.

Franki, Sophie Goseniuk, and Mary Soova were now in grade five, while the Kaditz twins trailed behind in grade four. However, Franki and the twins were still best of friends.

The first day of school was a gruelling experience as the junior room had a heavy enrollment this year. Katayna faced thirty-two defiant children. They were all used to a male teacher and felt this woman would be an easy mark. Franki felt very secure having his sister as the teacher and began to take advantage of his position.

At recess, he and the Kaditz twins ran to the corner of the schoolyard and made some huge cigarettes using old newspaper and dry aspen leaves. When they came back to the classroom after recess, the boys smelled like three sausages that had been cured in a smokehouse. It was quite obvious they had been smoking. When Katayna asked them whether they had been smoking, they confirmed they were. Franki was quite certain his beloved sister Katayna would not strap him since this was the first time in his short life that she had caught him smoking.

Katayna was in a quandary. How was she to deal with these three defiant urchins? She went next door to consult with Mr. Starchuk, the senior room teacher and principal. His advice to her was that they be strapped for disregarding the strict policy of "no smoking" in or out of the schoolyard.

"I am determined not to ever administer corporal punishment as long as I am a teacher," Katayna protested adamantly.

"I know corporal punishment is not good. I certainly don't like it, but you handle it your own way, Miss Stry-Ker. However, when your students walk all over you, I'll be the first to say I told you so!' Starchuk was not pleased with this strong-willed female, his subordinate teacher.

Yet he was very attracted to her.

She pondered how she was going to handle this situation and not lose the respect of this huge horde of children who were assigned to her. What made matters even worse was that Franki, she felt certain, was the instigator of this whole mess.

Well, she thought, let's fight fire with fire. She walked to the edge of the fence. She scooped up dried aspen leaves and put them in a bucket. She then found old newspapers and rolled fifteen large cigarettes using the dried leaves. She called the three boys out of the class after assigning Mary Soova, whom she could trust, to be the supervisor in her absence.

She handed each boy one aspen leaf cigarette and lit them. She then commanded them to smoke. Their eyes became as big as saucers. They could not figure out what this crazy teacher was doing.

"We're not supposed to smoke, you know, Katayna. That's against school rules," blurted Franki.

"First of all, Franki," she said in a stern voice, "I'm Miss Stry-Ker while we're in the classroom. Can you remember that?" She was visibly upset. "Why were you smoking during recess? Since neither of you will answer, I will solve this problem. You will smoke your fill. If you want more, I'll make you more cigarettes. Now start smoking!" she commanded.

One . . . two . . . three cigarettes later the boys were coughing and pleading for mercy. "Katayna . . . I mean, Miss Stry-Ker . . . please, my throat is sore . . . ," pleaded Franki.

"My eyes feel like someone put hot coals in them!" cried Oni Kaditz, rubbing them gingerly.

"Yes, mine too." Harry appealed to Miss Stry-Ker for mercy. She could see that they were turning green and looked ill.

Soon Franki started to vomit . . . Oni and Harry followed.

"Will this teach you a lesson or will you continue to be foolish and smoke some more?" Katayna pressed.

"No, no, please, no more. We'll never smoke again!" Word got around the school very quickly that this new teacher was different. Indeed, she didn't strap, but her punishment was very effective. Mr. Starchuk, even though he would never have dealt with problem that way, told her that he respected her method of handling a touchy and messy situation.

No other child ever tried smoking in Miss Stry-Ker's class again, and Franki realized he would not receive any special favours in this classroom. He knew he had to toe the line. The others figured if the teacher treats her own brother in a tough manner, they too had better behave. And they did.

CHAPTER THIRTY

Franki Is Stricken with Illness

Katayna completed her first year of teaching and began her second term. The children had settled in well. They adored this tall, statuesque, and beautiful young lady. Katayna was every bit as beautiful as her mother had been at her age. Students respected her because she had a steely determination but they also knew that her main objective was to impart knowledge and, most of all, to teach them to be good citizens of the Dominion of Canada. Canada was a wonderful new land. Her parents had chosen to settle here and for this Katayna was very grateful.

Every morning they saluted the Union Jack, saying proudly, "I salute the flag, the emblem of my country, and to it I pledge my allegiance and all my love and loyalty." Then they would say the Lord's Prayer and sing *O' Canada.* Finally there was a health inspection. One student was chosen to walk down the aisles of desks to check the hygiene and cleanliness of the hands and ears. Since, in each case, the health inspector was every bit as poorly washed as the other students, he or she would find few rejections. The only person who found problems with almost every other student she inspected was Sophie Goseniuk, whose mother used to keep her extremely clean. Since she never had to do any yardwork she had beautifully groomed hands and clean ears.

When Sophie was the designated inspector Katayna dreaded the results because almost the entire class was sent to the one white enamel washing-basin located in the cloakroom that served as the washing facilities. Everyone would have to scrub their hands and ears in cold water with homemade soap. This took up to half an hour and certainly cut into the teaching time. Katayna would have to find some method to solve this delay. Furthermore, the children absolutely despised Sophie, who was an arrogant and rude child. The older she got, the more unbearable she became. That is, all the children despised her except Franki. He had some unusual fascination with this lovely little creature. He compared her to some of his father's unbroken mares and felt he would someday deal with Sophie. He felt this temperamental female could be trained.

On this day, he was feeling very, very weak. His vision was blurred . . . his joints ached terribly . . . his skin burned and was discoloured. Sophie walked down the aisle, arriving at Franki's desk which he shared with Oni Kaditz.

"Okay, turn your hands over, Franki Stry-Ker!" she commanded. "Don't be so lazy!" Then, noticing that something was wrong, she quickly alerted Katayna. "Miss Stry-Ker!" she shrieked, pointing to him. "Franki looks sick . . . look at him!"

Katayna came running over to Franki's desk. Just as she did he fell out of his seat onto the floor. "Oh, my God!" she whispered, going down on her knees to cradle his head in her hands. "Oni, run over to Mr. Starchuk and tell him to come here fast!" she instructed her student.

Within seconds Mr. Starchuk was in the junior room and kneeling beside Franki, who was comatose by now. Katayna dispatched Oni and Harry Kaditz to run to the Stry-Kers' and get Mikhail to come with the car to drive Franki to Dr. Allison.

When the boys came breathlessly racing into the Stry-Kers' yard, Tainka was the first to spot them. "What's wrong, boys?" she asked in alarm.

"Franki is dying in school, and Miss Stry-Ker wants Mikhail and Paul to come quick with the car!" Oni panted, breathless from running.

"And take him to see Dr. Allison!" Harry cut in, always second to speak.

Tainka was very upset. Stammering incoherently, she ran into the blacksmith shop where Mikhail and Paul were fixing some part of their precious threshing machine. It took only minutes for Mikhail and Paul to start up the Chevrolet with their greasy hands. Tainka hopped quickly into the back seat.

She was praying to God to spare her baby. "Oh, if only I had given him more attention! Oh please God, don't take him away from me!" The Chevy engine roared down the road to the school, a quarter of a mile away.

Katayna was already cradling Franki in her arms. It took less than half an hour to get him to Shady Hollow Hospital, where both Dr. Liston and Dr. Allison were making their rounds. They both came immediately to attend to the unconscious boy, whose temperature had by now leaped to 104°F.

Tainka could not control herself. "Oyee, oyee, oyee," she wailed loudly, wringing her hands anxiously. "Please, God, not another child. You must know this one has been chosen to serve you. Please let him live!" she pleaded. The other three children who had accompanied her tried to comfort their grief-stricken mother but to no avail.

"He'll be fine, *Mamunia*," Mikhail assured her optimistically.

"Yes, *Mamunia*, he's a strong boy. It's probably the measles," Katayna told her.

They patiently waited for four hours. The doctors worked ceaselessly to bring down Franki's fever and to diagnose his illness.

Finally, Franki began to regain consciousness and his fever began to break. It was determined he had been stricken with an allergic reaction to a specific bacteria . . . Rheumatic Fever. All four Stry-Kers were told how serious this disease was and that Franki would have to be hospitalized for a few weeks.

Tainka remained with Franki that night. Katayna's heart was heavy because she could not stay with him also. She, Mikhail, and Paul returned home to report the sad news to Evan, who had just returned from one of his horse-breeding circuits. Although visibly upset and grief-stricken, he did not cry. He had cried when Maria had died and was determined never to let that happen again . . . because, after all . . . it would be a weak, spineless man who cried, in his opinion.

"Do our tragedies never end?" Evan was on his knees talking to God. "Please, Heavenly Father, I beg of you, spare this child. He has been such a good boy and for this I thank you. If you will spare him I, too, will agree to have him become a priest to serve your ministry! Please, God . . . in the name of Jesus Christ," Evan pleaded sincerely.

CHAPTER THIRTY-ONE

Franki Recuperates

Franki remained in hospital for two weeks. His joints ached so badly that he could not even walk. The family visited him twice daily during visiting hours, between 2:00 and 3:00 p.m., and again in the evenings from 7:00 to 8:00 p.m. Katayna did not insist that Franki keep up with his school lessons as she could see he was in excruciating pain. Besides, Dr. Allison had prescribed total bed rest.

After Franki returned home the doctor was adamant that he was not to attend school for at least two months. Katayna started coaxing Franki to keep up some of his grade six lessons, otherwise he would be left so far behind Mary Soova and Sophie Goseniuk that he could not catch up.

"That might not be all bad," said Franki to Katyana. "Then I'll be in the same grade as Oni and Harry Kaditz, my best friends!"

"Perish the thought!" exclaimed Katayna. "The three of you are a handful now . . . whatever would I do if you were in the same class?"

"Well, I'd enjoy it much more and I wouldn't have to referee Mary and Sophie all the time. That Sophie is some kind of girl! Some days I could just choke her but on other days I think she is so pretty," Franki confided.

"Your mother had better not hear you say that you are noticing how pretty girls are . . . you know what career she has planned for you. She reaffirmed that you would go to serve God when you were unconscious . . .

when you were stricken with Rheumatic Fever. And now our father is singing the same tune."

Franki, perplexed, did not respond.

Another month passed. Franki became very bored reading the books Katayna brought home for him to read. He could not appreciate *Oliver Twist* by Charles Dickens even though Katayna felt he should become familiar with the classics. He much preferred *Tom Sawyer* and *Huckleberry Finn*. One day, when he was particularly bored, he wandered into the storage room where the *scranya* was stored. In it were all sorts of treasures: his mother's precious possessions from the old country, her brightly coloured sash which Evan had woven for her in Austria before they emigrated, some of her colourful *babushkas*. Covering everything was Evan's large buffalo fur coat. On top of the buffalo coat sat a bundle of Christmas cards from Rosie Soova, one for each year since Maria's death. Every year there was an invitation to visit her rooming house and stay. He noticed that she called her rooming house "The Pearl's Oyster."

As Franki dug through all the items that were stored in the *scranya*, he found some articles which he'd never seen. He discovered a canvas package stored at the bottom of the trunk. It had been carefully tied and appeared as though it had not been opened for years. Gently untying the numerous knots in the long, thick linen string, he carefully unfolded the canvas package. There he noticed some old letters and a string of brightly coloured beads from the old country, beads that were very old. Examining the envelopes, he saw they were all addressed to Miss Maria Stry-Ker. He never knew his dead sister but had heard many wonderful stories about her. He was also aware that *Mamunia* had changed drastically after Maria's death and he had known for a long time that he was not a wanted or welcome addition to the Stry-Ker family at his birth, although he had more love from Katayna than any normal child needed.

His curiosity got the better of him. He began to read the letters. There were five letters and love notes from Stephen Chomiak, Maria's betrothed. There were also four Christmas and birthday cards from him to Maria. Even at this young age he could sense there was a spiritual bond between these two young people who had died so tragically. He had often seen their graves side by side at St. Olga's cemetery. Once a year at a special service, *Mamunia* and Mrs. Chomiak set *paska*, apples, and oranges on their children's graves. This was a sacrificial offering along with prayers for the dead.

"No wonder he lost all will to live after she died," thought Franki.

He then opened the first three letters from Rosie Soova. He had heard so many stories about her. Rosie Soova had been a very good friend of Maria's. He had also heard that there was a mystery about her and that young Jewish teacher, David Newhouse. I wonder what happened there, Franki thought.

Although the family heard from her once a year at Christmas, no one knew what had really happened to Rosie Soova. She always lived in Edmonton as far as anyone at Shady Hollow ever knew. His curiosity overwhelming, he began to read the letters. The first was dated May 1, 1916.

Dear Maria,

It is now two months since I last saw you and spoke with you. I am sure the gossips in Shady Hollow have completely condemned me as I know my own father has. What a lonely feeling it is for me, Maria. David Newhouse was going to marry me, but when he told his mother what our intentions were, she tried to discourage him and sent him away to Montreal for one year. I know he'll come back to me, but I have not heard anything from him since he left.

I have found a place to live and work. I am a maid in a place called The Pearl's Oyster. Two sisters who were both named Pearl own it. It is funny that both their names are Pearl. They told me it happened when their father went to register five children at the same time. He had forgotten there was already a little girl named Pearl in their family, and so he registered another baby girl by the name of Pearl. There is not much difficulty because we call one Pearl and the other one Penny. They are also of Ukrainian descent and are very good to me. There are three other beautiful women who live here—Veronica, Lily, and Helen. Our house is located on the main road when you come from Shady Hollow, 96 Street and 107 Avenue. It is easy to find. Please come to Edmonton, Maria. That is, if you are not embarrassed to be my friend.

Until I receive a letter from you, I hope you are fine and life is going well just as you deserve. I have heard from Billy Makovitsky, who comes here quite often, that you are getting married soon to Stephen Chomiak. He is a very nice young man and I'm sure he will treat you well. Please write if it is in your heart to do so.

Sincerely, Rosie Soova

The next letter was dated June 1, 1916.

Dear Maria,

Thank you very much for replying to my letter. It was like a gift from heaven. You have always been such a good friend to me. You are also a nice person and so good to me over the years.

I am feeling particularly lonely during this period of my life as David has not contacted me and I do not know how to reach him. His mother will not give me his address in Montreal. She says the agreement was that we were to have no contact with each other for one year and she will not bend on that decision.

I have always shared my deepest secrets with you and so I will once again. I have to tell you this one as well. I am pregnant with David's baby and now more than ever I need to reach him. I have not told Mrs. Newhouse about my condition but shall decide whether it would be appropriate to do so in the next few months. The sisters Pearl and Penny, and Veronica, Lily, and Helen, have told me to tell her, but I shall decide for myself soon.

I wish I could see you and talk to you in person as you were always so understanding and made me feel like I was really important. The women here are now like my family, but you have been closer to me than a sister.

Maria, I am sorry to burden you with my problems. This is such a happy time in your life, only one and a half months until your wedding. Please be sure to send me a wedding picture. Until I hear from you again.

Sincerely, Rosie Soova

And the last letter in the package was dated June 15, 1916. It was a very short one.

Dear Maria,

I guess you have not had a chance to reply to my last letter. You must be very busy with the wedding plans. I am sending you some ivory silk material and damask veiling for your wedding outfit. Only special ladies in Edmonton wear silk for their wedding and I feel you are very special, so please accept this wedding present from me.

*I shall wait to receive a wedding picture. I hope
your special day will be sunny and happy and your marriage to Stephen will be wonderful! By the way, I have
told Mrs. Newhouse about my condition. She said she
would tell David and is coming to Edmonton to see me
soon.*

Sincerely, Rosie Soova

After reading these personal letters to a sister he had
never seen nor known, Franki felt a little guilty. But his
guilt was superseded by his curiosity about Rosie. He
vowed he would someday meet this mysterious woman.
From the letters he read he felt he would like her a lot.
He carefully put the letters back in the canvas package in
which they had been wrapped all these many years, but
he kept the coral beads. He then placed the letters in the
same location in the *scranya*. As he walked out of the
kumirka (storage house) the sun was shining brightly. He
was definitely beginning to feel much healthier.

CHAPTER THIRTY-TWO

After a two-month convalescence period, Franki returned to school. Everyone welcomed him heartily, except Sophie Goseniuk.

"I'm not happy to see your ugly face again," she told him sarcastically, a sneer on her face. "You are not only ugly but now you're stupid because you missed so much school!"

Katayna was just entering the school when she heard these rude and hurtful remarks. The anger inside her boiled over, making her lose her patience with Sophie. Grabbing the girl, she shook her with such force she heard Sophie's teeth rattle.

"Why are you such a deplorable and rude child?! Do you not think that comments such as you've just made are hurtful to others?" she shouted. She felt an urge to strap this awful brat, an action she had never taken during her young teaching career. But common sense prevailed. She could see no purpose in strapping Sophie as she was sure it would not change her ways and her parents would more than likely report Katayna to the Superintendent of Schools and to the School Trustees. She did not wish to have a blemished reputation because of an incident where she lost control of her temper.

This incident, however, made her decide that Franki should not be put back into the sixth grade with Sophie. Once Sophie started picking on someone she would not stop; the stress on the little boy would be too great.

Franki was very pleased about this decision. He was now in the same class as Oni and Harry Kaditz, his best friends.

His grades were excellent, as he had covered much of the same work last year. He had never been happier attending school, being in the same class as the Kaditz twins. He was also starting to take a very keen interest in serving as altar boy at St. Olga's Greek Catholic Church. This pleased Tainka and Evan no end.

Easter was a very special holiday at the Stry-Ker home. It meant the renewal of their faith through the symbolized resurrection of Christ.

Tainka and Katayna began to decorate *pysanky*, Ukrainian Easter eggs, using a *kistka* (a simple stylus to draw on eggs using hot beeswax). After the designs were drawn, the eggs were dipped into coloured dyes of green or red. Crepe paper submerged in hot water was used to extract the colour. Onion skins also submerged in boiling water were used to get a rich golden-yellow shade. Before the eggs were dipped into this coloured water, it had to be cold, otherwise the wax used to draw the intricate designs would melt and the patterns would be spoiled. Franki enjoyed drawing Easter eggs; he drew beautiful and artistic designs.

The prelude to Easter was Palm Sunday, when the pussy willows were picked and blessed. During this week Tainka baked *paska*, a special Easter bread which would be blessed on Easter Sunday and also *babka,* a sweet bread.

Tainka kept a special wicker basket which was used only for blessing the food for Easter Sunday. Along with the bread there was a dish of grated horseradish symbolizing the bitter suffering of Jesus Christ before he died on the cross. There were also the dishes of butter and cottage cheese, a ring of homemade *kobaska*, the coloured *pysanky* eggs, and a chunk of roast pork. In the middle of the *paska* was inserted a beeswax candle made by Evan. This candle was lit when Father Kohot blessed the baskets after Easter Sunday mass.

On Good Friday every adult fasted. The children, however, were allowed to eat lenten dishes. Franki chose to fast along with the adults. The church service was very sad as the procession circled St. Olga's church three times, carrying the *Plachinicha*, a shroud of Christ in his tomb. The shroud was laid at the altar which was draped in black banners. All the parishioners crawled on their knees to the altar to kiss the Holy Shroud. Franki stood at the altar holding a lit candle next to Father Kohot, who was getting very old and forgetful. He relied more and more on Franki, even to whisper some parts of the mass, which the old father would forget. Father Kohot usually heard confessions on the Saturday preceding Easter Sunday.

On Easter Sunday white and cheerfully coloured banners replaced the black banners. Father Kohot, with Franki at his side, led the congregation as he carried the shroud of Christ's *Plachinicha* outside to circle the church three times. They all stopped before the closed church doors which represented the closed tomb of Jesus Christ. When the doors were opened—to symbolize the resurrection—the Divine Liturgy began. The congregation filled the church, as did the aroma of the food baskets that would be blessed later. All through the mass, Father Kohot repeated *Xristos Voskres* (Christ has risen); Franki and the rest of the congregation responded *Voistynu Voskres* (truly He has risen).

The Easter services took almost three hours. No one, except small children who had not gone to confession, could eat food or even drink water before taking communion. This was an extremely difficult sacrifice for many people, especially the children who had confessed. As Franki watched the congregation assemble to receive communion, he saw Oni Kaditz keel over and faint, his limp body falling in front of an elder parishoner who owned one of the benches in church. This parishoner was an extremely ignorant and insensitive woman. She would not let anyone get in her way when she was going to take communion. Kicking the limp little boy out of her way, she began to fall to her knees to receive communion. Franki nudged Father Kohot, who also could be pompous while at the altar. The old Father looked over at Franki and saw the distress in his eyes as he pointed to Oni. The priest quickly poured some water out of the communion pitcher and onto a sacrament cloth. Going over to Oni, he placed the cloth on his forehead and dabbed his lips with the moist cloth. By this time, Oni's mother Annie noticed her poor little boy's plight and took him outside, where he soon regained consciousness. She gave him a small drink of water that she had brought with her to be drunk after communion. Annie knew that church rules were not as important as the well-being and safety of her own child. Saddened by the hypocrisy he had witnessed, Franki vowed that when he became a priest, he would work toward changing this outdated system, even if he had to go on a crusade to Rome to do so.

CHAPTER THIRTY-THREE

1932 – Katayna Plans the School Dance

After the Easter holidays the school re-opened. Katayna Stry-Ker and John Starchuk, the principal, were discussing the annual spring school dance. Young and old who lived in the school district of White Sands Creek eagerly awaited this usually successful and fun-filled event. Most times the Pushinsky brothers' orchestra played. They would normally charge $5 per night but since Katayna had become a teacher, they would be donating their time. Joseph Pushinsky, Helenka's husband, was Katayna's brother-in-law and he knew that every cent raised would be put toward buying extra library books or some other supplies for the school because the school board could not afford to buy any extras during this miserable Depression.

A committee had to be struck to organize the lunches. Tainka and Pashka Borischuk always headed that committee. This year Pashka Borischuk was nearing seventy-five years of age and was not willing to prepare lunches, as her health was failing noticeably. Tainka asked Josephina Lupski, their Polish neighbour, and Annie Kaditz to help.

Paul, Mikhail, and Mikhail's friends, the Romanian Fred Radjec and Paul Lupski, were placed on the setup and cleanup committee. The students were put in charge of printing tickets and selling them in advance. The dance was to take place on the first Saturday in May before spring work started. There was over a month to prepare for the dance but the excitement was already mounting. The dance was one of the most important events of the year for this area. Even some people from Shady Hollow would come, in Billy Makovitsky's car. John Starchuk was planning to ask Katayna to be his steady girlfriend on the day of the dance. He felt certain that this old maid, who was now twenty-two years old, would be grateful that a man with his looks, education, and possibilities for the future would want her.

One week before the dance Pashka Borischuk became ill. Tainka went to check on the Borischuks, a task which she had been doing daily for the past year. She found Pashka, her old friend, in bed and in grave condition. It appeared she was paralyzed down her left side. Her left eye remained open. Theodore was too weak to climb the hill to the Stry-Kers to get help. He was seventy-nine years old now. Tears were streaming down his cheeks as he could not help his wonderful wife, a woman who had saved so many lives in these parts and had attended countless births over the years. Tainka, immediately recognizing the seriousness of the situation, ran home to get Mikhail to come with the car. Tainka, Mikhail, and Theodore Borischuk rushed Pashka to Shady Hollow Hospital, where Dr. Allison administered to her almost immediately. It was ascertained that Pashka had had a severe stroke and was incapacitated down her left side. She would have to remain in the hospital. Dr. Allison expressed his concern that she might not survive and that another stroke would surely be fatal. Theodore Borischuk would not leave her bedside. He remained there until he was completely exhausted. Tainka also would not leave Pashka's bedside—this woman had been more than a mother and a friend to her since she had come to Canada. Tainka would do everything in her power to save Pashka.

As the dance night drew nearer, Tainka declined to attend. She went to the Borischuks and packed a few necessities for Theodore, making room for him at the Stry-Ker home. Exhausted as a result of sitting at Pashka's bedside for four days and nights, he reluctantly consented to stay in their home—but only until Pashka came home from the hospital. Pashka, under Dr. Allison's care, was recuperating ever so slightly, although her speech was very slurred.

The dance night came and the Pushinsky band started to play. They would always begin with peppy polkas, followed by foxtrots and waltzes. At most of these social occasions, Katayna started dancing with her brother, Mikhail. He was still quite shy with women; he would only dance when his sisters asked him. Helenka chose to dance with the other brother, Paul, who was even more shy until he'd consumed enough moonshine to loosen him up. Helenka's husband, Joseph, played in the orchestra and only danced one or two dances with her throughout the entire night. She had many opportunities to dance with other men, but did not feel it was the proper thing for a respectable married woman to do. However, it was fine to dance with one's brothers or sisters. The orchestra usually played a waltz before lunch. Later in the evening the single men would choose a partner for lunch and this same young lady would be expected to be escorted home by him after the dance. John Starchuk was heading toward Katayna. She could see him coming in her peripheral view. What was she to do? He was Russian Orthodox and she was Ukrainian Greek Catholic. Even though it didn't matter very much to her, it certainly was a big factor to her *Tato* and *Mamunia*. She ran over to Helenka, who was near the orchestra and close to her husband Joseph. She asked Helenka what to do. Her sister advised her to go with him.

"Go, for God's sake! You're not expected to marry him just because you have lunch with this man!" she explained in exasperation. So when John Starchuk asked Katayna for the lunchtime waltz, she consented to go. The lunch, which Annie Kaditz and Josephina Lupski had prepared, was contained in small brown paper bags with three sandwiches in each bag. The sandwiches were made of white bread buttered, with mustard spread on top of the butter and a piece of baloney in each. These supplies were bought at Makovitsky's store at Shady Hollow. Each bag also contained two cookies that were baked and brought to school by a few of the children's mothers. The bags were sold for twenty-five cents each.

As Katayna and John Starchuck ate, sharing one bag of lunch, the tongues were already starting to wag. "It won't be long until those two are married!" the women whispered to one another.

"There may be a wedding at Stry-Kers this summer," one lady said. The others nodded in agreement. Evan regarded this possible union with disapproval. He had absolutely no patience with anyone who mingled with people from other religions. What was Katayna doing? Had she completely taken leave of her senses? Feeling a bit old and desperate, he made a mental note to talk to her next day. He went over and asked the Widow Hunkowski to dance. There were rumours that he had been intimate with this woman for many years. Evan and Tainka had not had sex for ten years now—not since the birth of Francis Nykola (Franki) when Evan had made his promise to God that he would never have sex with Tainka again. Since she would not use any means of birth control because of her strong Catholic convictions, he had found other outlets for his sexual needs. Widow Hunkowski was only one of these, but she was the most convenient.

After lunch the orchestra played a melody they had just learned . . . the Charleston. Helenka had also just learned how to dance this fancy dance. Even though people in Edmonton had been dancing the Charleston since the 1920s, it was a new dance in these parts. Helenka had taught Katayna the steps. To everyone's delight, the two of them got up and did the dance; they were both excellent dancers. They looked like twins. Helenka, however, was heavier set and now wore her hair blonde, using peroxide to get it that way. Helenka had always liked Maria's blonde hair and had envied her sister while she was alive.

As they were dancing the doors suddenly opened and Corporal Seymour and Constable McLennan, dressed in their official RCMP uniforms, entered the hall. They stood at the back of the school and watched. The Pushinskys continued to play and Helenka and Katayna continued to dance the Charleston.

Corporal Seymour, in his usual manner, sneered at the people in attendance. But Constable McLennan took a special interest in Katayna. As the dance came to a halt Katayna went to John Starchuk. They agreed to approach the Mounties to see what they were doing there, as it was obvious it was on business. Corporal Seymour told Starchuk and Katayna that someone had reported that moonshine whiskey was being sold on the school grounds; they were there to check out this complaint. The two RCMP officers did not like to disturb a social event of this nature deliberately, but if a report was lodged it was their obligation to investigate. John Starchuk left the room, walking in stride with Corporal Seymour. Constable McLennan followed with Katayna at his side.

"Have we met ? . . . Your face looks familiar," he said to her.

"Yes, we have, Constable. The first time was when my brother and I reported the Popilsky beatings seven years ago. I have seen you many times since then in Shady Hollow."

"You dance a pretty mean Charleston . . . Katayna," he complimented her.

"Do you know how to do the Charleston?" she asked.

"No," he replied, smiling down at her, "nothing quite that fancy. I'm only good at waltzes and foxtrots. But, frankly, I'm not bad at these dances."

They walked in silence for a while. Slowing his pace, he allowed Corporal Seymour to get out of earshot. "Would you be interested in accompanying me to a dance sometime when I'm off duty?" he asked Katayna. Katayna, having had a crush on this man and secretly loving him all these years since the Popilsky incident, was sure she had died and gone to heaven.

"It would be a pleasure!" she replied enthusiastically.

"Well, I'll let you know about a week before the dance . . . to give you time. I hope it won't interfere with any other social plans you may have." Rusty McLennan was genuinely impressed with Katayna. And he made no effort to conceal his interest and admiration.

As they walked, Katayna stole a glance from under her lashes. His red hair was even more copper than she remembered. His dark brown eyes were soft and warm this night, not the dark piercing kind she remembered from the first time they met. They caught up to Corporal Seymour and John Starchuk in time to hear the Corporal barking orders and wanting to know which vehicle was Louie Kaditz's. John Starchuk showed them the Kaditzes' Model T Ford truck with a red painted box on the back.

Although the Mounties searched the vehicle thoroughly, they could not find what they were searching for . . . moonshine. Katayna had suspected that it might be moonshine whiskey, as the rumours around Shady Hollow were that when Metro Soova was jailed Louie Kaditz had taken over his customers, becoming very financially secure as a result. A pop bottle full of moon-shine sold for twenty-five cents. Louie Kaditz was too clever to leave his supply on the truck. He used to distribute bottles in the early afternoon and leave them in designated places agreed to by the buyers. Usually the moonshine was placed along every second fence post or near the well or in the school barn manger.

The Mounties checked other vehicles, shining large flashlights into the cars. In a few they found couples necking or being even more intimate. They opened the vehicles, checked each one, then continued on to the next. After about half an hour the Mounties left. As Constable McLennan walked away, Katayna returned the tender smile he aimed in her direction. The people in attendance started to talk. A few young men told Louie Kaditz that the Mounties had searched his truck particularly. Louie, visibly anxious, soon got Annie's attention, collected the twins and went home.

The music continued to play. John Starchuk danced one more dance with Katayna. When he asked her to go home with him, however, she politely declined. She came home with her father and brothers Mikhail, Paul, and Franki. Evan was puzzled. She had had lunch with John Starchuk, so why hadn't she gone home with him? Oh well, it was best to leave well enough alone. He wouldn't have to lecture her about religious differences after all, he thought, breathing a sigh of relief.

CHAPTER THIRTY-FOUR

Two weeks went by. Katayna had not heard or seen Constable McLennan. Beginning to feel depressed, she told herself that if she didn't hear from him for another week, then she would have to believe that he had changed his mind. She should have suspected that Corporal Seymour might be behind this whole delay of Constable McLennan. After the search at the school, Constable McLennan, unable to contain his enthusiasm for Katayna, had shared his excitement with Seymour.

Corporal Seymour had been less than impressed. "You are a complete idiot. Why do you wish to get involved with these Bohunks? They're ignorant and they should associate with their own kind. . . . Your Scottish parents would be flabbergasted. Boy, am I surprised at your bad judgement!" he had scoffed.

Constable McLennan was still intimidated by Seymour, as he was his superior and could therefore drastically affect his future. A week went by and then another. There wasn't a waking hour that Rusty McLennan wasn't thinking of Katayna. "Why did Seymour have to interfere with my private life?" he thought. After all, Rusty McLennan had served in the RCMP for eleven and a half years—three in Athabasca and eight and a half in Shady Hollow. He had saved most of his earnings. The RCMP had a twelve-year marriage restriction for young constables. Also, a cash saving had to be shown as well before marriage permission was granted by the RCMP hierarchy in Ottawa. He had only six months to serve before his twelve-year restriction was lifted. He could also show a $5,000 savings. "For God's sake," he thought, "my mind is thinking about marriage." This had never occurred before. Rusty McLennan had taken out many girls during his time in the RCMP. Most were from Edmonton, where he would go on his days off. Granted, most were also Anglo-Saxon girls. He had never been this infatuated with any of them as he was with Katayna. He decided to write to his father, who had achieved the rank of Assistant Commissioner and was stationed in Ottawa.

After spending five weeks in the hospital Pashka Borischuck was discharged by Dr. Allison into Tainka's care. She did not insist on going home but agreed to stay at the Stry-Kers along with Theodore. Tainka nursed her with the greatest of love and compassion. Pashka, unable to walk or eat on her own, was also incontinent. Tainka willingly spent most of her time tending to her needs. She would feed her every meal and change her soiled diaper. They even purchased a wheelchair in which she wheeled Pashka outside for fresh air and sunshine. Theodore, depressed to see his loving wife in this state, spent most of his time holding her hand.

One sunny afternoon in late June, while Pashka was in her wheelchair and Theodore and Tainka sat on a bench in the shade of a tall birch tree, an RCMP car drove into the yard. It startled all three of them—this had never happened before. Police usually drove into farmers' yards when there was trouble or to notify people of the death of a member of the family, primarily if they had been in an accident.

The tall, handsome Rusty McLennan opened the door and stepped out into the sunshine. He was not wearing a hat as he approached the three people sitting in the shade.

"I'm looking for Katayna Stry-Ker. I was told she had already left the school. Is she at home?" he asked courteously.

Tainka understood some English but it was limited. Pashka and Theodore understood even less. However, between the three of them, they understood he was looking for Katayna.

"Go to in house," Tainka gestured, pointing to the house. "She in dere."

Was Katayna in trouble? they wondered. Maybe those Goseniuks had reported her . . . maybe she had finally strapped that horrible Sophie of theirs! They waited anxiously to hear what the visit was all about.

Rusty and Katayna spent about half an hour talking in the house. The moment he left, Tainka went in to question her daughter. Katayna told her that Rusty had asked her to go to a dance at the Trocadero in Edmonton and that she was planning to go this coming weekend. It was understood, she quickly added, that she would stay in a hotel and that she would be in her own room. Rusty would stay with his friends in Edmonton.

"Surely, this has to be the worst thing that's happened in this family since Maria died!" cried Tainka. "Not only is this crazy daughter of mine planning to go out with an Englishman. She's planning to spend a weekend away from home in Edmonton in a hotel. You just wait until you father hears about this!" she warned her daughter grimly. Tainka did not distinguish between English, Welsh, Irish, or Scottish . . . they were all English as far as she was concerned. They were not what she wanted her children to be involved with in life.

Angered, Katayna defied her mother, something she had never before done. "Mother, when will you stop living the standards of the old country? What's the difference if I go out with an English or a Ukrainian man? I'm over twenty-one years of age and I can do what I want. Everyone is saying I'm an old maid anyway!" Twenty-one years was the age of consent in the province of Alberta.

"Stop talking back to me! Have you completely taken leave of your senses?" demanded Tainka, flushed and furious. "I can't even talk to those people . . . what good would that be if he came here? Your dad also would have trouble talking to him!"

"Whose fault is that, anyway? You've been in Canada for over thirty years. You're a Canadian now, so why haven't you made any effort to learn to speak English? Every time we children try to talk in English you and *Tato* stop us. Why don't you learn English?" she challenged her mother hotly, and ran out of the yard toward the artesian well in the distant valley of the farmstead. Smoking had now become a habit of hers and in her agitated state she desperately craved a cigarette.

Pashka Borischuk had heard this whole exchange. Normally she would not say a word, but since her stroke she was not as diplomatic as she had been before her illness. "Tainka," she began in her slurred speech. "What you said to Katayna was wrong. Maybe it is time for us Ukrainians to integrate into Canadian society. We are living in an English-speaking country. Queen Victoria, the English Queen who opened Canada to welcome all of us to immigrate here, perhaps expected us all to learn English. Your children all speak English well, and Katayna is a teacher. Look at their point of view," she advised her friend reasonably, struggling to continue. "Can't you see in her eyes how much she loves that young policeman? I've never seen Katayna look like that. Support Katayna, Tainka. She's a good daughter. And . . . you know how angry Evan will be when he hears about this. If you both condemn her you can be sure she'll leave home. The idea of staying in Edmonton for the weekend in a hotel is not such a good idea . . . but there must be some other way." Exhausted from this speech, Pashka put her head back in her wheelchair and fell asleep. Tainka gently wheeled her into the house and put her to bed.

"Oh, God," she whispered to herself. "What an exhibition in the presence of this poor angel. Maybe there is merit in what she said. She is so very wise."

At supper that night Katayna was very reserved. Tainka waited for her to say something but nothing was mentioned, no word was said. Finally, when the rhubarb pie was being served, Tainka casually announced, "That young policeman, Rusty McLennan, was here today."

"What did he want?" Mikhail asked.

"He came to see Katayna. He is apparently interested in her," Tainka explained.

"Of course Katayna told him she wasn't interested!" Evan boomed as though Katayna wasn't even in the room.

With that comment Katayna jumped into the conversation. "I most certainly did not! I happen to like Rusty McLennan very much. Furthermore, I respect him and his position."

"You stupid idiot," barked Evan. "Why does this family need to get involved with an Englishman! You find yourself a nice Ukrainian Catholic boy . . . one we can be proud of and understand."

Pashka gave Tainka a quiet look of disgust, saying nothing. But Tainka picked up the cue. "I think we're over-reacting, Evan. After all, this man is not asking Katayna to marry him. We certainly do not own our children, Evan, and maybe it's time we let go. The English are not bad people. Look at Dr. Liston and Dr. Allison. They've saved so many Ukrainian lives! In fact, they saved our own son's life. Even though Dr. Liston was not able to save our Maria, he did try," she reminded him.

"If any child of mine marries an Englishman, I don't want to know them as my child!" Evan retorted adamantly. "Those bastards called me a Bohunk once too often when I worked at Medicine Hat. I'll never forgive them!"

Tainka knew it was futile to pursue this matter further. She knew Evan would have a brain haemorrhage if she even mentioned the weekend in Edmonton—the weekend Katayna was planning with Rusty McLennan.

The next day, Tainka and Pashka discussed the matter. Franki, sitting in the parlour, overheard them. Tainka said she could cover for Katayna, that she would have to tell Evan she was going with Rusty McLennan, but she absolutely drew the line at staying in a hotel room.

"It's too bad we don't have relatives in Edmonton where she could stay," fretted Tainka as she and Pashka wondered how to solve this dilemma.

"I also don't know any reliable people with whom she could stay," Pashka admitted.

"What about at Rosie Soova's place?" asked Franki, who would have done anything for his beloved sister Katayna.

"What do you know about Rosie Soova?" inquired Tainka.

"Oh, that she was a good friend of our Maria and that she sends us a Christmas card each year inviting us to her place. What does she call her rooming house— The Pearl's Oyster or s . . . something?" He was stammering, not wanting to reveal he had read Rosie's letters to Maria.

"You know, that's not a bad idea!" Pashka exclaimed, looking at Tainka. Tainka nodded in agreement and relief.

When Katayna came into the house, Tainka broke the news to her daughter and assured her that she would be supporting her. At supper that night, she encouraged the children to speak English as she announced that it was time she learned the language well. Surprisingly, no resistance came from Evan. Pashka Borischuk gave Tainka a loving look of approval.

A week passed. Early one morning, just before sunrise, Theodore roused Tainka. His beloved Pashka had just suffered another massive stroke. She was barely alive when Tainka got to her.

Tainka grabbed Pashka's hand and held on firmly, tears streaming down her cheeks. "Always remember how much I loved you, as you were a daughter," her friend told her weakly, her words slurred. "Thank you for looking after me . . . be more tolerant of your children . . . and give Katayna. . . ." She was unable to say more. Pashka had taken her last heavy breath, almost ten years to the day after Maria's death. Bidding the second person closest to her heart a silent goodbye, Tainka lowered her forehead onto Pashka's lifeless hands and wept quietly.

Mikhail drove to Shady Hollow to fetch Dr. Allison, who signed the death certificate. Once again, the church bell at St. Olga's rang its mournful toll. Most residents of Shady Hollow were sorry to see this wonderful woman depart from their midst. She was laid to rest near the Stry-Ker plots reserved for Tainka and Evan, near Maria and Stephen Chomiak. Before one month had passed, Theodore Borischuk would follow his wife Pashka in death. Tainka was not surprised. She had always known these two people were inseparable. Oh, how she would miss them both.

Their will bequeathed their quarter section to Tainka. At this point the farm meant nothing to her, as she would much rather have had the Borischuks back in her life. She continued grieving very deeply, again experiencing a profound depression. One day, as she knelt praying at the graves of Maria, Pashka, and Theodore, a spiritual presence came upon her. It was a feeling of tranquility and inner peace. She felt their spiritual presence urging her to go on with her life, to continue for her family's sake and for those who were depending on her strength.

CHAPTER THIRTY-FIVE

Edmonton in 1932

Canada, like its neighbour to the south, the United States, continued to experience the tough Depression. Canada's Prime Minister was R.B. Bennett, a westerner from Calgary, Alberta. His foolish motto was that he could "blast his way" into the markets of the world. The American president, Herbert C. Hoover, was also incapable of helping his country out of the Depression, because after the terrible stock market crash in 1929, people in the U.S. who usually led in business were afraid to invest. World markets were dried up.

Tainka had a long talk with Katayna. She realized that her daughter was deeply in love with Constable Rusty McLennan.

"As long as he doesn't make a fool of you, Katayna," Tainka warned her. "You've heard of many other girls where a man takes advantage of her and then leaves her with a broken heart. Many times they even become pregnant!" As though this was the worst curse any single girl could suffer. She was not quite sure how she was going to convince Evan that he should not stand in Katayna's way.

About a week went by. Rusty McLennan had visited the school to see Katayna almost every day and spent the lunch hour with her. John Starchuk, the principal, knew his opportunity for a future with Katayna had passed him by. On this lunch hour, Rusty kept pressing Katayna to set a weekend date to go to Edmonton with him but she kept delaying her answer. She would not admit she was afraid of the confrontation she would have to face with her father, Evan Stry-Ker, should she insist on going. Rusty, however, sensed there was a problem.

When Katayna went home, she pressured Tainka, saying that she wished to go the following weekend. At supper, Tainka carefully studied Evan's mood. He had just returned from one of his horse-breeding circuits. She suspected he had paid Widow Hunkowski a visit during his absence because Rudy, the horse, came trotting home pulling the empty cart behind him. The cart did not have Evan on its seat. The stallion, Shascha, and the teaser stud, Kudlee, must have been tied up better and could not escape. The widow lived only one and a half miles away from the Stry-Kers so the horses knew their way home at this short distance.

As a matter of fact, Evan was looking very sheepish. He came home leading the two stallions and walking angrily in front of them. This may be the time to broach the Katayna and Rusty situation, Tainka thought. She had never again mentioned his indiscretions since the terrible fight before Helenka's wedding. She also knew his feelings on not getting her pregnant again. Hence, he abstained from having sex with her, and she did not blame him for having to satisfy his sexual needs. Nevertheless, she always considered him to be an over-sexed being and many times she wondered why she had ever married him. Oh well, it was too late for those kinds of thoughts.

Everyone was eating peacefully, including Evan, Mikhail, Franki and Paul. The whole family seemed pre-occupied this night, and there was silence around a table that was usually filled with interesting conversation. Also, they had started haying and the men were tired from pitching hay all day. Franki was looking curiously at Katayna and Tainka. He knew these women well enough to know that there was something each one wanted to say, but they were hesitating. Evan looked down at his plate without speaking a word.

"Did you all forget it will be St. Peter and Paul's feast day on July 12? Maybe we should go to Mundare for the celebrations. It will give Franki a chance to see the seminary at the same time. While we go to Mundare, Katayna would like to go to Edmonton," Tainka carefully explained.

"Woman, why don't you tell the whole thing . . . Katayna wants to go to Edmonton with that English Mounted Policeman . . . isn't that closer to the truth?" Evan boomed.

"So what if it is?" Tainka challenged.

"Is that what you want, that our daughter becomes a laughingstock around Shady Hollow? It isn't enough this Englishman will use her and then throw her out like a worn-out old dish rag, but he has to do it in Edmonton for the whole weekend!" Evan was becoming very angry and Tainka needed to say something to placate him.

"If she stays at a place with friends, what would be wrong with this? She can stay at Rosie Soova's place . . . Rosie invites us every year when she sends us the Christmas card. Don't you think she'd like at least one of us to visit her?" Tainka felt this was the lesser of two evils.

"Do you people think I'm a child?" Katayna butted in. "Do you not feel I have some moral standards? It makes me feel terrible to see how little you trust me. Father, I'd never want to hurt you, but can I ask you why the horse and cart came home without you? If we're talking about morals, let those beyond reproach be the first to preach them!" She wanted to hurt Evan and she certainly did.

"You do what you want . . . you have a sharper tongue than any of my other children and God will punish you for talking to your father in this manner!" With that accusation Evan left the table. Katayna promised Tainka that she'd stay at Rosie Soova's rooming house. The next day, she told Rusty they could go on the July 12th weekend. Evan expressed no more objections but refused to have further conversations with Katayna.

On Saturday morning Rusty McLennan drove into the Stry-Ker yard in his own personal car. It was a neat, dark blue coupe with a rumble seat. He came into the house and was introduced to Franki and Tainka, the only people in the house.

"Mrs. Stry-Ker, I promise I shall protect Katayna's honour and reputation. I will have her home on Sunday evening," Rusty told her sincerely.

"What is he meaning?" Tainka asked Franki.

He translated. When she understood better, she smiled at Rusty and apologized for not understanding English better.

"You be a good boy to mine daughter," was all she could say. She told Franki to tell Rusty the rest—that she would be very disappointed if he did not live up to his promise.

As they drove out of the yard, Katayna told Rusty that she'd be staying at a friend's house. He asked her for the name. "Rosie Soova," Katayna replied. "Remember her father is in jail for attacking the Popilskys? Rosie owns a large rooming house called The Pearl's Oyster. I believe it is located somewhere on 96 Street and 107 Avenue."

"Oh yes, I remember indeed. I'd rather you don't stay there. Do you know what type of a rooming house Miss Soova owns and operates?" he asked her.

"I believe it is an ordinary rooming house which provides room and board to its tenants," she replied, as this was her knowledge about the place.

"No, no, Katayna, it's a high-class house of ill-repute . . . a whorehouse. And yes, it's called The Pearl's Oyster.

That's the last place on earth I'd take you to!" Rusty was adamant.

"Oh God, what will I do now?! I promised my mother I'd stay with Rosie. No one at our place knows that Rosie owns a whorehouse. At least I don't think anyone knows," she ended meekly.

"Let's keep this our little secret, Katayna, and let's consider this on our way to Edmonton. But for now, let's enjoy each other's company," he suggested, smiling at her warmly.

The roads were in poor condition as frequent rains that summer had helped in creating deep ruts. This condition was also aided by the large steel wagon wheels that primarily travelled these roads. All the municipalities were suffering a lack of funds for any public works projects during this deep Depression. It took them four hours to reach Edmonton—four of the most enjoyable hours either one of them had ever spent in their entire lives.

Upon arrival, Rusty proceeded to travel down 97 Street and into the Highlands development down 111 Avenue. There on Ada Boulevard, facing the North Saskatchewan River, stood a beautiful large home. It belonged to the Andersons, friends of Rusty's mother and father. Geoff Anderson also hailed from New Brunswick. He was a successful businessman who owned a coal mine north of Edmonton. As Rusty introduced Katayna to Millie and Geoff Anderson, they eyed her with approval. Katayna was dressed in a blue cotton suit with a white blouse. Her dark hair was beautifully coiffed, and her manners were perfect.

She had taken an etiquette course at the Camrose Normal School for Teachers. "What an asset that course has been," she thought.

"How long are you two staying in Edmonton?" inquired Millie.

"Just until tomorrow," Rusty replied.

"As you know, you are both welcome to stay with us. We have lots of room for you both because our children are all gone now," Millie offered. "In separate bedrooms of course!" she added, laughing.

"Let us have a private conversation, please," Rusty requested so he could discuss the offer with Katayna. They both moved to the window for a moment to consider the offer. In a few moments, he walked back to the Andersons. "Both Katayna and I would be very happy to spend the night here," he accepted, "in separate rooms of course!"

The Andersons were going to a banquet that night and apologized for not being able to host them. Rusty explained that he wished to escort Katayna to a special dinner at the Wedgwood Room at the McDonald Hotel and then follow it with dancing at the lovely new Trocadero Ballroom.

During dinner they both expressed their love for one another. Rusty asked Katayna if she would consent to be engaged at Christmas as his twelve-year service in the RCMP would be up then and the marriage restriction lifted.

Katayna couldn't have been happier. The whole evening was like a fairy tale, but the dance at the Trocadero Ballroom was like living a dream. The lights were dim and the large mirror ball spun during the waltzes. Rusty was an excellent dancer and he was a master at the Viennese old-time waltz.

His tall, beautiful frame held her tight, moulding her well-shaped body against his. They made a spectacular couple and received many compliments from other dancers who watched them intently. Katayna wore a beautiful, floral-printed full-skirt dress which she had borrowed from her sister, Helenka. She looked every bit an elegant lady.

When they returned to the Andersons in the wee morning hours, Millie and Geoff had long before gone to bed. Rusty escorted Katayna to her designated bedroom. Holding each other tenderly, they kissed passionately then, breaking the kiss, he gently but firmly pushed her away.

"Katayna, I won't have the will power to control myself soon, so let's say goodnight until I see you tomorrow," he told her, his breathing ragged. Reluctantly, she agreed. She cleansed her face and washed herself, applied her Pond's cold cream, and fell into a wonderfully deep sleep in a comfortable bed covered with a thick feather down comforter. The sheets and pillowslips, crisply ironed, were an irridescent white. Katayna felt like royalty.

In the morning, during breakfast with Millie and Geoff Anderson, they expressed their gratitude for their hospitality. Both the Andersons privately told Rusty how very impressed they were with Katayna. Rusty and Katayna spent the rest of the morning and early afternoon sight-seeing in Edmonton and then headed back north on Highway 28 to Shady Hollow.

Early Sunday morning at the Stry-Ker home, Tainka awoke shortly after four. She stoked the fire in the stove and proceeded to bring the cows home from the pasture. As always, the trusty collie Roger accompanied her. Roger would normally bring the cows home by himself, but this was even too early for him to function.

When Tainka returned from the pasture she awakened Mikhail and Paul and the morning chores began. The mass at St. Peter and Paul's Greek Catholic Church in Mundare commenced at 10:00 a.m. It would take them at least two hours to drive south across the North Saskatchewan River by ferry at Pakan to get to mass on time.

By 7:00 a.m. chores were finished. Evan was finishing his shave. He still used a straight razor which he sharpened on a thick leather belt, a habit that he had never broken since serving in the Austrian army.

Franki, dressed in his Sunday-best suit, was ready and waiting. He did not even want to eat breakfast; he was too excited. He'd be seeing the seminary for the first time.

By 10:00 a.m. the Stry-Ker car had reached Mundare and was parked. All five members of the family proceeded to church, with Franki leading the procession. There were a few places left to sit in various pews but none together. Franki and Tainka proceeded to go to the front pew, where one space was available at one end and another at the opposite side.

The church was crowded, as the Basilian Bishop was conducting the service on this very special day. Three seminarians were being ordained today. Four other Basilian fathers accompanied the Bishop. This was the most spectacular church event any one of the Stry-Kers had witnessed to date. At the closing of mass the seminarians took their vows and promised to serve God, as they lay with their faces to the floor in the presence of God. Something in Franki moved him to new heights. This spiritual experience left him with a profound feeling that this was the life he wanted—such deep mystery . . . such purity . . . such holiness.

Mass was followed by special prayers at the beautiful grotto. A dinner was served afterwards. Father Kohot, the Shady Hollow parish priest, took Franki to see the seminary, much to Tainka's pleasure. They were happy that there would finally be a priest in their family. Tainka was ecstatic. What an honour this would be. Evan was thrilled as well, but he would not express his feelings out wardly.

Mikhail and Paul were also pleased that their little brother had chosen the priesthood. He certainly had no interest in farming. This was something they could not understand. Who in their right mind would not like working with the precious land, the machines, and the soil? After all, wasn't this the true Canadian dream?

That evening at the Stry-Kers' home several people were in a euphoric state . . . certainly Katayna, as well as Tainka, Franki, and possibly Evan. Katayna did not elaborate why she did not stay at Rosie Soova's. She lied that Rosie was not at home, and even if she had been home, there was no room at the rooming house. The maid said that the rooming house was full. Evan appeared very relieved, but he was still not speaking to Katayna.

She told them about the Andersons and what wonderful people they were. Mostly she emphasized the separate bedrooms in which she and Rusty were accommodated. This satisfied Tainka.

Franki told Katayna about his experience at Mundare and about his decision to become a priest. Katayna shed a tear as this little boy, now ten, spoke like a grownup. He was more of a son to her than to Tainka, but now Tainka was taking a very keen interest in her son . . . the future Father Stry-Ker. Oh, how pleased her mother in the old country would have been. Tainka already had all sorts of visions of his ordination. She was shaken back to reality when she saw Katayna's tears.

"Why are you so sad? Did Rusty McLennan mistreat you?" she asked her daughter.

"No, no, *Mamunia*, he treated me better than I could imagine . . . I know now that I love him very deeply and he loves me. We are planning to get engaged at Christmas." She would not reveal why she had tears, as she knew how much Tainka wanted Franki to be a priest.

"Don't you think you and this Rusty are rushing things?" her mother went on, worried that her daughter might be making a mistake.

"Why, *Mamunia*? We know what our feelings are. You've always accused me of being an old maid, haven't you? I should confess to you that I've loved this man since the first time I saw him. That was after Helenka's wedding when Metro Soova injured the Popilskys and Mikhail and I drove to Shady Hollow to report the incident to the RCMP. That's eight long years ago!" Katayna explained assertively. "Don't you think that's a long time to love someone when you don't know if that someone even knows you're alive?"

Tainka remembered the words of her dearly departed friend, Pashka Borischuk, and vowed to support Katayna in this relationship. She was also learning much more English, though she still had little confidence in speaking the language.

CHAPTER THIRTY-SIX

It was 1933. The Depression was bad and the economy was taking a further downturn. Eggs brought five cents a dozen, homemade butter sold in the stores for ten cents a pound, hindquarters of beef were ten cents a pound, while butchered and dressed hogs brought $4 per carcass. Wheat was selling for 25 cents a bushel if anyone could sell it. In the late 1920s it had sold for $3 a bushel. There was, however, a ray of hope. The United States had just elected a new president, Franklin D. Roosevelt. His motto was to help small businesses to thrive and competition to flourish. He also wished to rework the government to aid the poor, to improve education, and to create a less crash-prone financial system. This was a tall order and there were incredible objectives to meet.

The Stry-Kers fared well even during the Depression because their farming operation was self-sufficient. There was always plenty of food. Many men who rode the rails ended up working at the Stry-Kers', clearing bush to make more fertile and arable land on which to grow cereal grains and hay.

Saskatchewan and southern Alberta turned into dust bowls. Cattle were dying because of a shortage of grazing pastureland. Grain crops did not grow because there was no moisture. The dust storms brought with them grasshoppers that ate whatever crops remained. People thought God had certainly abandoned them.

While Canada suffered under this severe Depression, Germany and Italy were flexing their muscles under the fascist rule of Hitler and Mussolini, respectively. Under these rulers, the economic fallacy of the corporate state was now gaining ground in these two countries. R.B. Bennett, Canada's Prime Minister, felt confident that he could "blast his way" into the markets of the world. No one could afford to buy gasoline . . . for those few who had an automobile. So they hitched horses to the automobile and used it like a democrat. Many people referred to these as "Bennett Buggies" in disrespect for Prime Minister Bennett, as most people blamed his poor leadership for the sad state to which the country was reduced.

During this dreadful time in Canada's history, there were some silver linings to the black clouds that loomed. Katayna Stry-Ker and Constable Rusty McLennan were very much in love. Katayna's courtship with Constable Rusty McLennan had intensified. He would visit the school as often as he could. On many occasions he told Corporal Seymour that he was searching for moonshine whiskey stills, but the Corporal always noted this was in the northwest direction of Shady Hollow and precisely where White Sands Creek School was located. Corporal Seymour most certainly did not approve of this union. However, his disapproval was nothing compared to the strenuous objections Katayna was receiving from her *Tato*, Evan. Constable McLennan's parents approved of her, as they had heard high praises from their son and also from their friends Millie and Geoff Anderson of Edmonton. The Andersons used to see Katayna frequently. She and Rusty had spent many weekends in Edmonton since they started going out and they always stayed with the Andersons. Rusty's parents were planning to come to Edmonton for Christmas, primarily to meet Katayna in person.

Katayna did invite Rusty to the Stry-Kers on a few occasions. Evan would ignore him completely. Tainka did attempt to communicate, as her English was becoming quite understandable. Mikhail and Paul were civil but not overly friendly, because this young policeman was quickly destroying their liquor supply sources. They particularly did not appreciate his snooping around Louie Kaditz's homestead. Louie was now supplying the best moonshine whiskey in these parts. Unknown to anyone, Louie Kaditz used to visit Metro Soova at the Fort Saskatchewan Jail. Metro shared his famous moonshine whiskey recipes with Louie. Their agreement was that Louie Kaditz put one quarter of the proceeds of his sales into a tin can. These savings were to be Metro Soova's nest egg when he finished serving his jail term. The other part to the agreement was that Metro would become Louie's business partner upon his release from jail.

Franki adored Rusty. He enjoyed talking to him and learning about New Brunswick and about his training days at the RCMP Academy in Regina, Saskatchewan. Rusty wished to accelerate the engagement date and Katayna agreed. They felt that marriage would be more in order and so the wedding date was set for January 1, 1933. His parents would be here and he and Katayna could finally be together every day. Katayna was simply ecstatic as she told her parents about her wedding plans.

"Rusty and I have decided to be married after Christmas!" she told Tainka enthusiastically. Her mother's response was cool and reserved.

"Are you sooure this *Angleck* is for you good to marry? Ya knowing they say, Ukrainians and *Anglecks* mix it like oil and vater!" Tainka avoided mentioning her deep apprehension about Rusty not being of Catholic faith. "Is it he be Catlic?" she finally asked.

"No mother, he is a Protestant!" Katayna replied as assertively as she could. She knew exactly what a fight this would create in the house, yet again.

"Ooyee, Ooyee, do you know of vhat your father vill tell?" Tainka was very concerned.

"We haven't discussed what minister will marry us . . . that's not as important as both of us being in love and promising to be faithful to one another . . . is it, Mother?" Katayna was becoming angry.

"It doesn't matter you say . . . .yes, yes, it does matter in this house. We are strong Catholics and have been since we came from the old country and that's what we've always been. How can you be so insensitive when your little brother Franki is soon to enter a seminary . . . to become a Catholic priest?" Tainka had reverted to talking in the Ukrainian language again, only it wasn't talking, it was more like screaming.

Katayna knew there was no sense arguing with her mother, as she would never concede this point. And she needed her support to confront her father, who continued to speak very little to his daughter.

When Katayna told Rusty about this dilemma he agreed to go see the Catholic priest, Father Kohut. The old priest was even more rigid. He explained that the only way he would marry them in a Catholic ceremony would be if Rusty agreed to take Catechism lessons and be re-baptized. These preset conditions were not agreeable to either Rusty or Katayna. They both felt it was best to be married by a Justice of the Peace rather than go through a religious fight.

When she announced her plans, Tainka and Evan both called her a Bolshevik, a non-believer . . . a heathen. Even Franki was disappointed that Katayna chose this route. However, he continued to support her.

"I tell you . . . you Bolshevik, who I raised, God will punish you for this . . . just you wait!" Evan warned furiously.

Rusty and Katayna found a small house to rent in Shady Hollow. She was not able to obtain a contract to teach in the village for at least the remainder of the school season so she would continue to teach at White Sands Creek School.

Christmas came. The school Christmas concert was a complete success, as it had been in previous years. This year it was even more special to Katayna because Christmas always brought a renewal of her deep belief in God. Even though she would not be married in a religious ceremony, nevertheless she loved her God.

Sophie Goseniuk and her parents bought some land around Pakan, and moved there because the land was better and more fertile nearer the North Saskatchewan River. Katayna was relieved to be rid of this obnoxious child from her classroom. Sophie would be attending the school in the village of Shady Hollow.

Tainka was secretly happy for her daughter because she saw how deeply Rusty loved her and how well he treated her. This was something she had never had with Evan. However, she would be defying Evan outright if she expressed her approval, so she remained silent. Everyone except Evan was going to the wedding in Edmonton on January 1, 1933. The Andersons insisted on having the reception at their beautiful home on Ada Boulevard.

On the day of the wedding Katayna wore a lovely ivory-coloured dress with a handkerchief hemline. Her veil was made of a very soft damask lace. She wore white silk stockings and soft leather shoes with a delicate strap across the bridge of her foot.

Her sister, Helenka Pushinsky, would be her Matron of Honour and Helenka and Joseph's only daughter, Emily, only two years old, would be the flower girl. Helenka and Joseph's three sons, ranging in age from three to seven, were also there.

Tainka, Mikhail, Paul, and Franki also attended from Katayna's side. Corporal Seymour was the best man.

Both Rusty and Corporal Seymour wore their formal red tunics. Their boots were highly polished and crisp Stetsons crowned their heads. They were a sight to behold. Edward McLennan, Rusty's father, also wore his formal red serge. His mother, Julia, was attired in a royal blue velvet gown and looked stunning with her copper red hair, similar to her son's. Her hair was beautifully coiffed. It wasn't difficult to see from where Rusty's genes had come. His sister, Angela, a registered nurse, could not attend as she still lived in New Brunswick and her work would not allow her absence.

The wedding ceremony took place in the Andersons' parlour in front of the large bay window that overlooked the North Saskatchewan River. The hoarfrost covered the branches of the birch, maple, and spruce trees and the white glistening snow created a scene like a winter wonderland. A Justice of the Peace conducted the ceremony beautifully.

It was obvious that Katayna and Rusty were deeply in love and very compatible. They spent their wedding night in the bridal suite at the McDonald Hotel, even though it cost Constable Rusty McLennan one month of his wages. The McDonald Hotel stood at the top of McDougal Hill. It was named after Canada's first Prime Minister, John A. Macdonald, and was owned by the Canadian National Railroad, which came to Edmonton in 1909. The hotel was called the Jewel on the Hill. Its majestic peaked towers with flags atop gave the building the grandeur of a gigantic castle. The hotel was beautifully appointed within, as it had been through all its years in business. The housekeeping was immaculate; the tall mahogany and brass front doors were polished twice a day. The bellmen always wore long red topcoats and peaked officers' hats.

Not only were these two people intellectually compatible, their sexual compatibility was phenomenal. They could not stop making love all night. In the morning they ordered breakfast into the room and continued to make love.

Katayna did not have to return to teaching until January 10, after Christmas for people celebrating the Julian calendar, as did her family and most of the people at White Creek Sands School. Rusty and Katayna were invited to the Stry-Kers to celebrate Christmas on January 7. Evan made the atmosphere particularly cool, but he did not create a scene or make an issue about the non-religious wedding ceremony that had just taken place. He just ignored Katayna and Rusty. This saddened Katayna. She could not understand why a man who professed such deep Christian faith could be this unforgiving or so lacking in understanding. He was also a highly respected school and municipal councillor. But there were rules for other people and there were rules for his own family. The latter were much more rigid and unforgiving rules.

Katayna spent the extra week setting up their home at Shady Hollow. As the week drew to an end she had set up a cozy, attractive little house with scented geraniums in the parlour and on the kitchen window ledges, plants that Tainka gave her daughter. Katayna had learned to sew quite well and made beautiful, frilly lace curtains for each room.

Rusty was even more impressed with his new wife. In addition to all her other attributes, she also kept a clean house and was an excellent cook. And so married life began for Constable McLennan and his wife, Katayna.

CHAPTER THIRTY-SEVEN

It was 1935. In the past two years Franki had skipped a grade and was now in grade seven. Since he had first committed himself to the priesthood his mind had not deviated from this chosen course. Consequently, he did very few farm chores, much to the disappointment of Mikhail and Paul. Tainka, on the other hand, encouraged Franki in reading of the Bible and other holy books.

Katayna had successfully obtained a contract to teach school at Shady Hollow the following school year. A new teacher came to White Sands Creek School—Nadia Krause, just graduated from Camrose Normal School for Teachers. She chose to teach at White Sands Creek School because she was a sister to Annie Kaditz and wanted to be near her sister and her family. The Kaditz twins, Oni and Harry, were delighted to have their aunt teach them. She was a gentle person very much like her sister Annie. Within a year Nadia had married John Starchuk, the principal. They established residency at the teacherage.

During the years 1929 to 1933, Canada's gross national expenditure declined by 42 per cent. Thirty per cent of the labour force was unemployed. One in five Canadians became dependent on government relief programs. The Prairie Provinces were affected worst of all because of their agricultural base and the low price of grain crops. Grain was the primary product, and it was exported. The total provincial income plummeted by 90 per cent. Sixty-six per cent of the rural population was forced into Relief Assistance programs in order to survive. The western provinces were technically bankrupt from 1932 onwards.

In this year, 1935, a political reform movement developed. William Aberhart, a preacher, headed the new reform group. It was called the Social Credit Party. Its platform promised to give every man, woman, and child $5 a month. Of course they were elected and started distributing the promised funds. This continued for several months until the federal government banned this program as being in contravention of the Banking Act.

As men continued to ride the rails in search of employment, the Stry-Kers' wealth increased. Evan's Clydesdales were now commanding the highest world prices for such animals. A breeding mare would fetch $100 and stallions sold for $150. This was a fraction of the original price Evan had paid for his mares and stallion from Bruderheim. Evan had now become quite an authority on Clydesdale horses. He was travelling to a number of Clydesdale farm exhibitions in eastern Canada and once even went to the U.S.A. Anyone wishing to have their mares bred now had to bring them to Stry-Kers. The studding fees were extremely high to people outside of the Shady Hollow district. He gave local people a thirty per cent discount; to people belonging to St. Olga's parish, the discount was fifty per cent. No matter how much his annual income, Evan always donated ten per cent to the church or to the poor. He often said that this was a cardinal rule with him, as outlined in the Bible.

Mikhail and Paul continued to farm successfully, buying more land as it was being sold for taxes because poor, unsuccessful homesteaders could not survive due to low grain prices. As land was purchased the readily available labour force was hired to clear even more brush from these lands, particularly during the winter months. The Stry-Kers continued to pay the men $5 per month as well as provide room and board. Tobacco was also supplied, as was moonshine whiskey. The workers were pleased to have this opportunity, as many others starved.

The Stry-Kers sold very little of their grain, as most was used to feed the large horses as well as the cattle and pigs. Evan's breeding mares now totalled twenty-five. He had two stallions to service these mares and these stallions provided studding services for others. The Stry-Ker Ranch, as it was now called, also raised about one hundred cattle and the same number of pigs, a profitable operation which Mikhail and Paul had learned from Louie Kaditz.

Their threshing machine contracting business was also successful and they were strong competition for the Pushinskys, Helenka's in-laws and husband Joseph.

Since Katayna had left home Tainka could not manage the workload of cleaning, gardening, and cooking, especially when there were up to six hired men at one time. A young Ukrainian girl from across the creek was hired to help Tainka. Her name was Anastasia Ozypko. Anastasia was an eager, hard-working girl, very willing to please. She had a pretty round-shaped face with brunette hair and crystal clear blue eyes. She was twenty years old. Tainka and Anastasia got along extremely well and soon Tainka started speculating that this girl would make a good wife for Mikhail. After all, this thirty-one-year-old son of hers should certainly be married by now. However, Anastasia showed absolutely no romantic interest in Mikhail and he showed none in her.

Spring came and Alberta's beautiful countryside began to awaken and blossom. The young white aspen trees, or poplar, as they were locally known, opened their shiny lime-green leaves. The green meadows and the mosses around the artesian well exuded an earthy and humid fragrance. A soft, fresh rain washed the hills and valleys as an artist first washes his canvas before creating a masterpiece. The Stry-Kers had planted maple trees around the perimeter of their farmyard. There was also a white picket fence where the house and root cellar were located. In the inner portion of this yard, a caragana hedge grew and flourished. This hedge was always kept trimmed so it had a lush green look and blended well with the honeysuckles growing near the house. The violet lilacs brought forth fragrant blooms in spring. Tainka, a confirmed gardener, enjoyed seeing the fruits of her labour as she watched her perennial flower beds begin to poke their healthy little heads above the soil. She grew sweet williams, iris, lilies, yarrow, and tansy. She used yarrow and tansy for medicinal purposes, an art she had learned from her good friend, the late Pashka Borischuk.

This was Tainka's favourite season. Everything was awakening from its deep winter sleep. Spring was also a time when most of the young animals were born on the farm. The hens would start clucking and sitting on nests full of eggs, and in three weeks there would be baby chicks chirping in the yard. Her favourite mushrooms, morels (May mushrooms), grew in abundance. Tainka loved geese, as she remembered them from the old country. She had acquired five female geese and one five-year-old gander. She wintered these lovely creatures, which she regarded more as her pets than as providers of a meat supply. In the spring her old geese would lay eggs and nest. After one month, a week longer than the hatching period for chickens, her geese were multi-coloured but the old gander was almost white. She often compared his moody disposition and amorous sex drive to that of her husband, Evan. This observation was her very own personal secret, not to be shared with anyone. In all the years she had had many colourful chickens, but no matter how she tried to mate her hens with various roosters, she could never get a colourful black-, gold-, and red-feath-

ered rooster like the one she had owned in the old country. That old rooster brought back so many memories . . .
he used to crow so faithfully every morning. So many
mornings he was already crowing when Evan was stum-
bling home from the *korshma*. Deep in thought, Tainka
walked toward the valley.

Every spring she would walk down to her favourite
spot on the farm at the artesian well. Roger, the collie,
would follow her everywhere. The geese would follow
her to the farmyard's edge and then stop and pasture the
young grass at the edge of the forest.

Tainka cherished the morels which usually grew
among the poplar trees. She would prepare these delicate
mushrooms with young dill weed and rich farm cream.
After sitting and enjoying the scenery and fragrance at
the well, she would go to her favourite mushroom
patches and pick the morels. After everyone had enjoyed
the creamed mushrooms she would dry the remainder
and use them as a delicacy for the Christmas Eve supper.
This year, because of the rains that came early, the mushrooms grew in abundance. She gathered them in her
apron as she continued enjoying the tranquility of the
forest.

CHAPTER THIRTY-EIGHT

As Tainka continued to pick mushrooms, she heard a rustle in the bushes nearby. Roger began to bark and growl aggressively. Peering at a clearing deep in a willow grove, she saw a figure from the past emerging. The frame was of average height but the body was extremely obese. The head, which was capless, appeared to be balding. The voice—there was no mistaking the voice. It was Metro Soova! Roger barked viciously and growled even louder. Metro Soova was carrying a .22 calibre rifle, startling and scaring Tainka as he walked toward her. She tried to control her fear and the dog's barking, but it was impossible. Metro Soova stopped and looked at her. Finally he spoke. "Tainka Stry-Ker, is that you?" he asked.

"Yes, and you are Metro Soova . . . I haven't seen you for many years!" She was still very frightened. She would not mention his jail term. "When did you come home?" It seemed like an eternity since that dreadful night after Helenka's wedding.

"Well," he answered, "I was let out of Fort Saskatchewan three years ago . . . but I did not come home for a while. What happened to me was a very dreadful experience and it's because of those son-a-beech RCMPs and those other English bastards! I didn't mean to scare you. I was just looking to shoot some partridge," he reassured her as he continued walking in the opposite direction. He bid her farewell in the Ukrainian Christian tradition, *Slava na vikee*. Surprised, Tainka could not stop trembling. She quickly made her way toward the farmstead, feeling resentment that Metro Soova had invaded her privacy. She did not trust him, particularly carrying a gun.

At supper that night the main discussion was about Metro Soova. The table at Stry-Kers these days seated at least twelve people. There were six workmen and, with the family and Anastasia, it looked like a small Ukrainian wedding. It was a happy time of day, as the men liked to joke after a hard day's work. It was also a time for discussions of the day's events.

Mikhail and Paul, who usually knew what was going on in the area, were the first to comfort Tainka, their *Mamunia*, when she told them about her meeting with Metro Soova.

Mikhail spoke first. "Don't worry about Metro Soova any more . . . they say he is as gentle as a kitten these days," he told her.

"Yeah, they say he was castrated in Fort Saskatchewan!" added Paul. This was indeed a profound statement for this shy young man to make, particularly in the presence of the working girl, Anastasia, who blushed profusely at hearing this comment.

"Paul, where do you hear these things?" Evan asked.

"When we play cards at the Kaditzs," he replied.

"Is Louie Kaditz your newspaper?" Evan questioned Mikhail.

"Well, it's not only Louie Kaditz who hears things. There are also my friends, Fred Radjec and Paul Lupski."

"Billy Makovitsky also plays cards with us and he knows everything. He's always going to Edmonton and hearing things," Paul jumped in to defend Mikhail. "They say that Metro Soova was very obnoxious when he came to Fort Saskatchewan to serve his jail sentence, and when the other inmates found out about what he did to the Popilskys, and that their six children were left almost orphans, they decided to sentence Soova in their own way. They say one day six of them caught Metro Soova in the machine shop and used a chisel to castrate him.

Others say that they used an old sardine can lid," Paul concluded.

"Who knows what they used, but he is castrated, because Domka Soova herself told that story one day when she was talking to Annie Kaditz," Mikhail stated. He was surprised that his mother or father had not heard this before, as he was sure Katayna must have heard the incident described to her by Constable Rusty McLennan, her husband. But, on the other hand, he never heard Katayna gossip, least of all where it might concern Rusty's work.

One of the workmen piped up with some unsavoury comments. "Ooyee, Ooyee, that would hurt like hell . . . Oh hell, he can't have fun no more . . . I wonder if it's like castrating a bull?"

"Soova was worse than a bull!" This comment might have possibly come from Mikhail.

Tainka noticed how uncomfortable Anastasia was becoming and asked the men to stop. "That will be quite enough about Soova," she told the men. "Maybe he has changed . . . . he gave me a Christian farewell . . . maybe he has accepted God in his life." She shrugged. At least she was able to stop the Soova ridicule.

Another discussion followed. Evan announced that Father Kohut was retiring and moving to the Basilian Fathers' Retirement Home in Mundare. The father was now seventy-five and was becoming very forgetful. Franki, when serving at the altar, also noticed that Father Kohut had very bad bladder control. A small bucket had to be kept in his change room near the sacristy where he could relieve himself several times during Mass. It was much worse during the cold winter months when mass was conducted at St. Olga's. Franki, feeling very sorry for the old priest who had served faithfully, was relieved to hear of his retirement. A young priest who had just been ordained at Mundare was taking Father Kohut's place. His name was Father John Stepka.

CHAPTER THIRTY-NINE

It was 1937. Franki, now fifteen years old, had completed grade nine. He had become a very close friend of Father John Stepka. Father John, as everyone called him, was everyone's friend but he was particularly fond of Franki. As he knew Franki would be entering the seminary, a special kinship was developing. He began to prepare Franki for the demanding schedule that lay ahead.

There did not appear to be an end to the brutal Depression in Canada. Hard times were still upon most families living in and around Shady Hollow. There was just no money. A cord of firewood sold for a dollar, coal oil was thirty-five cents a gallon, and cattle prices at market were only two cents a pound. The Stry-Kers were paying only ninety-five cents for fifty pounds of flour. With a crew like the one they had to feed, much flour was consumed. Tainka's chore of baking bread in the large *peech* was taken over by Anastasia. Her bread was light and airy, with thick brown crusts sealing in the soft, tasty inner portion of the loaf. She kept the sourdough in a special way, in a spot that was not too hot where the starter dough would get overly sour, yet not too cool where the precious starter dough action could be killed. She always saved and used potato water to moisten the flour while making the dough.

Franki had gotten over his loneliness for Katayna after she married Constable Rusty McLennan and moved to Shady Hollow. It took about a year. Evan still was not speaking to Katayna or Rusty. Consequently, the couple did not visit often. Franki spent a few weekends at their lovely little home in Shady Hollow.

Now that Franki was preparing for the seminary, his mind was occupied with little else. He was beginning to interpret the Bible differently from some of the explanations given by Father Kohut. He often wondered if the old Father used to interpret the Bible to suit his own philosophies.

At supper one night, Franki made his announcement. He had talked to Father John a few weeks before about entering the seminary. The previous Sunday after mass, Father John told him that he had made all the arrangements, if it was agreeable with Evan and Tainka.

Tainka was ecstatic. "Of course this will be wonderful with me! After all, I promised you to God when you were born!" As far as she was concerned, the decision was made, so what was there to discuss, anyway?

Franki would be much taller than his other two brothers. He was almost six feet tall now at only fifteen, but he was as skinny as a beanpole. Tainka looked at him closely. Tears filled her eyes, because right there in front of her was a spitting image of her own father. Franki was a true Grosko. She could now see where his genes came from . . . from her own father who had drowned so many years ago. He had the same high forehead, same dark brown hair—almost black—and he had dark brown eyes, soft as a young fawn's, framed by thick lashes and eyebrows. His cheekbones were high and already there was evidence of facial hair, which would be dark. He would have a blue beard just like her dead father . . . why hadn't she seen this before?

Then an incredible guilt came over her. Why hadn't she given this child more attention? Why had she been so unfair to this boy? And yet now she wanted to send him away to the seminary.

Evan knew there was no hope in hell for him to even raise an objection. After all, he had let Tainka have her way with their youngest son since his birth. He also knew very well that she had had little to do with his rearing. Katayna was his surrogate mother. Katayna, who dared to defame the Stry-Ker name by getting married by a Justice of the Peace. He still fumed when he thought of it. It will serve her right, he thought smugly. She will never get to see her precious Franki when he enters the seminary. Maybe it's time she had her own children anyway, Evan thought unpleasantly.

"Evan? Evan! Why aren't you saying anything?" Tainka interrupted his thoughts. Evan looked up at her. "I have no objection to Franki becoming a priest in this family. Go, son, and may God be with you." He looked at his son directly. "I understand it's a very hard life, and you must be extremely dedicated before you can even hope of being ordained . . . ."

"Yes, *Tato*. I have been told that by Father Kohut and now by Father John. I'm expecting that it's not an easy life. I feel I have made the right decision," he assured him.

"When will they accept you?" Tainka asked,

"At the beginning of the next school term in September." Franki replied.

Mikhail and Paul looked at each other and smiled knowingly. They had always thought their youngest brother would be better off in his books and spiritual involvement. So both brothers also gave him their blessings. On July 12, the family once again travelled to Mundare for the celebrations of St. Peter and Paul. Franki took a special interest. Soon, this would be his new home.

The spring dance at White Sands Creek School was coming up at the end of May, and Mikhail and Paul asked Anastasia to come with them. Tainka was not sure which one of her sons Anastasia was more interested in, as she never said anything to indicate how she felt. On the night of the dance Mikhail, Paul, Anastasia, Evan, and Tainka went to the dance. Franki, already taking seriously his vow of celibacy and sacrifice, did not go.

Helenka's husband Joseph Pushinsky and his brothers once again provided the dance music. This time Joseph had his oldest son, Peter (named after his own father), playing in the band. He played the guitar. A natural, he played with his whole being and tapped his feet and smiled a lot at the crowd. Helenka was so proud of her eldest son. At eleven, he was indeed turning out to be a handsome lad. There was, however, no similarity to the Stry-Ker family; this one was definitely a Pushinsky. Her other sons, Joseph Jr. and Evan (named after her own dad), were a mixture of genes from the Stry-Kers and the Pushinskys. Emily, however, was a true Stry-Ker, or was she a Grosko? She looked like her Baba, Tainka.

Annie Kaditz was now heading the lunch committee. She was much more involved with school affairs since her sister Nadia Starchuk and her husband John both taught school here.

As the music started, it was shy Paul who Anastasia asked for a dance, much to Tainka's surprise. They danced practically all night, with the exception of one dance that she had with Mikhail. They ate lunch together and had the "home time" waltz together. It was quite evident that the two were very fond of one another. Tainka and Evan were very pleased. After all, both were Ukrainian and Catholic even though the Ozypkos belonged to another parish.

The relationship moved quickly. Anastasia, twenty-two, and Paul, twenty-four, had fallen in love. The wedding date was set for the last weekend in August, before Franki left for the seminary. A big wedding was planned, as it was quite obvious this would be the last wedding at the Stry-Kers. Mikhail, it appeared, would remain a bachelor along with his Polish and Romanian friends, Paul Lupski and Fred Radjec. Franki was to become a priest and wouldn't marry, so this wedding would be a huge celebration.

Anastasia was the Ozypkos' eldest child so her family was also planning a large celebration. Paul and Anastasia's wedding day was sunny and bright. Surely the gods were looking down on these two young people.

The couple exchanged their vows in the presence of old Father Kohut, who had baptized Paul. The young Father John also officiated and Franki provided all the altar assistance.

The *brama* (celebration gate) was decorated in spruce boughs. Many waxed paper roses and brightly coloured crepe paper streamers hung on the fresh boughs. Helenka's children and many others were grabbing streamers and running around the yard in happy games. Emily, Helenka and Peter's daughter, was once again a flower girl. Her Auntie Katayna sewed her a light-blue organdy dress. It made her look extremely feminine as the puffed sleeves had many tiny ruffles on them. The skirt was long and covered with ruffles from the waist to the floor. The wedding was a wonderfully happy event. Most people who had come to Helenka's wedding were also invited to this one. Tainka once again had Mikhail drive her to the White Sands Creek Reservation, and she invited Paul and Mary Tatonga. Cochees Sinclair had moved off the reserve, as had Louie Demers and Gabriel Laboucane. But the greatest surprise was that Paul and Mary Tatonga's lovely daughter, Teresa, who had been taken to the residential school, had been found. She had joined the sisters of the Sacred Heart and was a nursing sister living in Vancouver. Mary and Paul Tatonga got to see her once a year when she would come to the reserve for a visit.

The young couple received many gifts. Most of these household items such as fruit bowls and nappies were in pink and green Depression glass. They also received $210 in monetary contributions. It was a small fortune for these times . . . these depressed times. Paul and Mary Tatonga once again gave this couple two pairs of the most beautiful, colourful hand-beaded moccasins.

Paul and Anastasia were given the Borischuk quarter section by Tainka, who had been willed the property by Theodore and Pashka. They upgraded the Borischuk home. Katayna helped Anastasia by sewing pretty curtains for the windows. A new floor was installed, as dry rot had eaten through the original floor. There apparently had been insufficient air circulation in the original floor. The home was located only half a mile from the Stry-Kers, so Paul and Anastasia slept in their own home but continued to work at the Stry-Ker yard and eat their meals together with the entire crew.

Mikhail and Paul, who always got along well, decided to share their partnership on a 50-50 basis. Tainka loved Anastasia as though she was her own daughter. She reminded her in so many ways of her dearly departed Maria, who had died it seemed so many years ago . . . in actuality, only fifteen.

CHAPTER FORTY

It was September 10, 1937, and Franki was finally leaving Shady Hollow to enter the Basilian Order at Mundare. He could not sleep all night. He had a formidable feeling that morning. He awoke and walked into the farmyard at 5:00 a.m. Even the animals were still asleep. The faithful collie Roger was first to greet Franki. He stretched and yawned loudly. He started heading in the direction of the pasture, thinking that was where Franki was heading to fetch cows for milking. No, it was not. Franki was headed for the Clydesdale barn and pen. Franki loved these huge horses of *Tato's*.

Zoria and *Zolota*, the first two mares Evan ever bought, were still alive even though he had stopped breeding them. He felt they should have as luxurious a life as possible in their retirement. They were the first two mares, which started his stable, and they deserved preferential treatment. Shascha, his first stallion, had long before been sold as Evan wished to have fresh blood in the operation. But every succeeding stallion was named Shascha; Shascha I, II, III, IV, and now V. In fact there were two Shaschas at the stable at present. Runty, the original teaser stallion, had been gelded since and was used as a pony whenever Helenka's boys came for a visit or for holidays.

This morning Franki wished particularly to say goodbye to *Zoria* and *Zolota*. Their necks were so thick that he could hardly hug them, but he tried. He nuzzled their velvety noses. These Clydesdale mares were beautiful; they had the blond markings usually identified with the Clydesdale breed. Their manes, tail hair and fetlocks were almost white, whereas the rest of their bodies were a dark tan. Evan always kept these two favourites extremely well groomed. "Oh, what beautiful creatures you are," Franki thought. "If I wasn't going to become a priest I'd take over *Tato*'s operation. After all, Mikhail and Paul do not care for these big horses." However, that was not to be. He was leaving for Mundare and the priesthood.

Soon the morning farm chores were done and everyone got dressed in their Sunday best. Evan, Tainka, Anastasia, Paul, and Mikhail rode in one car. Franki rode in Rusty and Katayna's car. Katayna was very sad this morning, as her precious Franki was leaving her. She knew she would miss him very much and would see very little of him after he entered the seminary.

After attending Mass at St. Peter and St. Paul's church, the family drove Franki to St. Basil's Basilian Monastery. As they drove up to the stone stairs of the monastery they noticed the large double oak doors, each over ten feet high. The doors opened and the friendly form of a tall, dark-haired man in a black cassock welcomed them. He wore the collar of a priest and introduced himself as Father Bill.

Franki collected his few personal belongings and kissed his mother, Tainka, and Katayna goodbye. He took very little with him, but among his sparse personal belongings were the red coral beads. These were the beads that he had found among his dead sister Maria's possessions in the old wooden *scranya*. He always meant to give them to someone special, maybe Katayna. He hated to part with them because these beads held so much meaning for him. He always wished he had met Maria, having heard so many wonderful things about her. Maybe the beads were just a little part of Maria. He always seemed close to her through the beads. He hugged his brothers, Paul and Mikhail, as well as Anastasia, Rusty, and his *Tato*. Escorted by Father Bill, he walked beyond the oak doors and looked back over his shoulder one final time as the large oak doors slammed shut.

CHAPTER FORTY-ONE

Franki was taken to the dormitory where he would be sharing a room with twenty other young men. They were known as monks. There were forty-five seminarians at Mundare this day.

The dormitory was built in 1922. The rooms contained high ceilings, plain walls adorned only by a crucifix, and several icons. The spartan metal single beds were located close together, similar to those found in overcrowded military barracks.

Each monk was provided with a night table that more than adequately kept the few personal belongings he had. The young monk's daily attire consisted of a simple black cassock.

Franki was placed between two other fifteen-year-old boys, Oleksa from Myrnam and Donalo from Mundare. The monks were grouped according to rank . . . the number of years spent at the monastery. Father Bill was their chief instructor and took special care in outlining the schedule that was established for Franki.

Since he was only in grade nine, he would have to complete his high school. Along with academic courses, he would take others specializing in theology.

Each monk was expected to specialize in some trade such as carpentry, shoemaking, printing, or tailoring. In 1933 a farm had been developed and some monks—up to ten—used to work on the farm and specialize in this area. Franki was not interested in farming, nor was he good at it. So he chose to specialize in carpentry.

A month went by. Franki could not believe the rigorous schedule the monastery demanded of its monks.

Every morning they would rise at 5:00 a.m. and were allowed one half-hour to wash and use the outdoor toilet facilities. At 5:30 the young men would descend the stairs of their dormitories and enter the chapel on the main floor. A short prayer of Angeles followed. After the prayer of Angeles the ceremony of the Matins prayer would follow for about an hour. The daily mass would then follow at 7:00 a.m. Mass usually took up to forty-five minutes and personal prayers continued in the chapel until 8:00 a.m. The monks would then troop to the dining room for breakfast. The dining room was a very plain large room with old rectangular wooden tables and worn wooden chairs. The only wall adornments were a large wooden crucifix hung on the long wall facing most of the tables, with icons of the Virgin Mary and St. Basil hung on either side of the cross. St. Basil was the patron saint of the seminary.

The meal was very sparse, taken in silence and consisting of milk and boiled buckwheat or oatmeal. No eggs or butter were served. Everyone participated in cleaning up the dishes. Some free time was allowed for the monks until 9:00 a.m. When school began, the first in Franki's group were memory classes. The purpose of this was to learn to memorize the mass . . . countless prayers . . . even passages of the Bible. These classes were followed by a series of others on liturgy, spirituality, church music, and formal Ukrainian language courses.

At 11:30 a.m. all monks trekked back to the chapel for another church service and period of reflection until 12 noon. Franki could not see why there were so many meditation and reflection periods, as he felt this tough schedule was designed for an unusual human being . . . one with complete devotion and dedication to God. It was only one month and he was already wondering what had compelled him to devote himself to God. Had he made the right choice? "Oh, God," he thought. "Why am I already thinking so negatively?" Much of his trouble was that he missed Katayna. He missed his family . . . and the Clydesdales. He was simply homesick.

The noon meal would follow, again as sparse as possible. There was none of his mother's or Anastasia's fancy cream dishes, *holuptsi*, or that wonderful bread Anastasia could bake. He was certainly becoming homesick, as were Oleksa and Donalo, although none would complain.

After lunch, when the dishes were cleaned up, they were actually allowed forty-five minutes for recreation. They were allowed to sing, talk, play checkers or other simple board games. Cards were not allowed as this could lead to development of the vice of gambling.

After recreation, every monk went to his designated place to do manual labour. Some tended to the garden; others cared for the animals or went to the printing shop. Oleksa chose to work on the farm, as he loved the animals. Franki and Donalo worked in the carpentry shop. Brother Sylvester, who held almost the same stature as a priest but had never been ordained, taught carpentry skills. Brother Sylvester had a marvellous sense of humour and used it effectively. He was also one of the finest finishing carpenters in the region. Both boys enjoyed his class most of all. They worked there until 4:00 p.m. Tea break usually followed, and at 4:30 p.m. everyone prepared for vespers, which took about one hour. Reflection period followed, yet again, and at 6:00 p.m. supper was served. At this time conversation was allowed. The supper meal was the big meal of the day and meat and eggs were served, albeit in small quantities. Whenever a lent was indicated on the calendar, which was at least four times a year, including the forty-day pre-Easter lent and on Fridays, no meat was served. During these periods of lent, the meals were not only meatless but also dairyless.

Academic study period took place at 7:30 p.m. until 8:30 p.m., followed by a fifteen-minute period for examination of one's conscience. At 8:45 p.m. everyone once again went to chapel for night prayers to end the day. This was followed by personal hygiene in preparation for bed. By this time of the day every monk was so tired because of the early morning start that snoring in the dorms was heard shortly after heads hit the pillows.

CHAPTER FORTY-TWO

For one year Franki was not allowed any communication with his family. Oh, how he missed everyone, especially Katayna. If only she knew what a tough life he was living . . . he was certain she would certainly not approve. He was feeling so sorry for himself that he felt a teardrop sliding down his cheekbone. His cheeks had been hollowing more and more each day in the past few months.

He had lost what he thought was about ten pounds since his arrival. There just wasn't anything rich and delicious to eat, food like his *Mamunia* used to prepare. There simply was no food served at the seminary which would allow anyone to gain weight. He was fully grown now, and at sixteen his height had soared to six feet two inches. Most of him, however, was legs. He looked gangly and his complexion was very pale. His normally dark-toned skin looked anemic. But still he persisted. He was going to become a priest if it killed him.

Father Bill and Brother Sylvester both noticed the change in Franki, and his appearance worried them both. They summoned him into Father Bill's office and inquired about his health.

Father Bill was first to speak. "Franki, are you eating? It appears to us that you've lost a lot of weight since you came here . . . you know that if your physical body is hurting, so will your spiritual body."

"Pretty soon the hammer in the workshop will be swinging you. How can I send you on that fencing detail? The sledge hammer will swing you!" Brother Sylvester attempted some humour, but received no response from

Franki. They could see young Franki was suffering from a chronic depression. They took him to the doctor at St. Mary's Immaculate Hospital in town. The doctor confirmed that his red blood corpuscles were very low and that he was, indeed, anemic. He prescribed a blood-building tonic but could see that much of Franki's problem was psychological, not physical. The doctor suggested that the boy be sent home for a leave. When Father Bill suggested a visit to Shady Hollow, Franki was delighted and chose the week during Ukrainian Christmas. Within a month, by taking the tonic and anticipating his visit home, Franki's colour had begun to return.

The same gruelling schedule at the seminary continued but it seemed to be so much easier to accept . . . easier because of his pending visit to his home in Shady Hollow when he would see his beloved family. Franki was excelling in his academic learning and writing examinations at the grade eleven level. His carpentry skills were also becoming impressive. He had built two small round plant tables, one for his mother and one for Katayna. These tables were to be given to the ladies for Christmas presents. The tables were meant to hold their favourite scented geranium plants.

Since his arrival, ten boys had left because they could not take the demanding schedule. Some ran away from the dormitory during the night; some just told Father Bill that they could not continue. Boys were free to leave any time, if this was their desire. Those who could last this gruelling schedule for three years could move to the next plateau—the level of a Postulant. At this point, acceptance had to be approved by the Order of St. Basil after an evaluation of the candidate's performance over the previous three years. The most important factor at this point was that the candidates show a keen desire to continue.

Christmas 1938 was one of the happiest Christmases in the memory of the Stry-Kers. Everyone of any significance to the family would be attending the celebration. Tainka told everyone that her son, the priest, was coming home for Christmas. She made Evan promise that he would be civil to Katayna, maybe even to Rusty. Evan was also sincerely looking forward to seeing his youngest son. In fact, he was very excited. He hitched two of his prize Clydesdale mares to his new fancy democrat and drove into Shady Hollow. As usual he went into the favourite meeting place at Makovitsky's store.

"Hello, Billy. I would like to order my usual . . . one ring of *kobaska* and a loaf of bread . . . one bottle of orange crush pop in the brown bottle," Evan ordered as he looked around the store. "Where is everyone?"

"Well, Mr. Stry-Ker, didn't you hear, most of the men are gone to the Ukrainian National Hall. There is a meeting. Some kind of man from Saskatchewan, name of Tommy Douglas, is speaking about a new political party, a party which will look after all people and treat everyone, especially the poor, in a fair manner. Fairness to all!" exclaimed Billy Makovitsky.

As Evan sat by himself in the hospital-green booth, he had time to reflect. "What is happening in this country?" he wondered. "Will this depression ever end?" But on the other hand, the Stry-Kers had managed to prosper beyond his wildest imagination. There was lots of cheap labour and lots of cheap land for him and his sons to buy. Then, in his mind, he heard Billy's words over and over again: "Fairness to all . . . fairness to all!"

He looked around Makovitsky's well-stocked store, at the ornate tin ceiling painted a dark marine blue (mostly to hide the housefly specks), and at the freshly oiled floor. He saw the huge potbellied heater that stood in the middle of the store. He noted just how well stocked the shelves were with groceries, dry goods, fabrics, shoes, clothing, and hardware needed for farm work.

"Billy, tell me honestly. Has the depression hurt you and your family business?" Evan asked.

After much thought, Billy responded. "Mr. Stry-Ker, I can say honestly that we Makovitskys have never suffered much, before or during the depression. But when I look at the books and see how much credit we have given to so many families around here, I can see this suffering. Some of these people will never pay us back because they can't. Their families have no food to eat, so how do we expect to be paid? It's a terrible time in Canada, Mr. Stry-Ker . . . maybe not for you, but it is for most other people." Billy shook his head at the situation.

About an hour passed. Evan had long ago finished eating the *kobaska* and bread, on which he spread mustard liberally . . . he had also finished drinking his Orange Crush pop. Soon the men were all coming into the store, after the meeting had finished at the Ukrainian National Hall. These men lived in the area and were of various ethnic origins: Romanian, Polish, Finnish, English, and Ukrainian. Even Doctors Liston and Allison were there. The Finnish farmers who had settled around the Radway region had brought Tommy Douglas, the young social activist, to Shady Hollow.

Just then, Tommy Douglas himself walked into the store. He was a brilliant young preacher whose foremost purpose in life was fairness and righteousness toward his fellow man.

As he talked, Evan could see what charisma he possessed. Everyone listened and hung on to his every word. Evan had been a Social Credit supporter of William Aberhart, but as he listened to Tommy Douglas speaking, he thought there was much sense in what this young preacher was saying.

Many of his neighbours could not afford to see a doctor, even though Doctors Liston and Allison also carried many accounts that were not paid. Tommy Douglas talked about a scheme whereby there would be a moratorium on banks, where they could not just order people off their land for non-payment of loans. After all, how could you pay when nothing was being produced? Furthermore, were people to die because they could not afford medical treatment? People were cheering on Mr. Douglas and the greatest "rah, rahs" came from Billy Makovitsky.

As Evan left Shady Hollow that day, his mind leapt back to the old country and to his childhood—to the bitter despair which he had left behind so many years ago. Why, it was already thirty-five years ago! His childhood had been about as dismal as any child's could be. He couldn't remember his mother. After all, he had been only three years old when she died. His father died when Evan was twelve, but he hadn't been any support to Evan during those twelve years. He could never remember receiving a hug from any of his family members. He had grown up with no affection shown to him and he had never seen a doctor until he went to see Pun Doctor Illia in Sosnitcha—and he wasn't a real doctor anyway. His brother Yatsko had tried to rear Evan as best as he could, but he had offered no love or affection. How could he, when he had never received any himself? At twenty, Yatsko had joined the Austrian army and Evan had to fend for himself. Evan had been fourteen then. He had almost starved to death. Even though he had tried to fend for himself by working for widows and old maids in the village, he could not manage. So his emaciated body had become wracked with scurvy and fever, until a concerned parishioner brought him to the priest's house. The parishioner had pleaded with the priest to take Evan into his employ and the priest had agreed. Evan's body was full of lice, as he slept in the hayloft and washed very infrequently. He did have a little food to eat, but only enough to barely survive.

In the winter, when the cold came, the concerned parishioner asked the priest to buy Evan a *koozooshok* (a fur vest). Evan remembered bitterly what the insensitive priest's response had been. "Did he earn a *koozooshok* from me? I think not!"

In the months following, Evan heard the priest's response over and over again in his mind, so in the next few months he had stolen eggs from the priest's huge supply and sold them on his own, in order to buy himself a *koozooshok*. Otherwise, he would have died of hypothermia. The old priest was so insensitive and unobservant toward to his poor urchin servant that he had not even noticed the new *koozooshok* which Evan wore. Oh, what bitter memories these were.

As the democrat bumped along the road to the Stry-Kers' homestead, the words "fairness to all" rang in Evan's mind over and over again. Then his thoughts jumped to Yatsko, his brother, who was still in the old country. Yatsko had survived the First World War. It was now also thirty-five years since Evan had seen his brother. The Stry-Kers got about one letter a year from one of the villagers of Sosnitcha, in the old country, a letter which Yatsko dictated as he was illiterate, as illiterate as Evan had been when he came to Canada. Evan had now become basically literate in the English language. He had had to learn in order to serve effectively on the Municipal Council and School Trustee Board and to keep up with what was going on around him in his adopted country. He loved Canada with all his heart because it was a country that had given him and his family a new start in life and countless opportunities. The last letter from Yatsko had mentioned that there were dangerous winds blowing politically, and he wondered if Evan would sponsor his immigration to Canada.

Evan began the process through his Member of Parliament in Ottawa, assisted by his Liberal friend, Mike Mikalik.

CHAPTER FORTY-THREE

Mikhail, Tainka, and Katayna drove across the North Saskatchewan River, south to Mundare, to pick Franki up for the Christmas holidays. They thought it was unusual for Franki to have a leave, as they had been told they could not see him for at least two more months, when his year would be served. However, it was a bonus and that was all that mattered. The car rolled along past the original Pakan Post Office, which was now only used for the local people. The Stry-Kers received their mail in Shady Hollow. They rolled further, onto the winter road over the frozen North Saskatchewan River.

Finally, Tainka got enough courage to ask Katayna the question. "How is Rusty treating you, my daughter?" She was surely expecting to hear Katayna had received a few beatings because, after all, he was an Englishman and not even a Catholic.

Much to her surprise, Katayna responded, "*Mamunia*, in all my dreams and imagination I could never be happier. I sincerely hope Rusty and I could have twelve babies and that they are all as perfect as he is!" Katayna had never been more sincere.

"Well, daughter, that makes me very happy. I can honestly say I was totally wrong about him . . . I am sorry about prejudging him so." Tainka remained silent after that.

Mikhail broke the silence. "Last night, when we played cards at the Kaditzs we heard something that you should maybe tell Rusty," he told Katayna. "Last night they said that Metro Soova is going to shoot Rusty and Corporal Seymour both together!"

"Why? Why? And who are 'they' that said that? Who are 'they'?!" Katayna demanded hysterically. The thought that anyone could harm Rusty was intolerable. Tainka tried to comfort her but to no avail. "Who said that, Mikhail? Who said that?" Katayna insisted desperately.

By this time, Mikhail was sorry he had even mentioned the conversation from the night before. "Louie Kaditz said it. He and Metro Soova see each other sometimes on business."

"God damn Metro Soova! God damn Louie Kaditz! How dare they even discuss my Rusty. He was only doing his job when Soova was arrested. You know that, Mikhail. You saw what he did to Milka and Todour Popilsky. Was he supposed to let him carry on . . . carry on in his cruel and sadistic manner? Mikhail, how can you have such terrible friends?" Katayna demanded, now in a rage.

Mikhail tried to defend himself, but to no avail. "Katayna, I don't pick your friends or your husbands, so don't you pick mine. Louie Kaditz is a fine man. He's hurt no one. He gives money to poor people all the time, and that's more than some of your friends do, or some others around this place!" Mikhail hardly ever lost his temper. He had almost blurted out "or your husband" but had restrained himself . . . and was pleased he was able to do so.

"All right, everybody, that's enough!" Tainka cut in. "Christmas is coming and we are going to pick up your brother, Franki, so let's try to be civil for his sake, if nothing else!" Her heart was heavy with this news that Mikhail had just given them, because she knew that Metro Soova was a vindictive man. All the years that she had known him, he was always sadistic and evil. She had thought that with his being castrated and doing prison time it would have made him a more mild-mannered person. But from what she had just heard, obviously not.

Neither Katayna nor Mikhail said another word. Soon the car rolled up to the tall double oak doors at the monastery of St. Basil in Mundare. A few minutes later Mikhail knocked on one of the doors, and out stepped Franki, holding the two lovely tables he had built for his mother and Katayna. Both women were astonished at how much taller Franki had gotten and also at how very thin and frail his body had become.

"Franki, Franki!" Katayna ran up to the tall beanpole of a boy. "I have missed you so very, very much!" She hugged him for a long period. She could feel his rib bones as she hugged him.

Now it was Tainka's turn. She also hugged him and could feel her son's ribcage. She was immediately concerned. "Aren't they feeding you here? You're just skin and bones, just like that old Debba we used to have, before she died!" She was trying to make light of the situation. Debba was the first cow the Stry-Kers had owned when they came to Canada.

Mikhail, still upset about his altercation with Katayna, just shook Franki's hand vigorously. The ride home was fascinating, as Franki told them about the seminary and how much he had to learn. Both women could detect that the hard and disciplined monastery life was difficult for Franki.

Christmas celebrations were wonderful. All the Yaworskys from Radway came. Helenka, Peter, and all their four children came. It was very evident that Emily was *Baba* Tainka's favourite grandchild. Evan was also proud to be the *Gido* to this lovely young girl with bright blue eyes and naturally curly raven hair. And Rusty and Katayna arrived. This was the first year that Evan relinquished his duties at the customary greeting and asked his youngest son, the soon-to-be priest, to take his place. Franki performed a beautiful and meaningful greeting.

Evan, Tainka, and all the others who spoke Ukrainian responded. Franki ended his greeting. "Let us all live with Jesus in our hearts all year long, let us help our fellow man, love our neighbours, and hold no vengeance toward anyone. After all, vengeance is not ours to take. We leave it to our Heavenly Father. In the name of the Father, the Son, and the Holy Spirit, Amen." He crossed himself three times with three fingers . . . the index, thumb, and forefinger to symbolize the Holy Trinity.

Evan now heard another repetition of words. "Vengeance is not mine to take . . . vengeance is not mine to take . . . vengeance is not mine to take." With that, immediately following the meal, Evan went over to Rusty and made his apologies.

"Roosty, I didn't know how to say dis nicely in Hinglish, bot I vont to apulidize for beeying sooch a stewpid fool . . . I be wary soury!" Rusty and Katayna felt surely their dreams had been fulfilled and that life after this would be marvellous. Katayna had never before heard her father apologize to anyone.

The ten-day holiday did Franki a lot of good. The colour came back to his cheeks and he gained a few pounds on Tainka's good, rich cooking. He was beginning to look like a handsome young man. During his stay a very special event occurred. Anastasia gave birth to a beautiful baby boy. They named him Evan after *Gido* Evan, as this was the first Stry-Ker to carry on the proud name. Little Evan was also blond and dark-eyed like his old grandfather. The baptism took place on the third day after Christmas, the feast of St. Stephen. Paul and Anastasia were extremely happy parents and beamed proudly at their baby. Uncle Mikhail was the proud Godfather and Anastasia's younger sister, Mary, was the Godmother.

Father John enjoyed baptism and wedding ceremonies most of all in his priestly duties. These were happy times and he revelled in telling humorous stories during his sermons, where he made people laugh. This occasion was no exception, after using holy water and anointing oils on tiny Evan. Mikhail was as proud a Godfather as you could find anywhere. He knew he would establish a strong bond with this little boy, a lifetime bond if he could. Franki marvelled at Father John's ability to hold a crowd's interest. This young priest was certainly a natural to his calling by God. If only he could be the same. "Oh God, oh God, help me to be worthy of you," he prayed sincerely.

Then Evan made the announcement that his brother, Yatsko, would be immigrating to Canada in a short while, and he was certain he would join them all for the next Christmas. Evan was more excited about his brother's arrival than he would have thought possible.

Franki returned to Mundare for another year and a half. It was a year and a half which he did not enjoy. The rigorous schedule was killing his spirit and he knew that another four years before he could be ordained as a priest would surely be the death of him. No matter how sincerely he prayed for God to guide him, he just could not continue. So, when the opportunity came for him to choose whether he wished to continue as a Postulant, he reluctantly declined. It was a decision he made all by himself. He had now completed his grade twelve studies and was a top-notch carpenter. He felt he could go into the world and make his own way. But how was he to break this news to his mother and father? This would be the worst hell that he'd ever experienced in his entire life.

Franki met with Father Bill before his departure from Mundare. He had always had a deep respect for Father Bill, who was in charge of the monastery.

"Franki, my son, you have been an exemplary student here in Mundare and I respect the decision you have made not to continue to our next level. The life of a Postulant does not get any easier . . . the calling must be genuine, otherwise you cannot succeed. Franki," he continued, "you are looking for something and it doesn't appear that it's here at the seminary. Perhaps if you leave for a while and search out there, your answers will come. Perhaps you will return and pick up where you left off. But, remember, if you take the marriage vows you cannot return, as you are well aware at the Basilian Fathers' vow of celibacy. My son, do you have any questions before you leave? By the way, where are you going?"

"Father Bill, I do not know. I can't go home to Shady Hollow because I'm sure my mother and yes, I guess my father as well, will surely disown me. After all, my mother has lived her entire life since I was born in a promise she made to God, and that was that I would become a priest and serve God. Honestly, Father Bill, I have tried so desperately to do so, but I just can't at this time. I know how heartbroken she'll be . . . *Tato* also . . ."

"Franki, Franki, God has never meant that you should live your life to satisfy someone else. He gave you intelligence and a will. He put you on this earth for a purpose and at this time your purpose is not to become a priest. It is obviously something else, but go out there and search for what it is. Your mother was also put here for a purpose. Perhaps one of her purposes was to give birth to you, for you will make your way in life. I can see you will help many people as life goes on. As well, you will learn many lessons. Hopefully, these lessons will result in serving your fellow man in ways other than being a priest. God understands—you know that he does. He's loving and giving and he will help your mother get over this situation. She made a promise about your life. She had no right to do that because children are only loaned to parents and God calls in the loan any time he feels it's appropriate. Franki, my son, do not ever feel guilty in life for someone else's decisions . . . for your own, perhaps, you have that responsibility, but not for anyone else's. Remember that, Franki. Now, son, where is it you are going?" Father Bill genuinely loved and respected this young man, and as he studied his handsome face he saw the strong determination in his eyes. Yes, he will do well out there . . . I know he will, he thought.

Franki had only a small knapsack for his personal belongings. This he hiked over his left shoulder. Father Bill slung his strong arm over Franki's right shoulder as he led him toward the vestibule, past the beautiful icon of Jesus holding his exposed heart, and out the tall double oak doors of the St. Basil's Monastery at Mundare.

"Goodbye, my son, good luck, and God bless you in your future travels," said Father Bill. It was a genuine blessing and farewell; Franki saw tears glistening in the Father's eyes. His destination was not discussed further. This was just as well because when the Stry-Kers came asking about Franki, Father Bill could tell them with sincerity that he did not know where he had gone.

CHAPTER FORTY-FOUR

Totally bewildered, Franki walked the wooden sidewalks of Mundare, for how long he could not say, until he eventually sat down in front of a confectionery store. He had ten dollars to his name, ten dollars that Father Bill must have slipped into his pocket when he gave him a big bear hug, just before he opened the huge oak doors. Franki was delighted because this would help him. He formulated a plan. Edmonton is where he would go. The only person that he had heard about there was Rosie Soova, at The Pearl's Oyster.

As he walked past the Mundare Hotel he heard the sound of barrels being rolled down a ramp somewhere nearby. Approaching the noise he noticed a big, burly man, dressed warmly, throwing empty beer kegs onto a new Ford three-ton truck. He was perspiring heavily. The back of the box was covered with a heavy canvass.

"Hello, mister, do you need help?" Franki asked.

"Hallo," a gruff voice replied. "You beechoo, dis somanabich vork is too much fur me alraddy!"

He sounded very much like Franki's *Tato*, Evan, so Franki spoke to him politely in Ukrainian. "My name is Franki, and I'd be happy to help you. I'm on my way to Edmonton."

The man grinned widely and replied in Ukrainian. "That suits me just fine. You help me with loading these empty kegs, then I still have some live chickens to pick up in crates, and then I'm driving to Edmonton. You may come along. By the way, my name is Bill Stawnychy. I'm the freight man in these parts."

It took them another two hours to finish loading the truck. Then they were bound for Edmonton. Bill was very familiar with the route, so he kept on talking to Franki without having to watch the road very carefully.

"Where are you going in Edmonton? Maybe it's on my way." Bill appeared genuinely interested.

"Well, I hope it is, because I don't know Edmonton at all. This is only my second visit to that city. I'm going to a place called The Pearl's Oyster. Rosie Soova lives there," explained Franki.

With that, Bill gave Franki a strange, even suspicious look. "You know Rosie Soova?"

"No, I've never met her. She was a friend of my sister, Maria, who died many years ago," Franki replied.

"So, so, you know nothing about Rosie or The Pearl's Oyster?" Bill questioned and appeared as though he certainly knew something about either Rosie Soova, The Pearl's Oyster, or both.

"Why, Mr. Bill? Do you know Rosie Soova?" Franki asked him.

"Oh yes, yes, I know her, but more important, I know where the house is. It's not far out of my way. I'll drive you there. As a matter of fact, a friend of mine who also owns a truck lives there. His name is Johnny Makar. You'll probably meet him there."

After two hours on a bumpy, poorly maintained road, Bill's truck rolled into the outskirts of Edmonton, into a little village called Beverly. Soon after passing through the outskirts of Edmonton, Franki could smell the acrid odour and smoke from many coal-burning stoves and furnaces. He saw streetlights, as it was now five o'clock and already darkness was falling. As the truck rolled further it got them to 96 Street. Mr. Bill turned left and headed south toward 107 Avenue, where The Pearl's Oyster was located. He stopped the truck in front of a beautiful three-storey house painted white with dark green trimmings around the windows and doors. The roof was adorned with cedar shingles and painted black. All along the front of the house, on the main level, was a screened-in veranda. It appeared abandoned as it was only used during the summer months. There was a white picket fence around the perimeter of the yard. The home looked well kept. Right by the entrance gate hung a big three-foot by five-foot sign shaped like a huge seashell. The sign read The Pearl's Oyster. All the letters were made in forms of tiny white pearls on a sky-blue background.

Mr. Bill had immediately taken a liking to this young passenger of his. He could see that Franki was apprehensive to go in alone, so he volunteered to go with him. "Hey, young man, do you want me to come in with you?"

"Would you, please, Mr. Bill. I'd be so grateful," replied Franki, relieved.

"Okay, come already, I can only go in and out because these chickens will freeze to death and the Farmers' Market will be very mad at me." Bill's Ukrainian wasn't perfect either.

Franki jumped out of the truck and followed Bill. He knocked on the door and a beautiful, very made-up woman answered. "Yes," she said gently. "Who are you looking for?" Bill began to feel uncomfortable and switched to speaking English. "Ve be lauking for the Rosie and if she be not hoom than is Johnny Makar hoom?"

"Why yes, Rosie is at home. Who may I say is calling?" The young lady had a gorgeous, voluptuous figure. Her bust was pushed up so that the cleavage could be seen immediately from beneath her form-fitting, long green velvet gown. Her delicate skin reminded Franki of *Tato's*

Clydesdale horse's noses . . . soft like velvet. As they were ushered into the parlour, Franki was flabbergasted. The contrast between this room and the sparse surroundings at the Mundare Monastery were phenomenal. All the front three windows were covered in elegant Chinese red velvet drapes with deep, rich swags fringed in wispy black tassels. The wooden furniture was rich and opulent mahogany. The sofas and chairs were covered in elegant beige tapestry upholstery. The little tables were a highly polished, rich mahogany wood. Lovely landscape paintings in rich golden gilded frames adorned the walls. A huge gramophone stood in one corner. The walls were covered with wallpaper which resembled a moiré taffeta material. The floors were highly polished oak covered in luxurious India area rugs. There was no sign of a crucifix or any saintly icons. There was a wood and coal-burning fireplace, which occupied the north wall of the room. It was masoned in clinker brick. The bricks were so intensely baked that the clay had turned into a glass-like substance, a mistake by the brickyard, but the mistake turned out well for affluent homeowners seeking clinker bricks for their fireplaces. Franki had never in his life seen anything as beautiful as this room . . . as this whole house.

Suddenly, in burst a tiny, pretty bundle of energy. In her stocking feet, she measured about five feet two inches in height, but she was wearing the highest heels that her tiny size-six foot could stand. Her hair was blonde, almost an orange blonde. Franki wondered why there were so many different colours of blonde on women. Her face was heavily made up—lots of lipstick and rouge—and her eyebrows were tweezed, creating pencil-thin brows. Even though she had a pretty face, the beauty she possessed lay primarily in her incredible personality.

"Woo, who do we have here, not one but two handsome gentlemen!" she exclaimed as she entered the room.

"Wait a minute, don't I know you?" Her comments were directed at Mr. Bill. "Yes, of course, you're the truck driver friend of Johnny, aren't you?"

"You be corract . . . and dis hair is Franki Stry-Ker from the Shady Hollow . . ."

Rosie turned white as a sheet. She was speechless for a few minutes. Then, regaining her composure, she ran up to Franki. "You're the youngest child of the Stry-Kers? But I thought you were studying to be a priest?!" she told him excitedly.

Franki was shocked at how much she knew. "Yes, I was. That is a long story and I'd be pleased to tell you if you wish to hear, but . . ." he hesitated momentarily. "I would like to stay here for a few days. I don't know anyone else in Edmonton . . . please, may I?"

"Oh, how rude of me, it's none of my business. Of course, you may stay in my house for as long as you wish. I've been sending invitations to your family for years . . . since Maria died, but no one has ever come." That wasn't quite the truth. However, who was she hurting by saying this, anyway? With that she ran up to him and gave him a big hug around his waist, as she only reached his shoulder. Franki liked Rosie right away. He knew she would become his lifelong friend if she wanted it that way.

Mr. Bill watched in silence as Rosie turned to him. "Can I get you a drink or some tea?"

"No, no . . . tanks wery so, Rosie, mebe unoder time. I have it chickens in mine trock and they be freezing to dead, so tanks. I be late fur the farmarski markit and to pick up beer kegs for Mundare Hotal from Bohemian Maid Brewery." Bill then turned to Franki to bid him farewell in Ukrainian. Franki expressed his deep gratitude and told Bill that he would never forget his kindness.

"Welcome to my house, young Stry-Ker. I can't believe you are Maria's baby brother! How old are you?" Rosie asked Franki when Bill was gone.

"I'm eighteen years old. I was born in 1922, six months after Maria died," replied Franki.

"Yes, yes, so much happened in 1922, some happy, but mostly sad, " Rosie lamented. If only she knew that Franki had read Maria's letters so many years ago, the letters that were so carefully put away in the old *scranya* from the old country. So neatly folded by Maria herself and kept in a special canvas pouch. Franki's heart was heavy for this little, friendly, warm bundle of energy. He wondered how many people knew what she was hiding.

"Come on, come on, young Stry-Ker. What do you want me to call you? Frank or Franki?" She spoke very rapidly, like there was not much time and she would have to say things in a hurry.

"Most people call me Franki, and I prefer that to Frank." He was so thankful to God that someone like Rosie had come into his life.

"Come, come, you must meet the rest of our little family at The Pearl's Oyster," she said as she led him into the large kitchen with white, ceiling-high built-in cupboards. There at the table was Cissy, her skin as black as highly polished ebony. Cissy was about five feet five inches tall, but no doubt she would grow another inch, as she was still young. Her dark chocolate-coloured eyes resembled an innocent fawn. Her teeth were white as snow and they were straight and even. She had a beautiful smile. As she looked at Rosie and smiled warmly, two pretty dimples showed in both cheeks. Cissy was rolling out a piecrust, getting it ready to make apple pie for supper. This was the first time in his life that Franki had actually seen a Negro, although he had read about them and seen pictures. The black Madonna icon came to mind . . . in the church of St. Peter and Paul at Mundare. He could not help staring at her. Rosie introduced them.

"This is Cissy. Cissy, this is Franki, a family friend from the place where I was born." She did not mention Shady Hollow by name. And then, as if on cue, in walked Veronica, who had answered the door when Franki and Mr. Bill came in earlier. Behind her were Helen and Lily. All three women were beautiful, with outstanding figures, yet they were all highly made-up. Franki thought that unusual, as women at Shady Hollow only used a little make-up for attending church or when they went to dances or weddings. Never had he seen women with such heavy make-up.

"Girls, meet the new member of our family." Rosie sounded proud to be introducing Franki. It appeared she too was developing a kinship toward him.

"Come, come Franki, I'll take you to your room," she said as she led the way, up one flight of stairs. He could see this level was as well decorated and furnished as the first level. They went up to the third level and there in the southeast corner was a tiny but well-appointed bedroom.

"The bathroom is down the hall. You'll have to share it with Johnny and Cissy. He lives up here and so does Cissy. You each have your own bedrooms. Veronica, Lily, Helen, and I live on the second level. We eat and entertain on the main level only. Franki, you can wash up and maybe take a little rest. That is, only if you want to. I will never tell you what you should do! Supper won't be served for at least another hour—you saw Cissy was just rolling out the crust for apple pie. I'd say maybe another two hours." Rosie turned and continued to talk. "I'm so glad you're here to visit me!" With that she turned and left the room.

Franki ambled over to the southeast window and looked out at the sights that faced him. He could see the

North Saskatchewan River valley at a distance and the activity on the streets of Edmonton . . . cars and delivery trucks, even some horse-drawn drays going about their business. There was much more activity than in Mundare or Shady Hollow. He decided he did not mind the city one bit; he liked what he saw and smelled. He liked the excitement of the city.

CHAPTER FORTY-FIVE

After Rosie left him, Franki did lie down and fell into a deep sleep. Suddenly, a soft knock on the door awakened him. "Franki, Franki, wake up! We're having supper now." It was Rosie.

Located on the main floor was an elaborate, formal dining room. The 10 foot by 5 foot mahogany table could accommodate twenty people comfortably. The high-back chairs with extravagant ornate carvings matched the table. The upholstery was a rich ivory and burgundy tapestry, and the cushions were soft and comfortable to sit on.

Sitting down, Franki looked around the table. Seated next to Helen, Veronica, and Lily were three older male guests. They were maybe only a few years younger than his *Tato*, Evan Stry-Ker. But they looked refined and their clothing looked well tailored and expensive. There was one other man seated next to him who did not look as refined. As a matter of fact, he looked like a downright rough character.

Rosie sat at the head of the table and began introductions. "I'm so happy to have a very special young friend visiting me today. He is a family friend whom I've looked forward to meeting for a long, long time. Ladies and gentleman, it is my pleasure to introduce Franki!" she said enthusiastically, directing her gaze toward him. She looked genuinely proud as she smiled warmly at him.

"Franki, around here we only use first names. You've met Veronica, Helen, and Lily a little earlier, and seated beside each of my girls is Jack, Jim, and Dick, and this man sitting next to you is Johnny Makar. He's one of our permanent residents, as I hope you'll become." Rosie rang a tiny bell, and Cissy began to serve the food.

First Rosie raised her crystal wine glass and toasted Franki. Everyone clinked glasses and took a sip of good vintage Bordeaux. She finished drinking the entire glass, then asked Cissy to pour another.

The ornate Tiffany stained-glass light fixture did not provide much light. This was quite deliberate. The four candles in the silver candelabra flickered gently, creating an enchanting atmosphere. Added to this was Rosie's china, which was Limoges, and her sterling silver flatware was a most elegant Gardenia pattern. The crystal glassware shone as the deeply cut prism designs reflected the colour of the rainbow in the flickering candlelight. The white linen tablecloth, along with white crisply starched napkins, was so white that the linen appeared to be almost iridescent blue-white. Franki thought of the tough work a laundress must have in keeping this table linen so immaculately clean. He remembered how hard his mother had to work when she washed the altar linens for St. Olga's church.

Jack, Jim, and Dick were deeply engrossed in a conversation about the status of the war that was looming in Europe. Many of Canada's young men were enlisting. The Ottawa government had approved The War Measures Act, which enabled the government to collect extra war taxes. It was September 3, 1939, that Britain had declared war on Germany. Canada followed suit on September 10, 1939. The Germans captured Poland on October 2, 1939, and the Nazis occupied Warsaw shortly thereafter. King George VI and Queen Elizabeth had visited Canada in June 1939 shortly before the war was declared. The Jewish people were being ostracized in Germany and word was getting out about the Jewish people's mistreatment by the Nazis. On June 2,

Canadian authorities did not admit the ship known as the St. Louis. It had a cargo of Jewish refugees.

Franki noted Johnny Makar did not participate in the conversation; as a matter of fact, he appeared to be in a bad mood and was definitely pouting. More to the point, he appeared as though he did not care to discuss the war. His shock of curly blonde hair looked like hundreds of golden curled straws. His blonde bushy eyebrows were also a wheat colour. Johnny had piercing blue-green eyes, high cheekbones, and a large and angular chin. When he smiled he had a large gap between his top two front teeth. His body resembled that of a huge lumberjack. He appeared to be clumsy, as he tipped his second glass of red wine all over the clean white table linen. Rosie rang the tiny bell again and Cissy came running. She saw the dilemma and quickly sprinkled salt on the awful red stain and covered it with an equally white napkin. She picked up Johnny's plate and flatware and placed it over the spot where the wine had stained the tablecloth.

"No fussy, fussy, that's all there's to it! Now we'll start eating dinner. Cissy, please," Rosie stated, as though these kinds of accidents were normal occurrences. The appetizer was a sumptuous sturgeon fish. Sturgeon, which was caught in the North Saskatchewan River, was prepared in butter and white wine, with onion and garlic. The main course was something Franki had never tasted. It was beef covered in flaky pastry. Rosie called it Beef Wellington. There were hot steaming bowls of creamed mashed potatoes, carrots, and onions in a white sauce. Franki had never seen better food anywhere. "Not even in Buckingham Palace!" he thought. The meal was topped off with homemade ice cream and mouth-watering apple pie which was served on a large crystal platter. Franki noted that Rosie had consumed at least five glasses of wine from the lovely crystal decanter. Everyone then proceeded into the parlour to take coffee and liqueur.

Franki watched as Rosie walked over to the gramophone, cranked the spring tight as carefully as she could, and placed the needle on the 78 rpm record. Soon the mellow sounds of Johann Strauss permeated the room. Almost in unison, Veronica, Lily, and Helen rose and coquettishly coaxed Jack, Jim, and Dick to dance the old-time waltz. As the evening progressed, Jack, Jim, and Dick became more and more intimate with the girls. Johnny, meanwhile, continued to pout and pour more and more liquor down his gullet. His voice was becoming slurred, and he was showing signs of aggression. Rosie, the ever-pleasant host, was also appearing tipsy.

She came over to Johnny and whispered in his ear. Johnny drank several cups of black coffee and soon appeared to regain some composure. Rosie continued to wind up the gramophone while the girls and Jim, Jack, and Dick kept on dancing.

Johnny came over to where Franki was sitting and asked him to come upstairs to his room, saying he wanted to get to know him. They excused themselves and climbed the two sets of stairs leading to the third level. Johnny opened his door and summoned Franki to come in. They sat at a small table that had two comfortable wooden chairs beside it.

Johnny stared out the window into the darkness. "Some day I'll be rich and be like those sons-of-bitches downstairs with the girls. I'll be able to afford one of Rosie's girls," he vowed angrily.

"What are you talking about, Johnny? What do you mean, Rosie's girls?" Franki was totally confused. So much had happened today. He had left the seminary at Mundare. He had come to Edmonton and met Rosie Soova for the first time and liked her.

"Are you ignorant or totally stupid? Don't you know you're living in a whorehouse!" Johnny appeared impatient with Franki's naivete.

"A what? A whorehouse? You mean Dick, Jack, and Jim are not boyfriends of Veronica, Lily, and Helen?" Franki blurted out, genuinely shocked.

"No, you stupid fool! Every night you'll meet another Jim, Jack, and Dick. They pay for the company of those girls and for whatever services they want the girls to provide. You know . . . . sex. I hope to hell you know what sex is!" Johnny spouted, shaking his head in disgust at Franki's ignorance.

Franki was totally bewildered. What a mess he was in. Not only had he left the seminary, which would displease his mother totally, but also now he was living in a whorehouse. "Boy, oh boy, I'm in a mess!" he exclaimed.

"You poor son-of-a-bitch, you are naïve. Where the hell have you been all your life?" Johnny was toning down a little, a touch of compassion for Franki coming through. "The worst part of this situation is that I'm in love with that damn bitch, Veronica!" Johnny confessed.

"Does she know?" asked Franki.

"If she doesn't then she's pretty stupid. She gives me a piece of ass once in a while and doesn't even charge me!" Franki knew enough to know that "a piece of ass" meant sex. He was totally bewildered because as far as he was concerned these were terrible, sinful acts. However, he was mature enough about the teachings of God to know that each person is given choices. Furthermore, he was not responsible for other people's moral values. Leaving Johnny's room in a state of bewilderment, he walked dejectedly to his own room, which Rosie had assigned to him earlier in the day.

It seemed as if doors were opening and closing all night long. Finally, when he looked at the wind-up clock

Rosie had placed on his bedside table, it read 5:00 a.m. He could hear noises in Johnny's room. "He's probably getting a 'piece of ass' from Veronica and not being charged for it!" he thought.

CHAPTER FORTY-SIX

Franki could not sleep beyond 7:00 a.m. His body clock was used to rising at 5:00 at the seminary. He was extremely troubled and tried desperately to figure out what to do with his life.

"Maybe I should get a ride back to Mundare. Mr. Bill will take me back to the seminary . . . no, no, that's being dishonest to myself. I don't want to be a priest, not now anyway. Maybe I'll take a year off and pray for guidance. Oh God, what a mess I'm in," he moaned.

He knelt down and did what he knew best how to do—he prayed. He talked to God. "God, oh my God, Almighty One. Please forgive me if I hurt you in any way. Please forgive me if I hurt my mother and father and Katayna. Heavenly Father, show me the way. Please point the way." Then he pulled out his rosary and prayed. He attempted to re-create in his mind the Stations of the Cross. When he finished, it was almost 8:00 a.m. Frankie washed in the bathroom down the hall. Hot water out of the tap . . . what a luxury. A flushing toilet . . . he liked this, not having to go outside to the privy. He came out of the bathroom and heard noises on the main level. As he descended the stairs he saw Johnny coming into the house.

"Where have you been so early?" inquired Franki.

"I've been outside starting that son-of-a-bitch truck. It's colder than a nun's heart . . . minus 30! You know some people in this life have to work. We're not all whores or priests!" Johnny said sarcastically.

Franki was very offended and let Johnny know that he was. "First of all, I'm not a priest. I'm not good enough to be one . . . so let's establish that first off. Secondly, I have no experience with women, but I know enough that I would never call the woman I love a whore!" Franki spoke in short, clipped, angry syllables to make his point.

Cissy was preparing breakfast. "Amen and Alleluia. It's time someone told off this stupid ox. Mon, does he think he's smart? Yeah, a smart ass, dat's all you are, mon . . . a big, old, smart ass stud!" She accused.

"Hey, Cissy, you better know where your place is. I won't put up with your sassin'." But Johnny was not quite so sure of himself when he spoke to Cissy.

"So what's you gonna do! Miss Rosie will tell you where to go, she will!" Cissy said simply.

After eating some cooked oatmeal and milk laced with rich farm cream, Johnny stood up and grabbed the lunch Cissy had made for him. He marched out the door to his idling truck. Cissy cleaned up the kitchen. Franki volunteered to help her but she refused his help.

"This here is woman's work," she said firmly. "If I need your help, Mon, I'll axe you for it . . . yeah, I'll axe you." Hearing that, Franki climbed the stairs to the second level. He couldn't hear anyone stirring, so he assumed they were all still fast asleep.

And why shouldn't they be, he thought, they got to bed sometime after 5:00 a.m. Franki went to his room and started doing what he most dreaded to do, writing a letter to his beloved Katayna.

CHAPTER FORTY-SEVEN

January 30, 1940
My Dearest Katayna,
    I cannot find the right words to describe my feelings. You are the first person I am telling that I have left Mundare and the priesthood.
    Katayna, I have asked God to forgive me and I hope you can find it in your heart to forgive me also. I just cannot live the life of a priest. It takes total dedication, total concentration, and total discipline to live the life of a monk at the seminary. Father Bill and I discussed my next step toward priesthood . . . to the level of postulant . . . and we both agreed I am not fit to go on, in my present state of mind.
    I left Mundare yesterday. Mr. Bill Stawnychy, a friendly truck driver, gave me a ride into Edmonton and the only place I knew to come was Rosie Soova's. I have since found out what kind of a rooming house Rosie keeps, but that doesn't matter at this point. She has been a kind and compassionate person to me and I like her very much, regardless of what she does for a living.
    Katayna, I hope this doesn't cause you a problem with Rusty. If you find it in your heart, please tell Mamunia and Tato about my decision. If you would rather not, then I'll also understand. In case I haven't thanked you for everything you have done for me during my whole life, I wish to thank you now . . . from the bottom of my heart. God bless you always.
    Love, Franki

He carefully placed the letter in an envelope that Rosie had left in his night table, addressed it, and went to ask Cissy where he might find the Post Office.

She directed him toward Jasper Avenue and 102 Street, well within walking distance. Before he left, Cissy gave him a four-cent Dominion of Canada stamp to post his letter.

"You won't have to break a big bill, Mon, to buy a measly stamp!" She must have sensed that Franki didn't have much money to his name.

When he returned at noon everyone was up and sitting at the kitchen table in their fancy morning wraps. They were all having oatmeal and freshly made coffee, and they were reading the *Edmonton Bulletin*. Their faces were not made up and all four ladies looked pale and washed out . . . no comparison to the previous night.

"Well, good morning, you handsome young man. Where have you been so early?" Rosie was her normal bubbly self. The other three just nodded and did not speak. All three, especially Veronica, looked as if they had been dragged through a knothole. There were circles under Veronica's eyes and what looked like a bruise on her left cheek.

"I've already written a letter to Shady Hollow and went to the Post Office to post the letter. I'm sure I won't be popular once they find out I've left the priesthood," Franki said dejectedly.

"Did you tell them you're staying here with me?" Rosie inquired.

"Oh, yes, and just how grateful I am that you took me in," responded Franki.

"That's good, yeah, that's good. Have you had breakfast? You look as thin as a rail. We'll just fatten you up a little," Rosie winked at Franki.

Veronica looked at Rosie with tears brimming in her eyes. "Last night there was an accident in my room. Jack fell on the night table and broke it to smithereens. He became so violent afterwards that he punched me in the face! I have a slight bruise, right here." She pointed to her left cheek. Veronica was more hurt than angry.

"That bastard . . . how dare he hit you! I'll deal with him in my own way! In the meantime, girls, remember he is no longer welcome at The Pearl's Oyster . . . not ever!" Rosie was furious, and what a pepper-pot she was when she was angry! She turned to Franki and mellowed. "You will have free room and board here for one month. After that, I hope you find a job. My monthly fee for room and board is twenty-five dollars per month. Is that fair? The same as Johnny pays." She looked at him questioningly.

"Very fair. I'm sure I'll find some work before a month, or do something. I heard those men last night discussing the war. They talked about young men enlisting for active duty. Maybe that would be good for me. My life needs some direction, and I've always admired the Air Force men . . . in their smart blue uniforms with the peaked officers' hats. Flying has always interested me," Franki added in a determined manner. He looked at Veronica.

"Did you say you have a broken table, Veronica?" he asked her.

"Yes, it's broken to shambles. Why do you ask?" she questioned Franki.

"Well, at the seminary I used to work in the carpentry shop. I know a little about building things." Franki did not like to brag, but he had become a top-notch finishing carpenter. "I'll need a few tools. I don't suppose you have any here?" he asked her.

"Oh, yes, I do," Rosie piped up. "Onc Dick couldn't pay me and brought me his tools instead. They're all somewhere in the garage, out back."

In about an hour, Veronica brought down the shattered table and Rosie and Franki took it to the garage. Everything was thrown in a heap against one corner, including a set of excellent saws, hammers, chisels, and clamps. There were no nails or glue. But what impressed him most of all was the black 1922 McLaughlin-Buick, which was also housed in the garage. Franki asked Rosie about the car, as it was in such beautiful condition.

"Could this be the same car people talked about . . . the mysterious lady who came to Maria's funeral . . . they said it was a huge black shiny car . . . could this be it?" he thought. Franki asked Rosie where he could buy a few more supplies and she directed him to the W.W. Arcade Hardware, south of their house. She stuffed a ten-dollar bill into his pocket and asked if that was enough.

Franki purchased the supplies he needed and decided to buy a few pieces of lumber so he could make some shelving and a workbench and clean up this messy garage, the only place at Rosie's that was not completely organized. Fortunately, it had a big heater in one corner. Franki fired it up with wood and then coal and it quickly heated the garage. He worked in the garage until suppertime. The tiny night table was repaired and looked even better than it had before the "accident." The only thing left to do was to sand off the old varnish and paint new coats onto the surface.

Rosie, not Cissy, whose job it was normally, came to call Franki into the house to prepare for supper. "Franki, Franki," she stressed. "You have much more time to do this . . . relax, relax . . . don't you know how to relax? You Stry-Kers have always been working fools! My, my, is that Veronica's table? It looks better now than before it got broken. You're a damn good carpenter, Franki Stry-Ker, damn good," Rosie stated. She was surprised, but mostly impressed.

Franki came into the house and noticed the transformation that had taken place. The girls once again looked like painted China dolls. Even Veronica's bruise on her cheek was covered by make-up. Their elaborate gowns, made of velvet, taffeta, and silk, were beautiful and they looked as beautiful as the mannequins he had seen at the T. Eaton's Department store. Franki noted that Johnny was not present anywhere in the house. When he inquired, he was informed that no one had seen him all day.

As there had been the night before, there were three different men this evening. These were younger men in dark navy blue Air Force uniforms. How coincidental, he thought, we just talked about the Air Force earlier today. And as the evening progressed it was "deja vu all over again." All three men looked different, talked different, yet Rosie introduced them at the dinner table as Jack, Jim, and Dick. Today the dinner consisted of a roasted goose with all the trimmings, including a tasty orange and cranberry sauce, potato croquettes, coleslaw, and honeyed carrots. For dessert, Cissy had prepared a Black Forest cake using preserved sour cherries, real whipped cream, and Kirsch liqueur. The only time Franki had ever seen a roasted goose was at Christmas or at christenings . . . at very special occasions. This was quite a new experience for him. Rosie once again consumed too much wine during the evening. After the meal, they proceeded to the parlour for coffee and liqueur, and once again Rosie wound up the gramophone and played Johann Strauss's Viennese waltzes. There was one difference . . . Johnny Makar was conspicuous by his absence.

Franki excused himself right after dessert was finished. He went up to his room on the third storey. About two hours later he heard Johnny's bedroom door open and close. He also heard faint music from the downstairs parlour. Franki knelt before a crucifix that he carried in his knapsack and prayed and prayed and prayed. "Please, dear Heavenly Father, show me the way. Guide me and give me strength to fulfill your wishes of me, and let me learn the lessons which I must learn."

He climbed into the bed and slept peacefully until 6:30 the next morning. After his morning grooming, he descended the stairs, tiptoeing so he did not wake the ladies on the second floor. As he came into the kitchen, he saw Johnny sitting at the large table reading the front page of the *Edmonton Bulletin*. The front-page headline read, "Stockbroker Beaten Savagely." A large three-column, six-inch picture appeared beneath the headline. The picture was none other than Jack . . . the Jack that had been here in this house, two days ago. The same Jack who "accidentally" broke the table in Veronica's bedroom. The same table he was now repairing. The same Jack who Veronica said hit her and bruised her left cheek.

Only now his real name was printed in the paper. The caption under the picture read "Fred Prentice, a successful and well-respected City Stockbroker, was found near his home last night, savagely beaten by unidentified assailants. Mrs. Prentice was walking the dog near their Ada Boulevard home and found her husband lying in a pool of blood." The police report stated that Mr. Prentice was in critical condition. He had sustained numerous blows to his head and body by what was suspected to be a blunt metal object, possibly a crow bar. The article continued on the subject of Mr. Prentice's success in the stock market since the Depression had ended a year ago.

Cissy was preparing thick bacon and fried eggs for Johnny's breakfast. "Hurry up, woman . . . my gut is empty. I'm so damn hungry I could eat the asshole out of a skunk!" Johnny was in a rambunctious mood this morning. He was "full of piss and vinegar," as he would put it, thought Franki.

"We missed you at supper last night," Franki told him.

"Yeah, yeah, I don't know who the hell missed me, but if it's any of your business, I had to work late. My trucking business keeps me busy. Yeah busy, you know. Day and night . . ." It appeared to Franki that Johnny had a sneer on his face as he made the insincere statement. "How the hell are you doing? Decided yet what you'll do with your life?" he asked Franki. He almost sounded as if he genuinely cared at this point.

"Well, no. I'm confused about that. I may even decide to go back to Mundare and to my studies in theology. Or I may enlist in the Air Force. I hear the Royal Canadian Air Force is looking for recruits to go and help the British fight the war in Europe. I don't know, Johnny, it is confusing at this time," Franki explained.

"Tealitigy or whatever you said . . . that priest thing, I guess you're talking about. Shit, that means those Catholic priests can never have a piece of ass, huh?" This was Johnny's first concern.

"If I was ever strong enough or dedicated enough to fulfill my vows after being ordained, yes, one of those vows would be celibacy," Franki explained.

"Franki, have you ever had a woman? I'll bet you sure as hell haven't, otherwise you wouldn't even think of living the rest of your life without it!" Franki knew for certain the "it" Johnny was talking about was sex. That's all that seemed to matter in Johnny's world.

Franki looked over at Cissy and then at Johnny. He could feel the blood rushing up his face. He was very embarrassed, as he had rarely discussed sex, never mind with a woman present.

"I guess not, you stupid son-of-a-bitch." Johnny

began to laugh hysterically. "We'll have to fix you up with Lily. She's always good for the first timers."

Franki tried to change the subject. "Johnny, do you know of any jobs anywhere here in Edmonton?"

"Rosie tells me you're a hell of a good carpenter. Over at the North West Industries where they're building planes for the war, there may be something there. When you know what the hell you're doing with your life, tell me and maybe I can help you look. I'll ask some of my buddies." Johnny had already wolfed down his breakfast. He appeared to be always in a hurry.

"Thank you, I'd appreciate any help. By the way, when did you see Rosie? I thought you worked late." Franki said.

"Rosie was still up when I came home, playing her gramophone, and the girls were still dancing with Jack, Jim, and Dick . . ." He winked at Franki as though they knew a secret that no one else did.

Cissy had Johnny's lunch all ready. Johnny ran his fingers through the shock of his golden uncombed, curly hair, and then slipped on his greasy cap and his Mackinaw jacket. He wore heavy felt *valinke* (knee-high felt boots). These boots were very popular winter footwear in Alberta during the Depression and continued to be popular now that the Depression was over.

When Franki and Cissy were alone in the kitchen (the other ladies would not be up for at least another two or three hours), Cissy looked Franki right in the eye. "You know, Mon, you're a pretty good person, even for a white man," she told him. "You shouldn't be so naïve. You have so damn much to learn. There are games being played all around you, so wake up, Mon, wake up! Johnny is not who he appears to be. He lives here because he has a job to do and you probably know he's sweet on Veronica. Veronica would give her eyeteeth to stop doing what she does, and so would Lily and Helen. Rosie doesn't sell herself any more, not for a long time already," Cissy confided.

"Yes, yes, I'm quite aware of what business goes on here at The Pearl's Oyster, but what does Johnny do here? I thought he pays Rosie room and board?" Franki didn't know whether he should even be discussing these matters with Cissy. He wasn't sure whom he could trust yet. He continued to question Cissy. "What are you doing here . . . do you?"

"Do I conduct this kind of business? No way, Mon, I'm studying in my spare time and I'll be a lawyer someday. Yes, the first black female lawyer in Alberta. All my folks' hopes ride on me. They never had sons, only daughters. I'm the eldest." Cissy sounded determined.

"Where do your folks live, Cissy? In Alberta?" Franki asked.

"Oh yes, I grew up at Amber Valley, around Athabasca, Alberta. My people are descendants of the American slaves. They ran away from the southern states in the late 1800s and settled around Amber Valley. There are quite a few Negro families living there. We are pretty rare in Edmonton," she proclaimed proudly.

"Yes, I know, and I apologize for staring at you when I arrived here. I had never seen a Negro person, ever in my life," Franki explained.

"And so, Mon, what is your feeling about people with different colour skin?" Cissy asked, sounding defensive.

"Cissy, I'm not very old, granted, but I have never felt any human being is better than another. To answer your question, God created all people and he loves all people. If I am to walk in God's image, and I try, believe me I try, then I should love all people. And Cissy, I do." Franki's sincerity was evident. "I hope you and I will become life-long friends, Cissy!"

"Franki Stry-Ker, Mon, I do like you. I only hope that some day all white folks will have the same attitude as you do. But I'm afraid that's a long time from now . . . a long time . . . yes, I'd like to be your friend, Franki Stry-Ker, Mon!" Cissy stated enthusiastically.

Franki finished eating his breakfast and then left the table, dressed in his warm Mackinaw jacket. He went to the garage to finish Veronica's table. Today he would start the first coat of varnish, so he lit the fire in the small wood and coal heater in the corner of the garage. Soon the warm air permeated the garage, and he began his varnishing job. This quiet place gave him an opportunity to reflect on his life and on how his decisions would affect others. He wondered when his letter would arrive at Katayna's in Shady Hollow.

CHAPTER FORTY-EIGHT

One week after Franki mailed the letter in Edmonton addressed to Mrs. Katayna McLennan, General Delivery, Shady Hollow, it arrived. It was Sergeant Rusty McLennan's habit to have breakfast with his wife. He always made the coffee in a Pyrex coffee percolator that they had received as a wedding gift seven years earlier.

Rusty and Katayna continued to love each other dearly. Theirs was truly a "marriage made in heaven." Everyone used to say that they were soulmates. Unfortunately, their union had not produced any children.

Katayna always said, "If God meant for us to have children, we will have them, but so far we haven't been blessed." She did see Dr. Allison about this matter, because they practised no birth control. Dr. Allison determined that her uterus was tilted too far forward so she could not conceive. She would have to have an operation to correct the situation. Rusty did not want her to suffer any pain. They would just enjoy each other's company as they had been doing all these seven years.

Rusty was promoted to the position of RCMP Sergeant and stationed at Shady Hollow. This detachment was responsible for providing policing service for five surrounding municipalities. Corporal Seymour, who had completed thirty years of service in the force, retired and moved to Victoria, British Columbia. His name was never totally cleared within the force and so he never attained a higher position than that of Corporal. His attitude toward the Ukrainians never changed . . . he hated them until his retirement.

Two other young officers were posted to Shady Hollow. They were Constables Mark Kuliba, who was of Ukrainian origin and hailed from Saskatchewan, and Samuel Ewing, from British Columbia. They respected Rusty highly and were happy to be gaining very valuable experience from one of the RCMP's most respected officers.

Most of the moonshine stills had been destroyed and the moonshiners jailed, but Louie Kaditz and Metro Soova had teamed up and were still producing the best brew for miles around. Their stills could never be found. Try as the RCMP did, they could not find them.

This morning Rusty and Katayna were discussing this matter.

"You'd think Louie would know better than to team up with the likes of Metro Soova!" exclaimed Katayna. "Why does Louie do it? He's got a fabulous ranch . . . I hear many head of cattle. He's got twins, Oni and Harry, doing most of the work. I can't understand his way of thinking. I don't know how Annie puts up with that stupidity." Katayna was visibly upset.

Rusty tried to console her. "Katayna, human nature is strange insofar as egos go. Louie is praised highly by everyone who buys his hooch. Let's face it . . . now that he's teamed up with Metro Soova, they've combined experience. Metro, the bum, has been doing this for over twenty-five years and Louie almost as long. I understand they can't keep up with the demand." Rusty was frustrated.

"Where in the world are they brewing that stuff? You've been watching them for years. Where are their stills?" asked Katayna.

"Who knows? I've had Sam and Mark tracking them twenty-four hours a day for one week and they did not lead them to the still. They just stopped producing for a week. They seem to smell the police and handle us like chumps. From what I'm gathering, they probably move the stills around . . . but, my dear Katayna, we have other work to do. We can't be wasting our free time on the likes of Metro Soova and Louie Kaditz. There will come a day when we catch them . . . just wait and see!" Rusty vowed determinedly.

They ate their breakfast. Katayna was dressed smartly in a tartan blazer, white ruffly blouse, and a plain black woolen skirt. Her make-up was beautifully applied right up to her highly coloured cheeks. Her dark hair, impeccably coiffed, showed no signs of grey hair. She was ready for another day in the classroom at Shady Hollow.

"Katayna, you are still the most beautiful woman that I've ever laid eyes on, and smart too!" Rusty told her sincerely. He loved her with all his heart and soul. She felt the same about him, although he was starting to show his age, his copper hair showing signs of greying at the temples.

He drove her to school, then proceeded to pick up the mail at the Post Office. The Postmaster, Harry Yaroslawski, a tall no-nonsense person, was of Romanian descent.

"Good morning, Sergeant McLennan. I have three letters for you this morning, and the *Winnipeg Free Press* and the *Western Producer.*" Rusty flipped through the letters and found one of them was for Katayna.

The return address was Edmonton, yet the name on the return address slot was Mr. Franki Stry-Ker. He was puzzled.

"What is Franki doing writing from Edmonton when he is supposed to be in Mundare? Strange indeed," he thought. He called in to the RCMP office and found that the Constables Mark and Sam had already brewed a fresh pot of coffee and were going about their daily business.

Rusty could see all was well. He told them that he had to deliver a letter to Katayna. He felt there must be some urgency in this letter; there was something strange about all of this. Driving over to the school, he tapped lightly on Katayna's classroom door. The children were just completing saluting the Union Jack. "The emblem of my country, Canada, and to it I pledge my love and loyalty . . . ." He tapped on the door again. A young grade three student answered.

"Hey teacher, it's that tall policeman!" he yelled excitedly at Katayna. "That there one who puts people in jail."

Katayna smiled, "Yes, thank you, Joe. That's my husband. His name is Sergeant McLennan, and he doesn't usually put people in jail. Only when they yell 'that there policeman'!"

She was quite amused by her young wards. Before closing the door she assigned a monitor. "Please be the supervisor, Joe, and see that the health inspection is done properly."

Rusty handed the letter from Franki to her.

"I thought this might be important . . . it's from your brother, Franki. But he mailed it in Edmonton, according to the postmark."

Katayna was curious indeed. She tore open the envelope and read.

My dearest Katayna,

I cannot find the right words to describe my feelings . . . Katayna knew instinctively that this was a serious matter and her instinct told her that people would be hurt. She quickly scanned the letter.

". . . *I left Mundare yesterday . . . ,* " she read in the third paragraph.

She quickly looked at the date at the top of the letter. January 30, 1940. Today was February 6, 1940 . . .

one week ago, she thought. Her troubled state showed in every stress line in her face.

"Oh my God. Rusty . . . he's left the seminary. He's left the priesthood and is living at Rosie Soova's place in Edmonton. Oh God, oh God, *Mamunia* will die of a heart attack!" Katayna was close to tears. Embracing her, Rusty tried to console her. The door flew open. "Okay, teacher, the health inspection is over and . . . boy oh boy!" he yelled at the top of his voice. "There are lots of dirty ears . . . like pigs . . . dirty like that . . . and hands too, and . . ." He started reeling off the names of the dirty kids.

Katayna by now was close to tears. She knew how difficult her task would be to advise her mother and father about what had happened with Franki. She could hardly wait for the school day to end. As soon as she dismissed the children, she ran home and started up the 1939 blue Chevy Coupe which she and Rusty had bought last year. She loved to drive this neat little car. Rusty felt it would be better if she went to Stry-Kers' alone, as this would be a private family matter to discuss and he did not feel comfortable in these situations.

She rumbled along the seven-and-a-half-mile dirt road trail. The road was clear of snow as Evan was still on the Municipal Council and roads under his purview seemed to receive preferential treatment—maybe because he was the longest serving councillor and his decisions were most respected.

As she drove into the yard she noticed Mikhail's car was gone. She hoped that Evan and Tainka were not gone also. As she proceeded into the house, she gave the Christian greeting *Slava Ichosoo Xristoo* (praise Jesus Christ).

"*Slava na vikee*" (praise him forever), Tainka and Evan replied in unison.

"Hello, Auntie Katayna," a little voice piped up. There, helping her grandmother to roll out bread dough, was Helenka and Joseph Pushinsky's sweet daughter, Emily. Emily used to visit the Stry-Kers once a week after school. She attended White Sands Creek School and loved to come to her *Baba* and *Gido* Stry-Kers . . . "to *Baba*'s for holidays" is how she described her visits. Emily was now almost ten years old. She was an absolutely beautiful dark-haired girl with blue eyes. Since her birth, Tainka had had a strong bond with Emily; the two were very close. She was an image of her grandmother. Emily also had the quiet and peaceful disposition of Maria, Katayna's dead sister. Helenka and Joseph's boys, Peter and Joseph Junior, mostly took after the Pushinsky family and enjoyed their paternal grandparents more. Joseph Pushinsky's parents lived on the same yard, so the boys had a very good rapport with that *Baba* and *Gido*. Evan, the third son, was named after his *Gido* Stry-Ker. He somewhat resembled the Stry-Ker family. Emily, on the other hand, had the true genes of the Stry-Ker family.

Emily came running to her Auntie Katayna, gave her a big hug, and planted a big kiss on her cheek.

Tainka was surprised to see Katayna on a weekday. Usually Rusty and Katayna visited the Stry-Kers on Sundays.

"How nice to see you, Katayna . . . is Rusty feeling healthy?" Evan was first to inquire.

"Yes, yes, Rusty is quite well. Of course his work never stops. I guess that's police work for you," Katayna sighed. She looked at Tainka, seeing the incredible bond that had developed between Emily and her *Baba*. Yes indeed, Katayna could see Maria in Emily's moves; just like a reincarnation of her dead sister. She dreaded telling her folks the news about Franki because she knew very well what a disappointment this would be to both of them. They had their hearts set on having their youngest son serve God. In recent years that's all they had in mind for the boy, especially her mother. She'd been talking about Franki's priesthood ever since the child was born. "It was so unfair," thought Katayna. "There were no other choices left for the boy." Katayna asked where Mikhail was this evening. "It's like always in the evening during winter," Tainka replied. "After Mikhail finishes chores, many times, like today, he doesn't even eat supper but goes to Kaditzs to play cards with Fred Radjec and Paul Lupski. I guess our Mikhail and those two will die bachelors."

"Well, *Mamunia*, if they enjoy their life, who are we to say that is wrong?" Katayna was, however, uncomfortable about the Kaditzs; she wondered if Tainka knew about Louie Kaditz and Metro Soova being partners in the moonshine business. There was that conversation when they drove to Mundare to pick up Franki at Christmas. In fact, it was quite a confrontation she and Mikhail had had that day. Katayna never revealed what she and Rusty discussed and what Rusty told her about his various cases, particularly not about Soova and Kaditz.

"And Anastasia and Paul . . . they took little Evan with them to the Ozypkos. Anastasia's mother is very sick," offered Evan.

Anastasia and Paul continued to sleep at their little house on the Borischuk's old homestead.

"I'm sure little Evancik [Helenka's third son was also named Evan, so to distinguish one from the other, Paul's son was called Evancik] is growing fast . . . he's so much like you, *Tato*. It's amazing . . ." Katayna knew the time was coming close for her to tell them about Franki. No more beating around the bush . . . no more procrastination. Okay, she thought, here goes. "I received a letter from Franki today," she stated as assertively as she could.

"Oh, is he sick? How is everything in Mundare?" inquired Tainka.

Evan sat in his favourite chair waiting with anticipation to hear.

"Well . . ." she hesitated. "That's just it . . . he's not in Mundare anymore. He's decided that he has to take a break from the seminary. He found it too hard to continue at this time . . ." Katayna attempted to leave a little hope for them to hang on to. And who knows, maybe Franki will actually go back, she thought optimistically.

"Where is he now?" Evan inquired tautly.

"He's in Edmonton and living at Rosie Soova's rooming house," Katayna told him.

"At Rosie Soova's?! What's he, crazy or what . . . for shame! *Bee iiho sluck trafit!* (may a curse hit him). *Bee iiho sluck trafit!*" Evan raged, and cursing his son.

In recent years, Evan only used this worst Ukrainian curse of all curses when he was furious. Turning white, he stood up, grabbed his hexagon-shaped woollen cap and buffalo coat, and stormed out the door.

"*Baba, Baba!* Why is *Gido* so mad . . . why *Baba* . . . why?" Emily was visibly upset. "Where is *Gido* going in the dark?" Tainka did not appear to even hear the child's questions as she burst out in a torrid of loud sobs as tears flowed down her cheeks—cheeks which today showed severe age.

Beside herself, Katayna attempted to soothe her mother, but no matter what she said, it didn't help, "Oh, it will be fine and he may go back. Thank God he's not sick," soothed Katayna. Nothing seemed to register . . . her mother was not listening and continued to create a scene.

Emily hugged her grandmother and kissed her. "*Baba, Baba,* please don't cry, please don't cry. You make me sad!" But there was no stopping Tainka.

Then Emily said something that made Tainka pause "Don't you love me any more, *Baba?*"

"Oh yes, child, I love you very much. You're one of my purposes to live. You're so much like my Maria!" With that she hugged Emily and held her tightly.

Katayna did not wish to be rude, but somehow she needed to bring her mother back to reality. "*Mamunia*, why are you so unfair? I've sat back all these years and said nothing. Maybe it's time you listened. Since Franki was born, you had very little to do with his upbringing. I took over and did most everything for him. Granted, you nursed him at first and that's very important, but I did everything else for him, changed his diapers, bathed him, played with him and most of all, I loved him like a mother. You made up your mind he was going to be a priest as soon as he was born. He had very little choice in the matter! Isn't that right, *Mamunia?*"

Tainka seemed to comprehend what Katayna was saying, but her eyes did not show forgiveness. "Had I known this was going to happen, we both should have died when I was giving birth to him. I promised God he would be a priest . . . God will punish him for this . . . I know he will!"

"*Mamunia*, that's quite enough! You made a promise for yourself—you cannot make promises for someone else. You go to church any chance you get. Isn't that what you learn in church . . . to forgive . . . to love your children unconditionally . . . not only when they do something that pleases you? Come on, *Mamunia*, don't be a hypocrite!" Katayna was becoming so tired. These kinds of confrontations she abhorred. She would have gone to the ends of the earth not to hurt her mother or father . . . but this was a matter of defending her precious Franki. Franki, who was like her own son, certainly not just a brother.

Tainka seemed to be calming down, perhaps mostly because Emily was still hugging and kissing her and begging her not to cry.

"Where do you think *Tato* went?" asked Katayna.

"Where do you think *Tato* usually goes when he's this upset? Why, to his favourite widow, that's where . . . he's never stopped."

"*Baba, Baba*, which widow? What else you said . . . who is she?" Emily was certainly paying attention to this emotional exchange.

"Oh, she's nobody. She's just a friend of *Gido's*," Tainka replied.

Tainka sat for about fifteen minutes staring into space. She appeared to be in a different world. Emily kept hugging her and gently cradled her face in her tiny hands and looked right into her *Baba's* eyes. Still no response. When she persisted, Tainka came out of her mesmerized state. Perhaps she had been thinking about the words of advice which her late friend Pashka Borischuk gave her before Helenka's wedding. "Be fair to all your children, not just to one." Tainka did not say, but in due time she smiled at Emily and showed her appreciation for the child's affection and loyalty.

Soon she appeared to come out of her self-pity and even looked a bit embarrassed about the way she had acted in Emily's presence. She knew Emily adored her and respected her. Tainka would try to be the best role model that she knew how to be. She knew her actions today had not been those of a good role model.

Katayna asked her mother if she wanted to come to Edmonton because she was planning to travel there the next Saturday, primarily to show Franki her support and convey her love, no matter what he chose to do with his life.

"Will you come, *Mamunia*? Just you and me. We will spend some time with Franki. You will also have an opportunity to see Rosie Soova . . . how long has it been . . . nineteen, twenty years?" Katayna coaxed her.

"Yes, yes, Katayna, its been a long time but I don't want to be seen in a house like Rosie operates, even though I would like to see my son," *Mamunia* replied.

"What kind of house, *Baba*? What kind of house does Rosie operate?" Emily was a curious child. Katayna was totally stunned that Tainka had even an inkling about Rosie's rooming house, The Pearl's Oyster.

"Emily, Emily . . . you ask so many questions." Tainka was reluctant to respond to Emily's persistent questions.

"What *Baba* means is that Rosie runs a rooming house . . . that means your Uncle Franki is living there and Rosie . . . Miss Soova provides his room, a place where he sleeps and eats his meals. It also means that there are other people living there, along with Uncle Franki." Katayna responded to Emily's inquiries.

That appeared to satisfy Emily. She went back to the big table and continued to roll out bread dough. Emily was learning from her *Baba* to make dough circles. Tainka would press the dough into circles with a cookie cutter, and then she would fry these dough circles in deep fat for breakfast the next morning. This was a family favourite, but most important it was Emily's favourite . . . and if Emily liked something special, you can be sure her *Baba* made it.

"And besides," Tainka suddenly thought of yet another excuse not to accompany Katayna on Saturday to Edmonton, "the men are going to be butchering a hog and it's hard for Anastasia to be dressing the meat by herself. Also, we will be making *otropkee* (finely cut-up organ meats prepared like a stew, with onions, garlic, and a thick brown gravy). Only I know how to make this dish properly. You know that little Evancik is a handful and is too hard for Anastasia to handle while we make otropkee."

Katayna knew she could not change her mother's mind, nor would she try. She thought it was quite an achievement that Tainka had stopped her hysterics.

Evan was another matter. Katayna had some tea with her mother and Emily. She was beginning to feel the fatigue and weariness resulting from this day's events.

Bidding them both farewell, she gave Tainka and Emily each a hug. Then, dressing in her warm winter coat, she went out to her car. The '39 Chevy barely started in the –25F temperature even though it had only been there for a little over two hours. After a few attempts, it started. Thank goodness Rusty regularly checked the battery, and she always covered the motor with an old horse blanket as soon as she arrived anywhere. Today had been no exception.

She wondered where her father could be on such a cold, miserable night. As she drove down the road heading for Shady Hollow, she passed Widow Hunkowski's place. There was no sign of Evan and no sleigh tracks leading into the widow's yard. She drove into Shady Hollow and past Makovitsky's store. There, through the window, she saw Evan and Billy Makovitsky sitting head to head in one of the hospital-green booths. They appeared to be in deep conversation. There was no sign of Evan's lovely team of Clydesdales, although his fancy sleigh was parked outside the livery stable.

She did not feel she wanted to interfere in her father's discussion. She felt she had aggravated him sufficiently for one day with the news about Franki.

CHAPTER FORTY-NINE

Evan and Billy in Politics

It was 1940. Evan had reached the age of fifty-seven. He wondered why so much always had to fall on his shoulders. Today he was particularly heavily burdened. The war in Europe was raging; hundreds of Canada's finest young men were dying. Hundreds of other young people on the war front in Europe were being slaughtered. He wondered why people had so much hate for one another . . . why kill each other? The American economy under their President was starting to improve dramatically. W.L. MacKenzie King was now Canada's Prime Minister. He represented the Liberal Party. He paid the American President, Franklin D. Roosevelt, a call on April 24, and found that the Americans were maintaining a position of neutrality toward the war in Europe. It was thought that MacKenzie King tried to persuade the President to assist the British, as it appeared the Germans were gaining force on all fronts. And yet, with all this trouble in the world, Evan was hit with this problem caused by Franki.

"Billy," Evan inquired, seriously. "Billy, how old are you now?"

"Mr. Stry-Ker, I'm thirty-seven years old," Billy replied.

"Whatever will you do with your life? Will you be operating this store for your mother all the rest of your life?" Evan asked him.

"I never gave alternatives any thought. The store and confectionery provide us with a pretty good living.

During the Depression we weren't suffering, but we were short of cash at times, because so many people didn't pay their bills. They just didn't have any money. So many people suffered during this awful Depression, Mr. Stry-Ker. I'm sure you know, being the Municipal Councillor and all, " Billy added. "Now that the war is on, the government is rationing everything. We have to take those stupid ration stamps from everybody. Only the families of soldiers are better off because they send all their coupons to their wives and children. They also receive their provisions from the armed forces. But god dammit, that's the way it should be . . . they are fighting in those front lines in Europe. That's no fun . . . a few of our own here in Shady Hollow have died on the front lines. But you know that, Mr. Stry-Ker." Billy sounded agitated.

He wondered what Evan Stry-Ker was doing in town at this late hour and it being so cold . . . oh well, it was none of his business, although he could see something serious was chewing on this man.

"Billy," Evan Stry-Ker finally asked, "have you ever considered running as a member of the Alberta Legislature? This new Social Credit government is doing a lot of good things for this province since they took over in 1936. There is going to be another election soon. Billy, we need someone we can trust as our representative . . . one of our own people, so our region is represented and we get some more money for public works projects. I know you were interested in what Tommy Douglas said when he was here. But in Alberta I cannot see a Socialist government ever being elected, because people from the old country think it's like the Bolsheviks in Russia." Evan's excitement was building.

"Mr. Stry-Ker, why don't you run for MLA for the Social Credit government? You've always supported them. That's well known, and you have so much political experience as Municipal Councillor and School Trustee on the White Sands School Board." Billy felt he had made an excellent suggestion.

"Son, I won't run for the legislature for two reasons. First I'm fifty-seven years old . . . too old to start as a provincial politician. Second, my education is not sufficient nor is my spoken English. I know how the Anglo-Saxons look at me in a funny way when I speak English. It's too late for me to change . . . or putting it another way, I just don't have any more fire in my belly to fight any more battles. Do you have that fire, Billy?" Evan asked him earnestly.

"I don't know, Mr. Stry-Ker, I really don't know. I must confess though that I have always been interested in every phase of politics!" Billy admitted. "Why do you encourage me . . . you have three sons and two sons-in-law and so many other people who would do better than me . . . why me, Mr. Stryker?" Billy asked.

"Billy, today one of my sons disappointed me terribly . . . the one that has never been good on the farm. The direction that he is going in, he will be good for nothing else. He'll be a bum. My other two sons are only interested in farming and have never expressed even an inkling of interest in politics. My son-in-law, Joseph Pushinsky, is a musician and farmer and has a family of four children to feed. And the other son-in-law, Rusty McLennan, is a Sergeant now with the RCMP. I don't think he would ever leave the police force or his built-up pension. He probably needs about another eight years, then he and Katayna can retire. Billy, there are no others who would be better than you!" Evan told him.

Billy felt very flattered. Old Evan Stry-Ker was highly respected in these parts. If he thought Billy had a chance to be an MLA, then maybe he actually did.

"Mr. Stry-Ker, there are some things that bother me. I don't know if I could live with the Social Credit philosophy. What exactly do they stand for?" Billy asked.

"Well Billy," Evan began, "the Social Credit movement started during the worst depression the world has ever seen. You know . . . that was only ten years ago. So, money reform was their major platform. They promised every Albertan $5 a month. Five dollars per month meant a lot to people who had nothing. Coupled with that, they promised that the goods people produced would be sold above what it cost to produce them. As you know, during the thirties farmers were paid well below what it cost them to grow their grain or raise their farm animals. Banks were ruthless. If a farmer missed his payment on a loan, the banker would call in the loan and repossess the property. People were left homeless and penniless. People were looking for hope . . . for something better than the dirt poverty they had. Social Credit gave them that hope. Social Credit promised not only $5 per month, but improvement for education and health programs. But the important thing was that they promised not to borrow money from outside moneylenders to operate the province. They promised they would pay, as they want no deficit budgeting. And most of all they told people that the harder you work, the more you will have . . . and, Billy, that is exactly what they did. So in my view, they are providing good government. I believe you would be a good addition to them," Evan ended.

After listening intently, Billy assured Evan that he would at least consider the suggestion. With that Evan got up to square up his bill for the Orange Crush pop, but Billy waved him on and thanked him for the confidence which he had expressed in him. Then Evan pulled on his heavy buffalo coat and his woollen cap and slowly walked to the Shady Hollow Hotel. There he registered to stay for the night. He did not want to discuss Franki with Tainka or with anyone else any further. Not tonight anyway. He was very disappointed with Franki's decision and the thought of his own son staying at Rosie Soova's Pearl's Oyster, well, that was the last straw. He decided he needed a few stiff drinks of moonshine whiskey. He asked the desk clerk whether he could get him a bottle. When he said he could, Evan asked how much and was told $2.50. My goodness, Evan thought, what an increase from twenty-five cents a bottle . . . the price it used to be before the war and before all the rationing took place. After drinking half a bottle of the hooch, he concluded that it was good stuff. Perhaps if he had known it was Metro Soova and Louie Kaditz's brew he would not have drunk it. He and Metro Soova had never been civil to one another since 1922 when Rosie Soova ran away with David Newhouse. Evan slept all night as though a mule had kicked him in the head.

For some reason in his drunken stupor he remembered his brother . . . his long-lost brother, Yatsko.

The Stry-Kers heard from Evan's brother Yatsko. He had escaped war-torn Ukraine and somehow got to Britain. Evan was sponsoring him as an immigrant. Evan was gladly paying all of Yatsko's travelling expense. Yatsko would be living as part of the family with Evan and Tainka.

CHAPTER FIFTY

Katayna Travels to Edmonton

Saturday arrived and with it a raging Alberta winter blizzard. Katayna gave the spring-loaded shade a quick pull, looked out her kitchen window, and saw that the temperature had dropped to –40, far below a level for safe travel from Shady Hollow to Edmonton. The winds were howling relentlessly, blocking the roads with mounds of white, crisp snow which was piling up in tall drifts. On Saturdays Rusty slept longer but he heard Katayna in the kitchen and knew she was planning the trip to Edmonton. He also knew how upsetting this whole ordeal with Franki and her parents had been for her. He had volunteered to drive the seventy-five miles to Edmonton to accompany her in her visit to Franki at The Pearl's Oyster. He was not one bit impressed with where Franki had chosen to live. He got up, dressed in his navy woollen wrap, and came sleepily into the kitchen. "Sounds like a terrible storm out there, Katayna. The wind has been blowing like crazy all night." He drew close to his wife as she continued to stare out the window. "You're not thinking of travelling in these conditions . . . are you?" he asked, kissing her warmly on her cheek.

"As anxious as I am to see Franki and to comfort him, I just think it would be irresponsible to be outside today. Why, we could both freeze to death just trying to get to Edmonton! No, I will not travel today," she replied despondently.

"Hey Kat." Rusty had taken to calling his wife that recently. He thought it suited her, although Katayna preferred being called by her full name. She did not like abbreviations of names. It reminded her of Mr. Horn, that horrible teacher at White Sands School, when he thought nothing of changing children's names, as he had done with Onyfry Kaditz, one of the twins, and started calling him Oni, or even changing her own brother's name from Francis to Franki. Maybe she'd tell Rusty one day that she preferred Katayna, but not now.

"Give Franki a telephone call. I'm sure Rosie Soova has a phone in that fine establishment of hers. Don't you think that would please him until you see him? He must be very anxious waiting to hear about what's being said by the Stry-Ker clan." Rusty too favoured Franki and regarded him as a son . . . a son Katayna and he did not have.

"Yes, Rusty, yes. I'll do that right now. Poor boy, he must be in such a state." She ran over to the wall telephone and cranked the little handle, which rang at the Alberta Government Telephone operator's office. The old operator, Miss McCormick, did not start working until 9:00 a.m. The switchboard sat in the front porch of her humble house located near the United Church. Miss McCormick also doubled as a missionary teacher when time permitted. She would travel to country schools along with her foot-pedal portable organ. She had a helper accompany her to teach children about the Bible. They also sang hymns with them and handed out lovely biblical readings in a pamphlet with a coloured picture of a biblical character. When the buzzer rang from Sergeant McLennan's house, day or night, Miss McCormick responded quickly, because she never wanted to be accused of negligence in police business.

"Buzz . . . Buzz . . ." The loud buzzer on the switchboard alerted Miss McCormick in her kitchen as she and her helper, Jane Smith, were finishing breakfast. Jane

Smith was a young mission teacher in training. She also helped Miss McCormick with her Alberta Government Telephones switchboard operator duties.

Jane went into the cozy winterized porch and saw that the call originated from the McLennans' residence. "I'll answer it," she called to Miss McCormick. "It's from McLennans!" she yelled as she clicked the little red lever on the board. "Good morning, what number are you calling?" she asked in her bright, cheery voice.

"Miss McCormick, I'd like to call long distance to Edmonton." Katayna replied. "I don't have the number. I'm calling a rooming house called The Pearl's Oyster. Could you get it for me?"

"Right away, Mrs. McLennan, and this is Miss Smith with whom you're speaking." Jane Smith quickly called the Edmonton long distance operator, who looked up the number. "Before I connect you, Mrs. McLennan, would you like the number for future reference?" Miss Smith inquired.

"Yes, yes, please. And thank you," Katayna replied.

"It's 41200 and the Edmonton operator is waiting to connect you."

It was 8:30 and, as usual in the mornings, very quiet at The Pearl's Oyster. Cissy had prepared breakfast for Franki. He was half finished eating when the phone rang.

"Mon, oh mon, these guys are starting to call at the crack of dawn. I wish they'd keep their pants on. Hello, this is The Pearl's Oyster." Cissy answered the first ring, before it roused Rosie and the other three girls. They would be in a bad mood all day if they were awakened before the normal time, at noon.

"Is Franki Stry-Ker there, please?" Katayna inquired. "This is his sister Katayna calling."

"Why yes, he's right here, ma'am. Franki, it's your sister. I think she said Katayna." Cissy handed the earpiece to Franki. It was a wall-mounted oak wood phone with the mouthpiece attached to the oak facing.

"Hello, Katayna. I guess you received my letter," he said sheepishly. "And what's the news on the war front?"

Katayna laughed lightly. "Yes, I guess the war front is an appropriate description. We, Rusty and I, were going to come to Edmonton today to see you in person and discuss this whole matter, but we're in the middle of a terrible storm here in Shady Hollow. What's it like in Edmonton today?" Katayna asked.

"It's a terrible blizzard here also . . . so as much as I'd like to see you, please don't drive anywhere in these conditions. It can wait." Franki was becoming very depressed but tried to put on a happy front.

"Did you tell *Mamunia* and *Tato* that I've left the seminary?" Franki couldn't contain his curiosity.

"Yes, I drove over there as soon as I got the letter. It arrived one week after you posted it. Franki, as you probably expected, they are very upset about your decision—*Tato* even more than *Mamunia*. He left the house as soon as he heard and drove to Shady Hollow with his Clydesdale team. Rusty heard in town that he didn't even go home the same night. Yes, they are upset, but Franki, you know I support you in any decision you make. Providing it is morally right, Franki . . ." she paused. "You know I don't like where you're living; I'm sure you're now aware what kind of a place that is?"

"Thank you for your support, Katayna. That means more to me than the support of *Mamunia* and *Tato*. You've been like my mother all these years, and I would never hurt you. Never. I will look for another place to live once I've decided what I'm doing with my life. Right now, I'm leaning toward the Royal Canadian Air Force. So many guys are signing up, and I'd like to help the war effort. I've always admired that branch of the armed forces, but that's not definite. Rosie Soova has been very good to me since I've arrived here. She's letting me stay here free of charge for one month. I hear there are carpentry jobs at North West Industries. You know they are building planes for the war cause. There are also jobs on the Canol Project, building the Alaska Highway with the American government. They are paying very well . . ." Franki sighed. "But I am too confused right now to make any good decisions."

"Franki, Franki, keep your chin up . . . times are getting better. It looks like that awful depression is on its way out. By the way, do you need any money?" she asked.

"No, not right now. Father Bill gave me some and so did Rosie. I intend to pay both of them back when I can. I'll ask you for some if I can't manage . . . thank you, Katayna." Franki was extremely pleased to hear his sister's reassurance.

"Franki, we'll be there to see you as soon as this storm breaks. In the meantime, God bless you and remember I love you, and so do *Mamunia* and *Tato*, although they have a strange way of showing it . . . Goodbye my dear." She hung up the phone and leaned her head back on Rusty's shoulder as he wrapped his arms around her warmly.

The phone went dead as Franki turned to Cissy. "Cissy, do you know anything about the Royal Canadian Air Force?"

"A little, Mon, mostly what I hear around here from those fly boys who come here once in a while. Why are you asking?" Cissy asked, puzzled.

"Well, Cissy, as you may have gathered, I'm in a real pickle. My mother and father are furious that I left the priesthood, and my sister is not pleased because I am living here."

"And you, Franki, what do you want, or does that matter? You know, Mon, I've had to struggle like mad to make it in life. It hasn't been easy coming here from Amber Valley, uneducated, and being a Negro has been two strikes against me right off the bat. Rosie Soova gave me a job. She pays me well, while I attend school by correspondence. And I have a very comfortable place to live and eat good food. Do you think, Mon, I really give a hang what people think . . . they will always think the worst. So who the hang cares, Mon, think of yourself . . . it's your life Mon." Cissy went back to her work, cleaning out the icebox.

"God," thought Franki. "This girl uses common sense. She'll make one hell of a lawyer." After listening to her sermon he knew she'd reach her goals in life.

On Monday, Cissy went to the Royal Canadian Air Force enlistment office, north of the Hudson Bay Company. She brought back an information package, all about how to join this illustrious force. At home, she slipped it into Franki's room and left it on his night table while he worked in the garage, doing some other furniture repairs for Rosie.

The storm raged on for yet another week. Franki read the package Cissy had left in his room, and decided that this was the life he would pursue. He would leave Edmonton and travel to far distant places, meet new people, and become a first class pilot. Yes, that would be a good career path for him. Only Cissy knew what his intentions were.

The storm kept pounding the area for another two weeks without letting up. Franki dressed in his Sunday best, the one threadbare suit he had to wear. Cissy freshly pressed his one tattered white shirt, got one of Johnny Makar's neckties, and helped him dress. When he looked in the mirror, the image that stared back at him, surpris-

ingly, was that of a skinny but impressive, handsome
young man.

"Well, do you think I'll pass inspection, Cissy?"
Franki's confidence was improving.

"Yeah, Mon, if you don't pass inspection, then I don't
know who will. You lookin' real good, Mon . . . real
good. Now go on and do your enlistin', Mon, and good
luck!" She slapped him on the back, and he disappeared
out the door.

As he approached the enlistment office, he saw a big
sign: "Royal Canadian Air Force Recruitment Office –
Welcome."

There was a huge Union Jack flapping in the cold
wintry breeze beside the sign. Franki's heart felt as if it
would jump right into his throat. A civilian female secretary greeted him and asked him to sit down. As per
instruction in the information package, he had brought
along all the necessary papers including his high school
general diploma, which he had received at Mundare, as
well as his birth certificate.

His appointment was for 10:00 a.m. Promptly at the
hour, he was summoned into the Sergeant's office for his
initial interview.

"Francis Nykola Stry-Ker . . . are you of German
descent, young man?" the Sergeant asked in an intimidating booming voice.

"No, sir, I am of Ukrainian descent, but my parents
immigrated from what was then the Austro-Hungarian
Empire in 1903. The name is Austrian, but we have
always spoken only Ukrainian, not Austrian," responded
Franki.

"I see, so your name has nothing to do with Germany.
Any relatives in Germany?" he boomed on.

"No, sir, I have never met any relatives from the old
country."

"Why do you wish to join the Air Force, Francis . . . is that how you prefer to be called, young man— Francis?" the Sergeant asked.

"No sir, people call me Franki, and that's the name I'm used to being called," Franki responded.

"That's not what I asked you, young man . . . what do you prefer to be called?" The Sergeant was a tough taskmaster.

"Franki, sir. I prefer being called Franki, sir." Franki answered, a bit intimidated.

"Franki it is, then. Why do you wish to join the Air Force?"

"I wish to serve my country. I love Canada and want to do my part in keeping it a free country . . . a democracy," Franki replied. He did not feel it would get him points by stating he would like to travel and meet new people, and this was a good vehicle to do it.

For the next hour Franki was questioned about himself, his parents, his involvement in Mundare, and Shady Hollow. The Sergeant learned that Franki's brother-in-law was a Sergeant in the RCMP because Franki talked about Sergeant Rusty McLennan.

Next came the rigorous total medical examination. The medical examiner checked his teeth, ears, throat, blood pressure, blood samples, urine samples and gave hime a penis inspection. Franki was not circumcised. The physician listened to Franki's heart, once with the stethoscope. It was curious to Franki that he repeated the heart test three more times. Then he looked at the lengthy questionnaire which Franki had completed.

"It says here you had rheumatic fever when you were young. Is that right, Franki?" queried the physician.

"Yes sir, when I was ten." Franki told him.

The physician completed the examination, and Franki was asked to return the next day at 10:00 a.m.

The following morning, the same Sergeant with the booming voice ushered Franki into his office. He was asked to be seated.

"Franki, we have reviewed your application carefully, as well as reviewing the results of your physical examination. You would be an excellent recruit, except you do not meet the physical requirements for the Air Force. Did you know that you have a serious heart murmur? The physician advised that your heart condition must have occurred as a result of the rheumatic fever that you had when you were a youngster."

The news of the heart murmur came like a blow from a sledgehammer over the head. Franki had never had problems with his heart all these years. Another rejection, when his hopes were so high. His morale was below anything imaginable. What a crushing experience!

"You are an impressive young man, and I noticed from your application that you excel in carpentry. We are looking for civilians of your calibre to work in airplane manufacturing." The Sergeant noticed Franki's dreadful disappointment and attempted to encourage him as best as he could.

"Thank you, sir. I appreciate the time you took with me. I'll be leaving now . . ." Franki had the presence of mind to show courtesy.

"Thank you for considering enlisting in the Royal Canadian Air Force, Mr. Stry-Ker. Sorry we couldn't do more for you." The Sergeant held out his hand in a final goodwill gesture.

CHAPTER FIFTY-ONE

That night at The Pearl's Oyster was a repeat performance of the dinner party with the usual Jack, Jim, and Dick in attendance. The dinner was Rosie's specialty, Beef Wellington as only Cissy could prepare it, along with all the trimmings. Johnny Makar was there, sitting in his usual chair across the table from Veronica. It was obvious he adored this woman and obvious too that if looks could kill, each Jack that ever sat beside Veronica and then bought further services from her would be dead! Franki walked past the dining room table, observed all the dinner finery as well as all the seated guests, but continued up the stairs to the second and then the third level.

He did not come down from his room again, as he wished not to participate in any conversations or even see anyone this evening. Even though suicide had never before crossed his mind, he was certainly entertaining that thought now. This was without question the lowest ebb of his young life.

Soon Rosie came trundling up the stairs to the third level and gently knocked on the door. "Franki? Franki, may I come in?"

"Yes, sure. Come in, Rosie. Please excuse me for tonight. I'm just not hungry. I just want to be left alone tonight." One would have to be blind not to notice Franki's depression.

Rosie came in and sat beside him on the bed. She was dressed beautifully, but her blonde-orange hair was growing away from the roots and Franki noticed much grey hair mixed in the dark growth.

"What's wrong, Franki? Are you not feeling well? What's wrong, my young friend?" Rosie asked him, her voice filled with genuine concern.

"It's nothing physical . . . it's something else. I'll probably feel better tomorrow, Rosie, but please leave me alone tonight." Franki couldn't hide his hurt.

Rosie knew her young friend was very upset. She would deal with this matter later. Now, she had a command performance to attend downstairs, so she would have to put on her happy face. Franki could hear at a distance the low sounds of conversation and laughter, followed by Johann Strauss's Blue Danube Waltz. Then the doors of Veronica, Helen, and Lily clicked behind them as they continued to entertain Jack, Jim, and Dick, providing them with the full services for which they had paid and which they expected to receive. He heard Johnny Makar's door slam shut until it shook the whole third floor.

"Why does he torture himself so?" thought Franki. "Why doesn't he just ask Veronica to leave this place with him? Then he could have her all to himself. Oh well, I have enough worries of my own. I don't have enough energy to worry about Johnny or Veronica. Oh God, is life really worth living? God, oh God, what am I to do?" He continued to feel sorry for himself. Suddenly, he heard a light tap on his door.

He didn't want to see anyone. Yet another tap sounded "Franki! Franki! May I come in . . . are you sleeping?" It was Rosie speaking in hushed tones.

She opened the door and entered. She had brought with her a tray of food, the crystal decanter full of red wine, and two crystal glasses. She pulled the little table next to the bed and invited Franki to eat and join her in a glass of wine.

"Franki, my young friend," she began in her rapid presentation of words, "we can't have any of our boarders starving. You're too thin anyway. Let's put some meat on those thin bones!" she insisted.

"No, Rosie, thank you very much. I just can't eat tonight. But I will have a glass of wine," he obliged. He and Rosie had one, and then another, and then another.

Soon Franki's heavy depression felt like it was lifting, albeit slowly. After much coaxing from Rosie, he told her the whole story of his rejection by the Royal Canadian Air Force. He couldn't believe how easily he could talk to her. She was not judgemental; she was warm and compassionate. "What a wonderful mother she would have made," he thought.

She made him feel like the refusal of the Air Force was less than significant in his whole realm of life. She said it with such sincerity that he believed her.

"Rosie, you're a special person, do you know that? You have such good qualites . . . why haven't you ever married and made some fellow happy for the rest of his days?" inquired Franki. Words were coming easier to him since he had consumed all that wine. Rosie walked over to the window and looked out for the longest time. When she returned she had tears streaming down her cheeks. The stress lines were also visible even though her face was lovely. As she continued sobbing, her cake mascara streamed down her cheeks in little black streaks.

"Dear, dear Franki, the nights that I cry bitter tears are countless. Life for me has been an ordeal over and over again. I knew your dead sister, Maria, when I was very young. Maria was a dear friend . . . in fact, she was saintly. Maybe that's why God took her from me . . . from us. You were born after she died. Before Maria died, my mother died and left me with a father who came from the pits of hell! I also had seven brothers and sisters to raise. Yes, I guess death for my mother was her only escape." She hesitated before going on, not sure whether she should trust Franki, but she did. "The night after my mother was buried, my father got drunker than he normally did and around midnight he came to the bed which I shared with my sister. He grabbed me by my hair and pulled me outside into the barn. I can still hear myself screaming to this day. Then he threw me down on a pile of hay and raped me . . . savagely. I had blood flowing out of me for several days. Imagine. I was only thirteen years old. He kept raping me until he married Domka Litikiw," Rosie sobbed.

"Did you tell anyone, Rosie?" Franki asked, horrified.

"Who was there to tell? We had no family in Canada. I suppose I could have run to your mother and dad's place or the Borischuks and told them, but I was only thirteen years old. I was too scared . . . he surely would have killed me. He was a very vicious man—in fact, evil . . . yes, an evil man. Oh God, Franki, I hate him 'til today and I wish him to suffer so much like I had to suffer all these years. I knew he was castrated when he spent time in prison after he was jailed for beating up the Popilskys . . . but he deserved more, much more. The convicts should have ripped the skin off his back in strips and salted it after each strip!" Rosie sobbed uncontrollably.

Franki tried to comfort her. His heart was breaking for the pain this little energy ball had suffered through no fault of her own. A bond was quickly developing between Franki and Rosie Soova.

"Rosie, Rosie. God, what you've had to live through. I must admit that you have intrigued me for so many years. I was hoping that some day I would meet you. When I was sick with the rheumatic fever, one day I went into the *kumirka* and looked into my mother's old *scranya*. I found some letters that you had written to Maria. They were all wrapped up in a canvas cloth and tied with a thin linen string. I was curious about this package, so I opened it and found your letters to Maria. She kept them, Rosie, because she must have treasured them . . . treasured you, Rosie."   He paused for a moment. "I read about David Newhouse."

"And that I loved him with all my heart and soul?" Rosie asked him.

"Yes, Rosie. What ever happened? Did you ever see David again?"

"Oh yes, Franki. I most certainly did . . . five years after I gave birth to the most beautiful baby girl, I saw him." Rosie was sobering up now. She glanced at the bedside clock. It was now 2:00 a.m.

"Yes, Franki, my young friend. Yes, I saw David again. But let me go back in time, a time that I regret until today. I found myself pregnant, right after Mrs. Newhouse sent my loving David to Montreal. We were going to see each other after a year . . . he promised. But that wasn't to be. After I found myself pregnant I reluctantly wrote and told his mother, Rachel Newhouse, in Calgary. She asked me to come and see her. She paid for a train ticket to Calgary. What a fool I was to go . . . yes, a true, utter fool. The two Pearls that owned this house before me took me under their wing and told me to stay here and have my baby and keep it. How could I bring a baby into a whorehouse? But I was also so confused without David. I thought his mother would surely help me when she found out I was carrying her grandchild." Rosie paused.

"Well, did she . . . did she let David know?" Franki questioned intently.

"One thing at a time," Rosie said. "You'll hear my whole life story . . . as I must confess to someone . . . someone I can trust, and you're so much like your dead sister, Maria Stry-Ker . . . whom I totally trusted." Rosie wiped the streaky mascara into a lovely white lacey handkerchief and continued.

"Upon the protest of the two Pearls, I got on the train and travelled to Calgary. When I got there Rachel Newhouse met me at the CPR Station. She was all concern and showed me some affection. I was so starved for affection that any bit of kindness was like a gift from heaven. She convinced me to stay in Calgary with friends of hers until the baby was born and that it was in the baby's best interest to give it up for adoption. I kept begging her to let me talk to David. I even tried reaching him by letter in Montreal. But I guess she contacted Abraham, her other son, and the letters I wrote were never given to David. He didn't have a clue that he was about to become a father. He was waiting patiently for one year to be over when he could come back to me as his mother had promised. As much as I tried, my letters never did reach him. My beautiful baby girl was born and I gave her away because I thought David never wanted to see me again. I never heard from him, and I couldn't bring her back here. I waited for David for one, two, three, four years but heard nothing—he never contacted me. I guess I didn't look too bad and the guys that were coming here looking for a whore were admiring me. I used to do the job that Cissy is doing now. The two Pearls told me to give up and make some money . . . they knew I wanted to finish my education, to become a teacher. Well, after four years I thought it was hopeless to continue to wait for David. I thought he was just not ever wanting to see me again and I had very little respect left for myself . . . very little. So I thought, why not? Maybe I could become something. I saw what money could buy so I decided to earn some of it for myself. So I started whoring. I saved $500 in one year, Franki . . . not bad for 1928. In fact, it was a fortune, but then the worst thing that could happen, did happen!" she lowered her head and stared at her hands on her lap.

Franki by this time was fully sober. He waited for Rosie Soova to explain the rest of her sad life's story, a story he had wanted to hear for so long.

Rosie continued. "It happened on January 7, 1928, five years after I gave my beautiful daughter away. I thought I'd never see her again. I always knew I'd see David somewhere, sometime, but God, not like I did, right on Sarah's fifth birthday. That's the name they gave her . . . Sarah. David came here to The Pearl's Oyster, along with our beautiful daughter, Sarah. I had been whoring for a good year. When he finally found me, I was a full-time whore. He wasn't aware that I was doing it. He did know what The Pearl's Oyster was—a common whorehouse. He never thought I would resort to that lifestyle, so he brought little Sarah along to find me. His hopes were that the three of us would go away to make a new life as a family." Her voice trailed off as she relived the misery of that moment.

"But how did he get Sarah when you had given her away?" Franki asked, perplexed.

Rosie looked at him sadly. "Franki, as you go through life, you will learn that the Jewish people never, never, never abandon their own . . . and so it was with Sarah, my baby. Mrs. Newhouse made it look as though I was giving her away, but in reality she herself adopted Sarah, unbeknownst to me. When David returned after one year in Montreal, he was stunned to see a baby girl at his mother's place. For years she would not tell him whose baby this was. She said she was raising the baby for a friend who died during childbirth. Only when she got very sick when Sarah was four years old . . . Rachel contracted tuberculosis and was forced to go into a sanitarium near Calgary to heal herself . . . only then, under great duress, did she tell David that Sarah was actually his daughter and mine. It took her another year to tell David where I was. That's when he rushed to Edmonton with Sarah, right on her birthday, to surprise me and take me away from all this. He didn't dream I was a whore. Yes, Franki, a full-fledged whore!" Rosie ended bitterly, a hard look in her eyes at the admission.

"And then?" Franki urged her on.

"And then he walked into the front door which you come through daily and into the same parlour which you see daily, Franki . . . he came with Sarah holding his hand and sees his loving future wife in the arms of a Jack—or was it Jim or maybe Dick? Who the hell knows! It was one of them. One of those low-down, stupid creeps!" She burst into a torrent of tears again. When she could stop her deep sobbing, Franki embraced her tightly, holding her, allowing her sorrow and regret to flow. When she could cry no more, Franki released her. At this moment, he knew that for the rest of his life he would protect Rosie. He was determined that no matter how anyone tried to hurt her, he would be there for her always.

"Good night, young Stry-Ker." Rosie hugged Franki and kissed him tenderly on his cheek. "I've shared more with you tonight than I have shared with any other living human being. I used to share much with your sister, Maria. Oh, God, you are so much like her. You know, Franki, you should have been a priest . . . you're so easy to confess to!" With that comment, she walked out his door, headed for the second level, and entered her bedroom.

Well into the night Franki heard Johnny's door open quietly and he knew that it was Veronica—Veronica coming to give Johnny his free "piece of ass" which would keep him satisfied for several hours. Franki fell asleep and slept longer than usual. It was 10:00 Sunday morning when he awoke. He rushed and washed quickly. He did not even stop at the kitchen, but Cissy did not work on Sunday anyway. He was fifteen minutes late for the ten o'clock mass.

CHAPTER FIFTY-TWO

After three weeks the blizzard stopped. Rusty and Katayna came to see Franki. By this time he had gotten over his depression about being rejected by the RCAF. He had got a job as a carpenter at North West Industries and was settling in well. He was determined that if he was not going to be a priest or a pilot, then he would become a successful businessman. And that's the direction in which he would focus his life.

The visit with Rusty and Katayna was like a tonic to Franki. He knew they both loved him, particularly Katayna. He knew she would do anything to make his life more pleasant. They picked him up at The Pearl's Oyster and Katayna genuinely enjoyed meeting Rosie Soova. She had heard from the family that Rosie had been a very smart girl while she attended school at White Sands Creek. She had also heard about how Rosie and David Newhouse ran away from Shady Hollow.

Rosie was her usual genteel self and tried to be a gracious hostess, but Rusty refused her hospitality. Instead, he took Katayna and Franki to the McDonald Hotel for lunch, where they had a long visit. Katayna explained that *Tato* and *Mamunia* had settled down considerably and were no longer talking about disowning Franki. In fact, they wanted to see him and wished to have him visit.

Franki told Katayna and Rusty about the Air Force rejection. He promised that he would come home soon, but not just yet. He was still feeling badly about the RCAF's refusal to accept him. He asked all about Mikhail, Paul, Anastasia, and little Evancik, and also about Helenka's Emily and her brothers, Evan, Joseph Jr., and Peter.

Katayna told him how close Tainka had become to Emily. She told him that Emily's disposition was just like Maria's was and that she looked just like her Baba. Helenka and Joseph Pushinsky were becoming very affluent farmers. Joseph's band was booked a year in advance. He now had his young sons Joseph Jr., Evan, and Peter all playing in his band. Joseph was teaching the boys to play trumpets and saxophones. He wanted his band to sound like the popular Glenn Miller Band. Billy Makovitsky and *Tato* were becoming very involved in politics and *Tato* was helping Billy to run on the Social Credit ticket. And, most important, Uncle Yatsko had arrived from England, where he had fled from Ukraine before the war erupted. He would stay at the Stry-Kers' for about a month.

"Why is *Tato* encouraging Billy to run on the Social Credit team? Isn't Billy interested in the CCF party . . . Tommy Douglas's party?" asked Franki.

"Because he can be elected as a Social Credit representative in Shady Hollow. People like this party. Albertans don't seem to take too well to the CCF. The only CCF member that's popular in Alberta is the fellow who lives around Gibbons . . . or is it Bon Accord?" Rusty added, trying to remember.

Franki was pleased to see his two favourite people, but he realized it was time for them to be travelling back to Shady Hollow. Katayna looked at Franki and could see he was changing. He looked harder and he was becoming much more interested in making money . . . becoming rich in business.

"Franki, never forget who you are. Please don't ever change your compassionate attitude toward your fellow man. You've always been so kind . . . so good," Katayna said, looking at her brother earnestly.

"Katayna, I'll never change about being kind, but I have so much to learn about the world . . . about business. I know now that I'll excel in business. Katayna, I'll be a success no matter what."

"Franki, please remember that success has its price. It's not all there is to life, my dear," Katayna told him. She hoped his life would be successful . . . but there was something that she did not like about his changing attitude.

CHAPTER FIFTY-THREE

1941

The war was still raging in Europe. Canadian forces—Army, Air Force, and Navy—were all involved in helping Great Britain as the Germans tried to batter this little island into surrender. They had captured Poland easily, and were rolling over the rest of Continental Europe without much resistance.

Evan Stry-Ker's brother Yatsko was now living with Tainka and Evan. Yatsko was an old bachelor now nearing seventy. His personal hygiene was terrible. He would think nothing of not washing his face before he ate breakfast. Nor did he wash for the rest of the day. He used the outdoor privy along with everyone else, but he would urinate and defecate on the toilet seat board. In the house, he would spit into a small bucket; he blew his nose from a distance, many times missing his mark. The mucus would land on the clean floor, which Anastasia washed and scrubbed daily.

Tainka was so fed up with Yatsko's presence and the way he had disrupted their lives that she spoke to Evan.

"Evan, please don't think I'm being unreasonable, but what on earth are we going to do about Yatsko? His bad manners and the stench coming from his filthy body are more than anyone can bear. Even little Emily doesn't want to come here from school because she says it stinks too much at the table and she can't eat or else she'll vomit! Our toilet always looks like a manure pile; Anastasia is cleaning it all the time. She can't keep up with it and Paul said it has to stop. He will not tolerate his wife always having to clean up this mess. What are we going to do?" Tainka was very upset.

Evan's mind was occupied with other matters. He was getting ready for the March 24 provincial election; his candidate, Billy Makovitsky, who was running for the Social Credit Party, was becoming a polished speaker. Their platform included a fundamental change in the monetary system.

Evan had stopped visiting Widow Hunkowski, as he had become impotent. He felt something serious was happening to his health, as he was developing bad sores on his legs. These sores refused to heal no matter how many herbs and roots Tainka applied. The usually reliable plant called *menyatka* (goat's weed), which Tainka picked in the muskeg hay meadows and applied as a poultice, did not help any more. Tainka also prepared tansy weed tea, which usually cured every ailment, but nothing helped. The sores continued to get worse and never stopped weeping. Tainka had urged him to go see Dr. Allison but Evan continued to refuse. He tried to focus on his current problem—his brother Yatsko.

"Yes, Tainka, we must do something with Yatsko, but what? He's my only living relative . . . my only brother. He did try to bring me up when my mother and then my father died. I owe him my loyalty, don't you think?" quizzed Evan.

"Evan, Evan, of course I don't wish to throw him out, but we can't live like this either. We're living like pigs. Let's have a family meeting with Yatsko present and let's come up with a reasonable solution," stated Tainka.

The next day everyone—Yatsko, Mikhail, Paul, Anastasia, Evan, Tainka, and even little Evancik—ate a sumptuous dinner. After raspberry preserves were served for dessert, Evan began the discussion.

"Everyone here has welcomed Uncle Yatsko into our family and we've lived together for almost a year. As in any family, problems do arise . . . our family has had many . . . God knows we have, Yatsko," he addressed his brother directly, just as Yatsko spit a big bolt of spittle into his little pile. "Yatsko, how do you like living with us since arriving here in Canada?"

"Evan, it's not that I'm not grateful or that I don't appreciate the expense you went through to get me to Canada. I am very grateful but I have never in my life lived in this kind of a house . . . I have never in my life lived like this with someone, and I'm almost seventy. I've always been alone. I've lived in barns, in chicken coops, never in such a big nice house. I'll tell you truthfully I'd be the happiest if I could have a little shack somewhere on this yard where I could once again be alone . . . I like being alone. Even if I do like all of you . . . there are just too many of you!" Yatsko was frightened to say this, for fear Evan would be angry.

Evan was immensely relieved at his brother's suggestion, which meant there was no need for a confrontation. Within a month Yatsko had his wish granted. He now had his own one-room cabin. It was a sturdy building with siding and trim on the outside and cedar shingles. The inside was finished with shiplap siding on the ceiling and walls and wood shavings in between the walls for insulation. It was twenty feet by twenty feet. They also built him his very own toilet. This was primarily for privacy and relief for the rest of the family. Yatsko wanted the inside walls painted yellow and blue, in the same colours as the Ukrainian flag, as Yatsko was indeed a Ukrainian nationalist. So the ceiling and the lower half of the walls was painted a cheerful canary yellow. The other half of the wall was painted blue, just like the Ukrainian flag colour. The floor was covered with a Congoleum carpet that made it easier to wash. Evan bought him a small cook stove, a little table and two chairs, a cupboard, and a 78-inch-wide mattress. On the washstand was a white enamel basin, which Evan knew would be used infrequently. A large icon of the Virgin Mary and baby Jesus hung over Yatsko's bed, along with a crucifix. Everyone was pleased, especially Yatsko, who loved his new little home and said he could never have had a better place, not even in heaven.

Evan used to hire one of the local farm girls to clean Yatsko's house and toilet once a month, and he paid her $10 each time. It was a wage that was well over the going rate; in fact it was what girls in these parts usually received for working a whole month. Yatsko's meals were prepared in the big house and usually carried to him by Mikhail or Evan. His clothes, whenever he changed, were washed by the cleaning girl. There was never another problem with Uncle Yatsko, and he lived happily by himself. He did come over to the big house for Christmas, Easter, and any other important holidays. He had learned that he should not spit or blow his nose during these times and he even changed his clothes for these occasions.

The Yatsko housing incident made Evan realize in what substandard conditions the Stry-Kers were living. Evan had known about electric lights and indoor plumbing for years. He liked visiting Edmonton and the Turkish baths. He liked the convenience of pulling a string and the lights would come on. So much better than lighting a coal oil lamp with a wick . . . which if not properly trimmed would smoke up the delicate glass globe; what a nuisance that was. But most of all he liked the indoor plumbing. As he was getting older, his body was less and less willing to accept the dreadful Canadian winter conditions where the thermometer dipped to -40 degrees Fahrenheit. Whenever he went to the outdoor privy he would have to drop his drawers and sit on the cold toilet boards. It was unbearably cold. But most of all he was starting to feel sorry for Tainka having to bear this cold; after all, she never asked for much.

"Goldarn, why am I so stupid? I have $25,000 in Canada Savings Bonds. I have $10,000 hidden in my old buffalo coat. How much can this cost to put in . . . how much?" Evan hitched his Clydesdale mares in their lovely ornate harnesses the next morning and rode off to see Billy Makovitsky. Billy was still campaigning for the election, but was usually tending the store in the mornings. Billy would know.

Billy Makovitsky did know, and he was trying to encourage people to better their lives. There were no farmers in this whole constituency who had electric lights or plumbing. A few had these conveniences in Shady Hollow, but you could count the number who did on two hands.

Billy said, "Evan, if you install plumbing and electric lights I will get everything you need through my store at wholesale prices. It will cost you half of what you would normally have to pay. Then, when I get elected, I will send people to your place to see what it's like to live 'modern like.'"

Evan was amenable to this suggestion because at this time he would have paid full price to have these conveniences. Tradesmen from Edmonton came over to the Stry-Kers' and performed the work. The plumbers dug a field for the sewage system and installed a three-compartment septic tank. They installed a huge claw-foot iron bathtub, a toilet, and a pedestal sink. The bathroom was located where Uncle Yatsko's old bedroom had been, before he moved to his own cabin. This was on the main floor of the house. With all the work and supplies it cost Evan less than $5,000 to install plumbing in his home.

The electricians installed the generators and banks of batteries in a winterized granary. The wiring was done in the house, in the cattle and pig barns, and in the chicken coop. Soon light bulbs hung everywhere and to Evan's delight there were light switches . . . he did not even have to pull a string. The generators, batteries, and all the electricians' wages and other supplies cost Evan less than $2,000. He was thrilled, but the person who was even more thrilled was Tainka. She had never dreamed she would ever be this fortunate.

CHAPTER FIFTY-FOUR

Franki got a job as a carpenter at North West Industries. In a very short time he was promoted to supervisor of his work crew. Even though he was paid $2 per hour, he was not pleased with how long it was taking him to save any money.

Johnny Makar continued to haul freight and could not keep up with the demand, as Edmonton, Alberta, was a bustling city. He was entertaining the idea of buying another truck and hiring a driver. Johnny had bankrolled $1,000. He thought if he could own a successful trucking company, then he and Veronica could leave The Pearl's Oyster . . . forever.

Franki had only saved $150 . . . a far cry from financial independence. At this point he couldn't even think of leaving Rosie Soova's Pearl's Oyster. Rosie still was not charging him room and board. Franki had the same arrangement as Johnny—work in lieu of paying your room and board charges. Franki did all the repairs around the house, while Johnny looked after other tasks . . . tasks that were never explained fully. It was a special arrangement Rosie had with Johnny. Franki guessed that Johnny was Rosie's enforcer and bodyguard.

Instead of taking the home correspondence studies, Cissy was now attending her last year of school at Victoria Composite High School. She would be writing her Grade 12 Departmental examinations. The success or failure of these provincial examinations would decide whether she could enter university. Rosie knew full well that Cissy would have a hard row to hoe in order to break the male dominance at the University of Alberta.

Further, the colour of her skin could create an even greater barrier.

Cissy was now only working in the evenings and Rosie gave her two days off on weekends so that she could study.

One day Rosie summoned her. "Cissy, I want to discuss a deal with you . . . an agreement which will make it easier for you and will benefit me. I will pay your university tuition fees . . . if, when you become a lawyer, you look after all my legal needs. What d'you say?"

Cissy didn't have to think twice. She accepted graciously and hugged Rosie with such great force that Rosie's breath was taken away for a minute. "God, ma'am, yes, Rosie. I'll look after you legally, and morally if I can [although she knew that morally would be an impossibility] as long as I live . . . you're some kinda lady . . . some kinda fantastic lady!"

It happened one night while Cissy was working in the kitchen. One of the Jack, Jim, or Dicks asked Rosie if he could pay for the services of Cissy. Rosie told him emphatically "NO. . . . NO, Cissy is never for sale."

He insisted. "Look, Rosie, everyone is for sale. What's a Negro bitch doing here anyway . . . in a whorehouse? Of course she is for sale. I feel like a little black ass; she probably much tighter than these banged-up whores you have here," and with his drunken hand he pointed to Lily, Veronica, and Helen.

At that comment Rosie, who was getting tipsy on wine, rose to her feet. She sobered up fast . . . like a speeding bullet. She shouted, "Get your Goddamn fat ass the hell outta here . . . get out and never come back . . . you, you fat son-of-a-bitch!"

Johnny and Franki were not home as yet; both were working late. The fat Dick rose slowly and saw that Rosie, the little pepper-pot, was furious. He would rather not tangle with her. So he grabbed his bowler hat and over-coat and scrambled out of The Pearl's Oyster. However, he did not leave the premises, as everyone thought he did. He lurked outside the house; he knew the routine because he was a frequent guest. He knew that soon the meal would end, the Strauss waltzes would begin, and soon after the girls would take their respective guests to their second-storey rooms. Veronica was left without a partner, as Dick would have been her client, so she was delighted. She excused herself and went upstairs alone. Soon Lily and Helen, with their Jim and Jack in tow, ascended the stairs. Rosie blew out the candles on the dinner table in the parlour. She peeked into the kitchen, where Cissy was just finishing washing the dishes.

"Good night, Cissy, I'm going to bed; this has been an awful, eventful night!" exclaimed Rosie.

"Yes Ma'am, I heard your altercation with that fat-ass businessman . . . I mean . . . was it Dick, Jack or Jim?" Cissy said quickly. She knew she was never to refer to the clients by their real names or by what they did in real life.

"That's okay, Cissy . . . tonight he was known as Dick. Oh, Cissy, I'm getting so tired of this goddamn rat race. After you finish university I will quit and move to some exotic place and try to find my own daughter . . ." She turned and went slowly up the stairs.

Cissy had heard through various gossips about Rosie's beloved David and his visit with Sarah, the little girl. That was so many years ago, here at The Pearl's Oyster.

Cissy put away the large Limoges dinner platter in the china cabinet of the dining room and returned to the kitchen. As she opened the door leading into the kitchen she was grabbed from behind. A big, clammy hand cupped her mouth and nose and twisted her arm back-wards and held her tight. She was disabled. His raspy drunken voice whispered, "Don't even try to scream you black little bitch or I'll kill you . . . I said I want a piece of black ass and I'll get it here and now. You're lucky a guy like me would even look at you!"

He was forcing her to the floor and she could feel his erect penis as he released his belt buckle. His big trousers fell to the floor. They were both now on the kitchen floor and he ripped Cissy's underpants off her body. She was still a virgin and wanted to remain that way. She was absolutely terrified, but even more she was furious that an ugly tub of lard like this creep would be the one to deflower her. By now she was crying hysterically, only no one could hear her. She was also trying to fight like a mad tiger. His stinky hand was clamped tightly over her mouth. This powerful ox of a man was so strong that she could not defend herself. She was rendered powerless as he straddled her in readiness to penetrate her. Just then the back door to the kitchen flew open and Franki came bursting in. He grabbed Dick by the back of his shirt. He was able to pull the fat ass off Cissy, whereupon the fat ass rose to his feet and tried to attack Franki. Franki then started punching him and with his knee kicked him as hard as his strength allowed into his groin area. The big tub of lard fell to his knees, both hands cupping his scrotum as he howled in pain. Just then Johnny Makar came running in. Cissy shouted to Johnny that she had almost been raped by this fat ass.

Johnny complimented Franki for saving Cissy. Johnny knew that if he had not returned at that moment Franki would have been beaten badly by the big fat Dick. Even though he was drunk, Franki was no match for this ox of a man. Johnny hauled the naked "Dick" outside and shouted back to Franki and Cissy not to follow him.

Rosie heard the commotion, as her bedroom was above the kitchen, and she came running down.

When she heard the story she stated, "Dick will be dealt with by Johnny, and trust me . . . there is no worst fate than that!"

In the morning the Edmonton Bulletin headline read: *Local Businessman Beaten Viciously.* The article went on to report that a well-respected businessman had been beaten. His penis had been so mutilated that it required amputation. The report stated that the man was in intensive care at the University Hospital. The police had no suspects.

Life at The Pearl's Oyster changed dramatically after this incident. Clients were screened more carefully, and now the service men visited more frequently at the establishment. Also, when Johnny worked late there was always another bouncer type of male in the house, usually a type that looked even more formidable than Johnny.

Cissy enrolled in a martial arts class, resolved to protect herself in the future. She was also even more determined now that she would become a good lawyer and help to jail scum like "Dick." She excelled in her studies and Rosie gave her as much time as she needed to study. Rosie hired another young, pretty girl to help in the house . . . a girl who had found herself homeless after her father had kicked her out after finding out she was not his blood daughter. He had also asked his wife to leave even though they had been married twenty-six years and she had produced six other children, which were his flesh and blood.

The girl's name was Sonia Clifford. She was sixteen years old and she had been born just outside Edmonton, in a village called Beverly.

CHAPTER FIFTY-FIVE

Sarah Newhouse had lived in Calgary, Alberta, Canada, all her life. Her grandmother, Rachel Newhouse, whom she called Nana, had brought her up. Sarah loved her grandmother because she was always gentle, loving, and understanding to the young girl. Coupled with this was the love and excellent tutoring she received from her father, David Newhouse.

Sarah was raised in the Jewish faith and tradition. She observed the ways of Judaism. She excelled in academic studies and in music; she played piano, organ, cello, violin, and flute. She attended school in Calgary at Western Canada High School until she graduated with honours in 1939. She was then sent away to a girl's finishing school in Montreal. While in Montreal she learned to speak fluent French. She learned many social graces and etiquette, more than her Nana and father could teach her.

David's father, Abraham Sr., had died many years earlier, before Sarah was born. Rachel had had a number of marriage proposals from Jewish gentlemen over the years . . . even some from gentiles. She was not interested in marriage; instead, her mission in life was to raise Sarah. She had done a marvellous job and so had her son, David.

Abraham Newhouse, upon his death, left a very large estate, which kept Rachel and Sarah in affluent surroundings and provided an above average quality of life. In fact, Rachel still owned half of the furniture store business with the Bernstein family.

David taught school in Calgary at Mount Royal College. He had never married . . . never even taken out another woman from the time that he had met Rosie Soova. Whenever Rosie was discussed his eyes teared up. Whenever anything unkind was said about her he would always defend Rosie and talked about her in the most complimentary terms. Many years earlier David's mother had stopped arguing with him about Rosie. Furthermore, Rachel would reflect often whether her religion was more important to observe or whether the happiness of her son was, as she watched how tortured his soul was over the years. Deep in her heart, she felt she had made a mistake about Rosie and David's relationship, but it was too late now. As his daughter grew he defended Rosie and it was hard to understand, particularly after he found Rosie in the arms of a strange man at The Pearl's Oyster many years ago when Sarah was five. He could not hide his hurt. But on the other hand, he had never stopped loving Rosie either.

He had aged prematurely and his hair had turned grey. His normally high forehead with its recessed hairline had been half-bald for many years now.

Sarah was a spitting image of Rosie, except she had David's reddish hair with tight curls. She was a ravishing beauty. Her thick tangle of curls were hard to manage. Both Rachel and David doted on her constantly.

In 1938, Rachel had gotten a call from her frantic daughter-in-law in Montreal to report that Abe Jr., David's brother, had gone on a buying trip and to visit some relatives in Continental Europe and she had not heard from him since he landed in Berlin, Germany. No one knew what had happened to him. Relatives in Germany said that they had not even spoken to him and they did not know where Abe could be or indeed what had happened to him.

A year had gone by without a word from Abe. His family was desperate to find out his whereabouts. They were worried sick, and so in July 1939 David flew to London, England, in an attempt to find Abe. He phoned Rachel from London telling her he was going on to Berlin as he had traced Abe to that city. They heard from David once more from Berlin in July 1939. War was declared in September 1939 by Germany. Rachel did not hear from Abe, David, or for that matter from any of her other European relatives. They heard wicked stories about Jews disappearing from their homes in Warsaw, Poland. But why, Rachel thought . . . this just couldn't be; in fact, she felt it was impossible. Nevertheless, both her sons were missing . . . so what was going on anyway? It was a complete mystery to her. She was grief-stricken because not just one son, but now both of her sons were missing. She had only two children, Abe Jr. and David. Now she had only Sarah. She did not give up hope, and daily lit her menorah in prayer.

CHAPTER FIFTY-SIX

Sarah Newhouse Visits Rosie

Cissy was enjoying a break from her studies. She had been accepted by the University of Alberta after much difficulty. The Principal of Victoria Composite High School had made many representations to the University Board of Governors. He asked questions such as: Why was this young lady being denied acceptance? She had the highest marks of any other entrant; her tuition was paid in full; she asked for no special favours; she was a co-operative and brilliant student at Victoria High School . . . so what was the problem? The Board of Governors finally came up with a lame-brained excuse . . . the arts faculty, the forerunner to entrance into Law was full. Before pursuing the matter further, the Principal did his homework and found the Commerce Faculty was not full. He approached the Board again and this time did not give them one inch of leeway. The Commerce Faculty was not full. Five more places were left . . . others who were already accepted had lower marks than Cissy. Mind you, they were all males . . . white males.

The Principal engaged Bob Oliver ("Red Eye Bob"), editor and top-notch investigative reporter at the *Edmonton Bulletin*, to advise him and accompany him to the meeting with the governors. The Principal also contacted the provincial Minister of Education for Alberta, the Honourable Alf Hooke, and advised him of Cissy's plight. After that, Cissy's acceptance letter came quickly, advising her as follows:

Miss Cissy Brown:
We are pleased to advise you that you have been accepted as a Commerce Faculty student. You are asked to contact the Dean at the Faculty of Commerce to confirm your attendance.

Cissy delivered her letter personally and she asked for a written receipt of delivery. The secretary to the Dean, Dr. Smith of the Faculty of Commerce, signed the receipt.

Cissy was making herself a pot of peppermint tea, from peppermint that she had picked in Rosie's garden and dried for her own use. She had just poured scalding water over the dried peppermint leaves in the teapot, when she heard a gentle tap on the front door. Cissy was working this day, as Rosie had given a day off to Sonia, the regular kitchen help. This was before noon and way too early for their usual guests to arrive, so when she answered the door she was surprised to see a beautiful young lady dressed immaculately. Her thick auburn hair was pulled into a "rat" which created a neat reversed pageboy. Atop her head she wore a small, black-rimmed felt hat, which crowned her beautiful face.

As soon as Cissy saw her she could not contain her excitement . . . for there in front of her was a young Rosie Soova. Rosie Soova with different hair. She was about five feet seven inches tall—five inches taller than Rosie.

"Good morning. Does Rosie Soova still reside here?" uttered Sarah in a soft voice, but with perfect articulation.

"Why yes, yes, Rosie lives here . . . who's inquiring, please?" Cissy tried to compose herself.

"I am Sarah Newhouse; I believe she'll know who I am," replied Sarah.

"Please come and wait in the parlour," instructed Cissy. She was pleased that she had already cleaned up the main floor and every piece of furniture shone from her lemon oil treatment. The hardwood floors were spotless and the thick India rugs were also put down after the night of the Johann Strauss waltzing.

"Would you like a cup of coffee?" Cissy asked Sarah.

"Why, yes, that would be nice. I have driven from Calgary this morning and have not stopped driving except to fill the gas tank at Red Deer."

"Do you take cream and sugar?" Cissy further inquired.

"Yes, please," replied Sarah.

"You must have been up early if you drove all the way from Calgary this morning!" exclaimed Cissy. "Why, isn't that almost two hundred miles?"

"Yes, about that," responded Sarah.

"Then you probably haven't had breakfast . . . have you?" questioned Cissy.

"No, as a matter of fact, I haven't. Some toasted bread would be very nice." Sarah stated.

"How about bacon and eggs . . . we have some nicely smoked bacon and fresh farm eggs." Cissy pressed.

"Thank you very much. I do not eat bacon, but a boiled egg would be much appreciated." Sarah was indeed pleased, because she was hungry.

Cissy got Sarah a cup of coffee and brought along sugar and cream in Rosie's best Limoges china. Before she started cooking the eggs and toasting the bread, she ran upstairs to Rosie's bedroom. She rapped on the door quite forcefully, as she knew Rosie would be dead to the world after consuming a lot of wine the night before. No answer, as she might have expected. So she gently tried the door . . . it was not locked. Cissy walked in and saw Rosie sleeping soundly. She had a cover over her eyes to keep out the light. First, Cissy tapped on Rosie's shoulder, but to no avail. She applied a little more force and shook her quite strenuously. Rosie started waking and knew instinctively that something serious must have happened, because Cissy would never have awakened her for any other reason.

"Wha . . . Wha . . . What's wrong, girl? What you waking me up at this ungodly hour?" Rosie stammered.

"Ma'am, Rosie, Ma'am. I'm shoo it's your baby girl downstairs . . . for she shoo looks like you, ma'am." Whenever Cissy became excited or scared she reverted to speaking in her own ways, forgetting elocution, which she had so carefully learned.

"Ma . . . My . . . what?" Rosie was coming to her senses. "What's her name, Cissy?"

"She says it's Sarah Newhouse!" Cissy stammered.

"Woo, you're right girl . . . it is my little girl." Like a flash, Rosie jumped out of bed and stripped off her nightgown right in the presence of Cissy. She pulled on her fitted corset, which held her ample breasts and derriere in shape. Then she slipped on a cotton frilly-sleeved dress, silk stockings, and slippers with medium-sized heels. She suddenly realized that Sarah was all alone downstairs, so she urged Cissy to go down quickly and she would follow immediately.

"I'll brush my teeth and wash my face and I'll be there right away!"

Even before Cissy finished telling Sarah about Rosie's message, Rosie was bouncing down the stairs. She went flying over to Sarah, grabbed her tighter than she realized, and hugged her for a full five minutes. To her surprise Sarah was hugging her back. Tears streamed down both Sarah's and Rosie's cheeks. They cried and hugged for almost a half-hour. Cissy did not interrupt them.

Then Rosie, in her rapid speech, asked Sarah if she had had anything to eat.

"Cissy already asked me. I'm sure she'll get me something," Sarah replied. She was crying and laughing as she could see this was indeed her mother, a mother whom her father loved so deeply. Just then Cissy appeared at the door and delivered the boiled eggs and toast, along with homemade gooseberry jam.

CHAPTER FIFTY-SEVEN

Rosie asked Cissy to tell everyone not to disturb them and to announce that there would be no dinner for Dick, Jim, or Jack that night. The two women talked until suppertime. Rosie held nothing back and told Sarah how it was that she gave her up for adoption. She told her about her life at The Pearl's Oyster. She also told her how much she loved David, her father, and that there was never another man whom she cherished as much.

"That's such a sad story . . . I'd like to call you mother, if you let me?" Sarah ventured.

"My dearest, dearest daughter, I couldn't be more honoured. How is your father?" Rosie asked reluctantly as she hoped against hope that he was not married.

"That's one of the reasons I'm here, to tell you that my father has disappeared in Europe." Sarah sadly replied. Then she told Rosie about how her Uncle Abe had flown to Berlin in early 1938 and David followed to try to find him in July 1939. She went on to tell Rosie that they had not heard anything from either one of them all these three years.

"You mean David has not been heard from for three years . . . Oh God, oh God . . . this is terrible news, Sarah!" cried Rosie. Rosie was so visibly upset that Sarah thought she would have a stroke. Her blood pressure was soaring . . . the pulsation of her blood vessels on her temples was very obvious. "What has your grandmother done to find them?" Rosie demanded.

"She's paid over ten thousand dollars to various detectives . . . those who usually do international work. They have all traced them leaving England and heading for Berlin and then the trail goes dead. You know we're at war with Germany and there is no co-operation between the two countries. We also hear some wicked stories about how Jews are being treated by the Germans . . . I hope these stories are not true," cried Sarah.

"Yes, child, I've heard similar stories and I had no idea my David was somewhere over there. Why, I thought he was safe in Calgary . . . my worst fear was that he was married." Rosie said sheepishly.

"No, mother, my father has always loved only you. We in the Newhouse family all know that!" Sarah exclaimed.

"How did you find me, Sarah?" Rosie inquired.

"With great difficulty. I finally gave my Nana an ultimatum . . . if she didn't tell me where you were, I'd leave her house and never come back. I have never given her any ultimatums in my entire life!" responded Sarah. "She told me, reluctantly."

Rosie asked Sarah to stay overnight, as she knew Veronica had now almost always taken to sleeping in Johnny's room. Sarah agreed; she had told her Nana that she would not be back for several days.

After Sarah was safely in bed and Rosie had hugged and kissed her for as long as she possibly could, she said goodnight. Rosie went into the kitchen and found Johnny, Veronica, Franki, and Cissy playing cards.

She asked Johnny to fire up the McLaughlin-Buick, which had sat there in almost new condition and was used very little.

She dressed in her best wrap and donned a stylish felt hat. She had toned down her make-up and looked very much like an elderly, genteel lady.

"The rest of you will please excuse Johnny and me . . . I have some favours to collect," was all Rosie would say.

The next morning, Rosie told Sarah that she had started her own investigation about David and, for that matter, Abe.

"Sarah, it could take up to a month before I find out anything. You are welcome to stay if you wish, for as long as forever." Rosie stated emphatically.

"Thank you, Mother, but I must get back to my Nana . . . she only has me . . . tell me, Mother, who is helping you find my father?"

"I would rather not discuss it further, my dearest child. I'm not being rude . . . but it is better for us all if you don't know!" Rosie was firm.

That afternoon Sarah left to travel back to Calgary.

Rosie's sources were superb: within one month she learned that David and Abe were still alive. They did not wish to be found because their lives would indeed be in great danger. In order not to spread David and Abe's whereabouts Rosie did not report to Sarah what she had learned.

Another month passed and Rosie got all her affairs wrapped up. Veronica would take over running The Pearl's Oyster for fifty per cent of the profits. Veronica and Johnny were planning to marry. The new girl, Sonia Clifford, was very willing to take Veronica's place entertaining Dick, Jack, and Jim.

Rosie transferred the $50,000 she had saved over the years to an English bank. She told Sarah she would be leaving Edmonton for a while to travel to Hawaii and would contact her upon her return. This of course, was not the truth, but she knew that she must keep her whereabouts top secret.

CHAPTER FIFTY-EIGHT

March 1943

Billy Makovitsky was elected as the member of Legislative Assembly in a landslide victory. He felt honoured to be serving as a representative for Shady Hollow. He could not have succeeded without Evan's coaching and experience in politics.

Billy hired Harry Chomiak, Teckla's youngest son, to work in his family store. Harry was a bright young man who had finished his grade twelve, farmed for a while, married a local girl, and found farming was not his forte.

Evan and Billy celebrated in Edmonton for one solid week. Evan frequented the Turkish baths and had long ago stopped visiting Rosie Soova's Pearl's Oyster . . . ever since his son, Franki, had arrived at Rosie's place after leaving the Mundare Seminary. Besides, he was now impotent. There had been an oath of secrecy sworn by all of Rosie's residents and until this day no one had revealed that Evan liked to visit Helen, the resident whore. She was the eldest of the three—Helen, Veronica, and Lily.

Evan's leech treatments, which were supposed to suck all the bad blood out of his system, were clearly not working. The sores on his legs were getting progressively worse and Evan, who had always thought he was inde-structible, was indeed worried about his state of health.

Every time he consumed copious quantities of moonshine whiskey, particularly Father Stepko's sweet communion wine, his condition worsened. He drank much more water these days and was urinating almost constantly. Many times he thanked God for giving him the good sense to install running water at the Stry-Ker home, as he knew he would never reach the outdoor toilet before wetting his pants. He was at the point where, against all his stubbornness, he would have to seek the help of Dr. Allison. But this celebration was his last big party before he would seek medical advice and he was determined he would enjoy it.

Billy and Evan discussed the bad provincial roads into Shady Hollow and the fact that there were no provincial government services in this village. Billy promised he would work diligently to ensure Shady Hollow and, indeed, this constituency would benefit, because after all it now had its very own Member of the Legislature.

Billy was a member of the Social Credit government, headed by Premier William Aberhart. No one could have guessed that this famous premier who charted Alberta's destiny in a very progressive manner, the man who led Alberta through the horrible Depression, would be dead within three months. Premier Aberhart died May 23, 1943, in Vancouver, B.C.

CHAPTER FIFTY-NINE

Rosie Soova, before departing for her secretive destination, tied up all the loose ends.

Cissy was looked after financially in order to complete Law at the University of Alberta. Veronica and Johnny would run The Pearl's Oyster in her absence. She signed a Power of Attorney to Veronica empowering her to run the house as though it was her own.

When Rosie departed, so did the heart and soul of The Pearl's Oyster. The usual laughter, joking, and family-type togetherness all changed completely.

Franki was heartbroken, as he regarded Rosie as his best friend and confidante. He no longer enjoyed living at The Pearl's Oyster. So after a month he told Veronica he would be moving into a place of his own. He rented a one-room suite at the Heckla Apartments for $25 per month. This was a rate he could afford.

Veronica was more than pleased because she had plans to make more money . . . after all, she was operating on a percentage basis. She now had two extra rooms on the third level, one vacated by Franki and the other by Johnny, who now shared her bedroom on the second level in what used to be Rosie's bedroom, above the kitchen.

Next she held a meeting with Lily and Helen and told them that if they wished to remain at The Pearl's Oyster they would have to accept the changes. First, they would be moving up to the third level and, secondly, they would be taking over the housecleaning and cooking duties. They could only keep their old clients and these Jims, Jacks, or Dicks would not be wined and dined as per the normal procedure that Rosie had established. She told them that the clients were demanding much younger women, such as Sonia Clifford, and she intended to keep up with the demand. She would be replacing them as soon as she found two younger, more attractive women.

It took Veronica one week to complete her transaction. Sonia Clifford brought in her friend, Jill, who was as attractive as Sonia. Johnny found a girl who was waitressing at the Royal George Hotel, whose name was Helen . . . they quickly changed it to Ellen so there was no confusion with the old Helen. Helen was now moved another level up and downgraded to housekeeper.

Helen and Lily were beside themselves at what Veronica, and in part Johnny, had had the gall to do to them. They wondered, in desperation, how they could reach Rosie. She would never stand for this . . . but no one knew where Rosie had gone and they had no choice but to live under these conditions for now.

A month passed by and the Jims, Jacks, and Dicks forgot about Lily and Helen. They all wanted to spend their time with Jill, Sonia, or Ellen. This infuriated Lily and Helen even more.

However, they held their tongues, as they knew that when Rosie got back, she would once again upgrade their positions and they would move back into the limelight.

In the meantime, Veronica had more than doubled the business, and she and Johnny were socking away the cash. He would soon buy his third truck, and Makar's Transport was born.

CHAPTER SIXTY

Franki worked at the North West Industries and was now in charge of a large contingent of men. His salary had doubled but he knew that even with a doubled salary he was still only earning $4 per hour, $40 per day—he always worked ten-hour days.

Johnny remained a close friend of Franki's and they would meet for coffee or beer weekly.

Johnny would always tease Franki about remaining celibate.

"For shit's sake, you crazy fool, we now have beautiful young girls at The Pearl's, why not treat yourself?"

"Johnny, I didn't live up to my vows at the seminary. I know now I'm not going back to Mundare and to the seminary, but the least I can do is remain celibate until I marry. After all, we expect that our women should be virgins when we marry them; why should there be different standards for men?" Franki was firm.

"Let me tell you, you are a stupid, stupid son-na- . . . yeah, well . . . you'll find out when you marry." Johnny stopped his teasing.

"Franki, do you want to make more money?" Johnny was very serious now.

"Yeah, yes . . . of course I'd like to make more money . . . at the rate I'm going I'll never amount to anything . . . what do they call us—those who carry lunch cans— Lunch Bucket Kings? That's what I'll be as long as I'm in this job, a Lunch Bucket King!" Franki sounded very despondent; he missed talking to Rosie, Cissy, and most of all Katayna. He saw her very infrequently. Her whole attention was now focused on Rusty, her RCMP husband. "Anyway, what have you got in mind, Johnny?" He was eager to learn.

"As you know, there are thousands of U.S. Army and Air Force people here in Edmonton." Johnny kept up with the changing times.

"Yes, I know, I see them every day. They're assembling and transporting planes from here, for the Russians." Franki stated. "For God's sake, Johnny, that's what I do."

"No, not only that, they're still building the Alaska Highway. What do they call it—Canol project or something like that. Yeah, well son-of-a-bitch, that means there are thousands of customers out there!" Johnny was excited.

Franki wished that Johnny would not swear so much, but he was not about to start changing him . . . "Customers for what?" he asked.

"Why for White Lightnin', Franki . . . boy, those Americans service boys like their hooch and they have lots of money. Yeah, Franki, we could be millionaires over night . . . son-of-a-bitch, you make hay when the sun shines," spouted Johnny.

"You know how illegal that is . . . we'd rot in jail for years . . . like so many moonshiners do. The RCMP are out to destroy moonshiners and bootlegging!" Franki was adamant.

"You are one stupid big *dupa* (ass). So why don't you go and ask the Bishop or confess to him. If I had to be afraid that everything is illegal, I'd still be loading freight at the CNR. You can see I'm not too badly off. Three trucks already . . . soon I'll have a whole fleet. This war won't go on forever, so why not? It's like shooting fish in a barrel!"

The Alberta liquor laws at this time were very stringent. Liquor was sold in hotels, where the men drank in separate rooms from women. Women were allowed to drink at a hotel only if escorted by a man but were segregated to a separate room. Hotel bars were open from 1:00 p.m. until 10:00 p.m.

The government ran liquor stores, and their hours were also very restricted.

The American servicemen were not used to these restricted conditions and would have been happy to have another supplier where liquor could be bought freely any time. This is what Johnny had in mind.

"My plan is to buy the stuff from Louie Kaditz. Louie and Metro Soova make the best moonshine whiskey in Alberta. Sell it on the base—you know your way around there, don't you? Or get one of the Americans as a partner. I haul freight to Shady Hollow now; I could haul the sugar there to them and bring back the hooch and you would sell it on the base, what d'you think?" Johnny had formulated a plan but Franki was not interested . . . not yet anyway.

"My brother-in-law, Rusty McLennan, is now the RCMP Sergeant in Shady Hollow. He has been trying to catch Louie Kaditz and Metro Soova for years. I could never get involved in such a scheme. I'd be betraying him . . . breaking the law . . . it's just not right." Franki stated.

"Well, if you'd like to make $40,000 in one year . . . and after one year we stop, before we're caught. Your whole future would be looked after. You could do anything you wanted after that. It's our seed money!" Johnny made some sense this time and he did not even swear. "Tell you what . . . think about it, Franki Stry-Ker . . . think about it."

A week had passed by before Franki and Johnny met again. Franki had been thinking about Johnny's proposal. Forty thousand dollars in one year was unimaginable, particularly when he considered that $1,000 per month is all he was netting in his earnings. Twelve thousand dollars a year . . . $28,000 less than if he bought into Johnny's scheme.

Franki even made the acquaintance of a young American Air Force service man. His name was Oliver Barris. He appeared to be a real go-getter; Franki noticed he would charge civilian people who wanted to get to downtown Edmonton ten cents to ride in the Air Force Jeep. Several times he saw four guys getting into the Jeep and leaving the base property. He would make forty cents and he was going downtown anyway.

Franki thought about how so many people were taking advantage of the opportunities presented during wartime.

When Franki and Johnny met again, the first question Johnny asked was; "Well, did you think about my idea for business?"

"Johnny, first of all, have you heard anything from Rosie Soova? It's almost six months since she's gone. I really miss her." Franki was genuinely concerned.

"Hell no. Veronica is making money hand over fist—who needs Rosie? Those old bitches Lily and Helen are giving us some trouble . . . complaining all the time. If it was me, I'd kick them out on their asses in the middle of the street . . . that's what I would do!" Johnny was not a compassionate soul. "Well what d'you think?"

Franki knew that Johnny wanted an answer, and with or without Franki, he would be selling "White Lightnin'" to the Americans.

"Johnny, I'd be a fool not to want to get ahead and I'll never do it on my wages. I'd like to start my own construction business, but it takes about $20,000 to do it. I'll go into partnership with you only until I make $20,000. You'll have to have a plan that almost guarantees the RCMP won't catch us. If you can promise me

these things then I may consider this business with you."
Franki was adamant about his proposal.

They met one week later at the Royal George Hotel
for a beer, in the gents' section. Johnny's plan for transporting the moonshine was foolproof. He explained that
he would get a custom-made gas tank for his big
International truck. The capacity of the tank was normally twenty gallons. Instead he would weld a separate
compartment into the gas tank, which would have a
cover and could only be accessed from inside an empty
gas tank. They could haul fifteen gallons of moonshine
on every trip, with a five-gallon capacity for gasoline.
They'd keep the gas tank full so that the inner tank could
not be detected. Each trip would gross them $600 if they
sold the moonshine for $10 a quart. With large amounts
like these, they would negotiate with Louie Kaditz to pay
him $1.25 per quart and provide him with the sugar he
needed. That was a profit of $8.75 per quart.

"Johnny is a superb businessman," thought Franki.
Human greed had grabbed him . . . grabbed him badly.
"So that sounds like a perfect plan . . . I don't think even
Rusty McLennan could figure out where we're transport-
ing the moonshine."

"We could make up to five trips per week to Shady
Hollow—that's twelve hundred quarts per month—our
profit should be over $10,000 a month. How's that for
business, Franki Stry-Ker!" Johnny was ecstatic with his
money-making proposal . . . this was like printing
money!

Their next step was for Franki to contact Louie
Kaditz. He did this by writing a letter to Oni and Harry,
Louie and Annie's sons, the Kaditz twins. The twins were
his friends from White Sands School.

Within two weeks the Kaditz twins wrote back. They
said that they and Louie, their father, would be coming

to Edmonton. This would be their first visit to Edmonton and they were twenty-one years old. They said they had always wanted to come for the Edmonton Exhibition and since it was in July they would wait and take in the Exhibition and Farm Fair. They wanted to buy a purebred Hereford Bull, as they were now breeding and raising purebred cattle.

CHAPTER SIXTY-ONE

Franki received a telephone call from Katayna. She advised Franki that Uncle Yatsko had died. He was seventy-five years old. Evan had found him in his bed peacefully lying there as though he had just fallen asleep. Dr. Allison said his heart had failed and he expired very suddenly.

Evan was heartbroken, as this was his only blood relative from the old country. The funeral was held in St. Olga's Church and Uncle Yatsko was laid to rest in the cemetery in the Stry-Ker row of graves. Only Maria had lain there all these years with Stephen Chomiak by her side.

When Franki travelled to Shady Hollow to attend Uncle Yatsko's funeral he met with Oni and Harry Kaditz as well as Louie, their father.

They met in a bunkhouse about a quarter of a mile away from Kaditz's big farmhouse. Louie thought that his wife, Annie Kaditz, knew nothing about his moonshine business. He should have realized that Annie's sister, Mary Starchuk, who was still teaching at White Sands School in the junior room, kept Annie apprised of all the goings-on in and around Shady Hollow. The children at school brought all the gossip from home and told Mary all of it.

Mikhail Stry-Ker, Fred Radjec, and Paul Lupski no longer came to Kaditz's to play cards . . . mainly because of Louie's involvement with Metro Soova. Soova was the most hated individual in and around Shady Hollow. Domka, Metro's wife, left a year after he had returned from prison at Fort Saskatchewan, Alberta. She could no longer tolerate his bad temper; he had started beating her on a regular basis. Domka had gained independence during Metro's ten-year incarceration and was much more capable of looking after herself and tending to the children's needs. Her cooking fame had spread to people as far away as Lamont, St. Paul, Gibbons, and Morinville—and even some families in Edmonton hired her. Ukrainian weddings were always very large affairs, and growing in size as the pioneering families multiplied. Many also attended funerals and Domka was hired as the cook for these events. She couldn't keep up with demand for her cooking services.

Domka still charged her regular fee of $25 for each wedding and funeral. On many weekends she had two or more weddings to consult on, particularly in the spring and summer months. So Domka did not have to depend on the support of a husband, as most other women in Shady Hollow were forced to do. In fact, Domka was salting away a large savings account at the Canadian Bank of Commerce in Shady Hollow. Domka was a shrewd businesswoman, mainly because she was forced to be. She also had a kind heart and was bringing up Metro Soova's children, her own, and the six children that Metro had fathered with her. All the children loved her, but all refused to have anything to do with their father. Other people, except Louie Kaditz, also refused to have dealings with Metro Soova. Louie's interest was selfish and self-serving. He knew that Metro Soova had a secret formula to brew the best moonshine whiskey ever made. Louie, no matter how he tried, could not match Metro's recipe.

As Franki sat on a rickety old chair leaning backwards on the two back legs, he rocked back and forth, until suddenly the rickety legs gave out from under him and crash! Franki went flying backwards, hitting his head on the rim of the slop bucket. All the remains landed on Franki's cleanly washed head and his new suit, which he had worn to Uncle Yatsko's funeral. He looked extremely funny as he sat spread-eagled on the floor, with apple peelings and peanut shells cascading down his face. Not only was he embarrassed, but the back of his head had a big goose egg on it, as a result of the fall.

"Damn, damn," he thought. "What am I even doing here . . . my head hurts, I am filthy dirty . . . what we are about to discuss is highly illegal. I should just walk out of here—this fall was a bad omen already."

His thoughts were interrupted suddenly when Louie Kaditz spoke in his clipped Hungarian accent.

"Young Stry-Ker, you von't have to pay me for the chair . . . just say I'm charotable. Now down to beeznezz. I'm hearing you be interested in buying mine moonshine?" No mention of Metro Soova's partnership with him, none at all.

"Mr. Kaditz, I'm here reluctantly. I don't even know if I'm interested right now," Franki said uncertainly.

"Young Stry-Ker, either you is or you is not . . . I have nother coustomers, so mack up you mind, vat vill it be?" Louie pressed.

"All right, Mr. Kaditz, my partner and I have this proposal." Greed had once again taken over. "The proposal is that we buy fifteen gallons of your best moonshine five days each week . . . that's seventy-five gallons per week. Let me ask if you can produce that much, first of all," Franki inquired.

Louie's eyes lit up like two 500-watt bulbs. "Jesus!" exclaimed Oni Kaditz—the first word he spoke since the meeting began. The twins were not allowed to talk when their father discussed business.

"Christ!" finished Harry. Oni always spoke first and Harry followed. In the past few years, Oni would start a sentence and Harry completed it. The twins were stunned.

"If I saying I be supplying this seventy-five gallons for one weeks, vat vill you pay me per these gallon?" questioned Louie.

"We are willing to pay you $5 per gallon. We will pick up the moonshine somewhere that the RCMP doesn't catch us." Franki stated emphatically. The slop on his clothing was drying off and he distinctly smelled strong urine on his clothing and on his person. He was sure someone had urinated into that slop pail that had spilled all over him. He was becoming very irritated and the more irritated he became the more determined he became in his negotiation.

"Five dollars per gallon—are you complete crazy for sure . . . I now be selling it for $10 for gallon. You be knowing mine is the wery, wery best moonshine in Canada. No, $10, not one cent less!" exploded Louie.

Franki's determination was growing. "Mr. Kaditz, please don't think me disrespectful, but you could never get this large an order from anyone in these parts. You do not have to sell on an individual basis any more; that's worth something. The other part of the agreement is that we will supply the sugar which you need for your brew. We know you could never get adequate sugar supplies because sugar is rationed and you could never produce the many ration coupons needed to buy enough sugar, am I right, Mr. Kaditz? Sugar is worth another $5 a gallon so it will still be equal to $10 a gallon. Take this or leave it, Mr. Kaditz. If you don't want our business, we'll take it somewhere else . . . there are still many moonshiners out of this RCMP detachment's territory . . . out of my brother-in-law's territory. In fact, we may be better off, as I know Rusty McLennan is out to get you and your partner Metro Soova. Yes, Mr. Kaditz, it's well known that Metro is your partner!" With that Franki rose to his full six-foot two-inch height and started to walk out. Franki had started filling out; he no longer looked like a beanpole. Working as a carpenter he had developed good strong biceps.

"Jesus!" quipped Oni.

"Christ," continued Harry.

"Father, does that mean we . . ." said Oni.

"Are you going into business with Franki?" continued Harry.

"I'm leaving and will be going back to Edmonton tomorrow. If you're interested, Mr. Kaditz, please let me know before I leave," Franki stated and left. He was relieved to get some fresh air.

When Franki got back to the Stry-Ker's home, Evan was still awake. He was sitting at the round oak kitchen table, the lovely old solid oak table which he had bought at a second-hand store when he worked in Medicine Hat so many years ago. He was smoking his Ogden tobacco home-rolled cigarettes, using Chanticleer papers.

Evan had forgiven Franki for leaving the seminary in Mundare, unlike Tainka. She was still quite hurt. Evan told Franki about his sickness. He had been diagnosed with diabetes. Every morning Anastasia injected him with insulin, and he had to watch what he ate. Evan was most unhappy at the way his life was taking a turn for the worse; he was depressed because of his diabetic state. Evan was restricted in his food intake as well as his liquor consumption—these were necessities in his life. He said he had almost starved when he was young and so he wished never again to be restricted in what he ate or drank. But he was told by Dr. Allison that it would mean life or death if he didn't change his eating and drinking habits, and he would be making that choice.

CHAPTER SIXTY-TWO

Franki was grateful that the Stry-Kers now had running water. Before going to bed he drew a hot bath, stripped off his smelly clothes, and piled everything into a large brown paper bag. He would take everything into the dry cleaners in Edmonton. After the bath he dressed in clean underwear and climbed the stairs to the girls' bedroom, which no one now occupied. This was the bedroom with the large dormer. Mikhail still slept in the boys' bedroom and he was fast asleep.

In the morning Franki woke very early, dressed himself in clean sports clothes and walked around the yard. Roger, the faithful collie dog, was still eager to go fetch the cows for their morning milking, only now he treated Franki as though he was a stranger. He watched him carefully and did not race ahead to the pasture. Going to fetch the cows for milking was now the role handled by Anastasia and she, Paul, and Evancik had not yet arrived from their place—the old Borischuk property, one-quarter of a mile away.

Franki wandered into the horse barn and saw a number of the beautiful Clydesdale mares. Zoloto and Zoria had died a few years before and were buried beside a peaceful stand of birch trees near where the Stry-Kers had been told was an ancient Indian burial ground. The Stry-Kers never disturbed that area, just in case it was genuinely a sacred burial place.

Evan no longer took his Clydesdale stallion Shascha on the breeding circuit. Evan had the stallion gelded and he kept him only for show. The Pushinsky boys, Evan's grandsons—Peter, Joseph Jr., and Evan—loved to ride

Shascha now that he was gelded and had become very docile.

During the summer holidays many towns in the surrounding areas held their sports day and parades. Evan participated in their annual parades; he was always pleased to accommodate everyone. Evan used to harness four Clydesdales in their fancy ornamental harnesses; he then hitched them to the ornate wagon and rode proudly atop the wagon with gold trim, on a specially built red-tufted leather seat.

"Good morning Franki," it was Mikhail. "What are you doing in the horse barn in your good, clean clothes?" he asked.

"Hello Mikhail, I'm just admiring these beautiful horses . . . I really miss these big animals." Franki replied.

"Well, they're just a big expense and now that *Tato* is sick, Paul and I have to look after them. If I could, I'd sell them all to the fox ranch!" Mikhail was angry at having to care for these lovely beasts. To him there was no beauty in them, just expense because they consumed so much grain and hay. Grain and hay that he could have fed to his beef cattle and derive some profit from when he sold them to the slaughterhouse. He knew it was futile to even suggest selling the Clydesdales. His father would not have consented to that, ever.

"Promise me one thing, please, Mikhail . . . promise me you won't sell them. When I become rich, I'll take them all because I've always loved them, just like *Tato* does . . . please, Mikhail," pleaded Franki.

"When you become rich . . . when will that be . . . when the moon turns blue!" Mikhail was annoyed.

"I've never asked you or *Tato* or *Mamunia* for anything, have I?" Franki pressed.

"No, no, you haven't . . . well, we're not going to do anything with them as long as *Tato* is alive; he wouldn't allow it. But you should know, *Tato* is very sick, he is not supposed to eat sugar or much fat but he cheats all the time . . . it's almost like he wants to die!" said Mikhail, with frustration.

Soon a small truck pulled up and there were Paul, Anastasia, and little Evancik, who was now attending school. But now he was on a summer holiday. They hugged Franki and little Evancik planted a big kiss right on Franki's mouth. Evancik was an adorable child. Franki helped them with morning chores and was convinced once again that he did not like farming.

They all ate breakfast together and talked mostly about Uncle Yatsko and how they all missed him since his death.

Then the talk got around to Katayna and Rusty McLennan. Katayna told Tainka that Rusty was on the list for a big promotion in Ottawa. He might get promoted to Sergeant Major. Rusty's father was now retired from the RCMP and he and his wife had moved back to Campbellton, New Brunswick. They would dearly love to have their son Rusty and daughter-in-law Katayna living nearer to them.

The only thing left for Rusty to do was to clean up the Louie Kaditz and Metro Soova moonshine business. Rusty told Katayna if it was the last thing he did, one day he would catch them and then throw that Soova back to jail, Louie along with him. Tainka did not realize her youngest son was now negotiating a deal with this unsavoury lot. Franki's heart jumped into his throat as he heard this news. He made no comment.

Mikhail explained how they had moved their card games to Fred Radjec's place because they did not like that Louie Kaditz teamed up with Metro Soova. However, Fred's place stunk to high heaven because he trapped wild animals, skinned them, dried the pelts in his kitchen, and then sold the dry treated pelts to furriers in Edmonton.

"He makes good money on those skins," Mikhail said. "You know, a funny thing happened to Fred this spring . . . he was missing one of his skunk pelts—it disappeared somewhere and Fred couldn't find it to sell with the others. So one day in the spring he was getting to the bottom of his sauerkraut barrel, and boy oh boy, what's there in the very bottom, but his lost skunk skin. Stupid bugger, huh?" Mikhail was laughing at his friend's untidiness; this story amused him a great deal.

"Uncle Mikhail, that's so awful," little Evancik piped up. "You mean he ate all the sauerkraut that was on top of that skunk skin?"

"Yeah, I guess he did," replied Mikhail, searching his memory as to whether he had ever partaken of a meal of sauerkraut at Fred's house since last fall, when Fred krauted the cabbage.

Franki noticed that Anastasia was pregnant again, but no one said anything and he did not feel comfortable in asking. Maybe Katayna would tell him. She always kept him apprised of family matters like these. There would be a large spread between Evancik and the new baby that Paul and Anastasia were going to have . . . at least six years.

Noon came and there was no sign of the Kaditzs— Louie, Oni, or Harry. Franki was relieved and was quite pleased that the deal was not to be. He would tell Johnny that he had proposed the agreement but Kaditz was obviously not interested. In the long run, it was all for the best. Franki reported this to Johnny upon his return to Edmonton.

One week later, when Franki came home at 8:00 p.m. from working at the base, there on his apartment doorstep were Oni and Harry Kaditz.

"We came today," said Oni.

"By CNR train," finished Harry. The twins still looked identical, both dressed like hillbillies. Overalls, GWG labels—new ones though—red and black flannel shirts even though this was July, woollen stockings which Annie had knit, and on their feet rubber shoes, meant to be worn over the top of dress shoes. On their heads rested brand new straw hats with green bands around the crown. No doubt Annie, their mom, bought her twins new outfits at Makovitsky's General Store in Shady Hollow. She still believed in dressing her boys identically even though they were twenty-one years old.

To describe them as "country bumpkins" would have been an understatement. After all, this was their first visit to Edmonton.

"How did you get to my place, boys?" Frank asked, delighted to see them.

"We walked," quipped Oni.

" . . . from the CNR station," finished Harry.

"Did you have trouble finding my apartment?"

"No, not much trouble," Oni stated.

"We asked many people," Harry continued.

"And then one man led us," Oni began.

" . . . right to your door!" his brother finished.

"Let us in, because I have to piss like a horse," Oni implored.

"I already did . . . against the tree, there in front of your apartment building!" Harry told him as though this was the most natural thing to do.

"No, for God's sake, don't piss outside in Edmonton. That's against the law!" Franki couldn't believe these two were so ignorant. "Come in, come in." He guided them to his small apartment. He had his own bathroom and led Oni to the toilet. Franki prepared a big bowl of scrambled eggs, then sliced some bread and buttered it. He still did not have one of those new-fangled electric toasters. Oni and Harry were very hungry, as they had not eaten all day.

After the meal the Kaditz twins discussed business. "Our dad told us to tell you . . ." Oni started.

". . . that he is interested in your . . . what you told him." Harry sounded unsure of himself.

"That he will sell you a gallon of moonshine for . . ."

"Oh, yes, yes, for $5 like you wanted, but you have to buy seventy-five gallons every week like you said." Harry finished.

"Well, what do you have to say for yourself?" Oni asked Franki.

"Well, as I told your father, I have a partner and we have to discuss this agreement further." Franki was disappointed that the Kaditz business deal was on because it filled him with much apprehension and uncertainty. Suddenly, Mikhail's voice rang out in his mind—the voice he had heard a week ago in the horse barn. "You'll be rich when the moon turns blue!" Yeah, that's exactly what he had said. "No one thinks I'll ever make anything of myself and so far they are right," he thought.

He used to see Mr. Bill Stawnychy, Johnny's truck driver friend, quite often—Mr. Bill who had driven him to Edmonton from Mundare when he had left the seminary. Mr. Bill told him that Donalo and Oleska, the boys that entered the seminary along with Franki, were going to be ordained during the feast of St. Peter and Paul on July 12 at Mundare. Franki felt awful about his failures. He would show the world what he could do!

He ran over to The Pearl's Oyster, where he found Johnny sitting at the kitchen table with Cissy, Helen, and Lily while the music of Johann Strauss emanated from the parlour. It was business as usual, but much more of it. Veronica was salting away as much money for Rosie as she had been making before her sudden departure, but

Veronica was also putting away fifty per cent for herself, after paying Sonia, Jill, and Ellen. Lily and Helen seemed, from the dour looks on their faces, to be very unhappy, bitter women.

Franki urged Johnny to go outside to discuss the Kaditz business deal.

"Johnny, Louie Kaditz is agreeing to sell his moonshine for $5 a gallon providing we buy no less than seventy-five gallons a week, but we must provide all the sugar he needs. Johnny, where are you going to get all that sugar, being it's rationed and all?" Franki asked.

"How the hell do I know . . . son-a-ma-bitch!" His shock of blonde curls looked more unruly than they normally did. He kept running his fingers through the unruly mess, like his fingers were a giant comb. "Let me sleep on it, let me think . . . I can get only a one-hundred-pound bag a week, that's all." What he really meant is that he could steal about one hundred pounds per week by shorting the customers to whom he was delivering freight. Johnny was very concerned. "Where did you leave these Kaditz twins?" he questioned.

"They're at my place. Who knows what they'll do next. Harry relieved himself against the elm tree next to my apartment . . . for all I know next they'll do it out of my third floor window. They are so ignorant!" Franki was visibly upset.

"Come on, we'll pick them up and let them have their first piece of ass. Those old whores, Lily and Helen, need to have something to do . . . hell, they're miserable!" Johnny declared. "And once more, maybe the Kaditzs have more brains than you when it comes to sex. They probably don't want to be celibate all their lives, huh Franki? Whada ya say?"

"You know, that's probably a good idea . . . but you can arrange it all!" Franki replied.

"What's to arrange? We pick them up, deliver them to The Pearl's Oyster, and they sleep with Lily and Helen. You have no room for them anyway, right?" Johnny asked cockily.

They asked Oni and Harry if they had any interest in sex. Oni and Harry knew what sex was but admitted they never had a woman and would not know what to do with one. Johnny assured them they would not have to worry and that the women they were to see would know what needed to be done.

The next morning Franki arrived at The Pearl's Oyster to pick up Oni and Harry to take them to the annual parade. Then he would drop then off at the train station, where they would board the train back to Shady Hollow. Franki found that Johnny's idea was a superb one—because Oni and Harry wore smiles from ear to ear. Helen and Lily, who were doing their housework, also appeared pleased. The trio walked to Jasper Avenue and lined up to see the parade. Oni stood on one side of Franki and Harry stood on the other side. They were about five inches shorter than Franki, although with their tall farmer-type straw hats they appeared almost as tall as Franki.

They were so excited and happy. "We decided . . ." Oni stated.

"That we will come to Edmonton . . ." Harry continued.

"Every month!" Oni finished.

"What made you decide you want to come back to Edmonton? I remember you telling me you didn't ever want to come to Edmonton. That you liked the whistling pines at your ranch . . ." Franki jokingly quipped.

"Franki, you're not as smart . . ." Oni started.

"As we thought you were . . ." Harry continued.

"Lily and Helen are much better to listen to than . . ." Oni stated.

"Whistling Jack pines." Harry continued.

"And they smell so much . . ." Oni went on.

"Better than our cows do!" Harry finished.

"Well, did you just listen to them? Is that all you did?" Franki was curious.

"Hell, no . . . you know, you are . . ." Oni started.

"Stupid, we did that thing called foocking and it was . . ." Harry continued.

"It was so real, real good and much fun!" Oni ended.

The parade started and Oni and Harry were so excited they could hardly contain themselves. They enjoyed the clowns, floats, and fancily dressed ladies. Their eyes lit up when the marching bands came along. The Edmonton Police Highland Band was one of the bands that came marching by, dressed in their Black Watch tartan kilts.

Oni and Harry were perplexed indeed. "What in the hell . . ." Oni started.

"Are those stupid guys wearing skirts for?" Harry continued.

"I never in my life saw such . . ." Oni excitedly said.

"A thing, is this the style in Edmonton . . . men wear skirts?" Harry continued.

"No, no, no boys. Those are kilts; the Scotsmen wear kilts when they dress up. Remember when my sister taught us geography, remember Scotland . . . part of the British Isles, remember?" Franki pressed.

"Oh yeah, but no one taught . . ." Oni started.

"That in Scotland men wear skirts!" Harry ended.

"Well, yeah, the Scottish do at events like this. Now enjoy the rest of the parade." Franki was thankful to God that he had expanded his mind more than his former schoolmates.

Oni and Harry also commented about the bagpipes. They thought they sounded like the tomcat when they castrated him. After the parade Oni and Harry went home, and told their dad that the deal was sealed and soon Franki and his partner Johnny would be bringing sugar and taking back moonshine.

Only where were they to get three more hundred-pound sacks of sugar, Frank wondered. That is how a third partner joined Franki and Johnny.

CHAPTER SIXTY-THREE

Oliver Barris was attending the State University of Kentucky in Louisville when the American government became involved in the European war effort. He was quickly drafted as a commissioned officer and assigned to the Canadian detail. He was two years away from graduating as a geologist. Oliver was not happy to be assigned to Canada as he had read how severe the Canadian winters were. He had also heard about the huge hordes of mosquitos in Alberta and in the rest of northern Canada. He heard this from other American serviceman assigned to build the Alaska Highway. They called it the Mosquito Run.

However, he had no choice, so Canada was where he landed. He wished to become a pilot, but his eyesight prevented him from following that dream. Oliver was assigned to look after Stores. He checked off all supplies that came in from the United States to the Edmonton post.

Oliver was five feet eleven inches tall, and his masculine face was very handsome, with a high forehead, a straight nose, bushy blond eyebrows, navy-blue eyes, and thick dark-brown lashes that framed his eyes. His chin was his predominant feature; it was square and jutted out like the Rock of Gibraltar. His neck was short and thick. His hair was a dirty blonde, and he wore it shortly cropped in a brush cut, according to military rules. All the ladies on the base who saw him would give him a second look, a look of approval. Oliver had a magnificent personality and could charm the birds out of the trees. He possessed a pleasing northern Kentucky accent and talked with a slight drawl and strong nasal overtones. But the most noticeable thing about him was his entrepreneurial spirit. He was becoming a regular taxi service, off site, and was raking in ten cents for every Jeep ride to downtown Edmonton.

Franki watched Oliver for several days and then one day he decided to take the Jeep ride to his apartment. He waited off the base for about half an hour and was just about to give up waiting and catch the streetcar which ran down Kingsway Avenue, when who should come roaring along in his military Jeep but Oliver Barris. He was in his olive green uniform, a smart military issue with a peaked cap.

Franki flagged him down with a wave of his hand. "Are you going downtown, sir?" Franki addressed Oliver.

"Yeah, I'm going in that direction," and he pointed southeast.

"That's exactly where I need to go, sir, to Jasper Avenue and 95 Street." Franki replied.

"Well, here is the deal. Y'all should know, I'm Ollie, not Sir, and I don't do this delivery for free . . . a ten-cent coin is okay. It's for my own charity." Ollie outlined his rules in his rapid Kentucky speech.

"Glad to meet you, Ollie!" Franki extended his hand and Ollie clamped his into Franki's.

A good, strong, handshake—a friendly shake.

Within a week, Franki learned that Ollie was in charge of all supplies on the base, including hundreds of pounds of sugar that arrived from the U.S.A. on a regular basis. Franki also learned that Ollie's dream was to become a successful oilman and then he would retire as a millionaire racehorse breeder in Kentucky's northern area.

Ollie's conversation would often mention the family in Kentucky. Of particular note was Alexis O'Neil, his sweetheart, with whom he had attended university. She was with the Sciences Faculty and eventually intended to become a veterinarian. Her dad owned a large stable of racehorses and bred some of Kentucky's finest racehorses for sale, mostly to aristocrats.

Ollie planned to follow in Fred O'Neil's footsteps, but he would make his own fortune first. And he was open to any business opportunity that was presented to him. Two weeks after Franki and Ollie met, Franki arranged to have Ollie meet Johnny Makar.

The draught beer at the Royal George Hotel was particularly tasty; much of this was due to the strict daily cleaning of the taps and lines leading from the kegs. No stale beer was allowed to remain in the taps and every night when the beer parlour closed at 10 p.m. the employees flushed the beer lines and taps with a lye and water solution. Then they flushed again with pure water. The next morning and throughout the day, the beer tasted fresh and delicious. The gent's beer parlour at the Royal George was Franki and Johnny's favourite drinking spot. Today Ollie joined them.

"Johnny, this is Ollie . . . Ollie Barris; he's the American I told you about . . ." Franki made the introductions.

"Franki tells me you're one helluva guy, and if Franki says that, then any friend of Franki's is my friend." Johnny swore very little at this first meeting.

Franki had forewarned Johnny about his swearing and that is possibly why Johnny held his tongue.

"Yeah, well, Franki has told me about y'all, Johnny, and I return the compliment. He tells me y'all's a pretty good businessman," Ollie responded. Ollie's Kentucky accent was more prevalent for some reason, Franki noticed.

Johnny was the spokesperson and explained the Kaditz moonshine whiskey deal.

Ollie showed great enthusiasm after he heard he could clear $40,000 Canadian dollars in one year. He would be well on his way to making his first million.

Yes, he told Franki and Johnny, he could get an ample supply of sugar and he had a captive audience to whom he could sell a good quality moonshine whiskey.

Ollie further commented on the archaic liquor laws in Alberta, Canada and what a great business opportunity this would be. He was anxious to begin and wanted to know how soon they could start.

Johnny had bought a piece of land—half an acre—in Beverly, just east of Edmonton, and he had established his trucking business there. He called it Makar's Transport. On the property was an abandoned building that he was using as an office. There would be room to store the sugar.

Ollie would include Makar's Transport on his list of delivery trucks which delivered to the base. That way Johnny could pick up the sugar whenever Ollie called him to say there was a supply.

Within one month, July 1943, Kaditz was ready to produce seventy-five gallons of moonshine whiskey per week, provided he was supplied with sugar. Kaditz also added to his demands that Franki and company supply the rye grain required to produce the hooch. It would be no problem to obtain rye, because that was the only grain that grew well on sandy soil, and since there was no market for the grain in the elevators, the poor farmers who grew it would be only too happy to sell it privately. Again Franki came to the rescue and named over a dozen farmers from whom they could buy the grain.

To avoid being detected by the RCMP, they would have Johnny pose as a grain buyer. The farmers were to be paid $2 a bushel, fifty cents more than any legitimate grain buyer would pay.

All the players were in place. Ollie, Franki, and Johnny were ready for business, in partnership with Louie Kaditz and Metro Soova.

CHAPTER SIXTY-FOUR

Mr. Bill Stawnychy, the truck driver from Mundare, saw Franki at Johnny Makar's Transport office and repeated to Franki that Donalo and Oleska would be ordained during the festivities at St. Peter and Paul on July 12, 1943. He told Franki that he had spoken with the two and they both invited Franki to attend their special day . . . their Ordination.

Franki had not been back to Mundare since he had left the seminary and was feeling sheepish about returning, but some force was drawing him back.

That night he telephoned Katayna and asked her if the Stry-Ker clan were planning to attend the celebrations at Mundare. Katayna was very happy to hear from Franki. She told him about the excitement in their house. Rusty had been promoted to Ottawa. She was so proud of her husband. She continued to love him so deeply, just like a new bride.

"Why yes, Franki, we'll all be attending, as we do every year. Why do you ask?" Katayna inquired.

"Because Donalo and Oleska are being ordained . . . I guess I would have been if I had stayed. They got a message to me, inviting me to attend. I'm apprehensive, I'll be honest with you," Franki was very unsure of himself.

"Franki, Franki . . . you're finding your way in the world, aren't you? You're serving God in other ways, so why not go back and help your friends to fulfill their joys." Katayna was always so solid and always gave him sage advice.

"What about *Mamunia* . . . how do you think she'll react, not seeing me ordained along with Donalo and

Oleska?" Franki asked.

"*Mamunia* will cry . . . as you might have expected. She'll probably even carry on, but as I've told you many times, wanting you to be a priest was her dream, not yours," Katayna continued.

On July 12, Franki borrowed the small Ford pickup truck Johnny had just bought primarily to be used for pickups at the air base. Since it was going to be a joint business, Franki was expected to pay his share toward the purchase of this vehicle, so Franki felt it was fine for him to drive it to Mundare.

He got to Mundare early and waited for the Stry-Ker clan from Shady Hollow to arrive. At 9:45 a.m. three cars pulled up. Katayna and Rusty's recent acquisition, a 1938 Buick, was a big car, and Evan and Tainka came with them. It wasn't new, as cars were almost impossible to buy during the war. Rusty had bought this car in Edmonton— his friends, the Andersons, had found it. It belonged to a widow friend who had passed away. In the other car were Paul, Anastasia, and Evancik. And in the third car were Helenka, Joseph, and their three handsome sons Peter, Joseph Jr., and Evan. In the front seat with Helenka and Joseph was their lovely daughter, Emily. Helenka was showering all her attention on little Emily, while Joseph was as proud as punch of his three sons. After all, they were now playing in a new style of band and changing the image of the old Pushinsky Band. The boys had learned to play the saxophone, trumpet, and clarinet. Their new sound was very much like the Glenn Miller Band.

They called themselves "The Pushinsky Soft Tones." Little Emily was now eleven years old and the boys were encouraging her to sing in their new band. Helenka tried to discourage this; she wanted her daughter to become a nurse, not a musician. But Emily was very interested in joining and singing in her brother's band.

The sight of his whole family overwhelmed Franki. They were such an impressive group. They all hugged Franki, and Tainka and Evan greeted him with the Christian *Slava Ichosoo Xristoo.*

"*Slava na vikee,*" replied Franki.

As Franki walked into the beautiful ornate church of St. Peter and Paul in Mundare, with its new stained glass windows and freshly painted icons, he could not control the shivers racing up and down his spine. Surely a spiritual presence was upon him as the choir sang beautifully in acappella harmony, with no organ to accompany them. The organs were common to the Roman Catholic faith and not used in the Ukrainian Greek Catholic churches. Instead voices blended to sing the heavenly four-part harmonies.

He saw Father Bill, his mentor from his seminary days. He had heard that Father Bill was being promoted to a Monsignor and would be joining the Bishop's staff in Winnipeg, Manitoba.

After mass the ordination ceremony of Donalo and Oleska began. Tainka started crying and then sobbed out loud. This, of course, was expected; Franki and the others knew why.

The ordaining ceremony is an old and traditional event which has changed little since the Catholic religion began. The postulants who are to be ordained are dressed in white vestments.

After mass and the ordaining ceremonies, the congregation proceeded to the Grotto and special prayers were said there. Most were directed to the Virgin Mary, Mother of God. The conclusion to this beautiful day was a dinner held outside in front of the field facing the Grotto, with long strings of tables and benches set up in a symmetrical pattern.

The ladies of St. Peter and St. Paul's church prepared the meal. It was mostly Ukrainian dishes *holuptsi, kolasha* (specially prepared cornmeal), *pyrogies*, breaded and fried chicken, *stewdanach* (head cheese), and the famous potato salad. Whether these Mundare ladies learned this dish from Domka Soova from Shady Hollow, no one would say, but mixed into this delicious dish was the same tasty yellowish dressing that Domka always made.

Franki enjoyed potato salad more than anything else. He was surprised that Rosie Soova, when she ran The Pearl's Oyster, did not know how to prepare this wonderful dish . . . after all, it was her stepmother who was famous for the Shady Hollow potato salad.

After the dinner the newly ordained priests Oleska and Donalo came to Franki and exchanged their Christian greetings, after which they both hugged Franki and thanked him for coming to their special day. They both expressed how pleased they were to see him. After more chitchat Donalo told Franki his first parish would be at Leduc, Alberta, just a few miles south of Edmonton. Oleska would serve parishes in and around Peace River in Alberta's northern country.

Soon Father Bill came to greet Franki. "Well, my son, have you found what you're looking for . . . is life treating you well?" Father Bill asked.

"No, Father Bill, I'm still looking, and life treats me as well as can be expected, thank you for asking," Franki replied.

"Has your search perhaps led you back here to the seminary?" Father Bill pressed.

"Father, in the church during mass I had a very moving spiritual experience . . . chills ran up and down my spine. It happened again during Donalo and Oleska's ordination, but whether that meant I should resume my studies here to become a priest, I do not know," Franki responded.

Franki bid everyone farewell, got into Johnny's delivery truck, and was about to leave when he saw his father slowly making his way toward him.

Evan was looking much thinner and his colour was ashen. He had never looked this frail and Franki was very concerned. As Evan hiked himself into the seat next to Franki he could hardly catch his breath.

"Francis Nykola, my son. Francis, I like calling you Francis as you were baptized . . . so much better than Franki as they all call you. As you can see I am getting sicker by the day and I want to put all my affairs in order before I die." Evan was so serious it brought tears to Franki's eyes.

"*Tato, Tato*, please don't talk like this . . . you're not old and you have many years left to live . . . how is your diabetes?" Franki inquired.

"No son, no, I can feel I am failing quickly . . . this diabetes is making me live in ways which I do not care to live. I cannot eat anything I like, I can't walk far, my bladder is failing and every day when Anastasia gives me that insulin, I feel like I'm half a man. Francis, my son, I would like to see you at Shady Hollow as soon as I can, before I die." Evan sounded very morbid. Franki bid his father goodbye and hugged him long and hard. As he travelled back to Edmonton in Johnny's light Ford delivery truck, the tears did not stop streaming down his cheeks. The day had been so extremely moving. It touched him to his inner soul.

When he reached Edmonton he had made up his mind. He would not be going into partnership with Johnny and Ollie; he would not make $40,000 in one year selling moonshine whiskey to the American and Canadian servicemen.

He drove to The Pearl's Oyster and told Johnny about his decision. He would not be their partner.

"You stupid son-of-a-bitch . . . what the hell turned your head? Those stupid priests in Mundare!" Johnny was angrier than Franki had ever seen him before. A better description would be livid.

"Damn it!" he thought. It is none of his damn business why I'm not going in with the partnership and that's final! "Listen . . . don't you ever again call me a son-of-a-bitch . . . you bag of shit. That reflects on my mother and she is a living saint, do you hear me? You couldn't even hold a candle to her. None of your damn business why I will not be your partner!" Franki caught himself yelling at Johnny. "And if you don't stop your stupidity I will tell Louie Kaditz not to sell any moonshine whiskey to you. Kaditzs do not deal with people they don't trust. And Johnny boy . . . they don't trust you!" Franki finished, got up and walked out.

The next day he saw Ollie Barris at the air base and asked him to meet him and Johnny at the Royal George Hotel. A cooler temper prevailed; Johnny Makar even apologized to Franki and promised never to call him a "son-of-a-bitch" again. "No," he said, "I'll call you a 'bag of shit' just like you called me." They all had a laugh and then discussed the parting of their partnership.

"Do you want to be a silent partner?" asked Johnny.

"No, not whatsoever . . . I want nothing to do with that business, do you hear, nothing! I'll be very honest with both of you—my conscience just doesn't allow it. Maybe I'll never be rich; as my brother Mikhail put it . . . not until the moon turns blue, but I cannot and will not be part of your business and that's final!" Franki concluded.

"Y'all leave us more to split." Ollie cut in. "Is there anything we can do for you?"

"Yes Ollie, as a matter of fact you can. I noticed all the crates in which the airplane parts are crated are now burned in big bonfires. All that wood is wasted. If I haul it away may I have it?" Franki inquired.

"Y'all be doin' us a favour . . . as you correctly say, it's all burned to ashes. I will arrange that you get it." Ollie stated.

On the weekend, Franki once again borrowed the light delivery truck and drove to Shady Hollow, just as he had promised his father he would.

Evan was home all alone as the rest of the family had gone picking orange top mushrooms, *kozaree*.

Evan spoke freely to Franki. "As I told you, son, I do not feel well and if God lets me live I will, but if he decides it's time for me to go, then I'll accept that also. Francis, you know how much I love my Clydesdales. Those horses have given me more pleasure in Canada than anything else . . . except of course my children. Mikhail and Paul do not like them and I know as soon as I die they'll sell them all. Since I know you love them as much as I do I want you to have them all. Do you want them, Francis?" Evan asked.

"I would give anything in the world to have them, *Tato* . . . I love them as much as you do, that's true. As a matter of fact that's all I like about farming—the Clydesdales. But *Tato*, I have no place to take them, and I have saved only $2,000. It will be a while . . ." Franki began, but before he could finish he saw his father open his canvas pouch and there were his Canada Savings Bonds. He counted out the bonds—each one was worth $1,000 and he counted to twenty. Franki was flabbergasted at the number of bonds his father had squirrelled away.

"I am giving you $20,000 worth of these bonds, Francis, for two reasons . . . first, I expect you to take care of my beloved Clydesdales and secondly, because we never gave you anything before and you asked for nothing. Mikhail and Paul have been willed all *Mamunia's* and my land. There are two sections of land. They have now acquired much more and have together six sections of land—that is 2,240 acres of mostly good black soil. I also gave them $10,000 to buy their first threshing machine and tractor. My will states that they must care for your mother until her death. I'm leaving $5,000 for Katayna because she also got nothing from us, and $5,000 for your mother so she has her own money. Helenka is richer than I am. Her husband, Joseph Pushinsky, is an excellent provider and has inherited most of the Pushinsky properties. So Helenka doesn't need my money." Evan continued to explain his plans to his son. "Francis, the advice I'll give you is that you use this money to buy land . . . buy all the land you can, because God knows they're not making any more of it. It will always be there; it can't burn, like buildings can. It grows food and the earth is our source of life . . . here my son, take these bonds and use them with God's blessings. As soon as you can, please take my precious Clydesdales away from here. I have discussed my plans with Mikhail and Paul, but more importantly with your mother."

Evan looked tired and asked Franki to make a pot of tea. He wanted to drink a cup of tea and then lie down for his afternoon rest. As they were about to drink their tea Franki saw Evan drag the sugar bowl close to his cup and when he thought Franki wasn't looking he quickly dumped four heaping teaspoons of sugar into it. Franki did not say a word, for it was not up to him to preach. When the rest of the family returned he did not mention the incident to them.

After the Christian greeting, Tainka was first to say, "Franki, it's so good to see you."

All the others hugged and kissed Franki.

"So, did *Tato* tell you about the Clydesdales?" Mikhail quizzed.

"Yes, he told me to take them; is that suitable with you?" Franki asked.

"The sooner the better, dear brother!" Mikhail continued. "They are eating me out of house and home!"

Anastasia looked like she wouldn't last until October when her baby was due and so Tainka was preparing the orange top mushrooms in rich farm cream, with dill weed and green onions.

This mushroom dish, served on Anastasia's light feathery bread with a crispy crust, was a feast fit for a king.

That evening Katayna and Rusty came visiting to Stry-Kers'. Following supper they all sat down and played card games and visited until late into the night.

Sergeant Rusty McLennan was showing signs of excitement about his upcoming promotion to Ottawa. He had received his letter of confirmation certifying that he was being promoted to Sergeant Major. Everyone, including Franki, congratulated him.

"When are you going to be leaving us?" Tainka asked curiously.

"I will be reporting to the Assistant Commissioner on January 1. We have six more months here at Shady Hollow before Katayna and I leave," Rusty responded. "My greatest disappointment is that I have not been able to catch and imprison those two scoundrels, Soova and Kaditz . . . but I've still got six months. You can bet I'll be working tirelessly to achieve my goal before I leave! You know that their moonshine operation is the last one left in these parts. We believe there are one or two in the Weasel Creek country and one for sure at Hollow Lake, Alberta. So you can see why I'm so anxious to get Soova and Kaditz arrested," Rusty concluded with utmost determination.

Franki could feel the blood rushing up to his face. God, was he pleased with his decision not to join Johnny Makar and Ollie Barris in the moonshine whiskey ring.

The next morning Franki travelled back to Edmonton. As he rode along the well-graded, gravelled highway, a public works improvement since Billy Makovitsky had become an MLA, he thanked God for his guidance.

He heard the words of Father Bill, who often used to say to the novices, "When God closes a door, he always leaves open a window." How true this was—his father, Evan Stry-Ker, had bequeathed him $20,000.

He would have lumber to start his construction company from the American crates that Ollie had promised to him.

He would go to church the next Sunday and pray a special "Thank you to God," a thank you for his intervention. Franki had started attending church regularly in Leduc because his seminary school friend, Donalo, was now the parish priest. And Franki truly enjoyed his sermons and his baritone singing voice.

Franki began looking for a quarter section of land close to Edmonton that he could buy, where he would relocate his father's precious Clydesdales. There was nothing available that he could find.

When the next Sunday came, Franki was getting dressed in his Sunday suit to attend church when he heard a knock on his door. There, standing before him, was Ollie Barris . . . Captain Barris, as was his rank. He was also Catholic and his background was French, but he had never attended a Ukrainian Greek Catholic mass as he was Roman Catholic.

"Good morning, Franki, mind if I come to your church? I never have been to a Greek Catholic church in my life. Time I learned all about it!" Ollie said.

"No, no, I don't mind one bit, my friend. Father Donalo will be very pleased to have a new visitor in his congregation. You may even understand some of the sermon, as Father Donalo has started using English for part of his sermon," Franki responded.

It took them three quarters of an hour to get to Leduc and as they approached the little church, Franki was amazed at how Father Donalo's congregation was growing. There was no room left to sit on the crude little benches, so Ollie and Franki were forced to stand.

Father Donalo had started choir practice and was developing a better than average choir. It was quite enjoyable. His own rich baritone voice carried all the way outside the church. Before his sermon started he made the announcements: what days the masses would be held; who had died in the parish; who had been married; who would be baptized; and then an announcement which Franki couldn't believe he was actually hearing. "And now if anyone is looking to buy a farm, a quarter section, our parishioner Walter Vaschuk is planning to retire because of health problems. Walter wants to spend the rest of his life in a warmer climate and so he wants to move to Vancouver, British Columbia. If anyone is interested Walter is here in church, please see him after mass . . . and now for our weekly laugh." He used to tell a joke every Sunday and had people laughing and many times holding their sides with laughter.

"There were three men that died and reached the Pearly Gates of Heaven and met St. Peter," began Father Donalo. "The first was questioned by St. Peter, 'Have you been faithful to your wife all through your marriage?' 'Yes,' was the reply. 'Well,' St. Peter said, 'You will be rewarded. I give you this shiny new Chrysler to drive around heaven.' The next man was asked the same question and he replied to St. Peter, 'Well, no I was unfaithful once . . .' St. Peter gave him a Model T Ford to drive around heaven. Then the third man was asked the same question and he replied, "No, St. Peter, I was unfaithful quite a few times.' He was given an old motorcycle to drive around heaven. Several days later, St. Peter saw the first man—the man who got the Chrysler—and he looked very unhappy. St. Peter asked him why he was so unhappy. 'Well, sir, yesterday I saw my wife up here and she was riding an old bicycle!'"

The joke was followed by serious teachings from the Bible. This day the teaching was about Jesus performing his first miracle at the wedding in Canaan. Franki admired how much Father Donalo's congregation was enjoying him. He also marvelled at how appropriate the sermon was. The announcement about the land was miraculous, to say the least. As soon as mass was finished, Franki found Walter Vaschuk and told him he was interested in seeing his farm.

Ollie and Franki got into Johnny Makar's light delivery Ford truck and followed Walter Vaschuk to his farm. It was located two and a half miles away from Leduc. The land had many rolling hills, a kind not found in other parts of Alberta. Ollie was particularly interested because while at the university, studying geology, he had seen many land formations and his knowledge of geological science told him that the terrain around these parts was very much like the terrain in Oklahoma, in the oil-rich part of the state, where oil was being produced in millions of barrels each year.

Ollie wondered aloud, "Has there been any oil exploration in this area?"

Franki replied, "I'm not interested in oil right now, only to buy some land where I can move my *Tato*'s beautiful Clydesdales . . . that's all!"

Walter Vaschuk was almost sixty years old. He had emigrated with his father and mother from Austria in

1895 when he was a boy. He had three sisters; only one was still alive and living in Vancouver. Walter had never married and was willed the one-quarter section by his father. His father bought another quarter section, next to the Podgorny land, in 1908. Walter was selling both his quarter sections for $15,000. He told Franki that the possession date could be within a month. He also told Franki that he believed the quarter section next to the Podgorny land included the mineral rights, but he wasn't sure.

On the yard stood a run-down two-bedroom house with no electricity or running water. A chicken coop, ice house, a big blacksmith shop, and a grain storage building were also located on the farmstead. None were in good condition, but what impressed Franki was that there was a huge barn, although it had never seen a coat of paint. It was in fairly good condition, with a tall hayloft on the second level of the barn. The barn could certainly accommodate thirty-six cows, as Walter Vaschuk used to sell milk to the Edmonton City dairy, so it could accommodate comfortably twenty-five Clydesdale horses. The hayloft would hold enough hay for one winter's supply for the horses.

Franki arranged to meet Walter Vaschuk during the week in Edmonton. He wished to consult Cissy Brown, who was studying law; perhaps she could tell him more about this thing called mineral rights. Maybe she could also advise Franki about a good lawyer in Edmonton to handle the transaction. Franki needed to see about the Canada Savings Bonds as the soonest some of them would mature was two years henceforth.

Cissy was so happy for Franki. She knew he had refused to be part of the moonshine whiskey business and told him how proud she was that he had done so.

Franki was forced to make a bank loan against the Canada Savings Bonds and the best interest he could secure on the loan was still one per cent higher than the interest he would be paid when the bonds matured. He borrowed $15,000, as he needed to pay Walter Vaschuk that amount for his two quarter sections of land. He did have $2,000 saved and would need some of this to buy a large truck for his own use. He needed a truck so that he could haul the wooden crates which he was getting from the American air force. He now had a whole yard where he could store his lumber from the crates.

Within two more weeks, Franki packed his few personal belongings from the Heckla Apartments and moved to his Leduc property. He called his place Paradise Acres. He was aware that Maria, his dead sister, and her husband-to-be Stephen Chomiak used to call their future home Paradise Valley. He hoped the name would bring him better luck than they had had.

Moving day also came for Cissy Brown. She wanted to leave The Pearl's Oyster because she did not enjoy living there after Rosie Soova left. And no one had heard or seen Rosie since she left two years ago. Veronica was a real tyrant, and ruled the house with an iron fist. She expected Cissy to work whenever she was there, which left her no time for study.

Franki made a deal with Cissy whereby she would take over his Heckla apartment. He also left her his second-hand furniture. It was fortunate that Rosie Soova had left Cissy $5,000. Cissy was so frugal that she still had $4,000 left in the bank. During the holidays she could now work for someone else instead of slaving away for Veronica and maybe she could put some extra money away. In the meantime, Cissy helped Franki clean up the old Vaschuk farmhouse. When they finished, it simply sparkled; it was far cleaner than it had been in years past when the old bachelor Vaschuk kept house. It was a cozy home, but a far cry from the Stry-Ker farmhouse or the luxurious Pearl's Oyster. But it was his very own property and he was extremely proud of his place.

Moving day for the Clydesdales was a difficult task. Franki explored different options for moving his precious Clydesdales . . . by CNR boxcar, truck, or having them walked from Shady Hollow to Leduc. Franki decided to have them walked. He had heard about a fabulous teamster by the name of Henry Warring from Gibbons. Horses obeyed him even though he was only five feet five inches tall; he had no fear of any horse. Henry used to be a jockey in the U.S.A. during the prime of his life. He was not a husky man, in fact quite slight, but he was as strong as a small ox. He chewed tobacco or snuff and the more excited or angry he got, the more he would chew and spit and spit some more. Henry agreed to move the Clydesdales at seven dollars per day, plus the cost of feeding and watering them at various farms en route to Leduc. He figured it would take him three days to get them to Leduc. He would cross the North Saskatchewan River at Pakan and ferry the horses across the river, then head cross-country through Bruderheim, Fort Saskatchewan, and south until they reached Paradise Acres. Before they left the yard, Evan blessed all the horses by sprinkling each one with holy water. He hugged his Shascha and cried out loud. Mikhail and Paul felt guilty that they did not have the same feeling toward these big beasts . . . the feelings that only Evan and Franki had for them.

It took three days, as Henry Warring had said it would. He delivered them in good condition; five of the mares in foal did not even look tired after this one-hundred-mile trek. Franki paid him ten dollars per day, three dollars more than he had asked for, and felt he got a bargain indeed.

Franki drove his International one-ton truck to work every day and every day there was a stack of lumber, which Ollie arranged to have Franki pick up.

CHAPTER SIXTY-FIVE

Life was going well for Franki, but life for Ollie Barris and Johnny Makar was overwhelmingly good—from a business prospective. The Kaditz moonshine was outstanding and sales for it were booming.

Because of the scarcity of a booze supply mostly caused by the Alberta government's strict rules, the illicit kind was being sold in great quantities. None was as good as the Kaditz and Soova brew.

Ollie and Johnny bragged to Franki that in three months they had each stashed away over $11,000. They were selling each quart for $8.50 unbeknownst to Louie Kaditz, to whom they were only paying $5 per gallon as per the agreement. This was the agreement that Franki had originally cobbled together with the Kaditzs.

"You could have been part of this money-making machine . . . pretty stupid aren't you, Stry-Ker?" Johnny Makar laughed at Franki.

"I wish you much luck . . . I'm perfectly happy doing it slowly. Have you had any trouble with the police yet?" Franki asked curiously.

"Hell, yes . . . that goddamn brother-in-law of yours, the dumb bugger doesn't know about the hidden tank!" Johnny appeared invincible and very cocky.

One month before Sergeant Major Rusty McLennan was to move to Ottawa, in November, 1944, it happened. Johnny Makar was bringing the sugar to Louie Kaditz's yard, where he usually went, when Louie waved him down. Johnny stopped the big truck. He always used his one-ton Ford because this was the truck with the doctored gas tank.

Louie said he wanted Johnny to deliver the sugar to Metro Soova's homestead because he thought the RCMP were snooping around his place too much and they had to change the location of their six stills.

"We have a safer place," he said. "We dug a big cellar under Soova's old log house on his homestead. We shored up the cellar walls because it's all sand, and in that cellar we have all our stills. Since his old log house is almost falling down, it's so old the RCMP will never think of looking for a cellar in a ramshackle shack, to find the stills. We'll bring the sugar and rye next time by horses, but so that we're not behind with our orders, Metro Soova has to start now . . . to make the brew on time. Do you hear?" Louie Kaditz seemed to be totally unfocused and stressed out.

"But Louie!" pleaded Johnny. "We can't take chances like this! You know the police, especially Rusty McLennan, are out to get us. It's not safe to be taking this big truck to Soova's homestead. They'll see us there. Don't you think in that head of yours?" Johnny was concerned.

"Vell, Johnny, you be tell me, vot to do? Vill you vait another month for the next moonshine?" Louie asked.

Johnny even now couldn't keep up with the incredibly good sales Ollie had for this illegal hooch. Another month would surely put them behind the eight ball and their regular customers would find other suppliers.

"Okay, goddamn it, Louie, just this once but never again, Louie . . . you hear?! It's your responsibility to make us seventy-five gallons of moonshine every week. I don't give a damn where your stills are hidden!" Johnny was not pleased, but he turned the truck around and asked Louie for instructions on how to get to Metro Soova's old homestead.

As they pulled into Soova's gate on the homestead,

there was about three inches of snow on the road. The heavy truck tires crawled over the snow. Johnny didn't realize that the tires were sinking into the sand. It was like sinking into a pile of loose salt under the cover of snow. The truck's back tire became embedded right up to its axle.

"Goddamn, Louie, how the hell am I going to get out of here?" Johnny threw his cap to the ground, exposing his blond curls. He swore a blue streak, as his big fingers combed his hair in frustration. Meanwhile, Louie Kaditz sat in the cab not moving a muscle. He was scared of this big, blond ape.

As Johnny looked for a log to try to jack up the truck, he saw a flash of light on the road, spotlights glaring. He closed his eyes and shook his head in consternation as he realized it was the RCMP. "Goddamn . . . goddamn!" he groaned, his bunched fists pounding on his thighs repeatedly.

"It's the RCMP!" Rusty McLennan's baritone voice rang out clearly. "We have you surrounded." He headed toward the truck, his form clearly outlined in his police car's spotlights.

Suddenly there was a crackling of broken branches in the forest. It sounded like a male moose crashing through the bush. Just then, before Rusty McLennan could react, a shot rang out. Johnny saw a flash as a rifle went off. He and Louie Kaditz watched in horror as Sergeant Major Rusty McLennan was hit in the chest with a shot from a .303 hunting rifle. The bullet entered his chest, striking his heart. The shot was as accurate as the shooter had intended. Sergeant Major Rusty McLennan fell to the ground, mortally wounded.

Johnny and Louie Kaditz stared at the dead policeman in frozen horror. They knew instinctively that it had been Metro Soova who had fired the fatal shot.

Constable Mark Kuliba and Constable Sam Ewing, who had accompanied Rusty, cautiously approached the men, their handguns drawn. "Stay where you are. You are under arrest! You are under arrest for attempted murder!" yelled Constable Kuliba before kneeling over Rusty to see if he could find a pulse, while his partner continued to aim his gun at the suspects. He could not. Slowly he got up and stared at the two frozen figures of Johnny Makar and Louie Kaditz. "Charge them with the murder of Sergeant Major McLennan!" he told his partner flatly, without taking his eyes off the suspects.

"No, no, we had nothing to do with this . . ." Johnny protested, as cold handcuffs were clamped on him and Louie Kaditz.

"Didn't you see . . . it was someone in the bush that did it? Not us, not us, for Christ's sake!" Johnny added. He was now positive that it had been Metro Soova who had fired the shot, but he was scared spitless to say so. The cops would find all the stills in Soova's cellar and he'd be in worse trouble than he was in now.

The two officers covered Rusty's body with a woolen blanket and carried him into the car. They proceeded to cuff Louie and Johnny to a large tree, then, with guns drawn, began to search for the person responsible for firing the rifle that had killed Sergeant Major McLennan. As they shone their flashlights into the forest, there on a large poplar tree, swinging by the neck, was Metro Soova. His eyes bugged right out of their sockets and his tongue protruded from his mouth like a long purple snake . . . a dead snake. Metro must have been prepared to do the dastardly deed because, as he had told many people, he would rather die than go back to Fort Saskatchewan prison.

The two young policemen cut him down and eased his body to the ground. Even though this incident had just occurred and the body was still warm, there was no life left in this miserable piece of humanity, so they carried him to the car and put his body into the trunk of one of the police cars. Then they led Johnny Makar and Louie Kaditz from the tree where they were restrained. They handcuffed each one again and shackled their legs with leg-irons and sat them in the other car. Constable Kuliba drove the car with the dead Rusty McLennan in the back seat and Metro Soova's body in the trunk. Constable Ewing drove the two prisoners in the other car back to Shady Hollow.

Louie and Johnny were charged with being accomplices to murder. No matter how thoroughly the police searched, they never found the stills on Metro Soova's homestead. After looking and searching in the fallen old log house they abandoned the search, as they found nothing. They looked inside the ramshackle shack, but there was nothing but broken old furniture and pigeon droppings. No one bothered to see if there was a cellar. As well, no one ever found the second chamber welded into the gas tank of Johnny Makar's one-ton Ford truck.

Breaking the news of Rusty's death to Katayna was left up to the Stry-Ker family. Constables Ewing and Kuliba drove over to the Stry-Ker farm because they were not strong enough to tell Katayna themselves. They knew Katayna too well to tell her that her beloved Rusty was no more. As tough policemen as they were, they could not handle this task. They both loved Katayna like a second mother, as she had treated them both like sons since their arrival at the Shady Hollow detachment. The family, after hearing the tragic news, formulated a plan. They would drive to Shady Hollow. Tainka and Evan were too distraught to go. Evan was crushed because in his own way he had a great deal of respect for Rusty. He was proud of Rusty's achievements and was sorry about

the shabby treatment he had given Rusty at the beginning of the relationship, so he could not face Katayna at
this time. Besides, he was getting physically sicker by the
day. Tainka was experiencing a shock similar to the one
she went through when her beloved daughter Maria
died. She also refused to go. Anastasia had given birth on
November 1st, to a new baby, Evelyn, so she would not
go either. Mikhail telephoned Franki in Edmonton.
After revealing the tragedy to him, he pleaded with
Franki to drive quickly to Shady Hollow, because if anyone knew Katayna, he did. It was left to Franki to be the
spokesperson to relate this horrible news to Katayna.

It took Franki only two and a half hours to drive his
old truck, exceeding all speed limits all the way. They
met at Makovitsky's General Store. Everyone—Mikhail,
Paul, Helenka, and most of all, Franki—were crying.
They knew they would have to compose themselves
before they went to see Katayna. After half an hour of
crying, they pulled themselves together and proceeded to
McLennans' home to see her, a task none of them would
ever have wished on their worst enemy.

As they approached the cozy McLennan home in
Shady Hollow, they saw Katayna looking through the
window. She was waiting for Rusty to get home. He was
supposed to have been home hours ago. As they
approached the house and knocked on the door, Katayna
quickly opened it.

She saw their sombre, tear-stained faces. "What is
it . . . is something wrong with *Tato* or *Mamunia*?" she
asked.

"No, Katayna," said Franki, the appointed
spokesperson.

"Then what . . . what's wrong . . . oh my God, not
Rusty, no, not Rusty!" She looked with desperate hope at
each of her brothers and her sister Helenka, hoping

against hope they would say that it was not Rusty. When Helenka grabbed her and tried to soothe her with a hug, Katayna became hysterical.

"No, no, no, no . . . not Rusty . . . God, how can you do this to me? No, not Rusty . . . why . . . we were so happy. Why Rusty?" Katayna cried and cried and sobbed and moaned. Two hours passed and the two constables, Ewing and Kuliba, came to see what they could do. They could see it was impossible to talk to Katayna. She was in a deep state of shock.

Ewing and Kuliba suggested getting Dr. Allison to come and give her a shot to sedate her.

Franki telephoned Dr. Allison, who was there in less than fifteen minutes. The news of Rusty McLennan's death spread like a wild prairie fire. The *Edmonton Bulletin* reported that Sergeant Major Robert (Rusty) McLennan of Shady Hollow had been shot to death by Metro Soova yesterday. Sergeant Major McLennan had helped to imprison Soova in 1929 for aggravated assault. Metro Soova hanged himself after shooting Sergeant Major McLennan in the chest with a .303 hunting rifle.

Johnny Makar of Edmonton and Louie Kaditz of Shady Hollow were arrested as accomplices to murder.

The rest of the story reported on what, where, when, and who else was involved. The why was never answered adequately because nothing about the moonshine whiskey was ever reported.

Katayna somehow lived through the funeral. She was like a zombie because of the heavy sedation that Dr. Allison had given her. She looked, walked, and talked like the living dead. Indeed, with all her heart she wished that she could have died. She agreed to the pomp and ceremony as befitted an officer of the RCMP. Rusty's body was embalmed at Park Memorial Gardens in Edmonton. In his coffin, he was dressed in his red serge;

his Stetson hat lay on the top of his casket. His face was prepared so well through embalming and make-up artistry of the funeral home that he appeared to be asleep. His thirty-nine-year-old face was as handsome in death as it had been in life.

The chapter on Rusty McLennan's life closed as his body was requested by his mother and father to be taken to Campbellton, New Brunswick. Katayna agreed, as she saw that both of Rusty's parents were in extremely deep grief. She felt that having his body near them might provide some small degree of comfort.

Katayna remained in Shady Hollow for two more months after the funeral, without once leaving her home. It had been the happy home which she and Rusty shared. She was hoping that all of the past two months were just a bad nightmare. But as things didn't change, she eventually accepted the truth. Rusty was gone forever. The RCMP death settlement provided her with about $10,000 and a small widow's pension. She also had the $5,000 inheritance from her father, Evan Stry-Ker. She sold her home in Shady Hollow and received another $5,000 from the proceeds of the sale. With this cash in hand she bade everyone a sad farewell. Taking some of her personal belongings, she boarded the CNR steam-powered train to Vancouver, British Columbia, where she boarded the ship *Orionna* and headed for Honolulu, Hawaii. There she climbed onto a cattle steamer and headed for her final destination of Kona, on the big island of Hawaii. She was quite positive that no one would ever find her there. She left no forwarding address. No one could reach her, not even Franki. Katayna had become a grieving, unforgiving, bitter woman.

The preliminary and pre-trial investigation started immediately after Rusty McLellan's death. Oni, Harry, and Annie Kaditz were questioned extensively and in separate rooms. All three swore that they knew nothing. They all stuck to that story . . . they knew absolutely nothing about this murder. No matter how the authorities pressed the Kaditz twins, they remained united . . . they knew nothing. They told the police officers who were investigating that they were plain, ordinary ranchers, and that if they wanted to ask them about ranching, they would be happy to oblige. They would give them all sorts of information about that subject, but definitely not about the murder or even about the moonshine business or the stills where this moonshine might be manufactured . . . no, nothing at all.

Johnny Makar's wife, Veronica, who was now in charge of The Pearl's Oyster, was no more helpful. She knew nothing about her husband being involved with the moonshine business, much less his involvement with the murder of a policeman.

Anyone that the police could find who was associated with Louie Kaditz or Johnny Makar claimed that they knew nothing about this matter either. Surprisingly, neither Franki Stry-Ker nor Ollie Barris were ever questioned.

The one serious charge that the police could pin on Louie Kaditz or Johnny Makar was that they were accomplices to murder since there was no evidence linking them to the moonshine business.

Johnny Makar worried about Helen and Lily at The Pearl's Oyster because of their hatred and resentment toward Veronica and him. But, surprisingly, neither one of these women was interviewed at any time during the investigation. Nor did Lily or Helen know about Johnny's involvement, otherwise you can be sure that they would have advised the police immediately.

Louie Kaditz and Johnny Makar hired a brilliant young defence lawyer, Duncan Stewart, who was making a big name for himself as a criminal lawyer. His friends used to call him "Sandy." Duncan Stewart had just recently left the Provincial Prosecutor's Office in the Justice Department, where he had served six years and made a reputation by winning most of his cases for the Crown. He started his own practice, and from that time on the Prosecutor's Office had great difficulty winning any cases in court when Duncan acted for the Defence, because he knew all their strategies and how their legal minds worked.

Johnny and Louie were charged with being accomplices in the capital crime of homicide; in other words, murder. Duncan Stewart would attempt to have his clients acquitted or, if he failed to win an acquittal, he would attempt to find them guilty of a lesser offence, thereby ensuring they would serve a moderate prison term only. He mulled over the criminal code and addressed topics under conspiracies, accessories, aiding and abetting, and finally, attempts—in this case, homicide. Duncan realized that his clients, just for being accessories, could serve a maximum sentence of 14 years. He researched how his clients could be accessories after the fact, which in this case they appeared to be, because Louie and Johnny were clearly sitting in the truck when the offence occurred. Neither of them took part, nor did they even know that the crime was going to take place. Duncan closely studied the three vital elements associated with accessories and found that neither Louie nor Johnny knew that the crime was to be committed (at least that's what they both had told him), neither intended to assist Metro Soova in committing the crime, and there was no act or omission intended to aid the criminal. The absence of all three elements should exonerate his clients. But he also knew of cases where a person was convicted even though that person was not charged with the crime initially. Duncan understood the dilemma he was facing. These two unsavoury clients of his were not well liked by a number of people—in fact, most people disliked them. At the same time, the man that was dead—Rusty McLennan, a Sergeant Major with the RCMP—not only held a high post but also was extremely well liked by most people. Duncan knew he had a tough case ahead of him.

The judge who would be hearing the case set the trial, to take up to a maximum of three weeks, in an Edmonton courtroom. The reason it would not take place near Shady Hollow was that an impartial jury from among the local citizens could not be found. The judge also felt it was a very involved case, with a high-profile RCMP officer having been shot. Thus he thought many witnesses would be called by both sides. The only problem for the Prosecution was that they could only find two witnesses for their side . . . Constables Ewing and Kuliba. Both constables stated that they saw Johnny Makar and Louie Kaditz at the scene of the crime but they had no weapons. Furthermore, the two constables stated that it was Metro Soova who shot Sergeant Major McLellan with a .303 hunting rifle. They testified that Metro Soova hanged himself at the scene of the crime after he shot the Sergeant Major and, finally, that they both cut the rope by which Soova hanged himself, lowered his body from the poplar tree where the deed had taken place, and removed the body from the scene of the crime.

"So how then is it that Johnny Makar and Louie Kaditz are accomplices?" Duncan Stewart asked. "Simply because they were at the scene? They didn't have weapons, they didn't signal anyone where the Sergeant Major was hiding, they didn't hold the Sergeant Major, they didn't, in fact, entice him to this area, where unfortunately he was shot. I realize what a great loss the death

of Sergeant Major McLennan is, folks . . . it's an unbearable tragedy . . . but my clients clearly had nothing to do
with this terrible incident. So they are not accomplices to
this crime in any way, shape, or form!" Duncan concluded forcibly.

The judge and jury listened carefully to the evidence
presented by both sides. Yes, indeed, there certainly was
plenty of reasonable doubt. Had the victim been any
ordinary John Doe off the street then Johnny Makar and
Louie Kaditz would have walked away from this trial . . .
free men. But because the man that was killed was a
high-ranking police officer and a well-liked one at that,
there was ugly public opinion against Johnny and Louie
by virtue of the two being at the scene of the murder. Of
course, if evidence had been provided that these three
scoundrels were involved in the moonshine business,
then the sentence would have been much stiffer.
However, none of that evidence was presented, nor did
the authorities know it.

Johnny Makar and Louie Kaditz were sentenced to
five years at the Fort Saskatchewan prison. Without the
brilliant defence of Duncan Stewart, they would certainly have been sentenced to at least ten years and up to
a maximum of fourteen years. Throughout the trial the
Judge had looked at Johnny and Louie with utter disdain. The jury, however, was right on the mark, and even
though they felt extremely badly about the killing of
Sergeant Major McLellan, they did due diligence and did
not rule against Johnny and Louie. Much of this was as
a result of the way Duncan Stewart had presented his
defence during the court hearing.

CHAPTER SIXTY-SIX

Franki held himself responsible for Rusty's death. He felt if he had not made the original deal with the Kaditzs all of the horror would not have happened. He was very bitter toward Johnny Makar and wished that Johnny would be dead. How could he have even concocted this crazy scheme? Franki also became an angry and bitter person. He threw himself into work in order to forget the gnawing pain burning inside him. Needless to say, the moonshine whiskey business came to an abrupt end. Ollie Barris was also sick about his involvement in this whole mess. He asked for and was granted a meeting with Franki. This time the meeting took place at the Alberta Hotel. They didn't even wish to be associated with places where they used to meet with Johnny Makar.

In his very pronounced Kentucky accent, as he spoke that way when he was upset or excited, Ollie began, "Franki, I can't tell you how sorry I am about the death of your brother-in-law, Rusty. I have the worst pain in my chest . . . God, I'm sorry, Franki." Ollie sounded and looked ill. "I am embarrassed and sick about ever getting involved in this mess. Honestly, I don't want one red cent associated with this business. I'd like to make arrangements with the Red Cross or some other worthy cause to give away anonymously every cent I ever made of this blood money. This horrid business . . . as long as I live I will never try to make a quick buck again. I don't need any blood money or for that matter this feeling . . . this feeling of guilt . . . of greed I actually possessed. Franki, do you believe me?" Ollie was pleading.

"I know how you must be feeling because I feel the same way, but only if you can imagine, one hundred times worse. I hurt a person who brought me up, who loved me unconditionally. How do you think I feel . . . pretty, pretty awful! I will look after her for the rest of her life and if I have to work night and day to do it, even that's not enough. She and Rusty had such a happy marriage. They loved each other more than any couple I know, and now she faces life alone. God, I feel so responsible for that. If only I had not dealt with the Kaditzs, Johnny could not have done this alone. Katayna is not well off . . . the RCMP has provided $10,000. She sold her house, the one they bought with Rusty's savings, in Shady Hollow. My father gave her $5,000 last year and she'll get a small widow's pension from the RCMP . . . very small. That's all she has . . . that's all!" Franki was close to tears.

"Franki, Franki, you're feeling so bad—yeah, and for good reason. But you know damn well if you had not arranged the meeting with Kaditz, Johnny would have done it himself. Johnny's like that, believe me. Johnny would have found a way. The fact is, you got out of it before you started, and I should also have done the same, but it's too late now this has happened and as sad as it is, it's happened and no one can undo it. Yeah, the best you can do is see that she is comfortable." Ollie was distraught. He was feeling awful. And Franki was indeed feeling one hundred times worse.

CHAPTER SIXTY-SEVEN

From the time of Johnny Makar's sentence and subsequent incarceration, accused of being an accomplice to the murder of Sergeant Major McLennan, his wife Veronica Makar became even more tyrannical. She was now running Makar Transport as well as The Pearl's Oyster. She worked eighteen hours a day travelling from one place to the other hiring truck drivers to take Johnny's place. The trucking business was a truck short as the one-ton Ford truck had been confiscated by the RCMP the night of Rusty McLennan's murder.

It was now almost three years since Rosie Soova had gone away, and no one had heard from her. Veronica was mercilessly bossing Lily and Helen around. Since the murder even Oni and Harry Kaditz stopped coming to Edmonton every month to visit Helen and Lily.

Veronica had just driven up from Makar's Transport in Beverly and entered the porch that led to the back door of The Pearl's Oyster, when she overheard Lily and Helen discussing her.

"That damn old whore, she's thinking she's better than you and me. She's now a big shot!" Helen spouted.

"Oh yes, she's now a big business woman with a murderer for a husband . . . boy oh boy . . . I hope the police will get enough evidence to hang him. Just wait until Rosie gets back!" Lily continued.

Veronica came bursting into the house and grabbed Lily by the hair and started slugging her with a clenched fist. The punches were delivered to the head. Helen jumped to Lily's defence and that's when the new bouncer came into the kitchen. He separated the women and as soon as he showed protection toward Veronica, she yelled at both of them.

"You miserable white trash . . . I want you out of this house by tomorrow morning, do you hear? Both of you . . . out by sunrise so I don't have to look at your miserable ugly faces again!" Veronica yelled. With that ultimatum she turned on her heel and yelled up the stairs to Ellen, "Ellen, get down here now!" The young girl came running down from the second floor, half dressed in her party finery in readiness for the evening to entertain Jack, Jim, or Dick. She was bewildered by all the commotion, especially Lily and Helen crying.

"Wha . . . what's wrong, Miss Veronica?" Ellen asked.

"Nothing's wrong that concerns you. Tonight you will serve kitchen duty . . . same as Lily and Helen have been doing. Only tonight; tomorrow I'll hire someone else for the kitchen. Helen and Lily are leaving us . . . leaving us for good tomorrow!" Veronica spat.

In the wee hours of the morning when Sonia and Jill had finished entertaining, and Veronica and Ellen, who had done kitchen duty, were fast asleep, Lily and Helen doused the hallway in front of Veronica's door with gasoline. They were so angry and vindictive toward Veronica that they didn't consider the danger in which they were placing themselves, the bouncer on the third floor, or Sonia, Jill, and Ellen, who shared the second floor with Veronica. For that matter, they did not consider how gasoline fumes evaporate and how combustible the whole area would become.

Lily and Helen were dressed in their woolen winter coats. They had their suitcases with them. The suitcases were packed and ready to go. All their personal belongings were in the suitcases.

As Lily lit the match, a big *whoom!* exploded and there were flames everywhere. In their haste they had splashed gasoline all over themselves and now both were on fire, like burning torches.

As they both started running down the stairs and screaming they roused the whole house. They ran outside and started rolling in the snow. The whole house was a flaming inferno because its wood construction was tinder-dry after years of existence. The house burnt like kindling wood. Veronica ran to her door but before opening it felt the heat and knew there was a fire that was quickly burning down her door. She banged on the wall to wake Sonia, who was in the bedroom next to Veronica. Sonia was already wide awake and had jumped through the second-floor window onto the frozen ground below. Veronica was the only one who had a ladder outside her window that led down to the kitchen window. She scurried down the ladder and found Sonia screaming in pain on the frozen ground. Jill and Ellen could not lift their frozen windows and didn't think to break them. They were sticking because of dried paint or frozen to the sills.

Someone, possibly a neighbour, had called the Fire Department and the fire trucks were starting to descend on The Pearl's Oyster. Veronica started yelling that three people were still trapped in the house and pointed to the windows of the rooms where Jill, Ellen, and the bouncer were located.

Ellen was saved, as she knew enough not to open her door to the hallway and the fireman brought her down on a ladder. Jill did open the door; perhaps she thought she could escape that way. She was burned to death, and so was the bouncer. Sonia sustained a compound fracture to her left leg. Veronica, toward whom the vengeance was directed, suffered only superficial burns and sustained no broken bones. She came out of this fire less injured than anyone else did.

Lily and Helen sustained third-degree burns to their bodies. Lily lived for one week at the University Hospital and then died. Helen survived, but she was rendered insane and spent the rest of her life at Oliver Psychiatric Hospital just outside Edmonton.

The house could not be saved by the Fire Department and it burned to the ground. The only thing that remained of The Pearl's Oyster was the charred sign, which swung sadly in the wind. Miraculously, the garage with Rosie's McLaughlin Buick was damaged very little. The car remained in good condition.

Many women in Edmonton breathed a sigh of relief and were happy this establishment was finally gone forever.

After a week Veronica hired men to clear the charred ruins. She left the sign hanging there and left the garage with the McLaughlin Buick inside it.

Veronica didn't miss a beat as she moved all her attention to Makar's Transport. Sonia, as soon as her fractured leg healed, went into partnership with Ellen. They bought a house two blocks from where The Pearl's Oyster was located and started their own establishment. It was not named Pearl's Oyster but rather The Shangrila.

Veronica had squirrelled away an incredible $30,000 each for herself and Rosie. She intended to honour the agreement she had with Rosie, although she did not know whether she would ever see Rosie again. But if Rosie did not return she would claim the entire $60,000 as her own.

CHAPTER SIXTY-EIGHT

Franki spent very little time in leisure activities. He worked at the air base for North West Industries ten hours a day and collected his lumber daily in the form of crates, which Ollie was still saving for him. His yard at Paradise Acres was starting to look like a lumberyard. He had been saving as much money as he could from his job and had built up his savings again to over $15,000 in total. He also had the $20,000 from his *Tato*, which had matured in Canada Savings Bonds. He designated $5,000 of these bonds for Katayna's use.

Franki had found ten lots in Edmonton's northwest section which were selling for $1,000 each. One had to buy the whole ten lots because the owner would not sell them separately. Ten thousand dollars would put a big dent in his savings. He and Ollie had become good friends and he discussed the lots with Ollie.

"What would you put on these lots, Franki?" Ollie asked.

"Houses, single family houses—can you imagine when and if this war ever ends, there'll be a building boom. Instead of everyone working for the war effort, everyone will be trying to make a buck. Men will come back from the war and they will need houses to live in . . . I am sure that will happen." Franki was indeed enthusiastic, more so than Ollie had seen him in recent months.

"I think you have a good idea . . . a good idea!" Ollie replied in his excited nasal Kentucky accent. "In fact, it's such a good idea I'll be your partner if you want!" He studied Franki very closely and detected reservation. "Franki, I have money which I saved honestly; the 'bad business profits' are in a trust. I need to discuss that with you. I wanted to wait until you had gotten over your grieving for McLennan. I thought . . . I thought, after you told me your sister Katayna was not that well off, that maybe she could use that money more than, say, the Red Cross . . . so I've got it sittin' in a trust. Franki, it's a lot of money . . . money she could use, but it's your decision." Ollie showed genuine concern.

"Ollie, I'd like you as a partner in my construction business as long as you let my name stand first on the incorporation. What I mean is, that it should be Stry-Ker and Barris Construction or Stry-Ker-Barris Construction or something like that. My reasons are personal." Franki stated. He wasn't about to tell Ollie that it was to show his brother Mikhail that he would be rich way before the moon turned blue.

The American wooden crates that Ollie gave Franki would provide enough lumber to build the first of many houses. Franki's yard was getting fuller by the day. "So yes, Ollie, you are legitimately my partner by virtue of being the lumber supplier. Your proposal of using the money which you made on the moonshine whiskey is somewhat more of a problem. You're right . . . it was made illicitly and I have a lot of difficulty with that, as you know, but let me sleep on it.

"Okay by me," Ollie replied and left. He had to get back to the base.

Franki pondered Ollie's proposal. Thirty thousand dollars could mean a lifetime of security for Katayna, although God knows where she might be. The thought of Katayna being alone left Franki in a cold sweat. Oh, how he would like to see her again . . . to comfort her, his sweet, wonderful sister.

Before he drove back to Paradise Acres he stopped in to see Father Donalo in Leduc. He explained that a person

. . . say his friend . . . wished to help someone who was in need, but the friend earned the money illicitly. What would Father Donalo's advice be?

As he might have expected Father Donalo replied, "You know the answer yourself. Illicit money should be given back to whoever suffered from losing it, and there's no other way."

"But Father, there are hundreds of people involved and what they bought they already used," Franki replied.

"Then the monies should be given to a needy charity or a needy person," Father Donalo replied.

They each drank a glass of brandy and Franki drove on to Paradise Acres. But when he got home he found that someone had been there and beaten two of his beautiful Clydesdale mares, which were in foal, so badly that they both had dropped their colts. Both would have delivered healthy male colts, which he could have sold as purebred stallions. Franki phoned the veterinarian first and then the RCMP to report the incident. The veterinarian arrived and treated the two beautiful mares. One was too badly beaten about the head and had broken ribs. One of the ribs had pierced the lung and the mare had to be put down.

Franki was totally distraught. He loved those horses so much and his father had entrusted them to him. He felt that he had broken the trust.

He thought, what a pity this was . . . to have had them walked by Henry Warring all the way from Shady Hollow and the mares didn't drop the colts. And then, when they were stabled safely in the barn, someone comes right into the barn and injures these innocent beasts. He'd been looking after them like a most precious possession. Why, why would anyone do this horrible thing?

Franki's thoughts were interrupted when the RCMP came to investigate this awful deed. They wrote down all the details and then left.

Franki decided he would have someone in the yard at all times so that his precious Clydesdales were not ever left unattended. But who . . . who . . . who would love these horses? Why yes, Henry Warring, the teamster who was semi-retired and living in Gibbons. But would he be willing? He would have to drive over to Gibbons the next day after work and find out. Then he got a message to Cissy, his friend, who was studying to be a lawyer. He would have her come and stay the next day if she could.

Cissy was delighted. "Why yes, mon," she cheerfully greeted him. "I thought you forgot all about me, Franki boy." Franki told her what had happened. Cissy was also upset to hear this awful news. Yes, she would stay, as she had written her last examination at the university and it would be nice to be in the country and enjoy the tranquility of country life.

"Do you own a gun?" she asked seriously. "'Cause if that thing comes along again, I'll shoot first and ask questions later."

Henry Warring agreed happily to work for Franki, as he loved these huge horses and missed working with horses. He had sold all of his own horses and still owned his livery stable in Gibbons but it was no longer open for business. He was pleased to work for $7 a day with room and board included. Cissy was pleased to cook for Henry and Franki. She polished up Franki's old house as well as she could, but it was impossible to do more. She occupied one bedroom and Henry the other. Franki made a place for himself in the old attic, which was unfinished. He was living in worse conditions than he had ever endured in his entire life.

"Franki," Cissy observed, "you got all this lumber around here and you want to be a builder. Why not build a prototype for yourself and get some experience? This house without toilet facilities is awful . . . real awful.

Mon, you're livin' like a homesteader. I've not seen the likes of this . . . sure I haven't, since I left Amber Valley, years ago!"

"You know, Cissy, you're right, you're damn right! It's time for me to do something about a suitable house and your idea of a prototype is excellent," Franki said with enthusiasm. He met with Ollie the next day and gave him an answer about the use of the moonshine money. "We'll make Katayna a partner, albeit silent, and the money you have will be her share of the business," Franki offered. Even though Franki had already a small $5,000 share for Katayna he told Ollie that he would add that amount to her share of the business and that would be used for working capital, with each one of them contributing $45,000. Ollie agreed overwhelmingly. Ollie also agreed to build a prototype of a house for Franki. "I wondered how much longer you'd want to live in that old rattle-trap of a house. Cissy is a pretty smart gal; when is she graduating from law?" asked Ollie.

"In two more years," replied Franki, "and if you're thinking what I'm thinking, yes, she will be our lawyer." Franki was pleased with Ollie's idea. He had heard about how the Negro people were being treated in the southern U.S.A. and had hoped that Ollie was not intolerant. Franki was also pleased that Ollie had a lot of knowledge about construction.

Ollie was a farm boy from Kentucky and had helped his dad build a chicken coop. But he figured houses were built on the same principle . . . only a little more complicated. To their surprise, Henry Warring knew everything about drawing plans and construction.

Within two months, Franki's home was framed and the rafters were raised as well. There were two bedrooms on the main floor and two bedrooms upstairs. Each room would have a dormer, similar to Stry-Kers' bedrooms in their farm home at Shady Hollow. The main floor also had a kitchen with lots of built-in cupboards; a living room, a dining room, and something Franki missed a lot—a bathroom.

One week after Franki's mares were so viciously beaten, the RCMP drove into Franki's yard and informed him that they had found the person who did the dastardly deed. They had had a report from the Ponoka Mental Institution that there was a missing patient and that the same patient was originally from the Leduc area. Upon further investigation they discovered that the patient's family were neighbours of Walter Vaschuk, from whom Franki bought the farm. The deranged patient had such hatred toward Walter Vaschuk that he wanted to kill him. When he could not find Walter Vaschuk he went into the barn and thinking the Clydesdales were Vaschuk's, he decided to hurt his horses. The patient did not realize that the farm had changed hands and now the property was Franki Stry-Ker's. The patient was transferred to the locked forensic unit at the Oliver Institution.

CHAPTER SIXTY-NINE

"The War Is Over," read the *Edmonton Bulletin*. It was a day of happiness in Europe and North America alike. The horror of the war was finally ended. Pictures flashed everywhere of happy faces, as families were once again reunited. There was also sadness as many families realized their loved ones would never return.

As Sarah Newhouse read the *Calgary Herald* and looked at all the pictures about liberation ceremonies in Europe, two faces struck her like a thunderbolt. There, right before her eyes, was the picture from Paris of the Liberation and in the picture were her mother, Rosie Soova, and her father, David Newhouse, with huge smiles, wrapped in an affectionate hug. She looked in bewilderment . . . in shock. She had been sure her father was dead by this time and she thought her mother was somewhere in Hawaii. Instead, right before her eyes, there was no mistaking it . . . her mother and father in Paris, France. They looked very happy and very much in love. Her father was wearing a beret and had a beard, but she could never mistake him, never.

Sarah let out a big scream. "Nana, Nana . . . look at this . . . can you believe this?"

"What's the matter, child? Are you all right?" Rachel Newhouse was concerned. "What's all the yelling about?"

"Nana, Nana . . . look at this picture . . . who is that?" she questioned her grandmother. She was now in a hysterical state.

Rachel Newhouse grabbed her reading glasses and peered at the picture.

"Why, my heavenly God . . . my God, that's my David, your father!"

"And Nana, look who he's hugging . . . see who it is," Sarah was ecstatic.

"It can't be . . . it can't be Rosie Soova!" Rachel hesitated. "I mean your mother, child!" This was the first time Rachel called Rosie, Sarah's mother. The two women hugged each other and tears of joy streamed down their cheeks.

Rachel Newhouse was now in her late seventies. She continued to be an attractive woman and looked young for her age. She had a regal look about her. After her bout with tuberculosis she had looked after her health. She ate only healthy foods and always made sure she had her eight hours of sleep each night. Perhaps for these reasons she continued to have an alert mind.

"They're alive, they're alive, and Abe . . . I wonder where is Abe? He has to be alive." Rachel was trying to convince herself.

That day both women went to the Synagogue and said high prayers of thanks.

Within two weeks Rosie Soova and David Newhouse appeared at Rachel Newhouse's front door in Calgary, Alberta. And as neither Sarah nor Rachel had stepped foot outside the door after praying in the Synagogue, both women scurried to the door. Rachel was slower than Sarah.

The door flew open and Sarah grabbed David with one arm and Rosie with the other.

"Father . . . mother . . . I knew I'd see you soon. I knew you were alive. I saw your picture in the *Calgary Herald!*" she announced, more excited than she had ever been in her life.

Then Rachel came to hug, first, her son and then, gently, Rosie. "Welcome, my daughter; can you ever forgive me? I ask you, can you ever find it in your heart to forgive me? Child, if I could reverse all these years, during which I have deprived you and David of your love for each other I would, but I cannot do that. I promise you only that I will always support you from now on," Rachel said with determination.

David and Rosie explained how it was that they found each other in Europe.

David began. "When I first landed in London, England, in July 1939, everyone warned me not to go to Germany, because Hitler and the Nazis were readying themselves for war. Everyone knew it except the English Prime Minister, Chamberlain. Those that knew I was of Jewish descent told me I was an absolute fool to set foot on German soil. I also heard that Abe was in Germany because I had phoned our relatives in Berlin and they were still there. But they were not inviting me to come and join them. In fact, they were discouraging me. So I thought I'd better do some more researching before I went over." David stopped and tears came to his eyes.

Rachel interrupted, "Abe, is he alive . . . David, I must know, David!"

"Mother, please listen to the whole story first." David was ready to tell his mother what happened to Abe. He knew he would have to, but he thought if he told her and Sarah the whole story, Rachel could perhaps be more prepared.

David went on to explain that he did not go to continental Europe before the war was declared and then not for a year. Jews were in grave danger . . . it was a fact, and it would have been suicidal to go over as Newhouse. Fortunately, David was a linguist; after all, he had taught languages at Mount Royal College. He spoke fluent French and acceptable German. He also now specialized in the Slavic languages. He learned that the Germans tolerated Frenchmen and so he arranged for a forged French passport and all the necessary documents enabling him to live in France. He boarded a fishing boat in Ireland and was taken to a little village on the French coast. There he was connected with the French underground and started working for them. It was a well-known fact that Jewish people were disappearing like flies and no one knew where they were going. David had to find Abe. The French underground had their network into Germany. Then word came back that the Newhouse relatives, along with Abe, could no longer be found at their Berlin address. Other Jewish people were scared; they were trying to escape Germany, but to no avail.

"In the hope of finding Abe, I started helping Jewish people escape. The French underground had several escape routes. None were very safe but the route which I was in charge of came through along the Baden Sea from Germany into Briggins, Austria, and then easily into Switzerland. Once the Jews were in Switzerland the Germans could not capture them. When the Germans occupied France, my route was changed to bring people directly from Germany to France. There were very few safe houses in France, as most people were scared to harbour any Jewish people, but of course some did," David continued.

"But how did you and Mother find each other?" Sarah asked curiously.

Now Rosie took over. "When my sources told me I'd have to be very careful when I got to London, and not to even think of entering Germany, I didn't accept that. If he was alive I would try to find my David. I had lost him once and if I could ever find him I'd never lose him again! When I got to England in 1943 the war was raging and the Germans had captured almost the whole of continental Europe; it was looking very grave. I had to spend $10,000 to pay bribes to various contacts, but even with those healthy bribes, the trail to David Newhouse went dead."

Sarah was totally spellbound listening to her mother. Rachel Newhouse, however, was looking extremely anxious and she was starting to fidget. This suspense was getting to be too much for her to tolerate.

Rosie continued, "No one knew where he was. But one of the contacts suggested getting in touch with the French underground . . . if anyone knew, they would know. That same contact suggested that I fix my papers to indicate I was of Irish descent, from Ireland...southern Ireland. It appeared the Germans were docking their U-boats there in Ireland and showed some tolerance toward the southern Irish. My papers were forged and I also boarded a small fishing boat and made my way to the French shore. I was dropped off on a remote beach along the ocean. I had two hundred French francs and nothing else. I was dressed like a charwoman. I made my way, surprisingly, into Paris. I made my contact with the person whose name I was given in the French underground . . . but to no avail. Neither he nor anyone else had ever heard of David Newhouse. I worked as a charwoman for people who owned a restaurant in Paris. I can't say anything exciting happened to me . . . the Germans never picked me up for questioning, nor did they even talk to me. Days and months passed by and no sign of David. Then, one day, while I was on my knees scrubbing the floor in the restaurant, there in front of me, as I looked up . . . there, looking down at me with those unmistakable eyes, was David . . . my David! I jumped and was about to yell his name, when I saw him press his index finger to his mouth, indicating for me to be quiet. 'Hello, Mademoiselle,' the voice said. I was certain it was the voice of David. He said, "I am Alphonse Archant and I'm looking for Gilbert Raquina." Gilbert and his wife Allena, who owned the restaurant, were in the French underground movement. He pretended he didn't know me and my heart sank, until he was sure there was no one else in the restaurant. He then picked me up from my knees, as I was frozen to the floor at this point. He picked me up bodily and hugged and squeezed me as hard as he could.

"He said, 'Rosie, I don't know how you got here, but I'm so grateful you're here. We must be strangers for now . . . for both of our sakes,' I understood. I thought this was a miracle, me finding David amid the horror of this war. I figured that my poor, dead mother—you met her Rachel, remember . . . Olga Soova—I felt that it was her spirit that was guiding me through this whole thing. How else could such a wonderful thing have happened during such a horrible time? We did see each other whenever it was safe, but that was very infrequently, and on VE Day in June we could be together again, forever! We'll never let anyone separate us again, Rachel . . . never!" Rosie was determined as she stroked her daughter's thick, curly auburn hair.

It was now David's turn to break the news about Abe to his mother. He went over to Rachel and hugged her tightly.

Rachel stiffened and asked, "David, is Abe dead? Tell me please."

"Mother," he started, "all those years with the French underground and saving hundreds of Jews, Poles, Ukrainians, Czechoslovakians, Yugoslavians, homosexuals, mentally retarded people—for all these people were in danger of death in Germany under Hitler's rule—all those years, Mother, my dearest hope was to find Abe. I wish I could tell you, Mother, that I know what happened to my dear brother, but I do not . . . I do believe that hope is slim, because so many Jews have died during this horrible war. There was news that our Berlin relatives are no more. Abe was with them. I know that much," David concluded.

Rachel excused herself; the tears were already streaming down her cheeks.

As events of the horrors of Auschwitz and Belzen concentration camps unfolded and reports came forth on how six million Jews had been put to death by the Nazis, the Newhouses learned that their beloved son, husband, father, and brother Abe Newhouse Jr. had met his death there in Auschwitz, along with their relatives from Berlin. They grieved, they wept . . . what was revealed about the horrors of the Second World War was to seal the destiny of David, Rosie, and Sarah Newhouse.

Rosie, David, and Sarah travelled to Edmonton after spending their first week together with Rachel in Calgary.

Rosie learned about the fire at The Pearl's Oyster from Veronica. Veronica also told Rosie that she had accumulated $30,000 in a bank account, which was her fifty per cent of the profits made during her absence. Veronica also explained that the fire insurance would not pay because the fire was caused by arson.

Rosie asked Veronica where she might find Cissy and Franki.

When Rosie and David visited the Heckla apartments they were told that Cissy was spending much time at Franki Stry-Ker's Paradise Acres at Leduc.

Rosie and David then visited the lot where The Pearl's Oyster had once stood. Rosie hugged David and looked at him fondly and commented, "It breaks my heart that people had to die in this dreadful fire . . . but David, I am pleased that this house is no more. It's as though all my sins have burned with it . . . it's as though someone up there really cares about me because, for the life of me, I do not wish to remember what went on here. David, my David . . . only God knows how much I love you!" Rosie was weeping out loud.

"And I love you, Rosie . . . I am also sorry for the loss of life in this fire, but you're right, it's just as well this place is gone."

Rosie took down the charred remains of The Pearl's Oyster sign and said she wanted to take it with her . . . and every time she forgot to be humble, she would look at this sign to remind her where she could still be.

They looked into the garage and there, as good as new, was her McLaughlin Buick.

"David, I'm going to sell this car and lot to Franki Stry-Ker if he wants it. I hear he's planning to become a contractor and he may want a lot in the middle of Edmonton," Rosie stated.

David and Rosie travelled to Franki's Paradise Acres and had a beautiful reunion with Franki and Cissy. They had to repeat the stories of how they found each other in Europe. Cissy told Rosie all about what happened at The Pearl's Oyster after she left.

Franki was more reserved. "Live and let live . . . there's too much hatred in this world, as evidenced by this awful war that's just finishing. Now if everyone could only remember to be more tolerant of one another."

"Said like a real priest!" Rosie commented as she winked at Cissy.

Franki's house was almost completely built, except for bathroom fixtures and hardware to hang the doors with, light fixtures, and other gadgets that were not available during the war.

Franki invited Rosie, David, and Sarah to be his guests overnight. Rosie and David graciously refused because they wished to spend their night at the McDonald Hotel—the same hotel where they spent their first night after running away from Shady Hollow, the same hotel where their daughter, Sarah, was conceived.

Sarah however accepted, because she was so pleased to see Cissy again. She remembered Cissy from four years earlier when she first came to The Pearl's Oyster to see her mother. Cissy was the first person to greet her and then she prepared her breakfast after Sarah's long drive from Calgary. Sarah was extremely pleased to hear that Cissy was soon to be admitted to the Alberta Bar, as a full-fledged Barrister and Solicitor.

CHAPTER SEVENTY

Ollie and Frank's Partnership

VJ day came later in 1945 and Ollie left the service as soon as the war was over but he did not move back to Kentucky. He quite liked Canada. He also liked his new partner, Franki Stry-Ker, but most of all he liked the opportunities in Edmonton . . . opportunities in abundance. Franki and Ollie called their company "Stry-Ker-Barris Homes (1946) Inc."

Johnny Makar was out of jail now and wished to renew the old friendship, which the three had enjoyed before Johnny was incarcerated. Both Ollie and Franki agreed they would continue to be friends with Johnny. But when Johnny asked to join the partnership they said no because they already had a third partner . . . a silent partner.

Their first project was the construction of a house similar to Franki's farm home. It would be their project home. They built these homes on speculation and even before the first one was completed, they had presold three for $6,000 apiece. The war veterans were buying property as they received assistance through the Department of Veteran Affairs. Each Canadian service-man who served in the Second World War received assistance for housing and for furniture purchase. They were also provided full tuition fees and expenses to attend university or trade schools.

Ollie would have received the same assistance or better to complete his university studies in the U.S.A., but for now he would put his completion of school plans on hold.

The next project for Stry-Ker-Barris Homes was a twelve-suite apartment on the old Pearl's Oyster site.

Rosie Soova had sold the lot to Franki, telling him he could pay her whenever he was able to at the agreed sum of $1,000 for the lot in the middle of Edmonton. It was a steal—he knew Rosie could have sold it for three times that price.

Both Ollie and Franki were aware that the low vacancy rate in Edmonton was now at three per cent. They also figured that new apartments would be more desirable than places like the Heckla apartments.

The apartment building was a tougher project, as it was more complicated than building houses. So they hired an experienced construction foreman, a tall Scotsman named Walter (Scotty) MacIntosh. Scotty was a top-notch construction man. He stood five feet ten inches tall and his burly frame was solid muscle. He had a handsome face with a ruddy complexion, red hair, and a bushy red moustache. He worked hard all day and played hard at night. He could consume a 26-ounce bottle of Canadian rye whiskey without appearing drunk.

He loved to dance and his favourite spot on weekends was the Trocadero Ballroom in Edmonton. It was an unusual spot for a rough, tough construction man because the dress code was strict . . . formal dress only. Ballroom dancing was what he liked best. He told Franki and Ollie about a fabulous dance partner he had met there. She was beautiful and could dance like a dream, but she remained a mystery to him. He only knew that she was a young widow, and that her husband had been killed in action in Italy. He had served there in the Canadian Army.

Every weekend he would invite Franki and Ollie to come dancing with him, but they would always decline. Ollie was in love with Alexis O'Neil from Kentucky and he had no interest in meeting someone else. Franki, on the other hand, was usually too tired to socialize although he did like ballroom dancing—dancing he had learned at The Pearl's Oyster with Rosie's Johann Strauss waltz evenings. He was spreading himself too thin with their construction business and Paradise Acres; he was working at least sixteen hours a day.

One Saturday, Franki received a phone call from Scotty MacIntosh who said there was a special Robbie Burns dance and banquet at the Trocadero and insisted Franki come with him as his guest.

Franki reluctantly agreed to go. He dressed up in his Sunday dress suit, the one he wore every Sunday to Father Donalo's mass at Leduc, Alberta. He asked Ollie if he would reconsider and come with him, but Ollie refused. After Ollie left the American Air Force Services he had moved in with Franki at Paradise Acres.

Franki fired up the McLaughlin-Buick, which he had bought from Rosie. He was so proud of his 1932 beauty. It had only five hundred original miles on it when he bought it and it was in excellent condition.

He got to the Trocadero and parked the car across the street. Scotty was waiting at the door and greeted him warmly.

Both men entered the fabulous ballroom. Franki was incredibly impressed. It was a sight Katayna had seen many years ago, a sight that he did not even know had impressed his beloved sister so many years before. He had not heard from Katayna for two years now, even though she was his and Ollie's silent partner, unbeknownst to her.

As they walked across the room toward a table at the opposite end, there at the table sat the most beautiful woman that Franki had ever laid eyes on.

Scott MacIntosh introduced them. "Franki, this is Sophie Hunter . . . Sophie, meet my boss, Franki Stry-Ker."

"My, oh my, you're not the same person as Francis Stry-Ker from Shady Hollow, are you?" Sophie inquired coyly.

"I am . . . have we met before . . . somewhere?" Franki stammered, as he was so smitten by this beautiful creature he could not even talk sensibly.

"Yes, of course, we attended school together at White Sands Creek. Sophie Hunter is my married name. I was Sophie Goseniuk then. Now do you remember?" she said sweetly as she continued to act coquettishly.

He was more flabbergasted than before . . . this beauty was actually the horrid brat . . . Sophie Goseniuk. She was the reason he had got his first strap in school from Mr. Horn. He couldn't believe she had turned out to be a sweet lady.

"Perhaps Scotty has told you I am a widow," Sophie stated flatly. "My husband was killed in the war."

Two dances went by and Scotty and Sophie were gliding along, dancing like two professional dancers. Franki could see she danced extremely well. He marvelled at her beauty. She also had a beautiful figure and was about five feet five inches tall . . . not too tall but also not too short. Her long ash-blonde hair was curled in a soft pageboy and her hair came down her forehead on one side just about covering one eye—the Veronica Lake look. Her eyebrows were tweezed almost completely and a thin line was drawn over her natural arch indicating an eyebrow. She wore heavy mascara, her long lashes were curled, and her cheeks showed a light rouge brushed over her high cheekbones. Franki was envious of Scotty, as he thought he had found an honest-to-goodness living doll.

Franki continued to watch Scotty and Sophie for about four more dances, and then the band started to play an old-time waltz. He walked over to a table where four ladies sat alone, and he asked an attractive brunette to dance. She was a wonderful dancer and so Franki asked her to join him at the table with Scotty and Sophie.

Several more dances went by and Sophie said, "Franki, since we're old school chums I think we should have a dance together, don't you?"

"If Scotty doesn't mind, I'd like that." Franki replied.

"No, no, go ahead and I'll dance with Suzie, here." Scotty agreed.

As they glided smoothly to the old-time waltz, Franki thought he felt Sophie deliberately rubbing her ample breasts against his body. He felt a stirring in himself and he kept a greater distance between them. When the dance was over, Franki walked Sophie back to Scotty's table. Then he told the brunette lady, Suzie, that he was tired and wanted to go home. He asked her if he could drop her off somewhere and she said no, she wished to stay at the dance. So he led her back to the table where she was originally sitting with the other three ladies. He said goodnight to Sophie and Scotty and drove home.

Ollie was still awake and wondered why Franki was home so early. Franki told him about his meeting with Sophie Hunter and that she was a former schoolmate. He also explained how attractive she turned out to be. He did not tell Ollie about what happened when he danced with her.

A few weeks had passed since the Trocadero dance and Franki could not forget the meeting with Sophie. He asked Scotty how he was getting along with her.

"She's a hard one to figure, Franki. Some days she's as sweet as a sugarplum and on other days she bites my head off. I thought it was because of losing her husband in the war, but that's not it, because she told me they weren't getting along too well anyway and that she does-n't grieve for him. So Franki, I dunno . . . I just dunno if it's worth it!" Scotty sounded perplexed. "I think she is a terrific dancer, good looking with her make-up on, but I can't handle the moods she gets into. I tell you, Franki . . . she's a hard one to give up, but it's better now I suppose than later!" Scotty concluded.

"Are you saying that you're through with Sophie; is that what you're saying?" Franki questioned . . . hoping to hear that was the case.

"Yeah, yeah . . . I guess that is what I'm sayin' . . . I don't need this . . . this!" Scotty didn't say what "this" was.

Within a week Franki had received a telephone call from none other than Sophie Goseniuk-Hunter. She invited him to a family wedding. She needed an escort, and that was all it would be. She didn't want to go alone because she would be uncomfortable, she said. The wedding was being held at her relatives' place. They lived at Lamont, Alberta. Franki attended the wedding with Sophie. Her mother and father were delighted to see him again, after so many years.

Sophie continued to phone Franki and always had one or another place where she needed an escort. She was always as sweet as sugarplums, although that's not what others were telling Franki.

Her landlady was uncomplimentary, so were her relatives, and so was Walter "Scotty" MacIntosh. "Don't get involved with her, Franki, or you'll be sorry. Listen, I like you and don't want to see you hurt!" Scotty would say. He said it several times.

Cissy Brown was graduating from the University of Alberta and invited Franki as a special guest. Cissy had met Sophie and tried diplomatically to tell Franki that Sophie was not invited, but Franki was falling head over heels in love with Sophie Goseniuk-Hunter and was not listening. At the convocation, Cissy wore her mortar hat and cloak with its scarlet-red trimmings. She looked every bit a lawyer, which she would soon become. When the time for congratulations came, Franki hugged Cissy, genuinely happy for her achievements.

Sophie rudely commented, "Congrats Cissy . . . I guess they let anyone into law these days, eh?" and laughed hilariously. She had had several drinks and it was obvious.

That's when Franki and Sophie had their first argument. Franki refused to talk to Sophie when she would call so she came to Paradise Acres; again just as nice as sugarplums. She always treated Ollie coolly.

That night she seduced Franki and that was the first night he had ever had sex. He honestly thought he had died and gone to heaven. What a thrilling time he had. She stayed all night with him and they had sex several times during the night.

The next day when she left, Ollie tried to talk some sense into Franki. Franki did not wish to listen to him either. He thought that nothing on earth could be better than the sex that Sophie had offered him.

CHAPTER SEVENTY-ONE

Mikhail was feeling very low when he called Franki. Whenever Mikhail telephoned, Franki knew something serious was at hand. Mikhail was a no-nonsense person and very frugal. Telephone calls cost money and should only be used sparingly, in his view. There was a new Alberta Government Telephone operator in Shady Hollow, Lizzy Husar, and Mikhail was spending much time now in Shady Hollow, mostly at the telephone office. He had reached the age of forty-two years. Lizzy Husar was about forty years old, an old maid according to Shady Hollow standards. She was a redhead, henna red, and had pretty turquoise eyes. She was indeed an attractive lady for her age. She owned and operated a clothing store in Shady Hollow, and it housed the Alberta Government Telephone (AGT) switchboard as well. But Franki did not know about Lizzy Husar just yet.

The telephone call was serious indeed. *Tato* had become very ill and might not survive. His diabetes was out of control and he was suffering severe dementia. He recognized very few people and he often hallucinated.

When Franki phoned Sophie to tell her he would not see her that night because he was going to Shady Hollow to see his sick father, she insisted on coming with him.

"I know your family . . . I'd like to see your father also. After all, it's like family . . . I've known you and your people so long." she insisted. Franki was flattered to hear Sophie assuring him how highly she thought about his family, so he took her along. The McLaughlin-Buick purred along on the smooth parts of the road, but even though these roads were gravelled, the grade was so infe-

447

rior that many mud puddles remained on the road from one rainstorm to the next. When they got to the Stry-Ker farm at Shady Hollow, Franki was surprised to see the whole Stry-Ker clan gathered around Evan's bed. As Franki looked around the room, there in real life was his sister, Katayna. He was thunderstruck.

Everyone acknowledged Franki and he introduced Sophie Hunter. "This is Sophie Hunter . . . most of you know her from when she went to White Sands Creek School. Do you remember Sophie Goseniuk?" Franki was very surprised to see a cool reception from everyone, especially Katayna.

Katayna walked over to Franki and coolly shook his hand; she also shook Sophie's hand, but her greeting to Sophie was even cooler.

Franki came to his father's bedside and knelt beside him. Evan was asleep and Dr. Allison was there, telling everyone not to wake him.

Just as everyone was leaving the room and Franki had risen to leave also, Evan's eyes opened and in a feeble voice he said, "Francis . . . Francis, my son. You've come to see me before I die. How are you?" he paused. "Your Clydesdales?"

Franki did not mention the two mares that had sustained the severe beating by the escapee from the Ponoka Mental Institution.

"Our Clydesdales are fine and are still as beautiful as ever, *Tato*. Two of our colts have won blue ribbons and I'm now showing them at the Edmonton Exhibition. I'm also doing well in my construction company . . . and did you see I have a beautiful girlfriend, Sophie Goseniuk? Do you remember her from when she was little?" Franki asked his father.

The old Evan's eyes looked clouded as he searched his feeble memory. "Something . . . something . . . I am thinking was wrong. Mr. Horn . . . that Englishman . . . Oyee, oyee . . . you Francis . . . You don't want Sophie . . ." His eyes closed again.

Franki was happy that Sophie hadn't heard what Evan said, as she had left the room along with the others. Within an hour Evan Stry-Ker, the patriarch of this family, expired, at the age of seventy-nine. Funeral arrangements were made with Park Memorial Funeral Gardens in Edmonton. People in these parts were now getting their loved ones embalmed. Franki insisted on giving Evan the best funeral that money could buy. More than a thousand people from all over the province attended. The Kuriak family from Star came and so did the Yaworskys. Kuriak and Yaworsky sat up during the three-day vigil in the Stry-Kers' house. They slept and awoke reminiscing about old times, about Evan's adventures, about what a tough life he had led.

Mike Mikalik, Evan's church friend and neighbour, sat vigil the first two nights; however, his poor health would not allow him to sit up the third night. Mike's wife, Annie, had died the year before. She died of a ruptured appendix, as she was as stubborn as a small mule and refused to see Dr. Liston until it was too late. Mike, even though he had been mistreated by Annie all through their marriage, missed her a great deal—his health was failing quickly as a result of his deep grief for his departed wife.

Widow Hunkowski came to view the body, but she did not come to the funeral mass at St. Olga's church. Father Kohut came out of retirement for this one special funeral. He was very feeble but he gave a wonderful eulogy. Father Stepko and Father Donalo from Leduc sang the mass. As an honorary server, Joseph Chomiak assisted with the provision of incense for the priest's *kaddilo* (the thurible, which the priests used to bless the congregation). The entire Stry-Ker clan came: Mikhail, who brought Lizzy Husar, the AGT operator, with him; Katayna, who had travelled so far to be here; Paul and Anastasia and their children Evancik and Evelyn; Pushinskys—Helena and Joseph along with their handsome sons, Joseph Jr., Peter, Evan, and the special grandchild of Evan and Tainka, Emily, who was so much like their first child Maria, whom they grieved for all their lives; and Franki, who did not bring Sophie to the funeral.

Evan was laid to rest in the Stry-Ker row of graves, right beside Maria, his only deceased daughter. The patriarch was dead and this was hard for everyone to accept. After the funeral, Domka Soova was hired to prepare a banquet feast that was served in the new church hall at St. Olga's parish.

Sophie did not attend the funeral, as she told Franki that his family treated her with no respect and that she felt the disdain that they had toward her.

After the funeral, when all the people had left, Tainka went to Evan's clothes cupboard, removed all his clothing and some books that he had been saving, and burned everything in a large bonfire. Little did she know that she burned, in that bonfire, $10,000 worth of Canada Savings Bonds certificates. Evan unfortunately did not tell anyone that he had hidden the Canada Savings Bonds in the books, which Tainka burnt. These were the bonds he had put away for his own funeral expenses. Tainka used her own $5,000, which he had left exclusively for her own use, for funeral expenses. Franki had offered to pay for the funeral entirely, but Tainka flatly declined the offer, explaining that it was her final responsibility to Evan. No one could explain why she had burned all of Evan's possessions, but some thought she held resentment toward him for his immoral conduct through life, and this last act of extrication was to wipe him out of her life forever.

On his way back to Edmonton after the funeral, Franki had a passenger—Katayna. Katayna was no more the loving, forgiving sister he remembered—not since she had lost her beloved, Rusty. She was cold and unreachable.

"I wanted to talk to you so badly, so many times . . . why haven't you contacted me all this time? Where are you living and how did you hear about *Tato*?" Franki inquired.

"Franki, I shall never forgive you for your involvement in the Kaditz and Soova affair. Do you think I didn't know about your involvement? Imagine the brother, whom I raised, helped to kill the only man I ever loved so deeply!" Katayna's eyes were cold as she spit out these words.

A cold dagger in his heart would not have hurt Franki more. This woman sitting beside him did not even resemble the Katayna he remembered.

He would have to defend himself. "Katayna, you're being unfair . . . I had nothing whatsoever to do with Rusty's death. If you know anything, you should know that!" Franki stated emotionally.

"You made the first deal with Louie Kaditz . . . it was done after you attended Uncle Yatsko's funeral . . . don't try to deny that. It's not becoming for a man that was supposed to be a priest!" Katayna spat back.

"I'm not denying anything, but I did not go through with the agreement . . . if you know all these things then you should know that." Franki was on the defensive.

"To me, Franki, anyone and everyone who was even on the periphery of involvement with that scum is responsible!" she screamed.

"Katayna, please settle down, you're the last person on earth with whom I'd want to fight. I'm trying to help you because of how good you've been to me during my life. In fact, you are a silent partner in my company and you have accumulated quite a profit. My company is legal and I work sixteen hours a day making it that way!" But Katayna interruped before Franki finished.

"I'm glad you recognize that you owe me something, and I'll not refuse to take my share from your company . . . that you owe me . . . that you owe me all right!" Katayna said, in her new commanding manner. "Now, Franki, I see you're involved with that witch of a woman, Sophie Goseniuk . . . are you totally out of your head or is your penis running your brain? Where in the hell did you find her again? Do you not remember the aggravation that she caused you in school? A leopard never changes its spots and you can be sure she's the same little witch—or have I gone too far down the alphabet?" Katayna was even more furious now.

"Goddam, Katayna, you're cruel . . . you're downright cruel. What's happened to you?" Franki was visibly upset.

"Life has happened to me, Franki. I tried to be a decent person before Rusty's death, but whoever controls life dealt me a tough blow. To answer your question, I don't think life has been exactly fair to me . . . so I'll take my share now. As far as Sophie Goseniuk is concerned . . . if you don't get rid of her then you deserve what you'll be dealt. And trust me, Franki, she will hurt you, she's that kind of person!" Katayna was more subdued.

She asked Franki to drop her off at Rusty's friends', the Andersons, in the Highlands of Edmonton, on Ada Boulevard.

As she was getting out of the car, she wrote down a box number and address where Franki could send her share of the company profits. He noted she lived in

Kona, Hawaii. There was absolutely no sign of affection, the kind that the old Katayna shared with him during his formative years.

CHAPTER SEVENTY-TWO

Franki was having many second thoughts . . . many apprehensions about his girlfriend. There did not seem to be anyone who had anything good to say about Sophie Goseniuk. Not only was there no one who approved of her; he was also finding her to be a very difficult person. She would come to Paradise Acres and refuse to talk to Ollie. In fact, she was downright rude to him and also to Henry Warring, the teamster who was looking after Franki's precious Clydesdales. It got to such a point that her condescending ways got the better of Henry and he served notice that he would be leaving the employ of Franki and of Paradise Acres.

"Henry, why . . . I know Sophie can be difficult sometimes but underneath it all, she is a fine person . . . give her another chance." Franki pleaded with Henry.

"I don't know where you're seeing another side of that woman," Henry couldn't even bring himself to call her by her name, "but where I'm coming from, she has no other side. She's downright mean. No one in all my born days has ever called me riff-raff. I don't deserve that. First of all, I know my job and secondly, I'm much older than her, so I deserve some small degree of respect . . . of dignity!" Henry's mind could not be changed, as he chewed his tobacco twice as quickly as usual. He chewed mostly for pleasure, but there was no pleasure today, only disgust.

Franki had a serious argument with Sophie. "Don't you ever be rude to anyone else on this yard! I won't tolerate your moods, do you hear?" Franki was shouting at her because he genuinely liked Henry Warring. Henry was doing an outstanding job for him. His Clydesdales were gaining much recognition because Henry knew how to train them for maximum showing at various exhibitions. Franki's purebred stock was now in demand all over Canada and he was getting requests for information from the United States.

The departure of Henry was only the tip of the iceberg. Ollie started telling Franki about how rude and inconsiderate Sophie had been to him and that he absolutely had no time for her. In fact, he had been looking for a quarter section of his own in and around Leduc.

Ollie used to talk to Franki often about a seismic bump in the rock which he perceived. He thought that in his travels around Alberta, he had nowhere seen that same seismic bump. Furthermore, he was aware that the Imperial Oil Company was doing seismic drilling around Leduc.

When Franki asked Ollie to be more specific about Sophie, he would only say, "I have no time for that moody bitch!" And that said everything that he felt about Sophie.

Franki also noted that Cissy had stopped coming to Paradise Acres. He had heard Sophie say some unkind things to Cissy, who was now articling with the Stewart Law firm. The clever criminal lawyer who won Johnny Makar and Louie Kaditz's trial, Duncan Stewart, was delighted to give Cissy articles and was giving her a full range of legal work to do. He now had four other lawyers working in his firm, each specializing in a different sector of law. After the Makar-Kaditz trial, Duncan Stewart was in extremely high demand to defend criminal cases.

Whenever Franki asked Cissy why she wasn't visiting Paradise Acres, she always used the excuse that she was too busy at work.

Fanki confronted her directly. "Cissy, does this have something to do with Sophie?"

"What do you think, mon, you are madly and blindly in love . . . do you think anything I would say to you would really make a difference?" Cissy replied.

Franki valued Cissy's opinion very highly. The two had become extremely good friends since their days at The Pearl's Oyster and he could see that Sophie had driven a wedge into this special friendship.

Franki took Sophie out to a formal dinner at the Wedgwood Room at the McDonald Hotel. He loved the elegance of the room, an elegance that had been there from the time the hotel had been built. He fully intended to tell Sophie that he was no longer interested in her romantically. And hopefully, they could still remain friends.

After a pleasant dinner Sophie addressed Franki. "My darling Franki, I know that this must be so hard for you to say . . . is it?" Sophie was coy and sweet again.

Franki figured she knew what he meant, but he could not have been more wrong.

"Then you agree that we're not meant for each other?" Franki stated.

With that she rose from her seat and started yelling at him.

"God damn you, you mean you weren't intending to give me a diamond . . . you use me and then leave me!" Sophie was out of control. She sat down again and almost in a whisper she said, "Well Franki boy, it's not so easy, I'm three months pregnant . . . with your brat. So you'll have to marry me, like it or lump it!" She had alerted the attention of everyone in the dining room and patrons were looking discreetly at Franki and Sophie.

To say that Franki was devastated would have been the understatement of the century. He was stunned. As soon as he could, he paid their bill and escorted Sophie out of the restaurant. She did not wish to leave, but he said he would go alone if she wished to remain.

They drove silently to Sophie's apartment and he walked her to the door. He did not want to come in when she asked him. His fury was rising; soon he would not be able to control himself and knew it.

He drove directly to Cissy's apartment at the Heckla, but when he got there Cissy was entertaining a handsome young Negro athlete. She introduced him.

"This is Jesus Jackson, Franki Stry-Ker, a long-time friend. What's the matter . . . you look like death warmed over . . . Franki, what's wrong?" Cissy was concerned.

"I'll tell you another time." Franki did not wish to discuss the Sophie fiasco in the presence of Jesus Jackson.

Jackson detected the tense situation and did not wish to interfere with the pending discussion. "I was planning to leave anyway. I have an early ball practice tomorrow. I must keep in shape . . . get my proper rest. It was real nice meeting you, Franki. Cissy, thanks for a real nice evening. I'll call you real soon."

After Jesus Jackson left, Cissy told Franki that she had just met him. They had been introduced by a mutual friend of hers from Amber Valley. Jesus Jackson came to Edmonton from Detroit, U.S.A., and was trying out as the pitcher for the Edmonton Class A hardball team. And yes, she thought he was one terrific dude.

"Now, what's happened to you . . . it's got to be pretty serious; I've never seen you like this!" Cissy cried.

Franki told her the whole sordid story. He was desperate for advice. "What now?" he inquired wildly.

"Sheesh! Oh boy, oh boy, are you ever in a mess, mon . . . Franki!" Cissy was always candid with him. "So what the hell are you goin' do . . . you're not going to marry the bitch, are you, or are you even thinking about it?"

"God, I sure would not like to, but what do I do?" Franki was obviously upset.

"Well, the first thing is get your companies in shape so she has no claim to anything . . . our law firm will do that. I'll do it personally, under Duncan's direction. Next, find out if she'll have an abortion." Cissy stated, without showing how concerned she really was.

"Yes, please get our companies in order. Do that tomorrow . . . as far as an abortion is concerned I do not condone abortions and I'd never encourage her to have one. I'll see if she agrees to my supporting her and the child without marrying her." Franki was starting to think rationally again.

They formulated the plans and Franki felt a little better.

When he got to Paradise Acres, Henry Warring, who still had another week to work, had a terrible message for Franki.

The Royal Alexandra Hospital had telephoned and asked Franki to come immediately. Sophie Goseniuk-Hunter had attempted suicide and wanted to see him.

Within one month, on February 1, 1947, a huge wedding was held at the McDonald Hotel, which Franki paid for entirely.

Sophie was decked out in a white gown with a white veil. Father Donalo married them in the little church in Leduc. The entire Stry-Ker clan attended. Emily, Helenka and Joseph Pushinsky's daughter, was a brides-maid. The boys, now in their late teens and early twenties, provided the music. Their band had gained notoriety as being of the same calibre as Glenn Miller. There were ten musicians—all young men—and they played several instruments each. Emily, against her mother's protests, sang with the band. The band had gone through several name changes but now it was called

"The Soft Sounds." Every band member wore a white dinner jacket, black trousers, white dress shirt, and black bow tie. Even Sophie approved of them.

All the friends from Shady Hollow attended. Cissy Brown brought Jesus Jackson as her escort. They were becoming an item. Even Johnny and Veronica Makar attended, as Franki had invited them. Tainka was totally disgusted to see Sophie in white; after all, she had been married before and everyone could see she was pregnant. "Where was the purity which was symbolized by white?" Tainka thought.

Katayna, even though invited, did not attend the wedding—as Franki expected.

The wedding night was a total disaster. Franki could not get an erection and Sophie knew the marriage was doomed even before it got started, but she didn't really care. She knew she would be well off financially—but she would not be as well off as she thought.

CHAPTER SEVENTY-THREE

Ollie Barris had closed the deal on the purchase of his quarter section of land on January 13, 1947. It was two miles from Franki's place. There were buildings on the property; they were in better condition than those on Franki's farmstead when he first bought his farm..

Ollie moved out of Franki's place just as soon as he could, within a week after the purchase. He had as little contact with Sophie as possible.

Ollie was also now engaged—to Alexis O'Neil from Kentucky. She had graduated as a veterinarian and was practising her professional skills at her father's thorough-bred ranch. Fred O'Neil was delighted to have a built-in veterinarian at the farm. She loved horses, as did her younger sister, Sandra O'Neil. The sisters were slated to take over the O'Neil estate after Fred O'Neil retired. Sandra was following in her sister's footsteps and also training to be a veterinarian.

Ollie had travelled to Kentucky for the engagement party; while there he received a phone call from Franki. It was February 13, 1947, a month after Ollie closed the deal on the purchase of his quarter section.

"Did you hear the news yet, from here, from Alberta?" Franki could not contain his excitement. "Imperial Oil has hit oil . . . it's shooting hundreds of feet in the air. It happened at four o'clock this afternoon. Your predictions were right, about your seismic bump, which you thought was located here. Ollie, you wouldn't believe what's happening here! Everyone is calling it Alberta tea . . . some are celebrating and calling it black gold, but whatever you call it, it means big money,

Ollie—honest to goodness money for you and me. Do you remember when we met Vern Hunter of Imperial Oil once in the Leduc Hotel?"

"No, I can't say that I do," Ollie replied.

"Well, at that time everyone was calling him 'Dry Hole' Hunter . . . he kept drilling test wells, one hundred and thirty-three in all, and they were all dry. Imperial spent over twenty-three million dollars in exploration wells . . . and now look at that, it was at the Turta place. They struck oil!" Franki could not contain his excitement. "The reason I'm calling you also is to tell you that Imperial Oil wants to drill on my land and on your quarter . . . what do you think?"

"Yes, of course I'm interested—I'm so darned pleased Franki, so damned pleased. We'll discuss this later, but how's life treating y'all buddy . . . I mean married life?" Ollie was genuinely concerned because Franki had not been the same person since he married Sophie.

"What's to say, Ollie . . . life has its mysteries here at Paradise Acres. I've started calling it Hell's Acres!" Franki replied.

He didn't tell Ollie that his prized German Shepherd watchdogs, which he had just bought from a pedigree kennel to guard the yard, had been poisoned. Someone had got the gopher poison down from the highest shelf in the blacksmith shop and smeared it on a beefsteak and then given it to the dogs. Sophie knew how much he loved these animals and how much attention he gave them. When he asked Sophie about it, her reply was that she knew nothing about it and besides it served them right—those dogs were vicious anyway and barked all the time. They disturbed her sleep.

Franki suspected that Sophie might have had something to do with it because she was acting more suspiciously then she normally did.

For a wedding present, Franki had bought Sophie a brand new 1947 Chevrolet with a sun visor on the outside. It had much chrome on it and she showed some appreciation when he gave it to her, but four months later when she was seven months pregnant she told him the car was very uncomfortable and that he should have got her a Cadillac. It had more room to manoeuvre. When he tried to explain that she would be thinner as soon as the baby was born and the Chevy would be fine again, she began to berate him for getting her pregnant in the first place. The stretch marks were ruining her body. Her lovely figure would never be the same.

Matters got worse until the baby was born July 15, 1947. She had a tough labour because the baby girl was over eight and one-half pounds. There was no bonding with the baby and she refused to nurse the child, who was placed on formula immediately. Sophie didn't really care what they named the child. It was obvious she looked like Franki. Would she mind if they called the baby Francine Marie? No, she didn't care what her name would be.

Father Donalo baptized little Francine Marie. The Godparents were Ollie Barris and Cissy Brown, even though they were both reluctant to accept this honour, as they knew they would have to have contact with Sophie and both dreaded the experience.

Franki loved his little princess. He made up for the love and affection she was not receiving from her mother. He had started calling her his one and only princess. Every day when Franki would come home he would pick Francine Marie up and carry her around, hugging and kissing the child. He loved her with all his heart and soul. The child made up for the horrid life he was living with her mother.

Sophie stayed home very little and would hire an older woman who lived nearby to baby-sit. She went out shopping most of the time and when she was not shopping she was drinking at the Royal George Hotel. She had started consuming a lot of liquor.

Then on October 22, 1947, when Francine Marie was just a little over three months old, Franki came home only to be told coolly by Sophie that the baby had choked to death.

He became hysterical and ran to the bedroom, where the baby crib was, and there laid out as though she were a sleeping angel was Francine Marie. She had joined all the other angels in heaven. Franki immediately called the RCMP and an investigation took place. Sophie appeared very distraught when the police questioned her.

She explained that she had wrapped Francine Marie in a little feather quilt that her mother, Mrs. Goseniuk, had made for her first grandchild. She wrapped her baby corner to corner in the quilt and then pinned the quilt with a safety pin. When she checked on the baby about a half an hour later she found her face down in the quilt. Sophie thought that Francine Marie must have tried to turn over and got smothered that way. The police could find no marks or bruises on the baby, no signs of abuse, so they believed Sophie's explanation about the baby's death. After all, the police figured, no mother could do away with her own child. They accepted Sophie's story but Franki did not. Neither did the Godparents, Ollie and Cissy. Franki buried his little princess in a white baby casket, which he bought at Park Memorial. There was a beautiful funeral. Father Donalo from the little parish at Leduc conducted the sad funeral mass. There was not a dry eye in the church. Even Father Donalo kept wiping his eyes with a white handkerchief he had clutched in his hand. The only one who was not crying was the mother, Sophie Goseniuk-Hunter-Stry-Ker.

At the viewing of the body, Franki looked for the last time at his beautiful little baby girl, as she lay in her casket. She wore her white christening gown and the little white frilly bonnet that Cissy had bought for her baptismal. Her long eyelashes were closed and her rosebud mouth appeared to have a faint smile. In her little hand she clutched at tiny pink rosebud. Franki threw himself on the tiny casket and would not let go. His brothers Mikhail and Paul, and much to Franki's surprise his sister Katayna, were there also. All of them tried to pry him away from the casket as he sobbed out loud. He finally left with Katayna as she once again soothed him . . . once again like the Katayna he remembered. The four Pushinsky boy cousins of baby Francine Marie acted as the pallbearers. She was buried at Edmonton's Beech Mount Cemetery.

The whole Stry-Ker clan attended the funeral. All their hearts ached for Franki because he was so overwhelmed with grief; they all worried for his sanity.

After a week of grieving, attending the cemetery most of the time, and not speaking to Sophie, he approached her. "You and I should never have been married, Sophie . . . the reason for our unfortunate liaison is now gone and as long as I live I never want to lay eyes on you again. Do you hear? Never again. To say I despise you, to say I hate your guts, would be an understatement. You are the most evil person I have ever met in my life!" Franki hated himself for being this way but he had an urge to kill Sophie—at the least he wanted never to lay eyes on her again—his wife, whom unfortunately he had married. He would not continue the agony of this marriage.

She responded with as much hurt and venom she possibly could. "You, look who's talking, the whoremaster himself. The man who couldn't make it as a priest . . . who lived in a whorehouse, the one himself . . . look who's talking! I also never want to see you again, you whoremaster . . . whoremaster, whoremaster, whoremaster!" Sophie was shrieking at the top of her lungs.

Franki came up to her with a clenched fist and was one inch from hitting her as she stood there and defiantly egged him on.

"Go ahead, hit me . . . just hit me. I'll sue you for everything, you whoremaster!" She kept on yelling as he walked out the door and slammed it behind him. He did not come home that night but stayed in a hotel room.

The next day he met with Cissy in her law office and prepared an agreement to rid himself of Sophie. He would pay her off and get a divorce.

When he approached Sophie with the agreement that he and Cissy had prepared, she would have nothing to do with it. She did not want a divorce. She wanted him to buy her a house in Edmonton on Capital Hill, because she said she always hated Paradise Acres, and she wanted him to support her. He knew that the only way he could get a divorce was if she or he committed adultery, and she would never do that.

So he asked her to find a house of her choice and move out of Paradise Acres.

She found the most expensive house that she could, along with the most elegant furniture money could buy.

He agreed to everything, against Cissy's advice. Cissy felt Sophie should sign an agreement with some finalized figures, but Franki wanted her out of his life immediately.

Several months had gone by and Franki was starting to feel that life was getting just a little more pleasant. Stry-Ker-Barris Homes was booming. In order to have an uninterrupted supply of lumber they bought and took over the operation of a sawmill in Athabasca, ninety miles north of Edmonton. They also branched off into all the sub-trades, their own electrical and plumbing companies. They hired their own tradespeople. Scotty McIntosh was still their head foreman and because of the excellent job he was doing they gave him a small share in the companies.

In the next few months Imperial Oil drilled on both Ollie's and Franki's farm properties and struck oil on both quarters.

Cissy Brown, who acted as the legal counsel to Franki and Ollie, was still trying to unravel the mineral rights issue on Franki's and Ollie's lands. Although Imperial Oil was paying them well for the oil they were taking off their lands, Cissy knew it would be much more lucrative if they were proven to own their mineral rights. Imperial Oil had their own brilliant lawyers on staff, lawyers who would try to prove that Stry-Ker and Barris did not own what was under the ground.

Cissy was reviewing the Turta case. This case was based on a mistake by the Alberta Land Titles office in failing to include the reservation of petroleum when the sale of a piece of farmland was recorded on the Land Titles office records. In 1908, the Podgorny family had acquired one hundred and sixty acres of land from the CPR. There was a faulty deed recorded on Podgorny's land. When he sold this land to Turta, only the coal was reserved to the CPR; the petroleum was not. At that time, neither of these two farmers could read English so neither of them was aware that a mistake had been made.

However, in 1942, when the Land Titles office was doing an audit of their records, the mistake was discovered. So, instead of notifying the farmers about the mistake, the authorities just made the correction, unbeknownst to the landowners. When Imperial Oil was assembling large tracts of land in the Leduc area, as seismic works showed there was a potential to hit oil in this region, it came upon the corrected titles in its land title searches and included these documents with others it sent to the CPR.

When the landowner, Turta, reviewed his title after Imperial Oil discovered oil on his farm, he consulted a lawyer by the name of George Steer. The case went all the way up to the Supreme Court of Canada. In a vote of six to three, the supreme justices found that Turta was a bona fide purchaser from the first owner, Podgorny, and therefore he was the owner of the petroleum rights.

Cissy Brown reviewed the land titles of Stry-Ker and Barris and was certain that their titles were handled in the same way by the Land Titles office. She was preparing the case for court and was optimistic she would win. After all, she lost very few cases.

Ollie and Franki could not believe the good fortune which was coming their way.

However, the more money Franki made, the more Sophie spent. Her expenses had doubled within six months. Franki kept paying and no matter how hard she tried to see him, he flatly refused. All interactions would be handled through Cissy Brown, his lawyer. Cissy continued to caution Franki about his open-ended agreement with Sophie.

Franki kept on saying he would pay as long as he never had to see Sophie again.

CHAPTER SEVENTY-FOUR

After Francine Marie was buried, Katayna had a long meeting with Franki and apologized humbly for her unacceptable behaviour after their father's funeral.

Katayna knew in her heart that the pain Franki suffered in losing his baby girl was very similar to the pain she herself had suffered when her beloved Rusty was shot. She still loved Franki deeply, as though he was her own real son, only she had not acted like a mother for the past several years.

"Franki, words can't express how sorry I am for treating you as shabbily as I have in the past few years since Rusty's death. I can't undo the hurt I caused, but believe me, as long as I'm alive it will never happen again." Katayna was very humble as she spoke. "And Franki, I hope we'll be as close as we used to be."

"Katayna, hearing those words takes a little of the pain away . . . of losing my little princess. Katayna, I know how you must have hurt after Rusty died; death is so final . . . how can anyone take my little angel . . . so innocent, just snuffed the life right out of her!" Franki was sobbing again, and Katayna comforted him lovingly. She made no comment, but she also suspected how Franki's little princess died.

Katayna stayed with her mother Tainka for two weeks at the Stry-Ker home at Shady Hollow.

Every day she saw Anastasia and Paul come to the Stry-Kers' to help with the daily chores. Anastasia was doing most of the housework as Tainka was getting older and could not manage. Paul worked with Mikhail as he had all his life. Evancik and Evelyn spent most of their time at *Baba* Tainka's and Uncle Mikhail's. In fact, they did not even want to go home at night. They enjoyed the electric lights and indoor plumbing at *Baba* Tainka's, as their home on the Borischuk place had none of these conveniences.

Uncle Mikhail was also very good to them. He would take them into Shady Hollow and buy them treats. He took them to all kinds of other events, such as auction sales, or to the movies, which were now being shown at a new theatre in Shady Hollow. On many occasions he took Evancik with him when he played cards at Fred Radjec's place. Evancik used to say he liked going there because Fred had many magazines to read and had all kinds of interesting junk, but he did not like how it stunk at Fred's place.

Mikhail's other friend, Paul Lupski, had enlisted in the army during the Second World War, and he had fought in the front lines. When the war ended and Paul came home, he was extremely shell-shocked and became a total recluse. He no longer cared to play cards with Mikhail, Fred, and their other bachelor friends.

Katayna observed these comings and goings at the Stry-Kers' and one day she asked her mother, "Why don't Paul and Anastasia move here into this big house with you and Mikhail?"

"I never asked them because I thought they want to be alone. Why would anyone want to live here with an old lady?" Tainka asked.

"Why . . . because you have a very big house for just you and Mikhail, and Paul and Anastasia have that little Borischuk house, without any conveniences. Don't you think it must be hard for them to come for the whole day and then have to go back there? I noticed the children want to stay here anyway." Katayna concluded.

"But what if Mikhail marries; where will he live?" Tainka questioned.

"When is he getting married, *Mamunia*? Has he ever said he would?" Katayna questioned.

"He hasn't said, but he has been spending much time with that Lizzy Husar, the storekeeper . . . the AGT telephone operator. Maybe I'll ask them . . . maybe I will," *Mamunia* stated.

At suppertime that night Tainka first asked Mikhail, "Mikhail, you're getting to be an old bachelor, as they say . . . they say it's time for you to get married. Seeing that you and Lizzy like each other, are there any plans . . . any plans to marry?" Tainka cautiously approached this subject.

"Lizzy and I are only good friends. She doesn't want to get married and I sure don't want to either. Look at what's happened to Franki and that Sophie!" Mikhail could not be more direct.

"Yes, Mikhail, but look at a good marriage . . . one like Paul and Anastasia's . . . like Helenka and Joseph's . . . like Katayna's was when Rusty was alive. There have been many more good than bad marriages in this family!" Tainka observed.

"Yes that's true . . . that's very true, but for me, it's better not to be married. I like to be a bachelor, I go when I want to go, come when I want to. No one tells me what to do . . . and I like it like that." Mikhail stated emphatically.

"Katayna and I were talking today that this house is so big . . . too big for you and me. What about moving here with us, Paul?" Tainka inquired.

Evancik and Evelyn, who was now four years old, both shrieked with delight. "Yes, daddy . . . yes, mama, we like it here . . . we like it better than at our place!"

Paul said he would discuss it with Anastasia and Mikhail. The next day, Paul talked it over with Anastasia. She felt they were spending most of their time at the

Stry-Ker house and she would like to move, but how would Mikhail feel? She did not want to upset him.

Mikhail was very pleased with this arrangement, as he and Paul got along famously and he liked Anastasia and both the children.

He suggested building two extra bedrooms onto the house and everyone would have their own. They would build the addition in the spring, and until then Mikhail would live in Uncle Yatsko's little house. That's where they now housed any workmen who helped during spring work or at harvest time.

The workmen could now live at the Borischuk place, Paul and Anastasia's house. The children were over-whelmed with joy. After helping Anastasia and Paul move, Katayna spent a few more days at the Stry-Ker farm with her mother. She could see that Tainka was starting to look older, but she still had much of her out-standing beauty. Tainka also had not complained that she had any major health problems. Oh, she had an ache here or some pain there and she moved slower but, by normal standards, she was doing extremely well for her age . . . she was nearing seventy years.

Tainka did tell Katayna that she had some arthritic problems, but nothing that she could not handle. She told Katayna about a garlic oil and cayenne concoction that she used to prepare. If she drank this brew regularly, her arthritis did not bother her.

Katayna hugged her mother for a long time and wished her God's blessing. She bid everyone else a farewell and travelled to Edmonton in a car loaned to her by her brother Franki.

Katayna then bid Franki goodbye. She sincerely thanked him for supporting her so lavishly, as she could not have afforded to live in Kona, Hawaii, otherwise. She could not have ever dreamed that she would have so much money every month. Katayna was sincerely grateful, but she worried about Franki and hoped he would not open himself to any more abuse or pain from Sophie.

"Don't worry about me. I'll be fine . . . just fine. And Katayna, you don't have to tell me you're concerned about Sophie because Sophie and I are finished . . . for as long as I breathe. Sophie will not come near me ever again. I promise you that." Franki sounded firm. "And now, Katayna, you promise me something. Every Christmas as long as our mother is alive, I want you to promise me you'll come home for Christmas. I know you can afford it quite well, so will you?" Franki pleaded.

"Yes, yes . . . I promise, for as long as *Mamunia* is alive and also as long as we—you and I—are alive, we'll see each other for Christmas," Katayna promised.

"One other question, Katayna. This has bothered me for years, ever since *Tato*'s funeral when you told me you knew everything that went on at Shady Hollow, but particularly when you said you knew about the meeting I had with the Kaditzs, about their supplying me with moonshine whiskey . . . Do you remember, Katayna?" Franki asked sheepishly.

"Why yes, Franki, I remember well. Was it true you had a meeting with Oni, Harry, and Louie Kaditz, the day after Uncle Yatsko's funeral?" Katayna inquired.

"Yes Katayna, I did indeed have a meeting with them, but then I backed out of the whole deal, but how did you know about the meeting? There were only four people there and no one was supposed to tell anyone," Franki stated.

"Franki, how little you know about a good marriage. Of course, how could you, you are married to Sophie . . . that's far from a normal marriage. In a good marriage two people hide nothing from one another. Louie Kaditz shared everything with his wife, Annie. You probably know that Annie and I have been friends for many years, ever since I taught her twins and your friends Oni and Harry. Well, Annie told me all about Louie's dealings with you, with Johnny Makar, and with Metro Soova. She corresponds with me regularly and visited me in Kona once. She did not tell me about that whole mess until about a year after it all happened. She pleaded with me not to incriminate Oni and Harry. And I thought, what's the use, it would only hurt my friend, Annie. There's been too much pain already. So, Franki, that's how I knew. Now I ask you to please keep this confidential."

She boarded the Trans Canada Airlines plane and it took off toward home—the home she now loved so much, Kona in Hawaii, U.S.A.

CHAPTER SEVENTY-FIVE

One year after Ollie Barris and Alexis O'Neil were engaged, there was a very big wedding, planned by the O'Neil family, to be held in Kentucky, U.S.A.

Ollie and Franki were reaching their first million-dollar gain. Their construction businesses were booming beyond all expectation. Scotty McIntosh was doing an outstanding job as Superintendent, a title which he had just been given.

The oil revenues from the successful wells which Imperial Oil drilled on their respective properties were flowing also, well beyond all their expectations.

Franki had hired a local couple to care for his Clydesdales, but they were a far cry from Henry Warring. His precious purebred Clydesdales had not won one ribbon since Henry had left. In fact, this present help knew nothing about training—training them in the proper stance and the proper walk for showing. Nor did they know anything about bloodlines. But they did provide tender, loving care to the horses.

With all the money Franki was making he could afford to build a huge house, and his small prototype would be used for the hired help.

Sophie had been a real thorn in his side. Cissy finally drew up a firm agreement that restricted Sophie's spending. Every time she spent over her limit, which was monthly, Franki and Sophie would go to court. She always claimed she needed more . . . much more spending money.

One day the hired help caught her near the Clydesdale barn. Franki had told them that if they ever saw Sophie near Paradise Acres they should phone the police immediately and then call Franki. There was a restraining order against Sophie, but laws meant nothing to Sophie. Laws were made for other people, never for Sophie. After all, she had literally got away with murder, so how could any order work against her? The legal wrangling in court would go on and on, but Franki was afraid that Sophie might try to harm the Clydesdales. So he bought another set of dogs—these were fierce, trained to obey only Franki or the two workers. They were Rottweilers. Laddie and Lady, he called them. Their names were very uncharacteristic of the dogs, as a lady or laddie they were not.

The Barris-O'Neil wedding was set for June 3, 1948. The O'Neils were a famous Kentucky family and many people throughout the States were invited. The Barris family was also large. Franki was chosen by Ollie to be the best man.

Ollie also invited Johnny and Veronica Makar from Edmonton. Ollie did have a soft spot for Johnny, even though he did not particularly like his business practices. Johnny and Veronica replied that they would attend.

The day of the wedding arrived and Alexis prepared to walk down the aisle. She had chosen an ivory, moiré taffeta gown, styled in a princess line cut with a full skirt that cascaded to the floor. Her shoulders were bare, but she wore an ivory lace bolero jacket, the same lace as her mantilla-style veil. On her feet were beaded white satin, high-heeled shoes. She was the picture of radiance. In fact, she was breathtaking.

Alexis the bride walked down the flower-laden garden path escorted by her father Fred O'Neil. They both walked slowly toward Ollie, with Franki standing by his side. Her equally lovely sister, Sandra, followed her. A string quartet played the classic wedding march as Alexis,

Fred, and Sandra neared the groom and best man. Sandra was dressed in a strapless turquoise gown in a Georgette chiffon. Her shoulders were covered in a thin shawl of the same fabric. In her hair was a string of ivory magnolia blossoms. Her strawberry blonde hair was swept up in a cascade of soft curls. As Franki glanced at her, he found her to be even more beautiful than the bride. Along with her beautiful face, she had a voluptuous, sexy figure.

The ceremony ended and the groom kissed the bride, they clasped hands, turned to face the crowd, and began to walk toward the reception area. Franki took Sandra's hand and the two followed the bride and groom.

When the reception was over, the dance music began. Ollie and Alexis danced the first dance; they were joined for the second dance by Franki and Sandra.

"God, no!" thought Franki as he guided this incredibly gorgeous woman around the floor. He had the same stirrings inside him as when he had first danced with Sophie, only more so. And he had promised himself that he was never going to be trapped by that feeling again. He muttered to himself, "never again."

After Franki danced with the bride and with Mrs. O'Neil, Sandra approached him to dance with her again. He did so . . . again the stirring was back, so as soon as the dance ended, he excused himself and went into the yard. He walked a long time and found himself in the large horse barns. What a difference from his own barn. There were men guarding these exquisite thoroughbreds. Not just anyone could walk into these barns. When he told the guards that he was with the wedding party, he was given permission to walk through but they warned him not to touch the horses.

Franki loved horses so much that he lost track of time. One and a half hours had passed since he had entered the barn, when he heard a voice behind him.

"I've been looking everywhere for my handsome best man and here he is, in his Sunday best, in the barn," Sandra spoke in a slightly nasal Kentucky accent—an accent that could charm the birds right out of the trees.

"Oh I'm sorry, I just needed to, I mean I wanted to see your horses. I have a stable of my own, but they're not thoroughbreds, they're big Clydesdales." Franki stated.

"Why yes, yes. Ollie told me all about you . . . I mean your horses." Sandra said, "Oh, and by the way my friends call me Sandi."

"Then Sandi it is." Franki replied.

"Here, Franki, let me give you a walk about—that's if you would like?" Sandi invitingly said.

"Yes, I'd like that very much, but what about your Sunday best? Aren't you . . . don't you care if you soil your lovely dress?" Franki asked.

"No, I'll be careful, and if I do soil it, we have cleaning shops here in Kentucky," Sandi chuckled.

So unlike Sophie . . . Sophie hated the barn . . . never went near the barn.

Sandi started the tour in the office and gave him a lesson on thoroughbreds. Then she showed Franki all the bloodlines from which their horses descended.

"I'm so impressed by your knowledge, Sandi. You are certainly capable of running this place by yourself, aren't you?" Franki asked.

"Well, you probably haven't heard, Franki, but Daddy will be asking Ollie to move here to Kentucky to run our stables. I'll help, of course, but I'll probably set up a veterinary office in our town, Lamourville," Sandi stated.

"No, Ollie hasn't said anything about moving here . . . not yet." Franki was surprised to hear this news.

As they walked back to the house, Franki teased Sandi. "You know, Canada is very short of qualified veterinarians. In fact, I could use one for my own herd of horses."

"You can never tell, Franki. I'm the adventurous one in this family, and I've always had an interest in the north," she commented.

CHAPTER SEVENTY-SIX

After the wedding Franki was leaving for Edmonton, and Ollie had still not told him anything about the arrangement related to him by Sandi.

As he walked toward the car that was to take him to Louisville to catch his plane, he was delighted to see Sandi sitting behind the steering wheel.

"I hope you're not disappointed, but I will be your driver . . . are you?" Sandi teased.

"Heck, no. I'm delighted!" Franki replied enthusiastically.

As they drove they discussed many issues . . . the history of Kentucky, the war that had just ended, how it affected the world . . .

"Franki, were you serious about a shortage of veterinarians in Canada?" Sandi inquired.

Franki was pleased to hear her say this. He had not even dreamed she would take him seriously.

"We truly are short of veterinarians. We only have one school for training students for this profession, in Guelph, Ontario—that's all the way on the other side of the country. There is a great demand for vets in the west, where Ollie and I live." Franki explained.

"I'm giving that some serious thought, Franki." Sandi said, uncertainly.

Sandi was very impressed by Franki. He was now twenty-six years old and had developed into an extremely handsome man. The beanpole body from his youth had developed into a strong muscular physique. His dark brown hair formed soft curls and he had started wearing a moustache, a bushy walrus moustache similar to the one his father used to wear. Cissy Brown had told him often that he looked like Clark Gable, the movie idol.

When they got to Louisville, he gave Sandi his address and telephone number at Paradise Acres and also the one at his construction office.

"Don't be surprised if I come up north . . . to see what it's like." Sandi. said, in parting.

But Franki did not think she would ever really come. When he got on the plane he reflected on his life. He was sure that he did not want to make any more mistakes . . . no more.

Ollie and Alexis flew to Florida for their honeymoon and after a month they came back to Edmonton.

Sandi's story was true. Ollie was indeed thinking of moving back to Kentucky. Alexis's father did ask Ollie and his daughter to take over the O'Neil stables because his health was failing.

Ollie asked Franki if he wanted to buy out his share of the business. Franki said he would but that Ollie should first ask Scotty McIntosh whether he would like to buy Ollie's share. Franki knew that he could get along well with Scotty, and after all, Scotty was probably a better manager than either Ollie or Franki—certainly a much better construction man.

Scotty was indeed interested and the sales deal was made. Ollie would take a payment scheme and concluded the sale of his share for one million dollars. This included the twelve-suite apartment, which they called "The Frolly." They took two initials from Franki and three from Ollie, then they added the "Y" to complete Frolly. They had built on Rosie Soova's Pearl's Oyster lot. There were a number of other similar properties in the deal. Cissy Brown handled the whole transaction.

Ollie would never sell his oil-rich land at Leduc. After a month had passed, Ollie moved to Kentucky, but he stayed in touch with Franki, almost on a weekly basis. During one of these conversations, he told Franki that Sandi was talking constantly about setting up her veterinarian office in Edmonton, Alberta, and asked Franki what he thought about such a proposal.

Franki told Ollie that he would help her in any way he could and that he did need a veterinarian for his Clydesdales. So she would have her first built-in account. Yes, he would help her indeed.

"You might have gathered," Ollie said—he had lost most of his Kentucky accent while living in Canada—"that Sandi has fallen head over heels for you, Franki . . . so just don't hurt her, you hear!" Ollie continued.

"Ollie, I said I'd help her . . . but listen my friend, I'm not making one commitment about my emotional feelings. I've made a mess of my life too many times in the past, and I just don't need . . . don't want to make a commitment to anyone at this time. You must believe me, Ollie," Franki could not have been clearer about his intentions.

Another month went by, and in October 1948 Sandi O'Neil completed her journey from Kentucky to Edmonton. Her father had bought her a new station wagon, a beautiful green Chrysler. It had wooden panels on the sides and lots of chrome. She brought along the equipment that she would need to open a veterinarian office. She spent her first night at the Leduc Hotel, and in the morning she telephoned Franki Stry-Ker at 7:00 a.m.

The hired lady answered the telephone at Paradise Acres. "Franki, I don't know who it is. It's a lady . . . sounds real nice, but sounds like maybe she's from somewhere else. Wants to talk to you."

Franki knew it was Sandi . . . he just knew. "Hello Sandi, welcome to Alberta. It is you, isn't it?" Franki said authoritatively.

"Yes, but how did you know?" Sandi questioned.

"One clue was, 'she's from somewhere else,' according to my housekeeper. And I guess the rest was intuition and wishful thinking," Franki replied. "Come and join me for breakfast; I'm so pleased you're here!" He gave her directions from Leduc to Paradise Acres.

She was there in half an hour, just in time for a delicious pile of pancakes that the housekeeper had prepared.

Franki's new mansion was just completed. His construction company was hiring the excellent cabinet-makers who were immigrating from Germany and skilled masons from Italy.

His cabinets were all completed in knotty pinewood, with a built-in breakfast nook in the kitchen covered in complementary fabric upholstery. In the kitchen were all new Westinghouse appliances in white, with a built-in oven and stovetop. The floors were done in stone by the Italian masons, stones which were polished slightly, but still retained the rustic, raw, granite look. The formal dining room could seat thirty people comfortably, as Franki intended to uphold the Stry-Ker Christmas, Easter, and other special celebrations in the Ukrainian tradition. The built-in china cabinet was finished impeccably with cherry wood and mahogany. The living room had huge windows, with built-in walnut wood planters lined with copper pots, and incredibly beautiful oak pegged hardwood floors. These were polished to such a degree that the floor looked like glass. India area rugs covered part of the hardwood floors. There were four bedrooms, two of which were designated for guests, and each had its own bathroom. Franki was proud to show Sandi his new home, and he invited her to stay until she found her own place.

She enjoyed her breakfast, and after that Franki took her to see his Clydesdales. She was immediately interested in these huge, beautiful beasts. She examined them very carefully and saw that several of the mares needed more attention on their hooves. She commented on how well groomed they were. She felt that half of the herd could place first in various international competitions. But she agreed with Franki that they needed to be more disciplined. They needed much training to compete.

"Are you interested in a contract to train them for show and competition?" Franki asked her.

"Yes, until I get myself established, a contract would be downright decent," Sandi agreed.

Franki asked her where she would like to set up her veterinarian office and she thought Leduc would be better than Edmonton, as she hoped to work more with farm animals than with small house pets.

After two weeks of living with Franki, Sandi found a space for an office in Leduc and started to establish her premises.

"Franki, I have not been able to find suitable accommodations for myself in Leduc, so if you don't mind, I'll pay you for rent here at your place. My veterinarian office is set up and I have had several phone inquiries. I don't know if they will actually be paying clients, but I hope they are." Sandi was excited about her new office.

Franki had to control himself with all the strength that he had within him. He had not broken down and did not show Sandi that he cared about her. He told her he would withhold her rent from the monies he paid her for looking after the Clydesdales and training them. The two Rottweilers, Lady and Laddie, were just getting used to Sandi. But if the housekeeper, or her husband, the workman, or Franki were not around, Sandi was not on safe ground with the dogs.

Cissy Brown and Jesus Jackson were regular visitors at Franki's, as were Johnny and Veronica Makar.

As the year drew to an end, Franki decided to hold a New Year's Eve party at Paradise Acres. This was for two reasons: first, to ring in the New Year, 1949, and second, Rosie Soova had now totally converted to Judaism and finally married her one and only love, David Newhouse. Rosie was a completely different person in her appearance than what she was as The Pearl's Oyster. Her peroxide hair was gone and she let her own colour take over—a distinguished salt and pepper grey. Her eyebrows had grown in and she tweezed very little. Her brows were now well shaped and were also salt and pepper grey. The stark thin line which she used to wear as eyebrows was long gone. She also wore very little makeup—perhaps a little lipstick and a tiny bit of rouge. She was now a respectable lady in society. The Newhouses—Rosie, David, and Sarah—were moving to the newly established nation of Israel. Franki wished to help celebrate their marriage and give them a farewell send-off.

Rachel Newhouse had passed away in the fall of 1948, mostly because of the deep grieving she had experienced for David's brother, Abe, who died in the German death camps. David, now fifty-five, and Rosie, a young looking forty-three, and their wonderful daughter Sarah were selling all their properties in Calgary and moving to Israel to help create a Jewish homeland. Besides, David was being honoured by Ben-Gurion for having saved in excess of one hundred Jewish people during the Second World War—over one hundred people who would surely have died if not for David.

Franki continued to adore Rosie and respect her like a surrogate mother. This woman had treated him so decently when he had nowhere else to go in 1942, when he first came to Edmonton from the Basilian Seminary in Mundare. She deserved to be honoured—highly honoured, in his view.

The whole group gathered. Scotty McIntosh and his girlfriend came, as well as many other friends. The table for thirty was full.

Franki introduced Sandi to everyone and said she was a friend and the new veterinarian in Leduc.

After dinner, as the evening progressed, Rosie called Franki aside and said, "I've heard about the hell you lived through, Franki, with your first wife . . . and the death of your baby girl. That must have been an incredible pain, but this young lady, this Sandi, is one special lady. You know, I've lived through a lot in my life, and the one thing I am for certain is a good judge of character. I do believe Sandi is a special human being . . . give yourself another chance, Franki; she obviously loves the ground you walk on!" Rosie said sincerely.

"Rosie, I don't deserve another chance; I've screwed up royally and I don't think God intends for me to have another chance." Franki sounded adamant.

"Franki, Franki Stry-Ker, my dear child," Rosie still spoke rapidly. "Don't you realize that if God didn't give people another chance, there would be no one left on earth . . . honestly, think about it!" she finished.

CHAPTER SEVENTY-SEVEN

After Rosie, David, and Sarah Newhouse said good-bye and wished Franki the best in his future life, they left to drive back to Calgary, and in one month they were bound for Israel. In appreciation for all that Rosie had done for Franki, he donated $100,000 toward the Israel Development Fund. This was the fund which David, Rosie, and Sarah Newhouse established before they left Canada. Franki was so happy for Rosie, because surely hers was the love story of the century . . . could he even hope for happiness such as she had now?

Sandi was keeping busy with the Clydesdales and had three mares entered at the horse show at the Edmonton Exhibition. Her veterinarian office in Leduc was also kept busy, so Franki saw very little of her, and he missed her tremendously. On Friday, he insisted she have breakfast with him and when she did, he asked if she would accompany him and Scotty McIntosh and his girl-friend to the Trocadero dance on Saturday night.

She enthusiastically agreed and told him she would be delighted. She liked dancing, especially ballroom dancing.

Saturday came and Sandi dressed in a breathtaking evening dress. It was black and hugged her body down to the knee. At the knee it flared out in cascades of chiffon net, to her ankles. Her strawberry blonde hair was swept up and she wore a huge aquamarine choker at her neck. It matched her turquoise eyes.

As they walked into the Trocadero all eyes were on Sandi; she stole the show. Everyone, including Sophie, Franki's estranged wife, was there. An elderly hotelier accompanied Sophie. He was from Vancouver, B.C.

The first one to spot her was Scotty McIntosh. "Hey Franki, over on the second terrace . . . look who's staring a hole through you!" commented Scotty.

Franki saw her and the hatred within him rose. He was going to show her. He danced every dance with Sandi and all eyes were on them, particularly on Sandi. She danced better than Sophie ever could and she looked so much lovelier.

Since the Trocadero was Sophie's domain—as she thought—her jealousy was uncontrollable. As Franki and Sandi danced by Sophie and her escort, Sophie blasted Sandi. "I see they are letting riff-raff in here now . . . what a pity!" She looked directly at Sandi. Sophie's escort was not proud of her and jerked her off the floor as quickly as he could. Sandi felt bad and Franki just told her to consider the source.

When they came home, Franki could not resist Sandi any longer. He kissed her and she kissed him back passionately. They fell into her bed; he had never experienced better lovemaking.

For three months they made passionate love . . . three, four, and even five times a night. One night as they were making love, Franki heard Lady and Laddie barking at the top of their lungs.

Soon Franki heard the workmen yelling at the dogs to stop. Franki grabbed his housecoat and ran outside. Lying on the ground was Sophie. Laddie had bitten her viciously on the back of her leg, drawing blood and mangling the calf muscle of her leg. She appeared very frightened . . . "for once in her life," thought Franki.

"What the hell are you doing here? Do you know what a court order is? I'll have my lawyer deal with you tomorrow. Now get the hell off my property . . . get!" Franki could not control his rage.

As she ran to her car she dropped a hypodermic

needle. Franki and Sandi had it analyzed at the government laboratory and found it was filled with anthrax virus bacteria—no doubt meant for the Clydesdales . . . or worse yet, for someone in the yard.

Franki reported the incident to the RCMP and they began an investigation. They charged Sophie with trespassing, violating a court order, and attempted murder.

Three months passed, and the trial had not yet begun. One day Sandi was in her veterinarian's office when Sophie walked in.

"You're the bitch my husband's been screwing . . . fine piece of dirt. You realize I'm still his wife?" Sophie spat out her venom.

"No, no, Franki and you have not co-habitated for a few years. Quite frankly, he cannot stand the sight of you. Now leave, do you hear . . . get out!" Sandi retorted.

"You bitch . . . you think you can scare me off. Well, you can't. I just about succeeded in killing both of you once . . . the next time I won't miss. Do you think I care about killing you? I killed my own child, so you will be nothing!" Sophie was shouting as she left the office.

Sandi was stunned . . . absolutely stunned. She had just found out she was pregnant and she still had not told Franki. She was so scared, the saliva in her mouth dried up . . . she could not even swallow.

Without telling anyone anything she locked the vet office and drove to Paradise Acres. She packed her personal belongings and told the housekeeper she was leaving for a few days and asked her to tell Franki she would be gone a while and to say goodbye to him. She then got into her station wagon and drove and drove and drove . . . mesmerized, in a state of shock

Sophie Goseniuk-Hunter-Stry-Ker certainly belonged in prison, at the very least. With the serious charges

against her, Cissy Brown, Barrister and Solicitor, was sure
that Sophie would finally pay her dues.

Cissy Brown was looking forward to the case,
because she had a personal interest in it. She was certain
that Sophie had got away with murder when Baby
Francine Marie died, but the police had not found any
evidence to charge her. This time there was plenty of evidence. The hypodermic needle containing the anthrax
virus had Sophie's fingerprints on it—the needle that she
dropped at Franki's yard. This was surefire evidence, and
Cissy was looking forward to the court fight. She had
taken over handling half of the criminal defence cases at
the Stewart Law Firm. Duncan Stewart handled the others, and both lawyers won most of their cases in court.

As Cissy prepared for this case, she had a visit from
Franki, who instructed her to drop everything. He was
most distraught about losing Sandi O'Neil. He had no
idea where she was and wished to spend all his time looking for her. Besides, he had other reasons.

"Cissy, I am completely worn out fighting with
Sophie. I hate the bitch, in fact I hate the ground she
walks on, and even if we win this case, I will have to see
Sophie in court. I do not want to see her ever again! So I
don't wish to pursue this case further," Franki instructed.

"You do not wish to pursue this case . . . am I hearing you correctly, Mon! You do not wish . . ." Cissy was
trying to finish her sentence but her composure was
quickly leaving her. "What the hell is the matter with
you, Franki Stry-Ker? Have you completely taken leave
of your senses, or are you completely gutless or what?"
Cissy's fury was mounting. "God damn it, Franki, you
infuriate me. You may not wish to see Sophie again, but
stop being so bloody selfish! It's not what you want, it's
that she has broken the law not only this time, but time
after time after time, and people have let her get away

with it. You, Franki, have always let her get away with it!"
Cissy stopped talking for a while. If her skin had been
white, it would have been red with rage, but her ebony
skin did not show her anger.

Then she started talking again, because Franki was
not responding. "Yes, I'm showing my anger, something a
lawyer should never do, but damn it, Franki, as you claim
to hate Sophie, I feel the same way about lawbreakers.
Sophie, on the other hand, is not only a lawbreaker, she's
evil! And those kinds of people must be dealt with. She is
morally and legally bankrupt!" Cissy was more like herself
now. "Franki, I have always cherished our friendship and
if you honestly wish to drop charges against Sophie then
I must do as I'm instructed by my client. As you are
aware, I am working closely with the Provincial Attorney
General's Prosecutor; I dunno if he'll want to co-operate."

"Cissy, I'd appreciate if you would try to convince
him to drop the matter. Earlier in your dissertation you
said Sophie was evil. I do believe that to be true; in fact,
I do believe she is the reincarnation of Satan! Whenever
I am within ten feet of her, the hair on my back stands
up. That is primarily why I refuse to fight with her or
even be in her presence. Fighting with the Devil is not
my idea of a fair fight, because evil scares anyone who
comes near it. Sophie has scared me all that she is going
to. She took away the most precious gift from God that
I could ever have had . . . my baby girl was angelic.
Sophie killed her own flesh and blood, only to punish me
because she knew how much I loved Francine Marie.
Knowing that she did that is precisely why I refuse to
deal with her any further. She has no end to her evil and
vengeance. She has no end, my dear friend Cissy, so if
you can't understand why I wish to drop this matter then
I can't be more clear." Franki's voice was almost inaudi-
ble when he finished speaking.

Cissy could only guess the pain that he had experienced during his dealings with Sophie. She could see the pain in her friend's eyes now. She could now understand, or at least try to understand, his pain. Even with all the pain she had to endure because of the colour of her skin, she understood that it was minor compared to the pain which Sophie had inflicted on Franki over the years.

"Franki, I will immediately begin the paperwork to quash this action. As you know, I won't have problems with the trespassing and violating a court order, but attempted murder . . . that's another matter." Cissy stated. After a week she was able to convince the Attorney General's Prosecutor to also quash the case. The main reason was that one of the chief witnesses had disappeared. And that was the truth. No one knew what had happened to Sandi O'Neil. The other witness, Franki Stry-Ker, would not testify. The courts could subpoena him, but he would refuse and would have to be jailed for contempt of court. Sophie's defence lawyer, who was every bit as clever as Cissy or Duncan Stewart, would crush the other two witnesses in court—Franki's workman and his wife. So, with those facts, the Prosecutor also dropped the action. And once again, Sophie Goseniuk-Hunter-Stry-Ker got away without being prosecuted.

1951

Emily Pushinsky graduated from university, not so much because she wanted a degree, but because her mother insisted she attend university. Helenka would always say, "You have to get an education in this country. I didn't go to higher learning, but my children have to." None of the Pushinsky boys cared for anything except music. Their band, The Soft Sounds, was now famous all over Alberta.

The boys, Peter, Joseph Jr., and Evan, all attended Olds Agricultural College.

They all achieved high standings and graduated with honours but among themselves they would say, "It's for Mama's sake!" And privately they had all hoped Joseph, their dad, would intervene, as he was pushing for their band to become successful. But Joseph rarely contradicted Helenka.

Emily graduated as a Petroleum Engineer. The convocation was a fabulous celebration. Uncle Franki bought her a new Chevy hard top Impala in a sky blue colour. Most important, he parted with the red coral beads which had belonged to Maria, his dead sister. Everyone said Emily looked like Maria, except that Emily had dark hair like her Baba Stry-Ker. Only now her hair was blonde since she started colouring it. Now Emily looked exactly like Maria, and it was uncanny how similar her disposition was to Maria's. Franki knew he was giving these precious beads to the right person. When he told Emily the story about the beads, she squealed with delight and immediately asked him to hook them around her neck. She didn't remove them that whole day.

The whole Stry-Ker clan was very proud of Emily. She was the first of the clan to graduate from university. Not only did she graduate from university, but for a woman to have penetrated the Faculty of Engineering was indeed an achievement. Imperial Oil was hiring her, and the company was happy to have her. Emily's heart's desire, however, was to sing with The Soft Sounds and she planned to do that, even when she worked at Imperial Oil during the day.

Three years had passed since Franki had seen Sandi. No matter how hard he looked or where he searched, no matter how he tried—oh God, how he tried, but to no avail—he could not find her. Sandi O'Neil had disappeared off the face of the earth. When he called Ollie Barris and his wife Alexis in Kentucky, the only thing they would tell him is that she did not want to be found and that she did not wish to see him. They would not say what the reason was that she did not wish to see him. Ollie, with whom Franki could always talk and share confidences, was totally cold in their conversations. He would only tell Franki to get another life and forget about Sandi.

Franki had hired private detectives, some of whom had been suggested by Cissy Brown, his friend and lawyer. Good private eyes who usually found their charges, they looked everywhere in Canada from British Columbia to Newfoundland. They looked all through the U.S.A . . . but no Sandi O'Neil. And her family would say nothing.

CHAPTER SEVENTY-EIGHT

November 1, 1952

Johnny Makar could not find a driver to take the northern route into Whitehorse, Yukon; Canada's most northwestern region.

Makar's Transport had now grown to a fleet of over fifty trucks, large transport trucks that did mostly long distance hauling through Canada into the U.S.A., mainly to California and Illinois, hauling cars and trucks from the auto manufacturers and produce from California. His firm successfully won the contract to deliver equipment up north to develop the Distant Early Warning (DEW) network, a joint venture between Canada and the U.S. governments. The DEW line, as it was known, was the major communication system, in the event that Russia would attack North America. A shipment of cribbing and communication equipment was expected in Whitehorse in four days, but no matter what happened, the authorities of the DEW line required the equipment no later than November 4. Try as Johnny and Veronica did, there was just no spare body to take this run. They now ran the trucking company together. A few of the extra trucks they purchased with Veronica's money, the $30,000 that she had saved when she ran The Pearl's Oyster. They required many drivers and had them, but on this occasion all the drivers were busy on other major runs or were in bed sick with a serious flu bug. The flu bug that was going around was so powerful that most victims had to spend several days in bed to get rid of it.

Johnny told Veronica that he would personally take the run. The roads were in terrible condition. Ice and snow blocked many parts of the highway. This stretch of road north of Edmonton, which ran through Dawson Creek, B.C., and then into Yukon was difficult in good weather conditions, but in these tough, wintry conditions it was dreadful. He travelled for three days straight, stopping only for an hour or two to catch some sleep and to fuel up. He was afraid if he turned off the motor, the engine parts would freeze. As he drove along the mountainous stretch of road between Toad River and Fort Nelson, the large transport loaded with DEW Line parts groaned as it climbed up the road alongside the mountain. There were very few guardrails in place. The sheer cliffs fell five hundred feet down through rocks and boulders: if a truck slipped over the side of a cliff it would have meant the end of the truck and certainly the end of the driver's life.

Johnny had never before driven in these terrible conditions, in all his twenty-five years of driving. There were storm warnings on the radio: Keep off the road if you can. Do not drive unless it's a matter of life or death.

"Yeah, som-a-na-biche . . . this trip is a matter of life or death," thought Johnny. "If I don't get these parts to Whitehorse, my trucking business be dead!"

He finally made it to Whitehorse, Yukon, late on November 4, 1952. He had driven four days without much sleep. But he did get the job done. He delivered the DEW line parts and was wondering where the one and only hotel was located. As he walked past a restaurant, near the hotel, and was about to head in for something to eat and a cup of coffee, he looked through the window and could not believe his eyes. He thought he saw Sandi O'Neil, except that her hair was as black as coal. Was it or wasn't it? He looked for a long time, staring through the frozen window, peering at her—yes, that face and that terrific figure were Sandi O'Neil's. It was no mistake. It *was* Sandi O'Neil.

"God," he thought, "I'm hallucinating . . . it can't be, in Whitehorse! What would she be doing in this god-forsaken place, in this dreadful cold?" But then he gathered his thoughts—why not, who would ever dream of looking for her here . . . in Whitehorse, Yukon, Canada?

He did not go inside because he figured if she saw him she might bolt and run away again. He would not risk that, not risk losing sight of her. His adrenaline started pumping with excitement; suddenly he was not tired any more. He rushed to the hotel where he would be staying that night. He asked if there was a telephone that he could use and was told the best phone was at the federal government office but the office was not open until the next morning.

Johnny Makar, for the first time in so many years, was as excited as a schoolboy who had gone on his first date! Sandi O'Neil . . . his friend, his best friend Franki Stry-Ker had asked him to be on the lookout for Sandi O'Neil four years ago. He and his other drivers carried her picture in their cabs all that time. He wondered how come his northern haul drivers had not spotted her before. Perhaps because they were looking for a strawberry blonde. On the other hand maybe he was wrong, maybe it wasn't Sandi after all. He walked past the restaurant again. It was called Monica's Best Foods.

When a customer walked out of the restaurant, Johnny asked him who owned Monica's Best Foods.

The person replied, "Jesus, you must not be from Whitehorse. Why, it's owned by Monica Travenier, there—right there!" He pointed through the window. "That's Monica Travenier; she's the best half-breed cook to ever hit these parts!"

"How long has Monica run this place?" Johnny inquired.

"Do you know her or what's your problem?" the customer became belligerent.

"Yeah, well I thought I knew her, but the girl had strawberry blonde hair . . . I guess its not her, eh?" Johnny did not wish to make anyone suspicious, not now—until he could get in touch with Franki Stry-Ker.

"Jesus, man, there ain't too many half-breeds with strawberry blonde hair, eh?" the man commented.

"Yeah, you're right!" Johnny agreed. Johnny continued to watch Monica. There was no mistaking it—this woman was certainly Sandi O'Neil. Her smile, her mannerisms . . . it's Sandi, all right! Johnny's mind was exploding as he talked to himself.

The next morning Johnny was waiting at the federal government station when it opened. He explained he had an urgent call to make. He found the only system in place was a two-way radio and it made verbal communication quite difficult.

He tried Franki at Paradise Acres and was told he had already left for Stry-Ker/McIntosh (1948) Homes Inc. The name had been changed when Ollie Barris sold his share to Scotty McIntosh.

The Whitehorse operator rang through to Stry-Ker/McIntosh. "Good morning, Stry-Ker/McIntosh Homes," a cheerful young voice answered.

The Whitehorse operator handed the headset and speaking microphone to Johnny. "Is Franki Stry-Ker there?" Johnny asked in a gruff voice.

"Yes, but he's in a meeting. Is that you, Mr. Makar?" she inquired.

"Yeah, it's me. Listen, I'm here in Whitehorse, Yukon. Tell Franki its an emergency and I need to speak to him now—do you hear? Now!" commanded Johnny.

In a minute or two Franki was on the phone. "Johnny, what's wrong; are you okay? My secretary said you're in Whitehorse." Franki was concerned.

"Som-a-na-biche, Franki, I'm okay, but you sure as hell will be much better when I tell you who I found!" Johnny didn't finish.

"Sandi . . . God, I pray . . . is it Sandi?" Franki was getting extremely excited.

"How the hell did you know? Yeah, I'm almost sure it's Sandi . . . but that's not what she's calling herself. Everyone here knows her as Monica Travenier and her hair is pitch black. Everyone says she is a half-breed, but it's her. I can tell by her smile and her . . . well, her body is still lookin' great!" Johnny explained.

"Johnny, Johnny boy . . . you can't know how happy you've made me. I'll be there as soon as I can leave, right away." Franki could not contain his excitement.

"Don't you be a fool, you hear . . . the roads are the worst that I've ever seen, and I been drivin' . . . you know how long. Wait till—" but Johnny was not allowed to finish.

"There's nothing on earth that will stop me from seeing Sandi. I've been searching for her almost four years. Do you think some snowstorm will stop me—not on your life!' Franki was adamant.

"Okay, okay, you stubborn som-a-na-biche . . . okay I'm sorry, I shouldn't call you that I know, but damn, I'm also excited. Can't you understand that you're no good if you're dead, and you sure as hell may be if you travel in this cold, miserable storm," Johnny cautioned.

The mobile phone went dead. Much of the dead transmission was due to the bad storms in Alberta and the Yukon.

Franki told Scotty McIntosh what the call was about and asked him not to tell anyone. He told Scotty he would be leaving for Whitehorse as soon as he could find a good four-wheel drive to drive up north . . . one with a good heater.

As he drove north the storm was raging in Edmonton. He headed toward Grande Prairie, but he could not continue because it was impossible to see, so he stayed overnight in Valleyview. The next day the storm kept on raging strongly and the temperature dropped to -50F.

"Damn cold." The roads were impassable and he had to lay over yet another day at Grande Prairie, Alberta.

As soon as the visibility cleared slightly, he got into the four-wheel drive and was off again. The roads were bad, but some trucks were already driving on the road delivering DEW line parts. No doubt trying to meet deadlines for their deliveries—no doubt these were Johnny Makar Transport trucks. Franki was fortunate enough to join a three-truck convoy and they all crawled slowly toward Dawson Creek, B.C.

At Dawson Creek the weather let up slightly and they were able to reach Whitehorse in three days.

Franki drove right up to the restaurant, Monica's Best Foods, and entered. There, before his very own eyes, was Sandi. Even though she had pitch black hair, he would have recognized her anywhere.

Sandi was serving four truck drivers their supper and joking with them. "Hey, Monica," one of them was addressing her. "When you gonna marry me? You're a hell of a cook and not bad lookin' either!"

All four laughed. "Careful or she'll kick us out. You know she never goes out; she's like a goddamn nun!" one said in a hushed voice.

Franki pulled out a wooden chair and sat down at a small table. His back was toward Sandi. She came toward him with four glasses of water for the truck drivers.

Franki turned to face her and their eyes met. She dropped all four glasses full of water. As the glasses came crashing to the floor, the broken glass made a terrible racket.

"Mommy, Mommy, you bad girl . . . you break dishes!" A little boy about three came running out of the kitchen. There was no mistaking whose genes this child carried. He had curly brown hair . . . his facial features were Franki's, but his eyes were like his mother's—beautiful turquoise.

Franki leaped up and ran over to Sandi. He embraced her and she hugged him back, hard, right there in the middle of Monica's Best Foods.

The little boy who tugging at her skirt. "Mommy, Mommy, who that man hugging you . . . bad man, go away, leave my Mommy!" and he went over and smacked Franki.

"Son of a gun!" the truck drivers said in unison. "She's not a nun after all . . . hey Monica, we have a run to make . . . where's our grub? Serve our supper and then hug anyone you want."

Sandi called into the kitchen and the cook came out to finish serving. She could not do it; her head was spinning with the events that had just occurred, and she could not talk, never mind control herself.

"How did you ever find me? I hoped you wouldn't, Franki, I really hoped you wouldn't!" Sandi looked very concerned. She clutched her little boy tightly and introduced him to Franki. "This little man of mine is called Nicky . . . Nick Travenier," she stated, holding her little boy.

"Sandi, are you . . . I mean the name Travenier . . . is that your husband's name?" Franki asked with deep concern.

"No, Franki, I never married. Nicky, this man is your daddy, the one I've told you about so often." Sandi was talking to her son. "I called him Nicky because your second name is Nykola . . . so he's actually named after you."

"Is this the man you said you love?" asked little Nicky.

"Franki, I changed my name to Travenier when I ran from Edmonton, when I knew I was pregnant . . . to protect the baby and me. I never wish to go back there, not as long as Sophie is within a hundred miles of my precious baby or me. She threatened my life, Franki . . . she scared me half to death," Sandi told Franki.

Sandi told Franki all about her encounter with Sophie that day in her veterinarian office at Leduc.

"Sandi, my dearest Sandi, why didn't you trust me to protect you? Sophie couldn't have hurt you!" Franki firmly stated.

"Well, Franki, she told me what she did to your baby daughter . . . to Francine Marie whom you loved so much. You couldn't protect your own child, Franki. I was scared silly she'd do the same to my baby." Sandi was still frightened as she spoke.

"Sophie will never hurt anyone again, Sandi . . . she's dead." Franki stated calmly.

He then explained that he had paid Sophie an enormous amount of money—one million dollars—soon after Sandi disappeared, much against the advice of Cissy Brown, his lawyer and friend.

But he explained that he wanted Sophie out of his life, forever, no matter what it cost him. It was worth it to him. Sophie knew at this point that she would never have Franki back again . . . not as a husband, nor even as a friend.

Soon after she was paid the one million dollars, she sold her house on Capital Hill and married a Vancouver hotelier and moved to Vancouver to live with him.

"Not even one year into their marriage, her husband caught her screwing his own son," Franki told her. "Sophie's husband owned a handgun; he shot Sophie and his very own son. He pumped the entire chamber into the two of them. He then reloaded the gun and shot himself. I am surprised you never read about this double murder and suicide. The tragedy was well covered in papers all over Canada."

"No, not all over Canada . . . not at Whitehorse, Yukon," Sandi advised Franki.

After relating the whole story, Franki showed no remorse for Sophie's death. But, he said, he had reluctantly forgiven her for all the hurt that she caused him. He said after forgiving her, his soul became lighter again, but he still felt she was a demon.

"May I give you a little hug . . . maybe even a big one?" Franki asked Nicky.

"Mommy, can he hug me?" Nicky asked.

"Only if you want him to, baby . . . only then," Sandi replied.

"No, Mommy, I don't want him to." Nicky clutched his mom's neck.

Franki stayed with Sandi and Nicky for a week, until the storm subsided. Johnny Makar visited with Sandi, Nicky, and Franki. Franki was now inseparable from Sandi—he would not let her, or Nicky, out of his sight. He had immediately fallen in love with his new-found son, but the feeling did not seem to be reciprocated.

Johnny drove back to Edmonton because his presence was needed at Makar's Transport office. The flu bug was still affecting their drivers and Johnny needed to drive down to California to pick up fresh produce.

During that week Franki persuaded Sandi to move back with him to Paradise Acres. It didn't take much persuasion.

As the week progressed Nicky started liking Franki . . . in fact, the two were gradually becoming inseparable.

Sandi sold Monica's Best Foods to the cook, on terms that were ridiculous—$100 a year for ten years. Sandi was going to give the café to her, but the cook insisted that she wished to buy it, "legal like," so Sandi agreed.

They packed Sandi's old Chrysler station wagon with some of the mementos she had collected up north— especially her beautiful soapstone carvings fashioned by the local Eskimo. She also had bought local paintings. A wonderful artist named Mona Trasher had done one of them. She only painted when her son was in trouble, and her work was breathtaking. One of Ms. Trasher's paintings was a night scene of the northern sky with an Eskimo paddling a kayak in the ice-cold waters; it was a haunting night scene.

Nicky decided he wanted to ride in the four-wheel drive with his father, Franki. Sandi thought it was just as well because they would get to know each other better.

They headed toward Watson Lake, and stayed overnight there. The next day they drove almost all day until they reached the mountains at Steamboat. The vehicles started climbing the treacherous roads into the mountains heading toward Pink Mountain, in the province of British Columbia. They were now at Trutch Mountain, the tallest peak on these roads. They found the roads passable, but still with very slippery conditions throughout.

The four-wheel drive operated well on these roads, but the station wagon was having some difficulty. Sandi did not complain because she was used to these driving conditions by now.

As they proceeded to the top point of Trutch Mountain, Franki and Nicky were driving behind Sandi. Then it happened. The horror of all horrors. The station wagon couldn't continue to ascend to the top of the mountain as it was a very steep climb . . . it kept slipping and sliding, slipping and sliding, closer and closer to the edge of the cliff. Franki could only watch in terror as the back wheels began slipping over the edge and suddenly, there was Sandi's station wagon hanging onto the road by only its front wheels, hugging the side of the embankment.

Nicky started screaming, "Mommy, Mommy! Mommy come back!" Franki grabbed a rope from the back of the four-wheel drive and told Nicky to stay in the vehicle. He ran over to the station wagon. He could see that any move would send Sandi and the wagon five hundred feet down the cliff.

He tried to compose himself, to not show Sandi that he was scared, that he was, in fact, hysterical. Sandi slowly rolled down the window and was crying uncontrollably, "Franki, Franki . . . don't let me die. Don't let me die, please!" she begged.

Franki was praying, praying silently. In his hysteria he remembered to promise God . . . to promise God on his father's grave, that he would never defy God and that he would donate, always donate at least ten per cent of all his net profits to help his fellow man. He would do this forever; he promised . . . as long as he would live, he would help anyone in distress or in need, as long as he was alive.

"Sandi, listen carefully . . . do not move, do not move, please!" Franki slid on his stomach as far as he could and tried to hand Sandi the rope . . . she almost grabbed it but this motion shook the wagon and it started moving downward. It was moving slowly . . . it slipped down about twenty more feet. By now Sandi was screaming with fear and then, to Franki's surprise, it stopped—as though the wagon was frozen in space. The wagon must have settled on a tree stump or a rock.

Franki lowered the rope . . . it was too short. God . . . too short by about three feet. Franki ran back to the four-wheel drive and grabbed the blanket inside the vehicle that he had taken for Nicky. In his hysteria he left the door open and Nicky got out. He came running after Franki and started crying when he saw his mother hanging on for dear life, thirty feet down the bank.

Franki quickly tied the blanket to the rope. It was just long enough for Sandi to reach. She grabbed it and as she was struggling to get out of the window the wagon started moving again. Miraculously, as though by divine intervention, the wagon stopped its descent again and Sandi got out the window just in time. As she did the wagon picked up speed on its descent and went crashing, plunging hundreds of feet down the cliff. The crash of metal on the rocks could be heard for miles . . . in this cold, God forsaken place.

Sandi was hanging on to the rope thirty feet down—hanging on for dear life, but only barely. Franki was pulling her up as quickly as he could. He kept telling her to hang on tightly but her arms were getting numb and she was losing grip . . . losing grip quickly! Her body was hurt and bruised as it crashed against the rocks while Franki kept pulling her up.

Nicky started screaming, "Mommy, Mommy, don't leave me . . . Mommy, I need you! Mommy, I need you!"

Sandi gained strength as she heard her baby call. She clutched the rope tighter and hung on, knowing that her life depended on this grasp. As soon as Franki could reach, he grabbed her arms and pulled her quickly to the top of the bank. He started crying uncontrollably and kissing her at the same time, as he held her tightly, while she lay on the frozen ground. He held her so tightly that he was scared he'd crush her. She was shaking with shock, pain, and the cold.

Nicky also bent over to kiss his Mommy. "Mommy, Mommy, I'm so happy God didn't take you . . . you are here. I love you Mommy . . . I love you!"

Sandi's arms, legs, and face were badly bruised by the scraping she had sustained on the jagged rocks below. She was having difficulty breathing and her chest hurt with every breath she took. She was also freezing and hypothermia was developing quickly, but she did not complain. Franki quickly swooped Sandi into his arms and carried her into the four-wheel drive. The motor was running throughout this whole ordeal and so it was very warm inside the vehicle. Franki cranked up the heater to full blast and as the heat began to flow into the vehicle the three of them held each other tightly. Franki and Sandi began to cry uncontrollably, while Nicky screamed with delight at having his mother safely in his clutches. Sandi continued to shake and had difficulty breathing. Franki then slumped over the steering wheel and silently prayed. He realized that God was present right here today, for truly this was a holy intervention that had saved Sandi. In his prayer he reflected on his life and asked God for forgiveness for all his indiscretions. He asked God to forgive him for leaving the Mundare Seminary and not fulfilling his vows. He realized today that God was a truly loving entity. Franki even asked God to forgive him for the hatred which he felt for his dead wife, Sophie. But mostly Franki asked God for genuine guidance so that he might be as good a person as one could be. He asked God to bless all future generations of Stry-Kers, particularly his son Nicky and his nieces and nephews.

As soon as Franki could control himself he made a bed in the back seat of the four-wheel drive and carefully guided Sandi into that bed. They had packed a quilt, blanket, and pillow for Nicky and now it would be very useful for Sandi.

Franki used his two-way radio to call Scotty McIntosh to tell him what had happened and to report that the three of them would be arriving the next day. Franki then drove with full speed, only stopping at Pink Mountain, British Columbia, to refill his gas tank and to get some much-needed nourishment.

Sandi was having a lot of trouble breathing and had no appetite. Franki asked her if she wanted to see a doctor, to which she replied "no." They drove as fast as possible to Grande Prairie, Alberta, where they registered in as nice a hotel as they could find and ate their supper. Franki drew a hot bath for Sandi and helped her into the tub. He could see her badly bruised body and was very concerned about her breathing. Sandi still insisted on not seeing a doctor, but she did say that she would see one in Edmonton if she wasn't feeling any better. When morning came Sandi's health was getting worse, but she still insisted on continuing to drive to Edmonton. Franki drove at record-breaking speed and they arrived in Edmonton in three hours. Sandi was looking ashen grey and Franki drove her directly to the Royal Alexandra Hospital.

When the admitting nurse saw Sandi, she immediately summoned a doctor. The emergency room doctor was a new graduate by the name of Morris Melynk. He was an excellent doctor and could see that Sandi was in distress. He ordered X-rays and blood and urine tests. The X-rays revealed that Sandi had three broken ribs. One of her rib bones had punctured the spleen and it had to be removed in an emergency operation. Her pancreas was badly injured as well.

Franki could not get Nicky to leave the hospital. The little boy insisted on staying with his mother. Dr. Melynk advised that Sandi must have complete bed rest. She was in intensive care, in very serious condition. Franki was totally overcome with depression but he knew that Nicky and Sandi were his responsibility and he would make sure that he was there for both of them. When Nicky fell asleep in Franki's arms, the nurses told him he should take the child home and come back when Sandi was in better condition.

As Franki drove toward Paradise Acres he could see many vehicles parked outside the house. He entered the house with Nicky in his arms and there were his family members from Shady Hollow—Tainka his mother, Mikhail and Lizzie Hussar, Paul and Anastasia, along with Evelyn and Evancik. There was also the Pushinsky family, Helenka and Joseph with Joseph Jr., Evan, Peter, and the youngest member of the Pushinsky family, Stephan. Emily was also there; a handsome young man accompanied her. He appeared to be of Middle Eastern origin, as his skin was a beautiful olive complexion. Emily appeared to be totally smittened by him. Franki could not help disliking this young man although he didn't know why. There was something about him. Maybe he was too smooth, too charming. Franki hoped that he was wrong, but this young man (who, he learned, owned a beauty parlour) was not the one he would have picked for Emily. Franki was so proud of Emily Pushinsky. He admired her for completing her engineering degree. She also had a marvellous opportunity to become a class A singer with her brothers' band. The now-famous band was to tour Europe in the summer. But who was he to judge, when his own choice of a first wife was one of the most dismal experiences that anyone could ever have had? Also he had to consider Emily's hardships before she entered University and he would be the last person on earth to try and control her life like his sister, Helenka tried to do.

Franki was not going to let this bother him. There were much greater worries at this time. His beloved

Sandi was in the hospital and he was worried sick, hoping that she would pull through this ordeal. As he continued to look around the room, he saw Cissy Brown and Jesus Jackson waving at him. Nicky was totally confused. He held onto his father's neck as tightly as he could while Franki introduced him to all these people. The O'Neils had flown in from Kentucky as soon as they heard that Sandi was coming to Edmonton with their first grandchild, Nicky. Along with them were Ollie and Alexis Barris. Nicky had never seen the O'Neil family either; they were strangers to him. It would take Nicky some time to get to know this big group of people, thought Franki. He also felt sorry for his young son, as so much had happened to his innocent life in the past week.

Father Danelo from Leduc parish was there, as were the Kaditz twins, Harry and Oni, along with their wives and their mother Annie. There were also telegrams of good wishes from his sister Katayna in Hawaii and from Rosie, David, and Sarah Newhouse in Israel. As the gathering began to thin out and people started to leave to go home, Franki thought how perfect an evening this would have been had Sandi been there with him. He took his precious son Nicky to the bedroom to put him to bed. The little boy knelt beside the bed to say his prayers. He prayed, "I miss mommy so much, God, that it hurts right here inside my heart," and Nicky pointed to his chest. "Please make her well."

Franki, with his arm around Nicky's shoulders and his head bowed, added fervently, "Amen."

CHAPTER SEVENTY-NINE

Nicky's prayers were answered. Within a week, Sandi was transferred from the intensive care unit at the Royal Alexandra Hospital into a private room on the medical wing. Her physical injuries were healing and she could hardly wait to hug her young son.

When Franki brought Nicky to see Sandi, the reunion was indeed a happy one. Sandi gently hugged both of her favourite men.

"How I have longed to hold you, Nicky . . . and you also, Franki. You are both so dear to me. I am so glad to be alive . . . so thankful to God, for it was divine intervention surely that saved me," Sandi said, almost in a whisper. It was obvious that her lung was still badly injured; her breathing was shallow and her breaths were short.

After an hour had passed, a nurse—her name tag reading Joanne—came into the room.

"Now gentlemen, you must let this precious lady rest. She's almost like new, but she still has a lot of healing to do. As much as I don't want to tell you to leave, I must at this time," Joanne stated.

Nicky refused to go home. "Mommy, Mommy, I don't want to go. . . . I don't want to leave you . . . I'm scared something will happen. Mommy, please, please!"

It hurt Sandi to the depths of her heart and she knew there must be some way for her baby to stay. She asked Joanne if he could sleep in her room. Sandi knew that Nicky was very fond of Franki, but of course Nicky was much more used to her. And since he was so vulnerable at this point she wanted to do everything possible to make him feel better. Nicky was also new to any family relationship other than the one with her. He did not know his maternal grandparents, the O'Neil's in Kentucky, nor did he know his paternal grandmother, Tainka Stry-Ker of Shady Hollow. He knew none of the Stry-Ker aunts or uncles, as all his short life had been spent in Whitehorse, Yukon. Franki had always slept with Sandi from the time of his birth. He loved his mother more than words could describe. Sandi also missed cuddling and holding her son.

"Nurse, I was hoping that perhaps an arrangement could be made for Nicky to sleep here in my room with me . . . is that possible? Perhaps a cot could be brought in . . . Since this is a private room we would not be bothering other patients. It would mean so much to me and to Nicky. He misses me so much . . . ." Sandi's voice once again became just a whisper.

Nicky's eyes became as big as saucers. "Oh Mommy, could I really sleep here with you? I could cuddle with you, Mommy, just like we used to cuddle, and you could read a Mother Goose story to me . . . yes, Mommy!"

When Nurse Joanne heard the pleading by Sandi and Nicky she was convinced that this arrangement might help Sandi to heal faster. The medical staff had been very concerned that even though Sandi's physical injuries were healing quite nicely, her psychological condition was far from good. On many nights Sandi exploded with screams: "Help me! . . . help me!" These screams lasted for more that half an hour at a time and it was evident that the accident had caused her a great deal of distress.

After consulting with Sandi's physician, it was agreed to bring in the cot. Franki could see that both Sandi and Nicky wanted some time together and he totally understood.

"I will be glad to bring Nicky here every day. We can have supper together and then the both of you can have a nice long rest. I'll come and pick Nicky up in the morning and maybe I could join you both for breakfast. As a matter of fact I'll have my own cook prepare breakfast and I'll bring it here . . . no one cooks better pancakes and poached eggs then Mary, my cook at Paradise Acres . . . what do you say?"

Sandi could hardly contain herself and Nicky was jumping hoops he was so happy. "Oh Mommy, I need my teddy bear . . . the one that Santa Claus brought me!" Nicky pleaded.

"Nicky, darling, if you want to stay here tonight, it will have to be without your teddy bear ... but if you want to go home with your daddy and bring your teddy bear for tomorrow, then you can do that ... it's your decision," Sandi whispered.

"No Mommy, I won't go home, I won't leave you . . . you better than teddy...you better, Mommy!" Nicky exclaimed.

The first night that Nicky spent at the hospital was the first night that Sandi did not scream, nor did her screams return while she was at the hospital. Her three-year-old baby was beside her sleeping on the cot. Sandi would get out of her hospital bed and rub Nicky's head and gently brush his hair with her hand. She was starting to feel better and the pressure which had felt like a heavy rock on her chest was slowly leaving her.

After a month had passed Sandi was ready to be discharged from the hospital. Franki was ecstatic, as now his life would be totally fulfilled. As he drove his new Cadillac to the hospital and picked up Sandi and Nicky he was beaming. "This is the happiest day of my life. I will have my special Sandi at home where I can love you forever and the extra bonus is having my wonderful very special son, Nicky."

When Sandi entered the lovely home at Paradise

Acres, a large bouquet of red roses, Sandi's favourite flowers, greeted her on the hallway table. The living room was full of fresh floral bouquets; the kitchen table held a huge vase full of red roses. There were bouquets of roses in the dining room on the large oak table, in the bedroom, and in the bathroom. The fragrance of roses was pure heaven to Sandi.

"Franki, this is so special . . . the whole place is wonderful! I love roses . . . you know that . . . these are so beautiful and the fragrance is like heaven—or heaven must be like this!" Sandi's voice was getting stronger; she didn't have to whisper any more.

Franki gently guided Sandi into the living room where a bottle of champagne was chilling in the ice bucket. He settled her into the soft and comfortable love seat and sat down beside her. Nicky came running after his mother and father and settled down between them. Franki poured the smooth Mums champagne into three glasses—one containing very little champagne.

He proposed a toast. "Welcome home, my dearest Sandi and Nicky." As he drank his first sip, he said, "May God help us never to get separated again, and may God grant you a full recovery, Sandi. I love you both with all my heart. I am the luckiest man alive to have both of you in my life." Putting his arm around Nicky, Franki tenderly kissed Sandi.

GLOSSARY OF UKRAINIAN TERMS

Since the Ukrainian language is written in the Cyrillic alphabet, the terms described below, and used throughout the book, are written phonetically, with the English translation in the right column.

Angleck	Englishman
Baba	Grandmother
babka	sweet bread
babushka	kerchief
boohigh	bull
borsch	beet soup
bouketa	corsages
brama	specially decorated entrance
cebulnick	flat bread covered in fried onions
Chi	tea
didko	demon
disiplena	discipline
fabrica	factory
Gido	Grandfather
golgone	rascal
holubtsi	cabbage rolls
Hopak	Ukrainian dance done mostly by men
kapusta	sauerkraut and chickpeas
kistka	stylus to decorate Easter eggs
klutka	community work bees
kobaska	sausage
kolasha	cornmeal
koluchi	special bread
koozooshok	sheepskin lined vest
korshma	village pub
krasaw	spotted
kumirka	storage house

kurva	whore
kutia	wheat dish served primarily at Christmas
kwos	sauerkraut juice
lidowna	icehouse
Mamunia	Mother
otropkee	Stew with rich gravy and finely sliced organ meats
paska	Easter bread
peech	outdoor clay oven
pischoha	special pet
plachinicha	shroud of Jesus in his grave
popravene	after-wedding party
pompuski	sweet buns
pun	revered mister
pysanky	decorated Easter eggs
rebka	little fish
russadnik	makeshift greenhouse for early planting
scranya	storage trunk
Slava Ichosoo Xristoo	Praise Jesus Christ – everyday Christian greeting
Slava na vikee	praise him forever – response to Christian greeting
Slavitee Iho	Praise him (Jesus) – Christmas greeting response
sluck taba trafit	May a curse fall upon you
sluck yahoo trafit	May a curse fall upon him
solonena	pickled pork back fat
spevake	singers
staray	old
starcey braut	elder who attends the priest during mass
starosta	match maker

Tato	Father
Ukrainske Vesta	Ukrainian News
valinke	knee-high felt boots
Vechnia Pomenit	Forever remembered – mournful song sung primarily at funerals
venok	bridal head-dress
Voima chaw & Sena & Shavatoo ho dooha, amin	In the name of the father, son and Holy Spirit, amen
Voistynu Voskres	Truly he has risen – Easter greeting response
vreeche	place a curse
Xristna Mawte	Godmother
Xrisnee Tato	Godfather
Xristos voskres	Christ has risen – Easter greeting
Xristous Ruzdieitshaw	Christ is born – Christmas greeting
Zelenee Shvata	Green Holidays – in June
zolota	gold
zoria	star

GLOSSARY OF CHARACTERS

Evan Stry-Ker	The patriarch
Tainka Stry-Ker	The matriarch
Maria, Mikhail, Helenka, Katayna, Paul, and Francis	Children of the Stry-Kers
Theodore and Pashka Borischuk	Stry-Kers' elderly neighbours and friends
Metro Soova	Neighbour of the Stry-Kers
Rosie Soova	Daughter of Metro and his first wife, Olga
David Newhouse	Jewish school teacher
Rusty McLellan	RCMP officer stationed at Shady Hollow
Domka Litikiw	Metro Soova's second wife
Milka and Todour Popilsky	Stry-Kers neighbours' and guests at Helenka's wedding
Louie Kaditz	Metro Soova's partner in the moonshine business
Oni and Harry Kaditz	Annie and Louie's twin sons and friends of Franki Stry-Ker
Ollie Barris	American Air Force officer and partner of Franki Stry-Ker
Cissy Brown	The Negro maid at The Pearl's Oyster
Johnny Makar	The enforcer at The Pearl's Oyster and a trucker
Teckla and Joseph Chomiak	Church friends of the Stry-Kers
Their son, Stephen	Maria's special interest
Veronica, Helen, and Lily	Girls who work for Rosie at The Pearl's Oyster
Father Bill	Franki's guiding light at the Mundare Seminary
Fred Radjec	Mikhail's Romanian friend

Paul Lupski	Mikhail's Polish friend and neighbour
Olana and Peter Pushinsky	First family to immigrate to Canada from Sosnitcha
Joseph Pushinsky	Helenka's special interest
The Kuriak family	First friends of the Stry-Kers in Canada
Mike Yaworsky	Mike was married to Tainka's sister in Austria
Sophie Goseniuk	One of Franki's interests
Sandi O'Neil	Franki's significant other

*Watch for Molly Anne Warring's second novel
"Paradise Lost; featuring Emily Pushinsky"*

Photo of Molly Anne Warring by Audrey Laschuk

ABOUT THE AUTHOR

Molly Anne Warring is the President of her own public relations and marketing company; Warring Channels Inc.

She has served on many Boards and Commissions as a Director and Chairman and she has worked in the private and public sectors. Molly Anne is a former broadcaster and an Accredited public relations practitioner.

She has also spent over 40 years as a volunteer serving in her community for multiple charities. For this effort she was decorated with the Queen Elizabeth Golden Jubilee Medal in 2003 and in 2005 she received an additional medal; The Alberta Centennial Medal of Distinction as well as being awarded the Premier's citation for outstanding community contributions. Also in 2005, she received a further award, the Centennial silver medal given to worthy Albertans. Her favorite charities are: Salvation Army and the Glenrose Hospital Foundation.

Molly Anne wishes to thank the multitudes of readers who have enjoyed reading; and have supported *Paradise Acres* in achieving the best seller's list for many weeks running, since the book's launch in May, 2005. She is extremely grateful to Borealis Publishing for nominating her novel for the 2005 Governor General's Award.

MEMBER OF SCABRINI GROUP

Québec, Canada
2007